A Moravian College and NYU graduate, Robert Honor has taught screenwriting at NYU's Tisch School of the Arts. His plays have been produced in NYC; he's currently developing a television pilot and working on his next novel. He lives in the New York City area with his family and their Great Dane.

For Lorie, Kav, and Jack.

Robert Honor

BOGART'S HAT

AUSTIN MACAULEY PUBLISHERS

LONDON • CAMBRIDGE • NEW YORK • SHARJAH

Ordering Information
Quantity sales: Special discounts are available on quantity purchases by corporations, associations, and others. For details, contact the publisher at the address below.

Publisher's Cataloging-in-Publication data
Honor, Robert
Bogart's Hat

ISBN 9781645363644 (Paperback)
ISBN 9781645363651 (Hardback)
ISBN 9781645368991 (ePub e-book)

Library of Congress Control Number: 2020923367

www.austinmacauley.com/us

First Published (2021)
Austin Macauley Publishers LLC
40 Wall Street, 33rd Floor, Suite 3302
New York, NY 10005
USA

mail-usa@austinmacauley.com
+1 (646) 5125767

In December of 2014, I embarked on the first of eight operations: two hip, two knee, three back, and a neck operation. This weekend warrior injured himself playing basketball, mostly. Mostly – that word always brings me to this – "They mostly come at night, mostly." One of my favorite lines from one of my favorite movies, *Aliens*. Credit the adorable urchin Newt for that quip, and either James Cameron or Gale Anne Hurd for writing it. There were probably a few other ways I contributed to breaking my body. Some of my hobbies included stumbling down stairs, slipping on ice, falling out of a canoe – oh, there was that skateboard accident.

Without the luxury of moving around much, getting soft, feeling weakened and then angry, I waded through and then eventually dove into this story I called *Lolly & Me*. By the way, the title *Bogart's Hat* came to me two years in. Wandering the streets of Gravesend, Brooklyn, where my parents grew up, I spotted an elderly man sitting on a beach chair outside a bakery my grandmother used to take me to when I was five years old. I approached the gent and asked him if he knew my father. Without missing a beat, he said he played stickball with him on West 6th Street about seventy years ago. He told me about the time he snuck into the old Madison Square Garden for a heavyweight championship bout in 1955: Rocky Marciano vs. Archie Moore. He was sitting ringside feeling like he had won the Irish Sweepstakes when he felt someone tap him on the shoulder. He looked up, saw a fedora and a cigarette; it was Humphrey Bogart himself. "Hey, kid you're sitting in my seat."

Inspired by his story, *Lolly & Me* became *Bogart's Hat* and from there I bend the truth in regard to Mr. Bogart's hat and its significance in my story. I've gone back looking for the gentleman to find out his name – to thank him. No luck. So, this is the point where I must thank all those people who helped me get through. And in case I've forgotten to mention you, I'll say what my old friend Christy Kelly says, "I blame myself." I hope you'll forgive me.

Thank you, Jeremiah Jurkiewicz, for the educational chat we had along the boardwalk, for your kindness and the discussion as we walked that brisk morning. Mark J. Honor, PA-C talked me through ER protocols. The always-exuberant Frank Rothman, thank you for sharing your expertise regarding the criminal justice system. Jim Farmer, Bayonne, New Jersey shines through thanks to you. Beth Gorrie and her fabulous non-profit organization, Staten Island OutLOUD for sponsoring my very first reading. And to Dick's Deli, no longer around but not forgotten, because a good cup of coffee is not to be underestimated, thanks. Thank you to the debonair Jeff Gallo for reaching out to Adam Coren of J.J. Hat Center for a discussion about hats, models and years, and period styles, etc. And thank you, Adam. Thank you to my new best friend Robin Locke Monda for designing a fabulous book cover. Fred's Restaurant at 83rd and Amsterdam appears between the pages. Owned by David Honor, my protagonist always has a good time there. To Keith Perkins, Renee James, Josh Apter, and Michael Ahn, who shared their enthusiasm for the book; they gave their time and unwavering support, thank you.

The name Venable Herman appears between the pages. He is actually Venable Herndon, one of my NYU professors back in the day. He's long gone, and I miss him, dear sweet man. Maggie Lally and Gary Garrison for lifting me up when I was down. To the family of the late Jack LaLanne. Mr. LaLanne made me do push-ups in the street when I was a kid. I reinvent the story somewhere in the book. It was one of the most charming mornings of my young life. The real Harry Kavanagh, my great uncle, was a kind and gentle man who was always quick to laugh. Uncle Harry, I borrowed your name here, but from where you're sitting, you already know that. Thank you to the entire production team at Austin Macauley. Thank you to Dr. Martin Quirno for putting me back together, and to my lifelong friends, the Nicholas family and the Denenbergs. I truly feel like a lucky man. Thank you, Bud. Your stories enriched my life and this effort. To Carmela, Helene and Kathleen, thank you for always supporting me; you may want to skip over the racy parts.

And thank you, Jesse Kornbluth, my very first writing teacher at NYU. Jesse would kick off his shoes and conduct the class with wit, compassion, and kindness. If Jesse had been anyone other than himself, I wouldn't have been secure enough to write a single sentence.

There are names between the pages that belong to friends and family members. I couldn't resist. Thank you, Moravian College, for setting me on a path; thank you, NYU, for keeping me there.

To my young men, Jack and Kav, you give me strength, make me laugh, and prop me up in so many ways – so proud of you both; you bring me so much joy. To my wife, Lorie, a passionate person with boundless energy and talent: an entrepreneur, feminist, activist, teacher, leader, mentor, mother, writer, my full-time editor, conscience, and Saturday-night fashion consultant. You are a soaring comet. I am a better person because of you.

Chapter One

"These days I seem to think a lot about the things that I forgot to do for you."
— Jackson Browne

As far as he could tell, the pancake was ripe and ready to go. Harry Kavanagh sighed. It was a long sigh. It was more of an internal moan, meaning something like, *here I am again*. Another day. Harry created his pancakes from scratch with organic ingredients. He licked the tips of his fingers before delicately rolling breakfast from the griddle. The pancake never made the trip to the plate because there wasn't one. Two-and-a-half bites later and *finito*, as Harry's ancient Uncle Sebastian would bellow to the annoyance of anyone standing so close they'd catch a whiff of the garlic he'd slipped into his Cheerios. Harry had perfected the size of his pancake over the last four years. He had that kind of time. He wasn't exactly living the life as some people suggested. Those people were usually the ones on the checkout line who coerced Harry into a conversation he didn't want to have. He wasn't working, and his wife and children were out of the house. Yes, his wife was out of the house. It softened the blow when he thought of it that way. Since his fingers had already been licked, Harry took the opportunity to comb his thinning eyebrows with his fingertips. Harry took a deep breath and another. It was all part of his routine on this morning and on every morning. There was no one around to mock Harry's pancake ritual, to chew him out because he was hunched over the stove, or because he was cleaning wax out of his ear with the same fingers that combed his eyebrows and rousted his breakfast.

Harry had learned a few things since he was a fat man. He'd lost 40 pounds over the last four years, due in great part to his grief. In his humble opinion, despondency was the best diet on the market. You wouldn't read about it between the pages of the supermarket tabloids. Harry wasn't the type to chitchat; he certainly wouldn't be sharing his opinion at a cocktail party. Did Harry really have to worry about being invited anywhere? No, absolutely not. Not these days. He shrugged to no one, reminding himself supermarket pancake syrup was his enemy. Well, maybe not his arch enemy, but a bad thing nonetheless. Harry learned all about high fructose corn syrup, the artificial everything, and whatever other foreign agents the corporate guys concocted to make up the slop. *For Chrissakes*, Harry thought, it was the kind of slosh that could wilt dandelions.

"Nothing on 'em, warden. I take my pancakes straight," Harry mused aloud; purposely sounding like a 1930s' mug who had been unfairly sent to the big house.

While Harry was eating healthier, his life continued to be generally unappetizing. On occasion, his two smart aleck boys standing on the doorstep of manhood would intervene, reminding him there were still a few things left in his life to cherish. Meaning the two of them, damn it. He could hear their voices mocking him. They were now in the business of joking and cajoling Harry out of his doldrums like the old souls they were becoming. And yes, they reminded Harry of their birthdays and holidays, because the old man would often get lost inside his own head. They emphatically endorsed the idea of Harry handing over some *guap* on those hallowed days, or whenever he saw fit. As far as Harry could tell, their word *guap* was the newest slang for cold hard cash. He loved his sons dearly, and so he permitted them to wag a finger and lecture him at length. Any occasion to be in their presence was time well spent, even when they treated him like an amnesia patient. They preached that proper nourishment would sustain his life and since they wanted him to be around for a while longer (although they didn't specify for how long), it would be a good idea for him to, in their own words, *chow down healthy*. How does one chow down on kale? Who was Harry to disagree with these charming and well-intended boys? They were all he had.

Well, there was Lolly, of course, his 5-year-old Great Dane. And thank goodness Lolly was incapable of butting in with words. Harry could barely manage two against one; three against one was out of the question. And so, Harry reluctantly got into this new habit of reading the nutrition facts labels. The actual lack of nutrition scared the hell out of him. Frightened him more than the prospect of his annual prostate examination with his primary care physician, Dr. Theodore "the wandering finger" Taylor. All things considered, Harry thought, if he could extend his life expectancy for a few moments longer, why not? The well-deserved applause would belong to those two harping sons of his, and a refrigerator full of organic vegetables, which once murdered in a juicer would turn into some truly horrible-tasting sap.

Harry used to have a high opinion of himself. It was customary for him to sit as high on his horse as possible. Somehow, he was once under the misguided impression that he was a sensualist. Perhaps he really wasn't a sensualist at all, but a sedentary, middle-aged man who believed he had an "adventurous" appetite? He did love food, travel, a good cocktail; the smell of the house when he or his glorious wife took over the kitchen. But that time had come and gone. Presently, when he ate, it was to live another day; having to endure without glorious aromatics, and subsequent *um-ms* after tasting the delicious Sunday sauce. He was nourished every single day since, and yet he remained profoundly unsatisfied. His senses were dulled, like his spirit. He wanted change to arrive sooner, but he couldn't seem to make it happen. It wasn't quite the same as getting back into the gym. Not that he'd seen the inside of his local gym within the last ten years.

Harry often ate without a plate and sometimes without utensils, so forget about place settings or honoring the standing reservation at his own breakfast table. Besides, the table was cluttered with local circulars, bills, and unread newspapers. His 19-year-old son Will was away at college and Jake, just shy of 21, was at Parris Island training to become a United States Marine. The latter was a shock to the system Harry wasn't quite over yet. After a couple of passionate appeals and uncharacteristic rough runs at him, which included Harry flinging his VCR player, probably the last in its line, through a window in a fit of exasperation, Harry finally gave up. He gave Jake his "blessing" despite all the screaming reverberating between his ears. He had concerns for his son's safety, naturally. He wanted Jake to return home whole and safe and healthy. What's a father to do? He wanted Jake to be happy, to follow his passion, but for *Chrissakes* he offered him a gap year in Tuscany. Jake wouldn't go for it. And what would his dear Felicity think about all this? Harry would never have the answer to this question since Felicity was not of this world any longer.

Harry continued to dine in front of the stove in solitude. He yawned and began cleaning the stovetop, vacantly dabbing the stainless steel with a damp napkin. He was tired. Sleep did not come easy.

Harry felt a warm presence against his lower back and legs. A soft appreciative smile washed over him. He was never really alone even during his darkest moments. The only woman he ever loved would never prance out of their shower with glorious wet hair ever again and his boys – their boys – were flung far from the nest. Thank goodness for his subtly intrusive companion.

"I'm so sorry, Lolly, but no pancakes for you. You know the deal, you're a big dopey dope. You already ate the delicious-looking dry kibble. No preservatives, no additives. Yum, right?"

Lolly bobbed her head, which was the size of someone else's dog. She began nudging him away from the stove, pushing him toward the door.

"Okay, I know it's time. All right, I'm going."

Lolly was a majestic looking creature: mostly black with an ocean of white on her breast. The old girl was getting grey around her muzzle. She had big soulful eyes the color of a muddy pond and the longest eyelashes – the envy of every teenage girl.

"Go get the keys, and try not to drool on them," Harry said, his voice laced with mirth.

Lolly pranced toward the foyer like a small horse, homing in on the brass key holder staring back at her in the design of snarling cats. She nosed the car keys free from the cat-tail hooks. By the time she delivered them to Harry, he was tying his laces sitting in his leather chair in the living room. Lolly dropped them in his lap and true to form, his keys were covered in *dog gerb*, as his sons would often remark in an utterly repulsed tone of voice.

"You're still a sloppy girl?"

Lolly didn't react to being admonished. She never did, because those admonitions were poorly acted. Lolly had a way of showing her appreciation. Thank goodness this Great Dane was not the licking type. Lolly showed her affection by leaning against and nudging the ones she favored. And when she absolutely demanded attention, she would jump up and down. *You haven't lived until you've witnessed a Great Dane jumping and huffing in place*, Harry thought, admiring her. He frowned at her. Lolly's long face looked back at him the same way she did every morning, thoughtfully. Those muddy pools were soaking him up, waiting for his next move. It was apparent to Harry that Lolly's loyalty was keeping him sane. He didn't know what he'd do without her. He loved the damn dog and couldn't imagine losing her or anything else at this point and time. It just wouldn't be fair.

Harry wiped the gerby keys in the folds of his oversized sweat pants. Felicity would have given him hell for going outside looking like a retiree from Palm Coast, Florida.

"You're a handsome man," she would say to him. "Why would you want to go out dressed like you're going to play checkers at the mall?"

At this point, it was a matter of comfort and ease for Harry. Felicity was all about Harry looking his best; being at his best at all times. Harry would put up a wonderful pretend fight and then change his clothes.

"Now, that's better," she'd say beaming, parting his hair with those long sensuous fingers of hers.

Harry felt himself sink deeper in the chair. Lingering there wasn't necessarily a bad thing. He was soaking up the warmth of Felicity's voice. His entire body felt embraced by a warm sun.

"Lolly, we should have named you Gerby," he said to her finally. Harry smiled at the memory of his sons complaining about Lolly.

"Ahhh, Jesus H. Christ, his beloved disciples and the Lord above, she gerbed all over me, Pops!"

"Will, didn't your mother and I raise you to be perfectly reasonable atheists?"

Harry didn't mind religion although he didn't partake much. He wanted the boys to experience life and make their own decisions later on down the road. He didn't understand how anyone could be influenced by a dopey televangelist who preaches he's deserving of a private plane because his God signed off on it. Paid for by the hapless parishioners, of course. In Harry's opinion, the landscape was cluttered with snake-oil salesmen selling cheap theology to a gullible and damaged population.

"Holy hell, Pops. Would you rather me use the words Mom used to say when she was mad at the world? Holy crap, Jake, remember what she said to the guy who was pissing…?"

"Will, watch your vernacular in front of our father," Jake said joking, putting special emphasis on the word *vernacular*, one of their father's most overused words.

"To the gentleman who was urinating on her rosemary plant in front of the house?"

"You don't want him to go there, Pops. I honestly felt sorry for the guy by the time Mom was through with him," Jake chirped. "It was gross. The gerb, I mean. Better you than me, you little idiot," he said to Will.

"Jake, you're not helping," Harry said, knowing the boys were having fun at his expense.

"I don't know, Pops. Everyone with the last name Kavanagh has a twisted smile on their face right now," Will volunteered. "Mission accomplished, right Jake?"

"Anything to make the old man smile," Jake added. "Right, Pops?"

"Affirmative," Harry countered, giving in.

The boys knew their old man loved the big dog, but they never seemed to have much patience for her. She was an inconvenience: having to walk her constantly, and there were those massive stools they were obligated to scoop off the streets. Harry supposed there was nothing more embarrassing for a teenage boy attempting to impress a teenage girl in a passing car than having to stand guard beside a Great Dane while it unloaded in broad daylight.

Harry tugged gently on Lolly's ear and whispered, "Let's go, beautiful. And by the way, I know the boys wouldn't admit this, but I bet they miss you." And without putting a leash on Lolly, Harry exited through the kitchen door. Lolly followed him at her own pace.

Chapter Two

Harry slid the passenger seat as far back as it would go so Lolly could ascend into the old Volvo without too much stress. With a boost from Harry, she took her rightful place beside him in the passenger seat. Lolly looked straight ahead, resembling an ancient gargoyle. The audience responses were well worth the extra effort it took Harry to help Lolly clamber onto the front seat. Horns honking and people gaping. "You need to put a saddle on that dog!" Harry was tired of hearing that one. But the wondrous expressions they would often receive traveling together in the car sometimes made Harry laugh. And it wasn't such a bad thing for a man struggling with a steady diet of depression to crack a smile every now and then.

"Now don't fidget or I'll demote you to the backseat," Harry said, wagging a finger at Lolly.

He followed through with a playful tap on the tip of her nose with his finger. Lolly looked at Harry dispassionately. She hadn't moved in the slightest. It was Harry filling the air with the sound of his own voice. It soothed him to think he was having a conversation with his 175-pound traveling companion who just happened to be his best friend. Maybe his only true friend. And as his B-team friends mentioned on many occasions, taking Lolly along for a joy ride was a good way for Harry to meet women. A new woman. To start all over again, beginning with a simple conversation.

Harry wasn't keen on the idea of showcasing his dog as bait to speak with members of the opposite sex. So, he never gave it too much thought. The woman thing was beyond his reach at the moment. The thought of meeting women, actually speaking to one with the intention of going out on a date, well, this made him feel clumsy inside. In his way, he was no different than his youngest son, Will.

Harry was 50 years old. His sons were away, and his wife was deceased. Felicity Kavanagh died four years ago in a horrendous car accident. She skidded off a deserted water-side road in her car midway between the Staten Island Ferry Terminal and the Verrazano-Narrows Bridge. The circumstances of the accident haunt Harry. There were many lonely days and on some of those days Harry wished he had companionship, but...there was always the bothersome *but*. When he tried to mull it around, his guilt always provided him with an easy escape clause. Harry still considered himself a married man. He was angry with Felicity for getting in her car with one-too-many drinks in her system. She knew better. He desperately wished she would have called him for a pickup. He used to say to her, often marveling, yet always slightly annoyed, "Why do you have a cellphone if you don't answer it? Why do you have a cellphone if you never call anyone?"

It had taken Harry a scant three months to remove most of Felicity's belongings from the house. His sons thought he was moving too quickly. He wouldn't agree at the time. Harry wasn't very agreeable then. He couldn't handle seeing Felicity's shoes, dozens of pairs, and her clothing, some of it vintage, with specific memories attached, mingling with his belongings. It made her seem alive, and Harry's grief told him otherwise. He felt teased by everything she owned. So much so, that his imagination often had him believing she would dance out of their shower with a playful glint in her eye. His anticipation died when he rid himself of all of her things. Later on, he agreed he'd made a grave mistake. He missed everything about Felicity, even the hairband she wore to her yoga class.

Properly closing her closet instead of opening it, Felicity said this, days before she died, "Are you thinking the same thing I'm thinking, handsome?" And her towel dropped to the floor, much to Harry's amusement.

"Hurry up, I'm cold," she complained, as he stared at his good fortune.

Harry was so profoundly in love with Felicity. His entire body ached for another moment with her. The closet was all his now. His grief deepened whenever he opened it. Was there a desire for Harry to move on? He didn't have a clue. This intrusive question was posed to him in many different ways and much too often.

Harry Kavanagh was never much of a mover or shaker. He was a playwright and college professor; having spent the last twenty years teaching the same courses at the university. He liked his job. There were never surprises and on average he enjoyed his students. He was comfortable with his life the way it was. All things considered, he was free from worry. He was fortunate enough to have a brilliant and talented wife who loved him, whom he loved, and those boys of theirs. Life was good. He was driven by the aspirations and the impulses of his wife. She planned their vacations, chose the house they lived in; she did the research and wrote the business plan that evolved into her successful boutique wine shop. That's the way it was – the way they danced the game of life together. He was content with Felicity tugging on the locomotive's horn. She moved their lives steadily ahead along the tracks. He was the clueless passenger who would occasionally awake and ask with the tone of an innocent, "Are we there yet?"

He gave Felicity's belongings to her girlfriends and donated the rest to community organizations. He kept her wedding band and engagement ring and a black and white handmade sweater she'd worn when they met at seventeen. She wore the sweater a few days before the accident.

"Looking like a resplendent teenager," Harry remembered telling her.

"Resplendent is the professor's way of saying I look good for an old broad."

In moments like those, her responses were uttered with a smile that made her look forever ageless. She was more than he deserved. Harry was looking forward to hitting the recreational vehicle highway with the beautiful old broad. He tossed the thought aside quickly. Did he think Felicity would ever step foot in an RV? She would prefer to spend the rest of her days dragging him around Tuscany. Not such a bad place to be sequestered. Hell, he probably would've never gotten married if Felicity hadn't chosen him. She practically picked him out of a lineup. Harry shook her smile from his mind when he felt his eyes getting moist. He looked over at Lolly who was watching him.

"Goddamn it. You remember her, don't you girl?"

In the solitude of his car, Harry's mind began to question his partnership with his wife. He'd done this before. He felt a flare of anger building inside of him. He spoke to himself on the exhalation, nearly running out of breath.

"How could she love a man like me? I've lived an unspectacular life, done nothing of great note, saved no one from drowning."

Lolly poked his shoulder with her nose. She looked at him with a deeper focus. Harry looked over at those big soulful eyes. "Okay, thanks girl. Okay."

There was an open-field dog-run behind Clove Lakes Park. A place where neighbors would have a few laughs, catch up on community news, or complain about whatever ailed them, which meant politics, ballgames, former spouses, or sometimes entitled children. There was always the option of going your own way, but it took effort. Once you dipped your toe in, you usually got what you got and dealt with it one way or another.

Harry shook his head in dismay when he saw Robert Devine in the middle of the field chewing on the end of an unlit cigar. Devine was plucking at the ass-crease in his trousers with his fingers; his appearance was sucking the life and temporary good nature out of Harry's universe. The hard-luck bystanders enveloped by Devine's negativism were his captive audience. The expressions on their faces dramatized their woeful existence in the presence of his low-rent mediocrity.

Devine worked for the state senator whose office was located in the St. George neighborhood, downtown Staten Island. It was a diverse, urban neighborhood, crumbling for decades, presently in the midst of an economic resurgence. The hilly landscape emptied at the ferry terminal, which deposited commuters into lower Manhattan. Senator Irene Roth's office was located several blocks from the Kavanagh abode and a stone's throw from Felicity's now shuttered wine shop. Felicity had been a sometime critic of the state senator, which usually triggered the senator's corpulent lap dog to froth back. Devine's attacks volleyed back in the form of barks of condescension and arrogance, which boarded on being threatening in nature. Nothing Felicity couldn't handle.

Harry believed Devine was nothing more than a glorified administrative aide. Yet Harry couldn't imagine how Devine's engorged fingers could possibly navigate a keyboard. Roth allowed Devine to act as her Pit Bull when it suited her. Devine enjoyed this role even though the payoff probably wasn't in his bi-monthly envelope. The growing speculation around the neighborhood was the results of the upcoming election would probably render Senator Roth a local citizen. On more than one occasion, Roth stormed out of community meetings when the questions asked didn't match her agenda or crib notes. The local newspapers, which no one confused with the *New York Times*, rarely challenged her. The big-city reporters and the one or two local ardent scribes would catch up with her in Albany and persist. Over time, she'd put off so many neighborhood people that some who hadn't taken part in the political process in years vowed to get off their La-Z-Boys to vote against her.

Over the years, Roth benefited from the apathy running through the pot-holed streets of the community. Small voter turnouts translated into victories. As Harry liked to believe, every rabid dog and disingenuous politician eventually reaches the end of the line. Roth's unemployment was in sight. This inevitability fostered an edginess among her staff. Their discomfort bled through their pores. And it didn't take much to set off a guy like Devine to begin with.

Harry regretted not making himself a cup or three of coffee before he left the house. He went to the dog-run to decompress and relax. He hadn't sniffed any of that yet. Harry doubted he had enough left in his tank to deal with a dark cloud who insisted on being called Bobby Dee.

Harry wasn't dressed warmly enough and he shuddered. "Lolly, is it too late to get out of the pool?" She didn't answer. "I asked you a question," he said playfully. Still no answer.

Harry mustered a smile as he watched Lolly jog off. Harry turned his back and ambled as far away from Devine as he could without leaving the grassy area. Lolly found a friendly pack of smaller dogs who were pleased to yip in her shadow, gaze up at her and sniff wherever she allowed them to.

"Harry Kavanagh, holy smoke, you're a hard man to find," a raspy female voice announced.

It was Emma Kendall, the self-proclaimed delicious-looking divorcee who owned and operated a gift shop in town. Harry thought he'd never catch a break until he noticed Emma was holding two cups of coffee. He felt guilty for a fleeting second, but he got over it when Emma handed him a coffee. Harry sipped it immediately. It wasn't very hot, but he decided to pretend it was the best cup of coffee he ever had.

"I know you like yours from Manoscalpo's. This is from my new favorite coffee spot," she said.

"Just the way I like it," he said fibbing through a smile.

"If I were holding a morbidly obese bacon, egg, and cheese *sangwich* in the shape of a lumpy football, now that would be something for Bobby Dee over yonder."

"Your language skills are off the charts. How do you really feel?"

"Let me explain it to you," she said.

"I think I get it, but if you insist," Harry responded, not so happily playing along.

"I would bark at him to go out for a pass. He'd go for it because he's a big fat slob of a man. And you know, he'd put his polyester trousers, made by small asthmatic children in China, to the extreme test by straining to fetch it. But you, my friend, you get a beautiful cup of coffee."

"Kindly do this man one more favor?" Harry said smiling falsely, sipping his tepid coffee. "First and foremost, thank you for the coffee and secondly, please keep your disgust at a lower decibel. I'm in no mood to breathe in his high-school halitosis this morning."

She made a face at him and quickly shifted gear. "Aren't you in the least curious how I found you here?"

"You're aware that I own a dog. This is a dog-run."

She frowned at him. "You disappoint me."

"Tell me the story. You can begin with once upon a time if you want," he said, trying to warm his hands against the lukewarm Styrofoam.

"Your words are shallow, but the appreciation in your eyes means much more to me."

"There's appreciation in these bloodshot old things?"

Harry felt uncomfortable when Emma's blazing smile seemed to brand him. A Jack Russell Terrier had discovered Lolly and began barking incessantly at her. The moment between them was lost, and Harry was grateful for the interruption. As the other dogs moved off, Lolly stood patiently as the little pest continued to sputter and yap.

"Who owns that little thing?" Emma asked, talking more to herself.

Harry turned back and realized Emma was frowning at him. Her frown softened into a smile. He noticed Emma's rather notable fur coat at first glance but felt the urge to say something about it now, to keep her from asking him out. The shoulder pads sown inside made her look like a cross between an aging Joan Crawford and the alien in a gorilla suit in the 1953 movie *Robot Monster*, considered by many to be the worst movie ever made. Harry wouldn't be sharing all of his thoughts with her.

"I can see you thinking. Stop making judgments; the fur is a fake, okay," she said to him, deflating.

He wanted to say, no kidding. Instead, he heard himself, "It doesn't really compliment you in the way you deserve." Harry was trying to be diplomatic for purely selfish reasons, however, he was plunging head-long into a no-win situation.

"It gets worse than that. For a second, I thought it was once a circus animal, or possibly a remnant from an old costume shop. It was an apology attempt from my former husband."

"Forgive me, but it's no way to apologize. Even I know it." He tried to hide his amusement.

"You're pissing me off, Harry Kavanagh."

"All right, Emma, get ready. I'm going to ask you the big question."

"This is the apology for putting your foot in your mouth? You're setting me up?"

"I'm tossing you a beach ball. Hit it out of the park. I like to hear you say it. You provided coffee. I'm giving you this opportunity. Forgive my smart aleck remarks. Go ahead then. I don't watch much television; you are the only reality show in town."

"Sure, you say it with fun, but there's no love in your eyes, Mister," she said flirtatiously. "So, as you know, I *am* the delicious divorcee. Since you're making me announce it, does it sound organic enough?"

"It sounds a little rehearsed," he said.

"You know, sometimes it's not what you say or how you say it, but it's how you feel. Regardless of how you're receiving it, despite the chill in the air, despite any and all rejections, I still do feel especially yummy, thank you very much."

"Okay then, before we move on, let's ask the other question you live to hear. How is your ex?"

She giggled and couldn't get it out fast enough. "He's sleeping on his brother's couch in Fort Lee, New Jersey. That's what happens to a husband who happens to have a venti-sized cheating problem."

The little-pest-of-a-dog continued to bark at Lolly. "Lolly, come on over here," Harry said, remaining slightly amused.

Harry liked Emma, in very small doses. She was one of Felicity's friends, as far as neighborhood friendships go. Felicity and Emma never seemed to be intimately involved, but they enjoyed each other's company in quick bursts and spent time gallivanting around the neighborhood together. Emma really shone bright after Felicity's accident and was very supportive during the family's subsequent ordeal. She bought Harry a new coffee pot, one of the more modern types, which he hadn't taken out of the box, and she also made many trips over with freshly-baked bread or cookies. She signed herself up for Lolly-walking duty, and in the beginning, she would drop the boys off at high school in the morning. At the time, Will was a sophomore and Jake a senior. The boys already had their driver's licenses, but they were traumatized by their mother's accident. Neither of them would get behind the wheel of a car for nearly a year. The drop-offs didn't last long. Harry sensed the boys were uncomfortable around Emma. She was essentially a stranger to them. He didn't think too much about it at the time. The boys were going through a lot. They were uncomfortable around a lot of people. But since the boys seemed to be unhappy, Harry decided to take over. Going forward, the last face his sons should see in the morning before school would be his.

It so happened his instincts were on target. The boys were slow to talk about their feelings in therapy sessions or with their father at home, but the ride to school was a different story. It seemed to bring along with it a manageable structure: limited time and short bursts of freedom. In the 7–10 minutes it took Harry to drive the boys to school, they struggled to put into words their feelings about losing the most important person in their lives. To his credit, Harry never censored the boys, and their discussions inside the car were never followed up at home. The morning sessions inside the Volvo turned out to be an important time for all of them.

Harry and Emma had gone out to dinner a few times, spread out over long periods of time (which was the way Harry planned it), and Harry did manage to enjoy himself. His Felicity was a funny, attractive, easy-going personality, with a laugh and a tilt of her head that made you feel like you were the center of the universe. Felicity was feminine, intelligent. She possessed a quiet dignity and a strong resolve. Emma, on the other hand, could be a loudmouth. She fancied herself as *the* center of the universe. She reminded Harry of an overly-ingratiating, boozy stereotype often dramatized in the black and white gangster movies of the 1930s and 1940s. A gun moll. A strong-willed, yet ultimately wronged person who genuflected before gangsters and tough guys; later on shooting them in the back. Harry never considered himself a tough guy. Funny thing, as far as Harry knew Emma didn't drink. Not a drop. The one exception was the night she kicked her husband out of the house. Emma, free of her husband, was completely comfortable in her own skin, whether she was clad in a bikini watering the shrubs in front of her house or in the hideous faux coat she was currently adorned in. She played tennis, was athletic, well read and possessed many eccentric talents. Harry liked her, but it was becoming more and more apparent Emma was pressing to become more than friends. Harry wasn't comfortable dancing the dance. He wasn't interested in going to the prom.

Lolly danced over and leaned on Harry. "Good girl," Harry said, stroking her.

"Hey, look at you, sweetie girl," Emma said patting Lolly on her side.

"So, come on, what's with this coat, Emma?" He must have contorted his face when he said it because Emma looked at him funny.

"I know you, Harry. You're thinking the only thing missing is a monster mask, correct?" She smiled at him and continued. "You know, it's nice to see you relax, or at least try." She hesitated, "In any event, I want to show you something."

"There's something else?" he asked.

Her tone held a playfulness that made him squirm. She stepped closer to him, leaned in and opened her hideous coat, giving him a peek at her shapely body. She was wearing nothing underneath, save a negligee.

"They say 48 is the new 47 and I think I wear it well. That is, the little that I'm wearing. What say you, my good man?"

Think was the operative word, because Harry was having trouble doing the thing called thinking. He felt his face flush with the redness of a boy discovered with a *Playboy* magazine back in the day.

"I uh," he stammered. Lolly looked up at him, awaiting his response.

"Don't expect Lolly to bail you out of this one, Harry."

Emma re-wrapped herself in the coat, not nearly as annoyed as Harry thought she'd be. She quickly changed gear and said, "I asked you earlier, how you think I found you here today?"

"Right, okay," Harry said in a wobbly voice.

Emma took a breath and pronounced, "I got up this morning wanting to see you. I woke up with you all over my mind. All over it."

"All over your mind? You make me sound like a raw egg that exploded on the top of your head."

"That's not the analogy I would have used."

"You're making me more uncomfortable. And I didn't think it was possible."

"It sounds decadent. But shut up, you have to know what I mean. I was thinking about you and Felicity too. So, I jumped out of bed, put this awful thing on because I knew it would cover all the juicy parts. Why else would I put something like this on?"

"If the important parts were covered in the first place, you wouldn't have had to borrow something from the Yeti's closet."

The Jack Russell Terrier sprang over to them and began yapping at Lolly. The big girl turned away, calmly dismissing the uninvited guest. Emma tried to shoo her away with a wave of her gloved hand.

"I pulled up to your house as you were driving away. I followed you here, took a detour to get us some coffee and here I am. I came to make you an offer – to offer myself to you. For us."

"I'm very confused," was all Harry could offer.

"The point is, on one hand, this is no big deal," Emma said. "We're consenting adults as they say and listen, this isn't me wanting to have a quickie for my benefit or yours. I don't feel sorry for you, Harry. I've had my share of quickies with my husband during the seventeen years of our disastrous marriage. Nobody benefits from five minutes. It's better to feed off each other. I can be a voracious person. Right now, I'm peckish and I was hoping you would dine with me."

The little dog continued to bark. "Will you stop it," Harry snapped at the terrier. He really wanted to bark at Emma.

"So, I came here to persuade you to come back to my place for a hot breakfast. If you know what I mean."

"Whatever comes next, please don't wink at me," Harry said.

"Jesus Christ, Harry, you're ruining it."

"Emma," Harry didn't know what he was about to say. His coffee was getting colder by the moment, and he was mortified by her offer. She watched him struggle to respond.

"No need for explanations, Harry," she quipped. "How about we decide something before I leave so there won't be any hard feelings?"

Robert Devine was approaching them; Harry was hoping to finish the conversation before Devine made his boorish presence felt.

"Okay, Emma. Sure."

"Let's agree that you'll take me up on my breakfast offer. When you're ready."

"Um, sounds like a plan," he said, sounding indecisive and disingenuous. And the word *breakfast* would never hold the same meaning for him.

"Hey, come here you little bitch," Devine's voice bellowed.

Harry's stomach sank; he knew he was about to get into something unpleasant with the state senator's sidekick. Emma whirled around at the sound of Devine's voice.

Devine sucked on his unlit cigar and said with a glint in his rheumy eye, "No, not you, honey. I was talking to the dog." Devine laughed so hard, his face reddened like a cartoon smokestack ready to explode.

"Excuse me?" Harry said.

"You're excused, Kavanagh. I'm worried about the little bitch. It's my friend's dog."

"You have a friend?" Emma could not resist.

"I'm bitch-sitting. I'm available and my rates are reasonable."

Emma snarled at Devine and nodded to Harry. "So long." She did an about-face and marched off.

"So long, Emma," he said weakly to her back.

Devine watched her walk away. He still had the sneer on his face when he turned his chins toward Harry. Harry was not smiling back.

"I don't suppose you read much, do you, Devine?"

"Oh boy, you got me pegged there, smart guy," he said in a mocking tone. "I mostly look at the cartoon pictures. Yup."

"Dashiell Hammett wrote this nifty little story, *The Glass Key*."

"Geez, Kavanagh. All you have to do is open your mouth and you bore the snot out of me."

"I don't recall if it was in the book, but when they did the movie, Alan Ladd, who plays Ed Beaumont, the good guy, he kicks this guy, somebody a lot like you, this boorish loudmouth. You'll get the picture even though you're a little slow on the uptake. He kicks this lout ever so subtlety with the tip of his shoe, right in the dope's shin. Beaumont's body barely moves when he bends his knee. It's a simple, quiet move. And you know what happens to the big, bad bully?"

"Let me guess. He takes the little wet-ass twerp by the throat and wrings his neck. Then he takes his lifeless body and uses it as anal floss after an all-day chili-eating contest. How's that sound?"

"The dope, a guy a lot like you who's always about five minutes from stroking out, he hits the deck, like a soiled, greasy bag of donuts. Not donuts made by a family-run bakery. No, they would be buoyant. He goes down hard like a heavy corporate donut that's been injected with additives and poisons you couldn't properly pronounce or digest."

"Ooh, you really know how to insult a guy. You must be a writer no one's ever heard of." Devine howled with laughter.

Harry continued, "It's because the shin, like your bloated stomach, is vulnerable. You would fold easy and go down hard."

Devine ran his hand over the coat protecting his large stomach. He sized up Harry and said, "What, are you going do? Punt me with your yellow sneakers, Kavanagh?"

"My sneakers are orange. I'm only suggesting how simple it would be to take down a bully."

They continued to go back and forth at each other. Their tone was getting increasingly loud and they were attracting attention. Some of the park-goers edged over to get a front row seat, leaving their dogs to frolic unsupervised and sniff among themselves.

That little dog began yapping again. Devine angrily reached down and plucked it, holding the dog uneasily, like a football player bound to fumble. He took a step closer to Harry.

"Yes? Is there something you want?" Harry's impulse was to step back, but instead he raised his chin attempting to make himself as tall as possible.

"I always thought your wife was the pain in the ass. She with her snobby ways." He eyed Lolly with trepidation. "But you take the cake. Why don't you put your horse in the stable, so we can see what kind of a man you really are?"

"Let me stop you there, Devine," Harry heard himself say. It was a quick response; he felt his heart beating quickly. "My wife was always the smartest person in the room. You didn't have the vocabulary or the intellect to keep up. Humiliating you came naturally to her."

Devine's face flushed. He took another step closer to Harry. Lolly edged closer to Harry. Harry was riveted by the food particles stuck between Devine's lower teeth. His breath was acrid.

"I don't care what you think of me, but don't you ever disparage my wife's memory again."

"Or what, Kavanagh? You'll throw yogurt at me?"

Lolly had been leaning against Harry, mostly disinterested, but she turned her head toward Devine and looked him over with a growing interest.

"My wife was more passionate about this community than most, including leadership, and let me give you a tip, Devine," nodding toward Lolly, "she is not smiling at you."

A resonant growl emanated from within the big dog. The little dog leapt from Devine's grasp and fled. Devine hesitated, frightened. Some of the spectators were enjoying Devine's imbroglio. He went white as a bleached sheet, took a few stumbling backward steps, and waddled after his ward.

Harry took a breath and decided there was nothing more to gain from cradling a cup of cold coffee. He noticed a little tremble in his hand. Harry and Lolly walked toward the car slowly, side by side like best friends sometimes do.

Harry was upset the rest of the day. He wasn't very good at letting things go. He tried reaching Emma, but she wasn't having any of it. He probably owed her an apology. He wasn't certain. He cringed at the prospect of hearing her husky voice so soon. But he wanted to check in and see if she was okay. If she was able to wash away the stench of one Robert Devine. Harry was all too aware that his hesitancy, or rather his refusal, to join in on Emma's reindeer-rutting games threw her for a loop even though she pretended otherwise. She offered him a roll in the hay. He wanted to magically rewind the morning, however, there was no guarantee a redo would change anything. Emma was unpredictable. Harry had come to believe he'd been treading around a landmine whenever they were together. If Emma picked up the phone, he'd have to tap dance, which might lead to a broader estrangement. Maybe some distance between them wasn't such a bad idea. When Harry realized the beep had already gone off, he decided that not checking in was the best message of all.

Devine was a big man with a bad temper. Harry had heard stories of his barroom beat-downs. Devine was usually the one on the giving, not the receiving, end. Harry supposed Devine's friends in local government tucked away those incidents, shielding him from a broader inquiry. Devine's breath stunk up just about every place he went, yet he never seemed to pay the price.

No one enjoys public humiliation. Harry hoped he didn't look overmatched. His boys told him he could be tough – that he had a surprising temper. While it rarely emerged, when it did, they recognized it as a sign not to mess with the old man. Harry wasn't so sure it was true. Harry couldn't stomach being trapped in a position where his dignity could be stolen from him. Harry didn't like to linger around the word *wary*, but yes, he was afraid of Devine. Harry was certain about one thing: if the big girl hadn't been by his side, there would have been a different outcome. Things probably wouldn't have gone in his favor.

"Thank you, Lolly. He probably would've kicked my arse if you weren't there," he admitted, patting her head.

That night, Harry was hopeful that his taste buds might rise from the dead. So, he decided to eat out. A local place. Place he'd never been to before. A restaurant that had always looked good from the outside. He was willing to give it a shot. He was in between paperbacks and nothing on television was currently sparking his imagination. He petted Lolly curled up on the floor on top of her blankets beside the humming dryer. Harry ran the empty thing on chilly nights because he loved to see Lolly lie so comfortably beside it, saddling up to its warmth. Fewer things made him happier than observing Lolly sleeping comfortably. Harry quietly exited through the kitchen door.

Harry's mind began working overtime the moment he sidled into the restaurant. He questioned his impulses when the manager greeted him with an insecure smile. The man with the dyed eyebrows had a look of near panic in his eyes as he scanned the room for a table. There were a few open tables. Harry couldn't understand the man's hesitancy. The manager took Harry on a circuitous walk to a table that had a clear shortcut as an option. *Things are not looking good*, Harry thought. It took fifteen minutes to receive the drink Harry so desperately needed. The cocktail glass had a lipstick stain on the rim. When the mussels arrived, it was clear they weren't properly cleaned. They were peppered with sand. The bread was as hard as a brick, and his lonely water glass longed for attention. Harry was blaming himself. He was not a happy Kavanagh. In fact, he was a miserable Kavanagh.

When the waiter explained for the third time that the chef had *graciously decided* to take the mussels off the bill, Harry decided it was time to throw in the towel. He floated enough cash onto the tablecloth to cover the sandy entrée and the sub-par everything else.

Apparently, he wasn't the only one looking for an escape route. As he headed for the exit, Harry noticed the waiter and the skittish manager were receding to the darkest niche of the restaurant. Perhaps to save themselves the indignity of having to ask Harry how everything was. In which case, Harry would have been obligated to lecture them until their ears bled lava.

There was something telling about the night's air. It was uncharacteristically humid for the time of the year. Harry's instincts were quickly confirmed. He turned up his collar the instant he was hit with a chilly blast of moist wind. Bad weather was not just brewing, it was already upon him.

Harry was fumbling for his car keys when he spotted a stooped figure in the shadows. Glancing to his left, he saw a man gagging on a cigarette. Harry recognized Corbin Reece, the medical examiner who lived locally. It was Reece's findings that reported the cause of Felicity Kavanagh's passing: death by drowning.

Over the years, Harry and Reece exchanged small talk whenever they crossed paths. Their discussions were brief, cordial, and solemn. After all, how many times did either one of them want to be reminded of Felicity's death? As time went on, Harry speculated that Reece's behavior and appearance had changed. He seemed more impatient – appeared physically unhealthy and was sometimes shaky on his feet, trying too hard to conceal his favorite habit of day drinking. Dead bodies were Reece's line of work. Had Felicity's death affected him more than the countless others over his long career? And if so, why? It struck Harry as odd. Or perhaps Harry was making this stuff up. Losing his wife unexpectedly, tragically, it created a lot of uncertainty within him. The ground beneath Harry's feet seemed unsteady every single day he stepped out of his house. *Why do I even bother to go out?* Harry thought.

Harry tried to deflect these thoughts as quickly as they came up. They made him uneasy, then angry, filling him with a heaviness that weighed his shoulders down. There was no mystery. Felicity had been drinking, which was not uncommon, she owned a wine shop, but she *was* driving. It turned out to be a deadly mistake. She was drunk, lost control of her car and drowned. Her car careened off the road and became partially submerged in shallow water. Shallow – but deadly – water, as it turned out. It was a horrible accident, an undeserving conclusion: the end of a beautiful life. And it was the end of their story, certainly. Harry couldn't accept the way she left them, and often tried to invent a conspiracy theory but there was none, period. Felicity controlled her own destiny and because of it, the lives of her loved ones were changed forever.

Reece flicked the cigarette into the street using his thumb. He did it with a flair of an experienced chain-smoker. He hacked a few more times and walked back toward the restaurant's entrance. Reece's impoverished complexion was evident even in the splintered night-light. He had lost more weight than Harry, but unlike Harry, Reece looked ravaged. The redness in his cheeks and nose had something to do with his keeping company with his best friend and constant companion, Jack Daniels. Reece led with his head bowed; he scratched the patches of eczema on his forehead. His hungry eyes searched for the door handle. He awkwardly stepped back inside the restaurant.

Harry observed Reece through the picture window, through the spaces in between the gold-trimmed calligraphy. Reece waved his hand like a sleepy magician. The bartender placed the ready Jack Daniels on the rocks in his hand. The handoff was executed with a flourish. The strangers crowding Reece applauded him. Despite the celebration, Reece wore his sadness like a musty overcoat. It was something he couldn't conceal from a keen observer. None of this was lost on Harry. Misery was in fact seeping through Reece's pores; it was his most faithful escort.

Harry had lingered long enough, but a funny thing held his attention. It happened quickly. At first, Harry thought he might have imagined it. Reece pivoted his head as he took a sloppy swig of his drink. He looked directly into Harry's eyes. *Call me.* Was Harry reading his expression correctly?

There were moments when Harry thought he would be swaying like Corbin Reece. Drinking until he was unsteady – head swiveling without his permission until his soulless eyes landed on someone else's wife at the end of the bar. With so many things in his positive column, there were days when Harry still needed to convince himself that he had a lot to live for. And that made him feel ashamed. He snapped out of his reverie and looked at Reece. Reece stumbled and dropped, disappearing from Harry's line of vision.

"Down goes Frazier! Down goes Frazier! Down goes Frazier." Harry conjured Howard Cosell's ringside chant from the famed bout so many years ago. The shocking sight of the undefeated champion of the world, Smokin' Joe Frazier, disorientated and helpless, feeling his way to the canvas with George Foreman looming over him, was cemented in Harry's memory.

There were demons looming over Corbin Reece. He was losing the fight. The bar patrons, many of them as intoxicated as he was, were stooping, wobbling, reaching for Reece, but with no real ability or genuine intention to rescue him. He was down for the count. No surprises here. It was all part of his final jig.

Harry walked away on an empty stomach, ticked off at how his evening had gone. He expected to be confronted with a stint of insomnia when he got home. He wished for a stash of paperbacks that he'd forgotten about. A cozy mystery to befriend him and guide him off to sleep. Harry wasn't looking forward to getting in touch with Corbin Reece. He shouldn't have wasted any time obsessing. Because the next time anyone wanting answers would think to pay Corbin Reece a visit, his lifeless body would be inside a box. And he wouldn't be breathing, which meant no talking either.

He had no way of knowing it, but Harry's unsteady feet were standing on the doorstep of his own magical-mystery tour. A real-life thriller, not a cozy mystery on the Hallmark Channel. He was about to go on a journey, as personal and painful as it gets. But first he had to remember where he parked his car. The wind kicked up a notch.

Chapter Three

Harry heard the pitter-patter midway through his miserable night. He wasn't sure if he'd been asleep for more than a five-minute stretch. The rain was not the only reason he was rousted. He had no one to blame but himself. His mind was racing. He was thinking about Felicity, worrying about his boys and trying to push the image of Corbin Reece from his consciousness. He was restless and couldn't land on a paperback. His stomach was making sounds he'd never heard before. It was as barren as his fridge. His biggest mistake was choosing bourbon before bedtime. Bourbon from a pint glass – neat; filled halfway. Two words never meant to hold hands: tall bourbon. It was not a bright idea. The tall bourbon was an aberration. Yeah, Harry should've known better. At his age, he knew that nailing down his sleep habits were as vital as breathing. Any choice made compromising sleep, well then, the fault lies with the instigator. Harry was guilty of sabotaging his night. Harry felt nauseated and generally unfit for any kind of duty. The wise choice would have been a glass of warm milk and some melatonin, but unfortunately, Harry was out of both.

While deciding on whether or not to remain a prisoner to his misery, Harry found himself drifting toward dialogue replaying in his head, from the Hitchcock entertainment, *North by Northwest*, written by Ernest Lehman. Harry held a special place in his heart for movie writers. In his opinion, few people seemed to know or care who the great movie architects were. The creator of *Robot Monster*? Yeah, some writers should be forgotten. But screenwriter Ernest Lehman wrote one of Harry's favorite films. But naughty ol' Ernie reminded Harry of his really bad idea when Martin Landau's melodious voice cut through the chaos in Harry's mind:

"Scotch, rye, bourbon, vodka? But first a libation, bourbon."

Forcing a bottomless glass of bourbon down Cary Grant's cultured gullet was the initial way Hitchcock's no-goodniks attempted to do away with the dashing gentleman.

But unlike Roger Thornhill, Harry wasn't coerced. He aided and abetted himself when he slung his legs out of bed. He reached for the glass and the bottle he kept hidden inside the bedside table drawer. The glass was dusty, but the bourbon was wet. Good enough. He polished off the nightcap like a glass of chocolate milk. If Cary Grant and Ernest Lehman glanced down from their jaunty corner table in the heavens, they would have mocked Harry with disapproving expressions. Party over, nothing good ever happens after the tall bourbon. *Doesn't everyone know that?* Harry could put a damper on a party in heaven. He wanted his mind to stop trifling with him. He wanted the bourbon to knock him out, but it sat in his stomach like a rusty anchor.

Harry tossed and tangled in bed until thuds of the rain above his head reminded him of the overmatched catch basins outside his house. During a heavy rainfall, the catch basins often clogged with neighborhood debris. Which meant toil and trouble. Lots of trouble, and wretched, lonely work for Harry.

The thought of the Barolo Harry should have savored three hours before sleep presented itself in his waking nightmare. Harry opened his eyes recalling that he hadn't sipped a glass of wine since Felicity died. There was no conscious rhyme or reason to it, it just turned out that way.

Harry dragged himself out of bed and looked out his window. Much to his dismay, he saw puddles of water escaping down the street, beginning to hug the curb. The water would rise to an unmanageable level if he didn't clear the debris from the gratings. He didn't want water seeping through his cellar windows. He didn't have the will to slosh around in a flooded cellar. There was a complication: some of Felicity's favorite Barolos from her boutique wine shop were stored in the cellar. About six cases from different winemakers, handpicked by Felicity. Clean and delicious, biodynamically produced beauties. Someone had to protect Felicity's *soldiers*, as she used to refer to the special bottles. He elected himself, naturally. Harry's temples began to throb at the thought of going outside.

Harry tried not to look at his reflection in the staircase mirror. He knew his face would be puffy and his hair pointed upward, making him look like he was wearing a dunce cap. He seemed to wake up looking like this on most mornings. He had to get rid of that mirror.

Years ago, Felicity remarked that Harry might still be slightly taller than their youngest son, Will. Will sniggered, replying, "That's because Pops wears a pompadour."

That was Will all over: quick, funny, unpretentious; he wouldn't let you get away with anything. Will was in a conservatory program at an upstate college. Will was a dancer, and Harry's other son was at Parris Island training to become a United States Marine. *Go figure?* Harry thought. Harry's expression grew serious: there are so many things one cannot foresee when staring in the mirror.

Harry realized he hadn't heard from Will and it concerned him more than the bloody rain. Maybe the old man had become too morose? Maybe Will needed a break from the shroud of sadness Harry cast over everyone? Harry's heart ached; he needed to snap out of it and do better. He needed his boys and he needed to work through his bereavement, so he could be present for them. Harry thought about calling Will. He quickly changed his mind. It was too early to call a college kid, and besides, Harry needed an infusion of caffeine so his mind and body would function better.

Harry took a peek outside. The rain was coming down harder and streaming down the street. He estimated that he had a little wiggle room before the situation became critical.

He hovered over the stove sipping coffee he made from his beloved Corning Ware percolator. He abhorred drip coffee makers and the dreaded French Press. And the thing Emma bought him? The blood in Harry's veins required honest-to-goodness perked coffee. Harry sipped his coffee as Lolly pushed her nose into his hip, possibly reminding him to stop procrastinating and get moving. The storm wasn't getting any friendlier.

Harry was holding a letter written by his oldest son, Jake. It was a quickly scribbled missive, fairly upbeat. Jake tells his father the nicknames gifted to his fellow recruits by those Parris Island "comedians," the drill instructors: Sweet Lips, Sweet Thing, Squid, Longfellow (*Don't ask, Pops*, Jake writes), The Ghost of Bravo Company, Creature, Fat Boy, The Prisoner of Ass-Co - Band-Aid, Peabody, Maniac, Cry Baby, Curtain Call, Tea Pot and there were many more. Harry laughed aloud as he read the letter. Jake's nickname was Ice Man – it made sense. Jake was the kind of kid who kept his feelings and emotions within himself. Unlike the easy-going and spontaneous Will, Jake was serious-minded; sometimes stoic. Harry hadn't seen Jake shed a tear in ten years. During his mother's wake and funeral, Jake comforted reeling friends and relatives. He comported himself with strength and with dignity.

Harry admonished himself. He felt his mood swoon. He hadn't thought enough about Jake's ordeal at Parris Island. This was not summer camp. This was serious business. One moment, Harry was laughing at his son's gift to him: a cogent, entertaining note, its sole intention to keep his father upbeat and unworried. The next moment Harry managed to manipulate Jake's gift into something akin to a lousy night's sleep.

Harry rested the letter on the kitchen table, dreading the thought of going outside. On nights like this, Harry's good neighbors finesse their curtains and then roll over on their Tempur-Pedic mattresses, assured Harry will make all the big, bad puddles go away. It would be nice if a neighbor emerged to assist Harry after all these years. Calling one neighbor? Or if someone handed Harry a cup of cocoa spiked with something from the top shelf as he slogged back to his house looking like a human sponge.

Harry scanned the neighborhood. Nothing but darkened windows. No one was coming to Harry's rescue. Harry and Felicity, their boys, they used to do this dirty work together. Somehow, they managed to make this miserable task family fun. Credit Will and his hijinks, often doing pratfalls and bawdy impersonations of their sleeping neighbors. He kept the family loose. Back then, the Kavanagh team was intact and on the job. The thought of taking on this homework without his family, well, it was misery.

"This is effing misery," Harry said. He smiled at Lolly apologizing, "Sorry for being in such a lousy mood."

Moments later, Lolly returned to her usual place as Harry, dressed for the apocalypse, exited through the kitchen door. The last time Harry cleared one of the basins, his rake snapped in half. He jogged to a neighbor's house removing a cheaply made shovel hidden behind bushes drooping under the weight of the heavy rain.

"Christ, this is a piece of crap," he said, snatching the shovel.

Harry awkwardly began clearing the basins with the shovel. Not the perfect tool for the job. He scraped away broken branches, potato chips bags, and Hostess Cupcakes wrappers. He winced when he saw some condoms heading his way, swimming for their lives. An incoming armada of plastic soda bottles in formation charged in his direction. Harry was forced to react like a goalie, under heavy pressure, making save after save, constantly in motion, clearing debris from the grating. He was more surprised by the endless fleet of soda bottles and the cake wrappers than the condoms.

"All this crappy sugar," Harry yelled in the storm.

His mind wandered to one of his impromptu stops at a gasoline station deli, one of those one-shoe-fits-all kind of an establishment where you can purchase anything from Q-Tips to motor oil. Harry stood on line behind a woman who ordered a small coffee with six tablespoons of sugar. She also ordered a bacon, egg and cheese sandwich with no salt. As she explained, the salt was no good for her hypertension. Harry shrugged spastically, as if involved in a contradictory conversation with himself. He managed to chuckle. The mysteries of life, he supposed.

Harry's hip-high boots and long raincoat kept the eclectic neighborhood cocktail from soaking his lower extremities. Murky water began whirl-pooling down the drain as the gratings cleared. The fast-moving swirling action and suction nearly swept Harry off his feet. No one was looking out for him; he had to be mindful of his every step. Harry had a silly notion of heading inside, but on cue, the heavens turned the lining of its stomach inside out and the vomitus continued.

Water seeped beneath the collar of Harry's raincoat. He felt the water cling to his shirt, sitting on his shoulders before it bled onto his lower back. He made the mistake of arching his back, causing the water to escape to a place it had no business going. The hard rain flicked his left ear like a seventh-grade bully's itchy-to-flick finger. He caught an instant earache. He was beginning to stiffen and hurt everywhere. He wiped his nose and eyes with his stiffening sleeve. This hurt more than it helped. Harry was trying to improve his visibility and make an attempt to restart himself. *Psych myself up*, he thought. It was a good idea, but his attempt was feeble. He fretted the angry night sky wasn't through with him. It meant Harry would be trapped outside for some overtime.

Corbin Reece was pacing in his galley kitchen. He was wearing boxers and a threadbare T-shirt pitted with perspiration stains. Reece looked at his socks and decided they clashed with his ensemble. He folded at the waist and yanked off both socks, inadvertently rubber-banding them into the sink. Reece felt light-headed and was forced to steady himself. He looked like he was doing a silent moment of prayer, which he may have benefited from. If only he knew.

Corbin Reece's night was already more miserable than Harry Kavanagh's. And it wasn't going to improve. His self-loathing jag was jump-started by Felicity Kavanagh's untimely demise. Reece kept hearing the word in his mind, *demise*, but he knew what it really was – the terminology was a familiar one, especially in his line of business – *murder*. She was murdered, and he knew who was responsible.

Reece's daily drinking was influencing his job performance as a medical examiner. As one would expect, not in a positive way. It was affecting every aspect of his life. *Credit the darker forces at play*, he thought. He often had nights when he dreamt of bullet-shaped slugs, those little monsters consuming him from the inside out. They exhibited razor-sharp teeth. They would burrow through his skin or emerge from his mouth and ears. Blood dripped from the corners of their upside-down smiles. They would leer at him, permitting him to remain alive long enough for him to recognize that he was a dead man. Every nibble at his nerve endings would cause him to scream. The nightmare would always conclude the same way: a painful and excruciating death. The ending he'd earned. Some nights, he'd bolt upright in his bed soaked in perspiration and urine.

In the case of Corbin Reece, there was no such thing as redemption. Not with the life he had lived. But he *did* want to try to square himself some if he could. He needed to tell the story. Was he driven by his selfishness and fear? He prayed – funny word, prayed – he prayed his impulse to tell his tale of woe would earn him a little time in the second, third, and fourth circles of hell, which he viewed as an upgrade considering the body of his past crimes.

Reece wasn't certain if his pathetic glance toward Harry Kavanagh at the restaurant was enough for Kavanagh to read his mind. *Of course, it wasn't. Why would it be?* Reece shook his head repeatedly, disgusted with himself. *Why the hell should Harry Kavanagh call me?* he thought.

Four years after Felicity Kavanagh's murder, Reece was a dead man bawling. He was forced to sell his house. All of his savings, gone. He was a single man who had made a decent living his entire life. He was relegated to a one-bedroom apartment in a building whose crumbling foundation caused the entire structure to lean. He was a knock on the door away from being inarticulately ordered to evacuate. The only reason he hadn't been directed to leave sooner was due to the startling incompetence of the Buildings Department. The other tenants, rational human beings all of them, vacated months ago. But not Reece. He silently prayed that the building would collapse on him in his sleep, killing his nightmares, delivering him an easy way out.

Reece popped a cigarette between his chapped lips. Descending in slow motion toward the hypnotic blue flame, he managed to light the cigarette on the stove. He felt his lingering hairs on his head singe. Then came the acrid smell of burning hair; it happens when one foolishly juts their profile into fire. Reece mopped his perspiring forehead with one hand and took a drag on his mentholated savior. He rested on the inoperable radiator by the window, planting his bare feet onto the linoleum floor. He reached for his cellular; it had Harry Kavanagh's number saved. He put the phone down and buried his face in his hands. He slowly uncovered his face, feeling the pull of an unseen tide. Like a werewolf being summoned by a full moon, Reece reluctantly shifted his attention toward the apartment's entrance.

Jaycee Singletary was poised under the uneven frame of the sagging doorway. The man was vampire-handsome, relaxed and put together despite coming in from a storm.

Singletary. The name was an alias. The man had dozens of aliases. He portrayed many characters and lived so many off-the-grid lives that sometimes Singletary felt the urge to review his past performances. At a private table for one, he would occasionally reflect on the small army of people who had occupied his mind and body during his adventures. This celebration always put him in good cheer.

Singletary was a creature of habit. He'd seek out an obscure public house where he'd mind his P's and Q's. He'd enjoy shepherd's pie and a Guinness while brushing through his mental files. Recounting with relish his many identities, his unique and bold experiences, the places he'd traveled, and most importantly, those souls who belonged to him for a time.

Singletary was a highly-functioning oddball, extremely intelligent; he covered his tracks like a modern-day Moriarty. He was in full career of a gloriously successful life on his own terms. He was unchallenged and unafraid. He had been a charmer, grifter, and a predator for most of his tenure on earth. He considered himself to be at the very top of his game. He was a narcissist who was constantly accessing his greatness. This was not his profession; it was not something he did to earn a pension. This was his noble calling. At his very core, Singletary believed himself to be an avenger. Those he chose to control, and bilk, were deserving of his attention.

"You don't look well," he said to Reece. The cadences in his voice did not reveal any particular place of origin. That's just the way Singletary designed it.

"I was getting dressed to go out. My date should be here any second. Maybe you should find your own date."

The slightest smile on Singletary's face was replaced by an elevated eyebrow. "This inkling of confidence and sarcasm. You nearly wear it well." He knew the change in Reece's attitude meant their relationship was close to their inevitable break up. "You're all grown up. This does not come as a surprise."

"Hooray for me," Reece said drolly.

"This is exactly what I'm speaking about. Your new-found sense of independence, your push back. It's time to go our separate ways. Breakups are emotional. Let's promise not to shed any tears. Business is always about the work at hand. And as it so happens, you owe me one last installment."

Reece was about to snap back, but Singletary's darkening expression convinced him to back down. Push back could prove to have a painful price.

"Okay, certainly," was all Reece could manage.

He dug for something in one of the rickety cabinet drawers. He tossed a bank envelope tied in a rubber band onto the table.

"I'm completely dry. My account is empty," Reece confessed. "You've taken the last of it."

Reece felt an odd sensation wash through his loins. Remotely familiar, terrifying, inappropriate. He was getting an erection. His reaction was driven by his escalating anxiety. A soaring dread was building up inside of him. Reece had experienced many failures with intimacy over the years, but this reaction right now, while seemingly out of place, there was some history to it.

When he was barely a teenager, his father ordered him onto the roof to clear the leaves from the rain gutters after an autumn storm. Reece's abusive father was afraid of no one and nothing, save for heights. The boy was terrified of heights as well but didn't dare mention it. Little boy Reece was reluctant to return to the damp earth with a surprise in his pocket. This surprise was brought on by his fear of heights and the searing terror he felt when he was in his father's presence. The man was unpredictable and violent, in particular, when he was impatient or thinking about getting drunk. So, Reece lingered up there on the roof, moving slowly, playing the waiting game. It was only after his father grumbled off to the corner gin mill did Reece finally negotiate his way down.

Many years later, blackmailed into the Felicity Kavanagh affair, driven by omnipresent anxiety, Reece would often experience an erection when fear began to consume him. The terror was instant Viagra without the benefit of a happy ending.

Reece moved from his seat on the radiator and slid into the chair at the table to conceal his mounting fear.

"Very good. Until next time then," Singletary said, putting Reece's money in his pocket.

"Next? I thought you were through with me?" Reece stopped himself. With nothing else to add, Reece nervously reached over and flicked his cigarette into the sink. He reluctantly lifted his eyes, daring to observe Singletary, who snapped the spell and looked away for an instant, lost in his own soothing, sociopathic thoughts. Eyes semi-closed, it was almost as if he was listening to a symphony through headphones.

Singletary was smiling to himself. Singletary's perfect smile widened until Reece noticed one of Singletary's back teeth was missing. Not there. What a surprise. A void amid all this perfection. It shook Reece from his submissive mood; it made him tremble with anger.

Reece rued the day that he met this odd and dangerous man in a Manhattan pub. He was drunk when he foolishly confessed his involvement in the Felicity Kavanagh affair. He had no idea that this seemingly sympathetic man was setting him up. It was from that moment on, this man Singletary, this lunatic, owned him, terrifying him, humiliating him, hurting him – squeezing him out of his life savings. Extracting and toying with his secrets. Subsequently drawing him closer to an imperfect ending every single day of their partnership.

Reece felt his erection fading; he unconsciously let out a short breath, which he followed with a snort, then a laugh. Singletary snapped out of his bliss and swiveled his face toward Reece. "You look like you're enjoying yourself. I believe that's against the rules."

"Let me ask you something, Mr. Singletary. Don't grifters have dental insurance?"

Singletary's fingers moved to the left side of his face. His eyes blinked when he did not ask them to. The ravaged man had taken him by surprise. Then everything became clearer to him. He needed to teach Reece a lesson.

Reece moved back to his radiator seat. He sat, removing his T-shirt. His eyes were locked with Singletary's. He was unafraid; it wasn't like him. Reece threw open the window and the room flooded with the chaos of the storm.

"You're not going to get anything else from me," Reece spat.

"You have vacation plans I'm unaware of?" Singletary spoke calmly, pausing between words to study the demeanor of his subject.

"I'm making my own decision for the first time in a long time," Reece said, looking out the window.

"The result is irreversible." Singletary paused. "As much as it repulses me to cause you any more pain, after your well-played remark, I think I deserve to have things go my way."

"What does that mean? I have no more money."

"Leave it to me to think of something."

"I came into this world without boxer shorts made in China and that's the way I wanna go out." Reece reached for a steak knife and sliced off his boxers. He slung a leg outside, straddling the windowsill. He was completely naked.

"Thank you for your service?" Singletary spoke it like a question. He was captivated by Reece's behavior. Singletary was accustomed to being the maestro, never an audience member. He found himself oddly transfixed and at a slight disadvantage.

"I am a coward," Reece said sniffling.

"Yes, you are."

"And many other things, but as far as you're concerned, I am not as stupid as I look."

"You'll have a hard time convincing me," Singletary said with a slight smile.

"The bloodletting is over. I filled three journals. Written all about you."

"You've lived the life of a criminal. The worst kind. You've earned my attention," Singletary offered.

"I've been shadowing you."

"No one follows me. No one knows me. You certainly don't know me."

"Overconfidence has a price. There's an especially steep price for sociopaths."

"Tell me all about it," Singletary said smiling, pulling up short of revealing his missing tooth.

"You're trapped until you find my storybooks. Find them before someone else does."

"I could simply leave after your departing flight and begin anew somewhere else. I've done this many times before."

"Yeah, but what a pain in the ass to start all over again. You have a compulsion to stay undisturbed. You're too tidy. And now you suddenly find yourself intrigued by a dead man's take on the great Singletary."

"Are you dead already? I hadn't noticed," Singletary said.

"Hungry for my thoughts?"

"Not really. Feel free to unburden yourself," Singletary said it calmly and with such an underlying tone of menace that Reece thought his erection would build again. He wanted to act quickly. This humiliating weakness was the one secret he needed to keep.

"I will unburden myself. And by the way, you're not gonna get far on that bullshit. Nothing but singles. So long, scumbag."

Reece pushed himself off the window sill and felt an immediate release. The sensation of flying gave him a rush. He knew he was smiling. The smile vanished quickly. He couldn't catch his breath. He ached to rewind his last seconds. But that was impossible. There were no do-overs allowed for someone like him. His prayer was a phony and he knew it. If there was someone receiving it, he or she would know it too.

Reece heard a dull sound. It must have been his brain hitting the street. And then there was nothing. Only blackness and silence. Because he was very dead. The next leg of Reece's trip was the tour of all the circles of hell.

Singletary stared at himself in a crooked wall mirror. He inspected the gap in the back of his mouth. His left eye began to twitch. When he blinked, the lid stuck; it remained closed. Singletary plucked his eyelid with his fingers until his eye popped open. He steadied himself; it took a second longer than he anticipated. His sphinxlike countenance slowly returned.

"Where does one find a good dentist?"

He inhaled, and his lean, hard torso expanded. He eased himself free from his self-hypnotic reverie and left the flat, stepping off confidently as if he were a Shakespearean actor exiting the great stage.

Harry Kavanagh was unable to keep up with the briny water ejaculating from higher ground. The wind was toying with overhead electrical wires, winding them up like jump ropes working the Double Dutch World Championship. Trees were swaying submissively. The rising water was nearing waist-high when Harry heard Lolly's bark resonating from inside the house. Harry was beginning to panic. The water had never gotten this high before. He was briefly comforted by his companion's plea heard above the din of the nor'easter. But something was amiss, something else. *What now?* Was Lolly sounding an alarm? Harry was distracted by shards of electrical sparks exploding from a transformer mounted on a telephone pole. The nightlight at the end of the street went out suddenly. He heard more short-circuiting sounds. The entire block was abruptly pitched into darkness.

Harry made the decision to get out of there. The water was too much to handle. He had to carry up those cases of Barolo before the cellar flooded. The hell with everything else. Suddenly, Harry's head began to throb. His body was twisting, recoiling. He felt unsteady on his feet. He imagined his body submerging into a deep pocket of icy water. He thought he could hear Bobby Darin singing "Beyond the Sea." It was Harry and Felicity's wedding song. The lyrics were muted, coming from a faraway place. Harry's inner ears began to sting. He realized then that he really was underwater.

Harry speculated he'd been hit in the head by flying debris. But it wasn't his immediate concern. It was imperative he will his dormant muscles to life. Harry discovered the shovel lodged under his arm. He tried to grasp it, but his hands weren't working. He had an idea and rolled himself over, facedown. His body was heavy; he felt like he had bricks in his pockets. The shovel was pressing against his sternum. His body's weight pushed off the shovel. Harry held out hope that with another push he would break the surface. Then the unthinkable happened: the shovel snapped, and there was nothing to impede his descent into the cold water.

Harry couldn't hold his breath much longer. He felt like he was going to die, and he was unable to think of little else but accepting his fate. The boys would be fine without him, he rationalized for one stupid, harried instant. Then he snapped back to his senses.

What the hell am I thinking? Today is not the day. Better not be.

Harry expelled the negative thoughts and managed to roll over, so he was facing the surface. But his energy was AWOL, and his lungs were about to explode. He looked upward into the murk and imagined he saw a sliver of light.

Holy crap, it's morning. The rain has stopped. I need a cup of coffee. Thinking about coffee at a time like this? Is this what happens when your head is floundering in icy water? Harry knew he wasn't thinking straight.

Harry saw a hand dive into the water, cutting neatly through it, interrupting his water-logged guesswork. He was floating upward, in the process of being rescued. Gently emerging toward the origin of the light.

The identity of Harry's liberator came into soft focus as he levitated toward the surface. The exquisite face appeared as soulful and as beautiful as ever. Harry's heart nearly detonated inside his chest.

It was Harry's wife, Felicity, and she was smiling at him, tenderly, with tears in her eyes.

"I've got you, Harry," she said. "I've got you."

Chapter Four

Nearly four in the morning. Young men were talking in their sleep and breaking wind, a lot of wind. This was par for the course. None of this bothered Jake Kavanagh before; he usually slept through the cacophony of snoring and everything else dished out by the other recruits. But he wasn't awake because of all the nocturnal distractions in the barracks. He didn't know how to explain it, but he'd been stone-cold awake because he was worrying about his father. He couldn't figure out why this night was any different.

Was he sensing something? Was Pops in trouble?

His father should have received his letter by now. Jake hoped the old man's mood was improving. He seemed to be emotionally stuck on this never-ending sabbatical of his. Jake couldn't help worrying about him. His father was aging like a sitting president. Jake questioned his timing, leaving for the Marine Corps when he did. Maybe he should have stayed behind to help the old man get a better handle on things? But Harry (he sometimes called his father Harry), Harry encouraged him to go. After the initial yelling and screaming was over, Jake knew his father would get over the surprise of having a son in the military.

"They'll be better for having you," Jake remembered Harry saying in a hoarse voice.

Not the typical advice from a college professor. And by the time he said it, the old man meant it. Sure, he was probably worn out by their confrontations and heated debates, and maybe Harry's acceptance was an act, but what's a father to do? In any event, Harry finally "coming around" made departing a little easier for Jake. His father was never a tough guy, but he had an understated strength that would emerge on occasion. Jake was eager for his father's restrained edginess to return, so Harry could feel the blood running through his veins and resume living. He also knew his father, despite his encouragement, was worried about losing a son. Jake made a promise to his father before he left. He was determined to play his part under any circumstances. Jake was going to make damn sure he'd come home to his father and brother when the time was right. They'd already lost enough. There would be no more losing.

Daybreak for recruits, Parris Island, South Carolina. It was seconds before 4 a.m. Jake's internal clock was right on target. His eyes were open and focused, cutting through the darkness, waiting for another grueling day to begin. The cold, harsh lights splashed on inside the barracks. Jake's feet hit the deck seconds before his rack mate. Seconds before anyone else's feet hit the ground. There was a drill instructor in his face already, yelling at him for some impropriety, real or imaginary. The DI's spittle rained across Jake's face, but Harry Kavanagh's kid didn't buckle. The drill instructor yelled at him again and Jake Kavanagh heard himself say, "Aye sir!" Still preoccupied with thoughts of his father, Jake inadvertently headed off in the wrong direction. Several drill instructors surrounded him, all of them hollering simultaneously. Jake waited for his mind to reset, for things to begin making sense again. He would self-correct. There would be no question about it. He had that kind of self-confidence.

The last thing on Will Kavanagh's mind was his family. He had been awake too. Lacking his brother's self-confidence, his inside words were bantering with anxiety, along the lines of *holy shit* and more *holy shit*. Frivolousness multiplied by a thousand all because Will never saw himself as a romantic lead.

Will was in his dorm room with a sleepover guest. His first sleepover guest ever. He was nervous, feeling tremendously insecure. Maybe it was the frontal lobe business he'd heard so much about? He should have paid more attention. Apparently, some boys are idiots for a really long time.

He felt like his idiocy was in full bloom. And at this moment, he thought he'd never be the same. He, *they*, made love last night. It didn't go entirely smoothly, not like in the movies: well-placed words and romantic touches at pivotal times. It was more like a comedy of errors, and he felt awkward and uncomfortable in his own skin. He wasn't sure if this was the way it was supposed to go. He liked this girl, this young woman; he cared about what she thought of him. He liked her before last night but didn't know how to approach her or what to say. Pratfalls and juvenile jokes work well around your family, but that kind of behavior, it's no way to become acquainted with someone your heart is pumping for.

Oh, my God, Will thought, *I feel like such a moron, or as Bugs would say, "What a maroon!"* He wanted to run, but he couldn't move, and besides, he had nowhere to go. His eyes were fixated on the coed asleep beside him. They should have been cramped in the excuse for a college-sized bed, except Julie Lambert, who was lean and tall, was somehow reposing perfectly beside him. Julie was on the swim team. He didn't know much more about her other than she was from New York City. After a stupid sip of grain alcohol disguised as

41

fruit punch and a few awkward opening sentences, neither was interested in discussing the other person's closeted vegan impulses. And there she was, sleeping face down next to him. He couldn't believe it. He marveled at her beautifully sculpted arm extending from her left shoulder, reaching beyond his waist. Her upturned palm was a lovely site. As beautiful as the rest of her.

"I can hear you thinking."

"I'm sorry. I didn't mean to wake you."

She rolled over and swept her hair away from her face. She smiled at him.

"What's wrong, Will?"

"I don't know, I just, last night. I was wondering...?"

"What? Should we talk about it?"

"Well, yeah, I suppose."

"You suppose? Okay, let's talk about it, you comedian."

"A comedian? Really?" His heart sank. "I mean, we don't have to talk about it if you don't want to."

She got to her knees and stretched out her arms. She knelt beside him and playfully tugged on his arm. He sat up expectantly. She took a breath that had a soft smile attached to it.

"I can tell you haven't been around girls in, you know, in that way. It says something really nice about you. I'm new at this too. Last night was silly. You made me laugh. I felt safe."

"Okay. I get that a lot."

"What?"

"I can make people laugh. I guess I've always been sort of a court jester. Comes naturally. I don't know if it's a good thing."

"I'm a big girl, and you still made me feel safe. Now, be quiet, please."

"Okay," he said a little too eagerly.

"At the party I sensed you needed a hug, so to speak. That's why I introduced myself. No expectations that we'd hook up, but you hugged me back. And I think I made you feel safe too. No matter how clumsy we were."

"Yeah, hugs count for something," Will shrugged.

"It was unexpected and profound."

"Profound? Wow. I never got that before. What do we do next?"

"Put aside our wedding plans until after breakfast," Julie teased.

"What?" He looked distressed.

"Shut up you jerk," she said, laughing at him.

There was a loud knocking at his door.

"That will be my roommate. Probably didn't sleep very well," he said.

Julie hopped over him and began sorting her clothes.

"I'm usually the one who gets kicked out," he explained.

"It's a new day for everyone then, isn't it?"

"The dawn of a new day. I like that."

"Where are we going for breakfast? I could eat a clown car," she said in an exaggerated deep voice.

"Somewhere off campus?"

"Sounds like a plan."

There was more knocking on the door. Louder than before.

"Calm down, Rog. Gimme five minutes," Will barked.

He heard a groan from the other side of the door. Julie was dressed in seconds. It looked like a dance. She was a whirlwind. Everything about her was impressive. She faced Will, frowning down at him. He hadn't budged from his spot on the bed. He was hypnotized by her.

"Are you going to stare at me all morning or are we going to get sustenance?"

"I'd like to do a little of both," he said, the smile on his face growing more comfortable.

Chapter Five

No one applauded when Jaycee Singletary entered the cluttered mom-and-pop auto supply store. For the sake of his own welfare, Singletary left his ride behind and walked two miles to reach his destination. Being stopped by a local policeman requesting his identification would set off a series of events that could end badly for all parties involved.

Singletary paused in the doorway to assess the landscape. As far as the kid at the counter was concerned, the 20-something slovenly kid enraptured by something inconsequential on his mobile device, as far as *he* was concerned, Singletary was like everyone else who entered his domain. He was another zombie. The kid barely looked up from his device when Singletary stepped inside.

Singletary immediately detected this cubby hole possessed the synthetic bouquet of a highly toxic soup. To put it plainly, the place stunk to holy hell. The looming pernicious presence meant that Singletary needed to get in and out as quickly as possible. He had a very sensitive nose and not much tolerance for the smellier side of life.

Singletary walked to the counter holding a worn-out pair of windshield wipers in his gloved hand.

He understood why the dulled-looking counter boy wasn't affected by the noxious air. This soup was the whiff he insufflated into his compromised respiratory system every second he was in the place.

"Excuse me, good morning. Can you recommend a suitable replacement?"

"Aisle three. Match it with the model of your car," came the deadpanned response.

Singletary eyed the mouth of the aisle. Aisle three was a disaster. It looked like merchandise had been carpet-bombed. Surviving supplies were strewn with unrelated bits and disembodied whatnots presumably belonging in other aisles.

"Would you mind choosing?" he said politely. When there was no answer, Singletary offered, "I'm daunted by the task at hand."

The kid spied Singletary with disdain. "What the hell, dude. Aisle fucking three. Want me to hold your hand? You're a big man-boy."

Singletary looked around the place and quickly discerned he was the only customer inside. It came as no surprise.

"I'm sorry, you're right. May I ask you, for my own safety, are those cameras operational?"

The kid put aside his phone and sighed his bad breath in Singletary's direction.

"Look mister, my douchebag cousin, Larry, what kind of fucking name is Larry? L-a-r-r-e-e," he proclaimed in a weepy sing-song way. "He's got these fucking cameras all over this dump. All of them useless, or probably fake. And how do I know that? Because every day I pocket some guap and nobody says nothing..."

"Guap?" Singletary interrupted.

The kid was wearing a Make America Great T-shirt. His flabby breasts were tightly confined beneath the straining cotton fibers. They were yearning to expand if only they were granted the freedom. As a result, the candidate's smiling face on the shirt appeared distorted.

"Guap means fucking money. And you know why I'm entitled to a bonus? Because I have to deal with lazy, dumb-ass punt-faces like you."

"The reasons for all your hostility young man are what?" The question was posed gently.

"Aisle three man. I'm not going to say it again," the kid grunted.

"Well, thank you for sharing your life's philosophy. You've given me little to ponder. My response can only be immediate and unforgiving."

The kid looked at Singletary, with a dopey look on his face – *What the fuck does that mean?*

Singletary grinned; he reached over and grabbed the kid by his hair. The kid let out a surprised yelp. Singletary used the kid's face like a gavel, pounding it on the counter. Blood shot from the kid's nostrils. Singletary led the whimpering "customer service representative" out from behind the counter by his hair like he was a dull-witted farm animal.

"Oh, look at us. We've arrived at aisle three," Singletary said, placing the windshield wipers in the kid's trembling hand. "The faster you accomplish this, the quicker your moneymaker will heal."

When the kid lifted his sobbing face, Singletary shook his head with some compassion.

"Hmm. You may need some reconstructive work. Although, personally I've always thought Chuck Wepner was a very handsome man. Be kind to yourself. Don't say anything insulting to strangers. That would be my advice going forward."

Blood trickled over the kid's lips, mingling with his bedraggled attempt at a goatee. Some blood eventually found its way to the T-shirt, staining the candidate's exaggerated hairline.

"Breathe through your mouth and you'll be fine. Hurry now. Hurry please."

Singletary kicked him in the behind and the kid, stumbling and moaning, staggered off to pick out a match.

"I'm ashamed of my behavior. It has been pointed out to me that I'm off my game. Perhaps my impatient reaction to your attitude proves the point. Perhaps. You must understand, you played a part in my behavior. Consequences for actions are a reality. It's a simple science. And where would we be without science?"

With his head down, the kid swayed back and handed off the new set of wipers. He slumped to his knees and prayed that the scary man would soon disappear.

Singletary whispered sympathetically, "Do yourself a favor, take a yoga class, read a book, and bathe occasionally. Whatever type of pornography and junk food you're addicted to, conquer it right now. Everything in moderation. Otherwise you will experience more mornings like this one. Oh, and don't forget, always be polite. Remember, providing poor customer service means your day is not going to go well."

Singletary reached into his pocket and removed several new bills from his wallet. He released them and watched them float to the floor beside his mentee.

"I have nothing against you taking what you deserve, but you haven't earned it yet. Put the guap in the register where it belongs. Remember to always give your very best self to Larry," he said as he walked toward the exit.

"I certainly hope my dentist has better manners than you."

The kid followed Singletary through blurry eyes. He fainted when he heard the front door close.

Harry Kavanagh's throat was dry. He rolled his tongue around the inside of his mouth and slowly separated his lips, which felt like they were sealed with Gorilla Glue. He inhaled and exhaled through his mouth. He heard himself groan, and he reached for the right side of his head. He fully expected something new and unusual to be in attendance there. And he was a winner, sort of. There was a bump on the right side of his forehead. More like a mound. He could have planted a flag on it, he thought. When he winced, he speculated his entire face might crumble like a Mayan clay mask. He thought he heard the hum of the dryer vibrating downstairs. That didn't make any sense. As far as he could tell, it was daylight. His thoughts traveled to Lolly. I have to take Lolly for a walk otherwise there would be a price to pay.

He intended to get out of bed, but his head was heavy. His eyelids became slits, shutting out the daylight. Harry rested back into a soft darkness. Soon he was adrift in a dream-like condition.

The purring sounds of the dryer were prominent. He felt embraced by its familiarity; he figured he hadn't wandered too far away from his own reality. An image of his Will popped into his head. He immediately thought of Chaucer's *The Miller's Tale* and of the character Absolon. The young squire was supposed to be a knight in training, but instead resembled a lovesick puppy who liked to dance and sing and put quill to parchment. That was his Will. Despite being a skilled martial artist, Will was not a fighter – possibly not a lover either. He was a real character: a generous boy, an upbeat and lively presence in everyone's life. Harry felt so much love for the boy. He could sense his mouth was forming into the shape of a smile. His face didn't crumble. Harry's thoughts of Will drifted upward like the balloon that got away.

Harry was aware his mind was trying to make sense of his current confinement. He had to get up. He had to figure out what happened to him. He willed himself to rise, but his body wouldn't cooperate. His eyes refused to open even after he'd asked permission; then he pleaded. His wish was not granted. Nothing, no movement. More easy dreaming. Not so bad.

Without discernible context or any warning, images of historical renderings of William Shakespeare popped into Harry's head. Then there was the sight of King James defiantly confronting the Puritans at the conference at the Hampton Court Palace, setting the style for his reign and the precedent for the creation of the King James Bible. These thoughts and images ran amok inside Harry's convoluted mind. *What a mess. Where did this come from?* These were the digressions of a compromised college professor. The images were quickly distorting into unrecognizable shapes, swirling faster in Harry's mind's eye, leading him through a corridor where he paused on the vision of his other son, Jake. He remembered Jake's birthday was March 24th. But the date had come and gone months ago.

Where am I going? What's my mind doing now?

March 24th was Queen Elizabeth's birthday, *the* Queen Elizabeth. *Oh, Jake and the Queen share the same birthday. That's how I got here*, Harry rationalized. Maybe. He was so confused.

Harry grimaced, and his face ached again; he heard sounds of industrial chains rattling wildly inside his pounding head. *Why? Who knows?* He wanted to open his eyes, walk downstairs, make coffee, and have a chat with Lolly over some shortbread cookies not named Lorna Doone. Because, well, because ol' Lorna was a cookie fashioned by Nabisco, that's why.

"No corporate cookies for me and my best friend," Harry heard himself speak.

Harry witnessed all the convoluted images in his mind quickly dispensing into a food processor, exploding within, distorting into unrecognizable shapes, swirling faster and faster, becoming liquid. Harry couldn't withstand the pain and the bedlam rattling inside his head. His body trembled. His left hand made a fist, and for the first time he became aware that he was perspiring. He bolted up in bed, folding at the waist.

"Will? Jake? Where are you?" His eyes popped open.

Harry felt the bump on his head, recalling the initial discovery. He had a headache. A real humdinger. As he dragged himself out of bed, he noticed the empty pint glass and the bourbon on his bedside table.

"Oh, that was a very bad thing to do to yourself, Harry," he said, whining.

He went into the bathroom without turning on the light. He slouched over the toilet and refused to look at himself in the mirror. He knew he looked like hell. He didn't need to confirm it. He flushed the toilet and swept some warm water on his face. He pushed off the sink and moved to the staircase remembering the wall mirror on the way down. *I'm going to avoid that one too.* As he gently padded down the stairs, another thought occurred to him. His boxer shorts and T-shirt – they weren't the ones he had on yesterday. The last thing he remembered was getting hit on the side of the head, outside in the storm.

"Was I hit by a piece of debris, a tree branch maybe?" he asked himself. He recalled sinking into the pool of rising water. Harry sat down on the bottom step to gather his thoughts.

Harry's elbows hurt, his knees throbbed, and he had that headache. He sneezed into the palm of his hand, which was a no-no, but there was no one around to rebuke him. Or was there? He had the sudden realization that someone must have rescued him, pulled him inside and put him back together. Not only was he rescued, he was subsequently carried inside the house, either assisted or hefted up the stairs to his bedroom, undressed, dried off and dressed. No small feat. He rose slowly and faltered toward the friendly sounds of the dryer.

Lolly was asleep beside the dryer. Harry opened the dryer without disturbing her and saw his clothing from the previous night, rolling to a stop, tangled and warm. He closed the dryer and Lolly opened her eyes and yawned. Harry padded into the kitchen and saw a note on the table:

Electricity restored at 5 a.m. Dog fed and walked. Clothes in the dryer.
Coffee on the stove. Advise going to hospital – you may have a concussion.

Harry rested both hands on the kitchen table before he sat down. He remembered the imagery of his wife reaching out for him, pulling him to the surface. It was fancy manufactured by his fertile imagination. It was a lovely gesture, a wonderful notion. He nodded subtlety, tipping his hat to his own inventiveness. Felicity saving him from his sorrow and giving him his life back. Granting him permission to move forward without worry or guilt. But it *was* nonsense, fantasy, he concluded. He shook his head and his expression soured.

He slid the hand-written note closer with the curve of his wrist and examined it. Harry thought he detected a light fragrance of lilac in the air. The handwriting was absolutely lovely, most likely written by a woman, he guessed, but by whom? Not by Emma; he'd seen her handwriting. She was a butcher. Last year's Christmas card looked like it was scribbled by a toddler speeding on Oreos. Another thought occurred to him. If a woman had rescued him, she had undressed him. She'd seen him as a helpless noodle and naked to boot. She would've been required to roll his exposed body around to turn him out. He could feel his cheeks burning with embarrassment and more. It went deeper than that. He was ashamed.

He had a good reason to be.

Harry had a dark secret he'd shared with Felicity and with no one else. As a child, he had been molested by an uncle. The man was an uncle through marriage, on the Kavanagh side of the family. As far as Harry could remember – and he hated to remember – it began when he was around seven and mercifully ended when he was eleven only because the predator divorced his aunt and moved out of state.

Throughout his lifetime, Harry struggled with many issues resulting from this form of evil. One of his more accessible feelings was shame. Harry always seemed to find the darkness on a cloudless day. Case in point, rather than focusing on gratitude, *he was alive after all*, Harry was fixating on a mystery woman. He was mortified that this someone, she saw him for who he really was: weak, vulnerable, and in his birthday suit.

"I have to work through this and be grateful first and foremost, right, Lolly?" Harry exhaled. Lolly stretched out and ambled over to his side. She deposited her head in his lap. He stroked her.

"But first, what do you say we have some coffee? And when I say we, I really mean me."

Harry rose from his chair and instead moved to the dryer. He removed his warm clothing and began to dress slowly, feeling every ache and pain in his body.

"Chrissakes," he said wearily. And with tears in his eyes, "Felicity, where the hell are you?"

Chapter Six

Harry returned to the house with Lolly. He undid her leash, and she made a beeline for her water bowl. Lolly was thirsty; she made a mess. Some of the water actually made it into her mouth.

"I'll see you later. You're a messy girl," Harry said to Lolly, rubbing the swelling on his head.

"Ooh, ouch."

He walked outside and headed for his driveway when it occurred to him he wasn't a very good candidate to get behind the wheel of a car. A decision Felicity would've made for him in an instant. The thought ripped through his head like a lightning flash. He put his car keys in his coat pocket and stood motionless until the sudden taste of bitterness in his mouth dissipated.

With a potential head injury, he didn't feel qualified to do much more than take his dog out for a short walk. Besides, Harry was distracted. Who the hell had rescued him? Why the mysterious disappearance? Questions to be answered another day, possibly.

Harry turned around facing the street and observed the goings-on in his hamlet. The silence inside his head was replaced by the exuberant sounds of the neighborhood cleaning up in the aftermath of a storm. *No one comes out the night of a storm, but apparently the entire neighborhood turns out to clean up the debris the next morning*, he mused. And his well-rested neighbors (because they slept peacefully throughout the night) seemed happy to be working together in teams, chatting and laughing, catching up on gossip or perhaps ridiculing their abysmal local sports teams. His neighbors were in the street removing errant tree branches and collecting the garbage can covers that got away. They swept piles of wet leaves and rubble and wiped mud off the tires of their leased automobiles.

"Hey, can I ask you a question? Did you use my shovel?"

Harry winced and turned his head to the left, ever so slowly. Not more than six inches from his face was his jowly neighbor, Dr. Arnold Fleck.

"That's actually two questions. Arnold and Fleck. What can I do for you?"

"That's Doctor Fleck, Harry. Did you use my shovel? Because it's broken, useless. I found it in the middle of the street."

Whenever Harry addressed his neighbor, the brooding podiatrist, he called him out in this way, Arnold and Fleck. It didn't have the ring of a successful comedy team from the old days; certainly didn't sound like a pair of trapeze artists either. In Harry's mind, it seemed like Arnold was always trying to catch up to Fleck, for what ungodly reason, who knew? Arnold and Fleck sounded more and more to Harry like *mucous* and *bile*. Harry was pleased with his choice. Dr. Arnold Fleck, the grandiose podiatrist with riverboat-captain's sideburns, was in Harry's view a walking, talking, human strain of flu. In plainer terms, he was a gigantic bore. Felicity had managed to dismiss him with a smile, which Harry was certain Fleck misinterpreted. It was her way; she was smarter and more patient than he. But Harry could never pretend. He had absolutely no tolerance for Fleck, and he wore it on his chest like a badge of honor.

"Did I break your shovel, Arnold and Fleck? Is this how we're starting off on this fine day?"

"Why do you do that to my name, Harry? Why?"

"Both names are yours – they're like conjoined twins."

"You're a childish jackass just like your…" he caught himself, then figured what the heck and continued, "like your boy, Will."

"While you were asleep dreaming of making Welsh Rarebit with toe cheese, I was cleaning the water basins," Harry said, staring Fleck down with a professorial frown.

"So, you owe me a shovel then."

"I owe you something," Harry said whimsically.

"What does that mean? You owe me something?"

"About your opinion of Will, you should be grateful I don't sic Lolly on you. I've got more pressing things to do."

Arnold Fleck peeked over his right shoulder and saw Lolly glaring at him through the kitchen door panels.

"Well, I mean, dancing, what kind of thing is that for a boy?"

"That boy happens to be a tremendous athlete, and he's been studying kung fu for over ten years. By the way, he does a marvelous imitation of you."

Harry enjoyed seeing Fleck squirming at the sight of Lolly. Harry walked away and climbed inside a black Escalade parked by the curb. Fleck came hopping after him, confused and somewhat outraged.

"Hey, this is my car."

"I'm aware, Arnold and Fleck."

"Cut the horseshit, Harry, and get out of my car."

"You did notice I'm sitting in the passenger seat?"

Fleck waved his stubby hands about, interrupting Harry before he could beat him over the head with Arnold and Fleck.

"Yes, yes. What do you want?"

"I want to be a passenger. Take me to the hospital, please." Harry pointed to the swelling on his head. "My reward for making sure you had a good night's sleep."

"Do you mean to say, you're getting your head examined?"

Fleck's face lit up with the expression of pure joy. Before Harry could answer, Fleck bounded around the front of his car and hopped inside with the energy of a teenager. He beamed at Harry and started the car. He tore away from the curb and drove erratically. Harry was certain, he was doing this on purpose, to annoy him and to settle the score.

"Slow down, Arnold and Fle…"

Harry couldn't take the contented look on Fleck's face as they weaved through the neighborhood. Harry swayed back and forth in his seat. Harry wagged a finger at Fleck; he tried to speak but decided to clam up, because he was worried he would get sick in his lap. Harry didn't have a choice in the matter. Something was on its way up, and there was only one way out. He lowered his window and began vomiting as the car sped onward. Through his blurred vision, Harry recalled something Will would say when he was a child. "Mommy, I'm gonna blow chunks!" Harry wiped his mouth on his sleeve and turned to face the jubilant-looking Fleck.

"You know what, Harry and Kavanagh? I win the day and that's all that matters," Fleck said victoriously.

Waiting in an emergency room was an uncomfortable experience. A reality show was blaring from the smudged TV screen mounted on the wall. Three judges, fully robed and with seemingly enough caffeine in their systems to challenge Usain Bolt, wrangled over the case before them. There was a lot of bellyaching from the bench; their ire was directed at the plaintiff and the defendant who were both *dumber than dirt*. This was a nearly extinct expression Harry had heard often when he was a kid. Usually uttered by one of his old uncles describing one of their bosses while they were all perched around his grandmother's Sunday table. They were his Italian uncles on his mother's side of the family. During the week, the men were hardworking brutes – laborers, subway track workers, butchers and the like – their hands toughened by callouses from years of repetitive work. On Sunday afternoons, they were gentlemen diners who were attired in starched white shirts with dark ties. They had Clark Gable mustaches and were showered with so much cologne you knew when they were crossing the street. More importantly, Harry recalled, these were kind and gentle men – always quick to roll around on the floor with their giggling nieces and nephews. Harry missed his Italian side.

Many of the relatives on his mother's family died by the time Harry was a teenager. The only one left was Uncle Sebastian. And on the other side of the family? There was no such thing as sitting around the table on Sunday at the Kavanagh abode. For one good reason, Harry's Irish grandmother was an atrocious cook. She'd sip Ballantine beer from a teacup and saucer from the time she got home from morning mass (she attended daily), and she continued drinking her special brand of tea all day long. By the time it came to making supper, she'd forget the little she knew about cooking.

Harry remembers his Irish grandma as one hell of a broad. Tough; to the point. You'd have to wrangle her to get a kiss out of her, yet Harry thought she was one of the most loving people he'd ever known. But because she was such a lousy cook, there was never any discussion of where the family would be on a Sunday afternoon. His Italian grandmother, on the other hand, was affectionate but she could be impatient and inconsiderate to Harry's mother. When Irish grandma died, his Italian grandmother danced around for days singing, *I'ma the only one.* Sundays Italian style meant fruit and nuts and finocchio (fennel) on the table, crooner Lou Monte singing something breezy on the Victrola while everyone waited for macaroni. Macaroni, synonymous with today's pasta. Pasta was the lingo Harry never heard until he was in college. Pasta, baloney! Macaroni could mean you were having spaghetti, penne, linguine or any type of – *Don't make me say pasta, even in my mind,* Harry thought. *Oh, hello? I said it, damn it!*

I'ma the only one – Harry thought about it for a second. Grandma Brazzano never liked competing with Irish grandma. Being the only grandmother left meant she was finally the queen. Harry was the only one now. He didn't feel like a king. Without Felicity, he felt diminished.

Harry leaned away from a woman sitting beside him when she unwrapped an egg salad sandwich. It smelled as old as the dawn of time. When the earth was forming, and everything was torrid and gaseous. Harry found himself turning toward the other television where the New York City Police Commissioner was ripping into Senator Ted Cruz from Texas for something he said on the campaign trail. It had something to do with the senator's idea to police Muslim neighborhoods using small squads – to root out terrorism. The commissioner, holding his tongue, still managed to say this about the senator: "He doesn't know what the hell he's talking about."

The mayor put his hand on the commissioner's shoulder before the angry cop could really let it fly. The commissioner walked away from the podium simmering while the mayor replaced him there, fielding questions. Back in the

CBS studio, Norah O'Donnell reminded her guest the senator there were no Muslim neighborhoods in New York City. The senator responded, saying something about Islamism and liberal henchmen, his two newest talking points. While he was pontificating, he never actually addressed O'Donnell's remark.

As Harry looked around the waiting room, he noted how slovenly and depressed everyone looked. The potential patients and some of the hospital staffers as well. People looked rumpled, tired, and downright miserable. Soiled and wrinkled uniforms and tired clothing appeared to be the norm; both men and women with few exceptions were hastily turned out for the day. Some people in the waiting room were clad in sweatpants; some others were wearing pajamas. Harry located a spot on his head that didn't hurt, and he scratched it. *People wearing pajamas as outerwear? The world is going to hell in a hand basket*, Harry thought. Another expression from Harry's youth, this gem from the Kavanagh side of the family.

There was this one guy; Harry estimated he was about 40. He was complaining to an elderly man who was sound asleep, slumping in the chair beside him. The blabbing guy wanted his social security money cashed out because, as he pontificated, he'd been working since he was nineteen. He wanted what he wanted. He thought he was entitled to have his cash forthwith. He swallowed a Kit Kat bar whole and daintily sipped Minute Maid orange juice from a half-gallon plastic bottle. He also mentioned in passing that he was diabetic. Harry wasn't sure if he was a patient, a mental patient or a waiting-room chaperon. A woman wearing sunglasses paraded into the room digging fries from a greased-stained paper bag. The man looked her over as if to say, *How you doing?* She nodded and tapped on her chest. "Heart palpitations," she said, as if she was imparting wisdom.

Harry squirmed in his seat.

"Kavanagh, Harry?"

"Thank you," Harry said. The woman eating the sandwich smiled at him revealing a mouthful of wreckage.

Harry was led into the triage area. *The air in here must be different*, Harry thought. The men and women were wearing recently laundered scrubs. Everyone appeared to be awake and present.

"To what do we owe the pleasure of your company today?" the male nurse sitting behind a monitor said.

"Today? You make it sound like I'm a frequent flyer."

"A figure of speech – we do have regulars."

"Do I look familiar to you?" Harry said, mildly annoyed. Then he took a breath. "Forgive my impatience. I've had an unusual night and…"

"Where are you going with the monologue, sir? We're a busy ER. Why are you here?"

Harry let his comments go although he wanted to kick the man in the shin. His head was pounding.

"I hit my head or was hit in the head last night. I'm a little light-headed. I vomited on my way to the hospital, but possibly because my neighbor was spiteful and drove like a lunatic."

"You should move."

"I should what? What did you say?"

"With neighbors like that, who needs friends, right?"

"You've reminded me, you're a very busy man, so let's stay on topic," Harry said, but what he meant to say was, "Shut your pie hole." His boys used to hurl this expression at one another when they were younger. When they were kids, fighting like brothers, slinging profanities; naively believing their parents were out of earshot. Not eloquent inner dialogue, but the thought seemed to pacify Harry in the moment.

The nurse made a face and proceeded to ask routine questions. He typed without looking at Harry. Then he finished off with, "Who is the President of the United States?"

"Barack Obama."

"Oh, geez, yeah," the nurse said with contempt. He slid his chair toward Harry and began checking his vital signs while observing the swelling on his forehead.

"So, what's it like?" Harry asked.

"So, what's what like?" the nurse said, wiggling his stuffed nose. He was having difficulty breathing through congested nasal passages.

"Being the president of the Scott Baio fan club. Intellectually stimulating?"

Harry would never get the answer to his question because the nurse shot up and left the room.

Harry was moved to a bed in the main ER. After some small talk with the medic who brought him back, the doctor arrived. She asked more of the same questions, running through the litany with efficiency and speed. He could not respond to all the questions, yet she kept rattling them off. Harry was uneasy.

"You're going too fast. Hold up please," Harry interrupted.

The doctor hesitated and took a good look at him for the first time. She took a breath and smiled apologetically. *Here it is, possibly a moment of humanity*, Harry thought. They were at an impasse; they took the opportunity to look at each other.

The doctor was somewhere in her 40s, possessing keen dark eyes with long hair pulled back tightly, corralled into some kind of a bun. *To describe her as simply attractive would demean her appearance and my own descriptive abilities*, Harry concluded. Harry was not a man of God, but he could be a man of faith and intuition when circumstances suited him. The doctor appeared to be uniquely appealing for reasons Harry instinctively knew would catch up to him the longer their interaction continued. On her end, the doctor thought her latest patient appeared to be lean and fit. She didn't meet many of those types in the ER. This man, however, her newest patient, her twenty-seventh patient of the day, he was almost handsome; potentially mannered – like a character from a PBS production without Ian McKellen's accent. She thought he wore his weariness a little too comfortably. Since she was musing about television productions with manners, she concluded that he sported this lethargy like an old smoking jacket. Not immediately off-putting. She snapped out of her reverie. She shook her head, appearing to apologize for being brusque. And then she made it official.

"I apologize. I'm guilty of chart-picking. It does work in your favor though."

"You mean you chose me?" He found himself answering brightly and not feeling guilty about it.

That lethargy she diagnosed in the man seemed to dissipate quite suddenly.

She answered, "Well yes, in a manner of speaking. I'm near the end of my shift and say if you swallowed a tire iron, well, stomach injuries could take all day. I average more than three patients an hour as it is. It's a lot for an ER doctor. Hanging out for several more hours would make my cat very angry."

"Well, it seems like this arrangement works in your favor. I'm a simple head case, is what you're saying?"

They smiled at one another. Harry caught himself. There was something there, in this woman's smile. Something he was drawn to. He noticed something about her the moment she walked into the room. Something emanated from within her despite the restrained manner. Three or more patients an hour, she must be good. Harry cozied up to people who were good at something.

"I understand you hit your head in the storm? Do you take any blood thinners or aspirin or warfarin? Were you drunk? Did you pass out?"

"Hold on, you're speeding again. The answer to most of your questions is no. But I did pass out or sort of pass out."

"Okay, did you hallucinate? For example, did you see the giant Stay Puft Marshmallow Man raging through your neighborhood?" Her bright eyes were anticipating a witty response from Harry.

Harry smiled, then he hesitated. He began to twist his wedding band with his finger without realizing it. She was about to call him by name but realized she hadn't taken the time to read his name on the chart. She scanned the top of the chart.

"Mr. Kavanagh?" The name meant something to her. It stopped her cold.

Harry noted her abrupt distance and was confused by it. He decided to answer in order break the spell. He watched her closely as he spoke.

"Actually, I was hallucinating. After I was hit by something, I fell into some water outside. Submerged and then I imagined I was being rescued by my wife. But it isn't possible." He paused, realizing he'd inadvertently placed her in a position to ask a follow-up question. Nonetheless, she didn't bite. She stared back at him, eyes blinking.

"Not possible because my wife is deceased."

The doctor's expression did not alter. Her expression remained clouded. She was troubled.

"Excuse me, Mr. Kavanagh, I'll be right back." She departed.

Harry waited another fifteen minutes before a replacement doctor arrived with his chart. He was in his mid-to-late 30s with gray flecks streaking through his otherwise jet-black hair.

"I apologize for the delay, due to no fault of my own," he held up his hand anticipating Harry's question. "Something came up and Dr. Armstrong had to leave. I don't know what you said to her, but a doctor rarely leaves after checking in with a patient."

"We seemed to have a cordial exchange." He didn't know what else to say, but he pressed on because he didn't appreciate the doctor's remarks.

"She explained to me that she sees more than three patients an hour. Maybe she grew weary of picking up everyone else's slack. How many patients do you see in an hour, doctor?"

"I'm going to ignore the question. Now, what's your emergency today?"

"Why don't you take a moment to read my chart." It was not a question.

Harry didn't know what to think about the woman's departure. He did know there was nothing useful to be pulled out of his replacement doctor. Harry was feeling deflated. He was more concerned about the woman who took a moment to smile at him. And then didn't. He believed it to be a genuine smile. Did he do something wrong? Had he offended her? Depressed her? The entire time Harry was questioning himself; he heard the second-string doctor jabber about the benefits of a CAT Scan.

Later that afternoon, Harry exited the hospital and stepped out into the sunlight. The CAT scan findings were negative, meaning he didn't have serious head trauma. He did have a mild concussion and was told to take Tylenol and given a prescription for something called Zofran for nausea he may experience later. He was instructed to return if the headache and vomiting continued. He took a taxi home, obsessing about Dr. Armstrong's warm smile and her vanishing act.

Unfortunately, the cab driver was the talkative type. He was yammering about how everything was terrible, from the New York Knicks to the New York Giants, the Jets; to his sanitation guys who for some reason only take half of his curbside garbage. This blabber and more from a guy who told Harry he has an aunt who spreads mayonnaise on corn on the cob. According to him, this was bad too, but not as terrible as his teams, hemorrhoids, taxes or worse, gay marriage. Harry rubbed his tired eyes and had to restrain himself from leaping out of the moving vehicle.

The driver took a side route, traveling down a narrow street. Yellow police tape was x-ed across the front door of Corbin Reece's crooked abode. The building didn't hold any special significance for Harry. He barely paid any attention to it as they passed by. The driver was singing about the terrible conditions of the roads. Harry closed his eyes, shutting him out, giving up on the memory of Dr. Armstrong's smile. He was going to try to plow through a power nap.

A few minutes later, Harry smiled as Lolly's face appeared on the other side of the window pane on the side door.

"Hello, beautiful old girl," Harry said.

Arnold Fleck came toddling across the street and caught up with Harry as he put his key into the lock. Harry's smile disappeared.

"What did the doctor say?"

"He told me not to hit my head again. Doesn't Arnold and Fleck ever go to work?"

"I keep my own hours. Say, if you need anyone to keep an eye on you, you know, in case you have a concussion. You have to stay awake, right?"

"Apparently, that's nonsense they say on TV. You're a doctor, you should know that?"

"Yeah, but I deal with the other end of the body. But listen, if you need anything. If you need me to come by…"

"What's wrong with you? Do you have head trauma?" Harry asked, frowning at Fleck.

"Okay, you don't have to be so ungrateful. Remember, you owe me a new shovel then. You could order it and I could come over and get it."

"You want me to order you a shovel, like what? Like you order Papa John's pizza? No one in their right mind orders Papa John's. We live in the pizza capital of the world right here," Harry said.

Harry was tired. Fleck was wearing him out; he was in no mood for conversation.

"Go home and give yourself a foot massage," he said to Fleck.

Harry opened the door and stroked Lolly who was happy to see him return. He reached for her leash.

After a short walk around the block with Lolly, Harry sat down at the kitchen table and wrote a letter to Jake. He didn't go into the details of his hospital experience. He kept it upbeat save for some complaining about the boorish podiatrist. He missed his boys, but he worried about Jake. He knew he was in for a tough haul. This career he chose was in its infancy. He did muse in his letter though, that he felt Jake was probably safer at Parris Island than Will was at an upstate college. He mentioned some news, reporting there was a sequel in the works for one of Jake's favorite childhood movies, *The Incredibles*. Harry joked, by the time Pixar completed the sequel, Jake might be finished with his commitment. Maybe they could go to the movies together, as a family. *As a family*. That is to say, if Jake didn't re-enlist and Will wasn't performing with the Moldova National Ballet.

Harry wrote three drafts of the letter. After making certain his despondency didn't bleed between the lines, Harry put the letter to bed by contentedly licking the Forever stamp, miraculously reduced from 49 cents to 47 cents. *There is hope for the world*, he thought. He immediately put in a call to Will but had to leave a message when he didn't pick up.

Harry wandered around his kitchen. From the television he heard Edward G. Robinson say, "Let's wrap ourselves around a little grub." It made sense. Harry hadn't had anything to eat all day, but he wasn't really thinking of food. It was a little after 4 p.m. and he was exhausted. He turned to Lolly. "I'm going to take a nap. If Arnold and Fleck pays us a visit, you have my permission to devour him. There's Pepto Bismol in the cabinet."

Harry turned off the TV. He headed upstairs and collapsed on the bed. To his surprise, Lolly followed him into the bedroom. The old girl didn't usually make it up the stairs. She looked at Harry lovingly. Harry smiled and said, "Okay." The bed creaked when the old girl climbed aboard. They both fell asleep immediately.

The sun was already setting outside, and all was dim inside the dank little hole. Jaycee Singletary was lurking around Corbin Reece's apartment. He'd been searching the tiny place for nearly an hour. No journals, nothing about him on Reece's laptop, no notes, damning pictures – there was nothing. Threats by Reece were meant to get under his skin. It was a bluff. Maybe or maybe not, Singletary was still not certain. The police hadn't bothered to confiscate his laptop or his cellphone. While it was a clear case of dive and die, the police were lazy and sloppy, in his opinion. The carelessness of the authorities was Singletary's gain. Singletary went through the cellphone meticulously.

Nothing on him. Nothing worth worrying about. With everything Singletary knew about Reece's connection to the Kavanagh woman's death, he was certain a clean-up team would be coming for the phone and the laptop. Not an official team. Not the authorities. No sooner did he finish his thought did he hear the approach of at least two oafs clomping up the stairs. They probably entered the vacant building through the basement as he did, but in their case without so much as one brain shared between the both of them.

"What amateurs," Singletary hummed. He'd been wearing gloves – there was no urgency to wipe anything. He placed the phone and the laptop on the table in the kitchen; both items would be clearly seen from the entranceway. He grabbed a bottle of dishwashing soap near the faucet and carefully poured it onto the floor. Then he hid in the shadows and waited.

The front door opened, and a pen light flicked on. Singletary saw the silhouette of two burly hatchet-men. The light found the items in question.

"Right there, what a piece of cake," he heard one of them say. A raspy laugh erupted from the other one as Singletary prepared to leave this chapter behind him. The men moved in quickly and clumsily toward the kitchen table. Their bodies immediately danced a jig when they reached the slimy liquid. They slid across the floor with their feet eventually pointing toward the ceiling. Singletary was descending the staircase when he heard the men grumbling and cursing. He regretted not taking the laptop and cell. There may have been something there to connect Reece to Felicity Kavanagh. Singletary was thinking about himself and the journals in the moment. He lost sight of the bigger picture. Information meant power. He *was* truly off his game.

Arnold Fleck parted his second-story bedroom curtains and spied Harry's house. The place was dark. The son of a bitch was sleeping it off. Fleck needed access to the Kavanagh house. He'd been desperate to get inside since Felicity Kavanagh's death, but it was impossible with that damn beast guarding the place. He'd often considered trespassing when Harry took the dog out for a walk, but he'd always lose his nerve. Those walks could last five minutes or an hour, there was no way of knowing. Time was running out on him. He was anxious. His skin would occasionally break out into a nervous rash. He couldn't live his life this way, constantly in fear of ruination. After all, it was that woman's fault, he rationalized. She was always nice to me. Not like that goddamn son-of-a-bitch Harry.

"Maybe we could have had something if she didn't drink herself into a fucking puddle and drown," he said out loud.

He threw the curtains closed and stomped his feet like a pouting child denied an ice cream cone. He punted his night table and it flew across the room shattering the full-length mirror on his closet door. Fleck ducked and let out a childish whimper.

Chapter Seven

State Senator Irene Roth opened her eyes although she'd been awake for some time. She contemplated her night table, which had a small army of over-the-counter and prescription drugs poised in formation. There were doctor-prescribed vials there such as Ambien, Valium, Ativan, and Xanax. When she wobbled out of bed, she inadvertently sideswiped an empty bottle of Benadryl with her toe. No one should be confronted with their own misery before a cup of coffee. And no woman should be repulsed by the sight of her own big toe. Those reflections reverberated inside her cloudy head.

She lifted her head slowly, swiveling it toward her bathroom where she heard the shower running. When she leaned into the doorway, she saw her 48-year-old boyfriend Thaddeus Calendar in the shower. He was masturbating.

"Hey," she said as a way of good morning. Her voice sounded sexy although she felt like she had hair growing in the back of her throat.

Calendar, a slender and physically fit man who was a runner and a swimmer, responded with a much more enthusiastic *hey* of his own. He was not dissuaded from accomplishing the goal at hand. He stepped out of the shower with a blush on his chest and in his cheeks. He kissed Irene Roth on the forehead, like she was a sexless schoolmarm. He proceeded to towel himself off.

"I wish you would've saved some of the morning mojo for me."

"I didn't think you were into it this morning, and unfortunately with schedules like ours, we have to make quick decisions," he said, drying between his toes.

She frowned. She thought his toes were much nicer looking than her own. "Since when am I not into it?"

When he didn't respond, she said, "I don't think I've ever dried between my toes." She said it as if she was longing for a discovery on an elusive treasure map.

He smiled at her. It was a distant smile.

"That might explain your athlete's feet," he said without looking at her.

This was not the kind of discussion that would recapture their once rabid sexual attraction. She shook her head with bitterness. He didn't notice. He didn't notice much about her these days.

Thaddeus Calendar, the handsome, naked man standing before her was a former criminal defense attorney and the current state senator from Brooklyn. A much more prestigious position than Roth's standing in Richmond County, otherwise known as Staten Island, or "The Shaolin," a nickname made famous by the rap group the Wu-Tang Clan.

Roth and Calendar "vetted" one another after a committee function just after she was first elected. Someone told Roth there would be a spread, so she lingered. She loved Buffalo wings, so she was hopeful. But Roth would come to nickname the Albany meet-ups as political abortions, or chandelier shit-scapes. The spread at the gatherings was hit or miss. Usually a miss. There were no wings at her inaugural buffet table.

Roth and Calendar were immediately drawn to each another. They shared a few celery sticks and flirted over a fetid sushi spread. They wisely turned their backs on the chum; as it turned out, it was responsible for the gastrointestinal hysteria that ensued the following morning. Making a hasty plan, they departed without the other, abandoning pasty-faced sycophants and bad suits collecting dandruff. Colleagues and constituents all.

"I bet you're the only woman in the room not wearing granny panties," Calendar said to Roth at the time.

"Senator, you're disgusting, and that comment is demeaning to women," she whispered.

"Senator Roth," he said in a deeper and more melodic tone of voice, "I have a place."

"Whoopee. A cave? A Neanderthal in a two-thousand-dollar suit? You are such a fucking Prince Charming. What's the address?"

Later that evening, they met at his hideaway, a locale she considered to be in the middle of the sticks. Calendar nicknamed the place the shed. It was a well-appointed cabin surrounded by a shabby forest, in a place called Cropseyville, not too far from the state capital. As it turned out, it came as no big surprise to Roth that Calendar had a nickname for his phallus as well. She stopped laughing at that handle a long time ago.

Heading to the shed on the first evening, Roth was filled with anticipation and trepidation. She had concerns about Calendar, least of which was his married life. He had a reputation as a hothead and power-player. He played around with some dangerous and notorious figures. There were rumors of double-dealing, back-door threats and even "gone missing" colleagues swirling around Calendar, going back to his days when he was practicing law.

She was on to him and his disingenuous smile, but the way his eyes swallowed her up made her forget about everything else. It didn't hurt that he had strong shoulders and looked great in and, as she would soon see, out of a suit. Irene Roth was lonely, and she was ravenous that night. He was a hard snack to resist. Calendar, the big shot from the *fahgettaboudit* borough of Brooklyn, and the junior senator from the Shaolin were friends with benefits since their fateful first tryst.

Calendar was a married man – to a television anchor on a morning cable news program. Three children together, one boy was in the United States Air Force and a girl in college; their youngest child, a boy, was in middle school. His pretend marriage and family life never seemed to interfere with their torrid affair.

But something was different now. A shift was occurring. Roth intuitively felt she was being left behind. She sensed she was on the verge of being cut from the team. And that wouldn't be such a bad thing, being let go. It would set her free. She could breathe on her own again. Calendar was a repellent man who tortured her in ways he didn't care to understand. Being unwanted by a man whom she loved and despised at the same time was one thing, however, feeling undesirable was the biggest blow. It was a crusher.

Maybe the douche has a new girlfriend, a much younger girlfriend? Probably.

Roth awakened that morning with Calendar grinding himself into her from behind. From his point of view, the morning began with promise: he was erect, and she was asleep. He quickly lost interest in her flesh and decided to begin anew under a hot shower. Roth "stayed asleep" until she could gather her composure.

Irene Roth had gained 17 pounds over the last few years. The curves in her hips were gone. Her brash confidence had given way to feelings of guilt and apathy so heavy that she had to drag herself out of bed each morning. Her history with this man was slowly suffocating her.

Calendar walked past her and into the bedroom. He began dressing without a care in the world.

"I don't smell any coffee."

That's because you spent your morning with your dick up my ass, she wanted to say to him. She calmed herself and said, "Sorry, got a late jump this morning."

"I'll shave at the office. I have a nifty new electric shaver."

"Nifty," she said. She took a breath and walked directly in front of his line of vision.

"Oh, hello." He tried to make it sound cheerful.

"It's time we end this, now. Don't you think? You're clearly not interested in me anymore. We're not the way we were. And a lot has happened. Too much for me to bear."

She heard a little of her old self in the voice vibrating from her body. While it was a surrender, there was a semblance of pride in her decision. The light receded from Calendar's expression. When he finished tying his shoelace, he stood up and held her shoulders firmly in his grip. His dark eyes inspected her face, watching the confidence drain from her features.

"I'm being strangled by unhappiness. I need to breathe again."

"That sounds poetic and tragic. Oh, no, no," he said quietly. "You shouldn't feel this way."

He kissed her eyebrow gently. It reminded her of the magazine article she should have finished: "How to Tame My Overgrown Eyebrows."

"You and I, we are attached by our hips."

"You think you're funny? At the hip, you nimrod." Her anger came spilling out.

"There's no danger here. Breathing is good. Take a breath."

"Thad?"

"I would argue there's jeopardy in distance. We depend on each other. What we have shared is sacred."

"And secret. Don't speak to me like I'm an evangelical fucktard," she said. "Don't pull that bullshit on me."

He moved his right hand from her shoulder to her neck. He caressed it. Then he put his other hand between her legs and parted her.

"Thad, you're frightening me," she breathed out.

"Nonsense. Give in to it."

He didn't have too long to wait before she became aroused. He caught sight of his reflection in the mirror and abruptly abandoned her. He swung around and moved to the mirror and began combing his hair with the fingers that were inside her. All intensity gone from his demeanor. Roth spat out an angry breath, standing there, shoulders tensed, legs spread in an unnatural position.

"Look, I'll see you at the shed on Friday and we can finish this. I can finish you off," he said with a schoolboy's leer. "I'll have Ursula send us her most gifted and discreet massage therapists. You and I will spend the weekend decompressing."

"Ursula, the former State Assembly woman and your former girlfriend who supplies women for men like you?"

He ignored the comment and said, "My wife is chaperoning our youngest on a school trip. Conveniently, she'll not be getting a massage this weekend. So, you're up next."

"Up next, how charming."

Roth turned her back on him and went into the bathroom. She felt sick. She poured herself a glass of water and drank it. When she looked into the mirror, she saw him standing in the doorway behind her, imposing; not a person to be trifled with. She raised the glass and toasted him looking into the mirror.

"To the shed and to many more happy endings," she said, trying to hide her disgust.

"Now, that's my girl."

"I'm not a girl." She whirled around and flung the glass at his head. He flinched when the glass shattered against the door frame. He smiled and winked at her. She watched Calendar remove a shard of glass from his lip. He reached into a bureau and pulled out a pair of her underwear.

"Darling, you don't mind if I borrow a pair of your granny panties? I know they've been battle-tested."

He dabbed the blood on his lip with her underwear.

"See you on Friday?" He departed with a nod and a half-smile.

Roth lifted the toilet seat and vomited what seemed to be everything she had left inside. Tears rolled down her cheeks. Her head felt like it was going to blow. She wiped her mouth with her bare arm and stumbled into the living room.

"Very ladylike," she blurted, opening the curtains of her pied-à-terre.

She scanned the St. George waterfront. The Staten Island Ferry Terminal below and One World Trade standing tall across the water in lower Manhattan. All this light streaming into her luxury apartment did nothing to assuage her mood. The short walk to her office meant she was marking another day in her life as an undesirable woman.

On the third day after his "warm and fuzzy" experience at the hospital, Harry Kavanagh woke up feeling a little better. His headache was gone, but there was something more to it. Harry rubbed his eyes recalling an old *New York Times* movie review written by A.O. Scott. Harry began chuckling because only he could conjure this type of memory before his feet touched the bedroom floor. The reviewer, mucking through his thoughts regarding the film *The Shape of Things*, spoke of writer/director Neil LaBute in this way – "Mr. LaBute has returned to his more familiar role as an anatomist of human awfulness." On many mornings pursuant to the death of his wife, Harry awoke feeling as if he was mucking through this bog of awfulness. Filling with anxiety and forever feeling like he would never become unstuck or have the impulse to exhale freely. *Thinking like this makes me feel better? What's so funny, Harry?* he thought.

But this morning was different for reasons he couldn't immediately figure. Yes, his aching headache was history, but there was a slightly lighter pulse springing from within him. As he looked around the room, he decided the colors seemed brighter. The morning light beaming through spaces in between the blinds was embracing his room with warmth. The light blue paint on the bedroom wall and the colors on the bathroom tile seemed unfamiliar and inviting.

Certainly, the days were richer when the boys were around; Harry was able to buoy them or vice versa. Will's subconscious commitment to being as limber and as humorously unpredictable as Ray Bolger's scarecrow from *The Wizard of Oz* (a reference only Harry could come up with, which would certainly earn Will's groans) and Jake's sturdy shoulders and pragmatic approach to life was a foundation from which Harry could rebuild his life on. But the boys were away. However, on this morning, Harry Kavanagh was feeling slightly elevated. *And that was what?* Harry finally put the words together in his head…*And that was good.*

"Let's leave the bog behind today, Harry," he said to himself. He looked toward his open bedroom door and shouted, "I hope you're making the java this morning, Lolly."

He rose from bed and swept some evidence of Lolly's hair off the bed cover. She had been sleeping with him ever since he returned from the hospital. Felicity would've never had it. She would have never tolerated Lolly's snoring or encroachment. The dog hair on the bed cover alone would have made Felicity a special kind of crazy.

Harry went into the bathroom and brushed his teeth. He dared to inspect his reflection in the mirror, but at the very last instant he decided it was not the way he wanted to begin his day. Why ruin this good feeling? Or as cherubic funnyman Lou Costello once said, in a one of those old movies in response to a similar dare, "Why should I hurt my own feelings?"

Under the hot shower, Harry observed steam rising off parts of his body he hadn't taken stock of in a long while. Harry suddenly became aware of how thin he had become. He inspected himself without too much criticism (which was a miracle). He decided he should finally make plans with this lighter version of himself.

Harry had been athletic in his youth – because in those days there were no excuses for not breaking a sweat. Tearing the knees of your dungarees was an expectation every parent had for their child. There was no such thing as jeans in those days. There was nothing fashionable about dungarees. Mothers used to call those durable dungarees play clothes. "Put on your play clothes," or "Take off your school clothes, and put on your dungarees." Harry heard his mother's voice blending with the voices of all the other neighborhood CEOs from that era.

Harry had recently read a story about the current generation of kids; some of them were developing carpal tunnel syndrome by age ten, caused by this around-the-clock video game hustling. For kids of Harry's generation, there was always Little League or choose-up everything else: softball, basketball, whiffle ball, and street hockey. Then there was touch football whereby the crooked, splintering telephone poles on the corners became the neighborhood end zones.

Harry couldn't recall the last time he did a sit up or rode a bicycle. He'd been a fat man for so long. Since he was almost feeling good, Harry decided there could be a sit up or possibly a pushup in his future.

He began to sing, "Take my hand, I'm a stranger in paradise," poking fun at his changeable mood. When he stepped out of the shower to dry off, he was surprised by the sight of Lolly sitting tall in the doorway looking at him as if to say – *You're a strange dude to begin with, but have you gone mental?*

"Oh, it's okay, girl. I'm not flying my freaky flag, as Will would say. Maybe I need coffee. Then you and I are going to take my orange sneakers out for a test drive. How about that?" The big girl yawned. She was quickly appeased and immediately lost interest. She turned away from Harry. Her huge chassis navigated its way out of the steamy bathroom.

In the kitchen, Lolly watched Harry tying the laces on his aforementioned sneakers. He took his last slurp of coffee. As he reached for Lolly's leash, there was a gentle rap on the door. Harry opened the door to find his 11-year-old paperboy smiling up at him.

"Oh, hello, Charlie," Harry said brightly. "Do I owe you?"

"No, Mr. Kavanagh. Oh, hello, Lolly," the boy's voice rose enthusiastically.

Lolly wiggled over to greet Charlie Perkins and stuffed her large head into the boy's groin. Charlie giggled as he handed off three newspapers bound in rubber bands to Harry.

"My father noticed you hadn't picked the papers off the front porch. He wanted me to check up to make sure everything was okay."
Charlie massaged Lolly's head and ears. Harry looked outside his kitchen door and waved to Charlie's father who was waiting in the car. The man shot back with a thumbs-up sign.

"Charlie, does your father always drive you around to do your paper route?"

"Monday to Friday, you know, school days, he does. On the weekends, I ride my bike."

"You know, when I was a kid…"

"I know, Mr. Kavanagh, my father says the same things. Even though he's a lot younger than you."

"There are days when I feel like everyone is younger than me, Charlie. Say, do you know what carpal tunnel syndrome is?"

"Car pool tunnel? Is it a ride? Sounds like fun."

"Oh, never mind. I'm just playing with you. Thanks for bringing the papers."

"Okay, Mr. Kavanagh. And see you, big Lolly girl. Oh, and hey, are you coming to my assembly like you promised? My father can't make it. He has to work, remember?"

"I'll be there with bells on."

"Huh?"

"That means I wouldn't miss it for the world."

"No, I get it, Mr. Kavanagh. I think it's funny because my instrument is the cowbell."

Charlie pushed himself away from the snuggling Lolly and ran back toward his waiting father.

Harry waved again to the dad and turned to Lolly. "Now see, that's some sugar for your coffee. Little Charlie Perkins. Good boy. I knew it was going to be a good day."

A rubber band choking the newspapers snapped when Harry tossed the bundle onto the countertop. Harry wasn't paying any mind as a front page unraveled to reveal the headline reporting the suicide of the Staten Island medical examiner, Corbin Reece.

A few moments later, Harry was taxiing the car with Lolly beside him. Harry still had the boy Charlie on his mind. Will was 19 and Jake was about 21. Jake was in the Marines for Chrissakes. Little Charlie Perkins reminded Harry of his boys when they were young and still innocent – young enough to tell them tall tales, grab an ice cream cone on the run; you could ask them to take out the garbage without collateral damage. The chaos would come later on with the arrival of muscles and moustaches. Harry nodded absently.

He drifted several years back when the family was intact – vacationing in Vieques. Jake was 11 and Will was about 9. They were all sitting on the deck of the rickety rental house watching the sun set when Harry turned and winked at Felicity. He shared a secret with his boys that evening. He told them he could read minds.

"No way," Jake exclaimed.

Harry asked Will to blindfold him and instructed the boys to take turns holding up as many fingers as they desired. Harry advised them to concentrate on the number. He would provide the correct answer by way of his humble supernatural abilities. The boys were astounded when time after time Harry called out the correct number. They never considered Harry's co-conspirator, their mother, sitting beside him. She tapped out their number with her foot against Harry's under the table. That night and many nights following, the boys demanded to know if Harry was really psychic. This teasing and cajoling went on for years. Harry wanted this innocence to be alive as long as possible. He would have eventually explained the conspiracy, however, as the boys grew older, they stopped asking the question. Harry wondered if they had forgotten about it or dismissed him as being a phony.

Whoop, whoop!

Harry jerked the steering wheel. He pulled over as the police cruiser with its flashing lights came to an abrupt stop behind his vehicle.

Harry turned to Lolly. "Okay girl, let's see what happens. I don't think there are any warrants out for my arrest," he said jovially. Harry inspected his rearview mirror and saw the cruiser dip to one side as the squat but powerfully built police officer pushed himself out of the car. His old uncles would have described this man as being built like a Johnny Pump, meaning he resembled a fire hydrant. Harry decided it was prudent to keep things light.

"Good morning, officer. What can I do for you?"

"You were swerving. What did you drink for breakfast?"

"I had a cup of coffee, milk, one sugar."

"License and registration."

"I jerked the steering wheel when you hit the siren. I was surprised."

"This is not a conversation."

"What would you call it then?"

"License and registration."

Harry complied. The cop turned on his heels and went back inside his vehicle to check on Harry's driving record. When he returned, Harry held out his hand, but the cop didn't part with his license and registration.

"Sure you didn't have Jack Daniels with your bacon, egg, and cheese?"

"I'm happy to take a sobriety test. Well, not pleased to, but willing."

"Maybe we should ask your wife if you've been boozing."

"My wife?" Harry quickly realized he was referring to Lolly. The cop hadn't actually looked inside the car and assumed the figure on the passenger side was Harry's better half.

"Okay with me officer, why don't you ask her?"

"She's your bag of doughnuts, you ask her."

"That's quite a comment, officer."

"Yeah, whatever."

"You're a hopeless romantic officer. Something they teach at the precinct or does this come from personal experience?"

Before the cop could protest, Harry turned to Lolly and said, "Dear, have I been imbibing the aforementioned alcoholic beverage with or without my Thomas' English muffins?" Harry shrugged his shoulders and smiled, "The lady won't say."

The cop gestured for Harry to step out of the car. The beet-faced cop shoved his brainpan inside the car. Much to his surprise, he came face-to-face with the drooling Lolly. The big dog put her big teeth on display and growled at the hypertensive interloper. The cop jumped backwards.

"Why didn't you tell me you had a fucking horse in your car?" He flung Harry's license and registration inside the car and handed him a ticket.

"What's this? I don't have a broken taillight," Harry said staring at the summons. He turned and watched the cop trudge off. When the seething, fire-hydrant-shaped "peace officer" arrived at the rear of Harry's car, he punched out one of the taillights with his gloved fist. Lolly immediately leapt into the backseat and began raging at the cop. Froth sputtered from both sides of her mouth, spraying the rear and side windows. The cop scrambled inside his car as quickly as he could, looking completely ridiculous as he did so.

Harry read the officer's information off the summons, leaned against his car, and said to the cop in a loud and deep voice:

"Officer Heastie, there's a big drug store right down the street. I hear they have a twelve-pack of adult diapers on sale. If you'd prefer to support a small family-run business, I'd try Bollmeyer's Pharmacy. Ask for Paulie."

Harry began to cough. The impromptu decision to use his big-boy voice was a mistake. He was clearly out of practice.

The police car revved its engine and came tearing alongside Harry, screeching to a stop. Harry pushed off his car and sprang to attention. The passenger window buzzed down, and the cop angrily pointed a finger at Harry. Shards of red plastic from the shattered taillight were impaled in the knuckles of his glove hand.

"Listen to me, you little dipshit. One more word and I'm going to snap your head backwards like a Pez dispenser!"

Lolly jumped into the front seat and began barking. The cop sped off, plowing through a red light, nearly colliding with an innocent vehicle minding its own business, meandering through the intersection.

Harry opened the door and collapsed into the driver's seat. His hands were trembling. Lolly was pushing her sloppy muzzle into Harry's shoulder. Saliva dripping from her mouth. She was gerbing all over Harry's sweatshirt. He didn't seem to mind.

"It's okay, Lolly. I should have played it smarter. But that guy, a guy like that, you have to believe that one day he'll get what's coming to him."

Chapter Eight

Harry and Lolly arrived at Silver Lake Park. His shakes were gone and Lolly was her more typical laconic self. The sky was gray; there was a low-hanging mist lingering in the air. Harry looked back at his car like he was abandoning his best friend. *What's playing on TCM today?* he thought. He considered heading back, but Lolly had already made herself comfortable sitting beside a park bench. Harry sighed, then instructed Lolly to stay put until he was finished with his run. *His run.* It sounded funny inside his head. He was prematurely taking ownership for something he hadn't attempted in years. Harry pretended to stretch for about thirty seconds and then hit the deck to try his hand at a few pushups. He surprised himself by counting off twenty-eight of them. He was slightly lightheaded when he got to his feet.

"Okay, kiddo, what do you say you and I blow this joint and grab some apple cider doughnuts? From the greenmarket. What do you say?"

Harry put his hands on his hips, waiting for her answer. "Lolly, you're not having any of this, are you, kid?" She looked beyond him, stoic as ever. "I'm really attempting this. Exercise, me? Go figure, as they say."

Lolly yawned in his face when he stroked her big head. "I'll be back sooner than later. You can bet on that."

No need to fetter the patient old girl; she wasn't going anywhere. Harry estimated the distance around the reservoir was about a half mile. He set out with more than a little reluctance. Lolly was fixated by the movement of Harry's orange sneakers padding off in the mist. Her eyes glazed over. She looked like she was falling under a spell.

After his second go-around the reservoir, Harry's brain began flashing distress signals to his body. They were being sent by express mail. Sweat pouring into his eyes; he became aware of his sore ear, the one bruised with his hardened sleeve on the night of the storm.

Harry wanted to push through. He decided he would try to keep his discomfort at bay by regaling himself with memories. Good memories, rather than obsess about the last two cable bills he may have misplaced. Or what he'd say to his wife's sidekick Emma Kendall, his openly peeved casual friend who wanted them to bypass the prom and get right down to Seaside Heights to do what horny teenagers do on the beach before and after the sun comes up. It was easier said than done. So much for good memories.

Harry couldn't help himself. He couldn't wrap his head around the gorilla-coat Emma wore at the dog run. His mind betrayed him, voluntarily flashing disturbing images of the two of them canoodling. She in the hideous pelt smothering him with it, and he mortified, clad in his least favorite garb, his birthday suit. His whole body ached. He considered abandoning this foolish charade of exercising his professor's body. He felt like lighting up his sneakers on the gas grill or trading them in for a pair of Sketchers or an orange-colored La-Z-Boy. Harry shook his head vehemently, disappointed by his too-easy-to-access negativity. Purchasing a pair of Sketchers? Harry decided it was akin to waving a white flag.

"Don't do it, Pop," he heard Jake's voice in his head. "Keep going; if I can wrestle with Parris Island, you can handle your neighborhood green space." It's something Jake would say.

Harry flung away his poisonous thoughts and kept on jogging. He concentrated and transported himself back decades, when he was teenager, a summer job between college semesters. He worked for a husband-and-wife team who catered commercial shoots.

Harry would take public transit from Staten Island to the Upper West Side of Manhattan. In those days, the Upper West Side was alive with the sounds of mayhem. Harry would catch the 3 a.m. ferry to Whitehall, then hop on the clamorous number 1 train en route uptown. In those days, the train windows were smeared with so much graffiti it was nearly impossible to see out of them. Harry routinely traveled amid the circus of down-and-outers: not-so-happy hookers, the hopelessly homeless, and drunken Wall-Streeters who were already pickpocketed, sleeping it off after a hazy stint at a strip club. And then there were the predatory city dwellers in the shadows seeking any opportunity to take advantage of the weak or compromised. Harry fought off a few muggers that summer – once with a piece of pipe that his grandfather fashioned for him for such a purpose.

"The only good'a insurance is'a one that donn'a cost'a nott-ting," his Italian grandfather told him.

"This pipe'a means'a good'a chance the bad'a guy no come back for no more."

His grandfather, Luciano Brazzano, nicknamed the pipe "the noncha." It translated to – don't you worry.

"Noncha worry no more, Harry."

Harry's new companion, the noncha, was christened around the old Victrola while Franco Corelli sang *Celeste Aida*. They clinked Flintstone glasses filled with homemade vino. Bitter-tasting wine his grandfather used to make in his cellar, in part by pounding down the grapes with his very own hooves. A tear welled up in one of Harry's eyes. He wasn't repulsed by the flashback of his grandfather's bulbous toes in the morass, but rather he was touched by the memory of the loving man. His grandfather had paws for hands and a heart the size of two people combined.

Traveling uptown at a time he expected to see Bela Lugosi, Harry knew he had to stay awake if he wanted to remain in one piece. He recalled soaking up the sensations of being perpetually on high alert. His nerve endings consistently tingled with anxiety and excitement. He was young and strong then and he felt alive. Harry suddenly realized he was feeling pretty good, or rather not so bad, on this run of his. He was successfully ignoring the nagging pain. The Sketchers became a fading memory.

Harry would arrive uptown at Gastronome, pick up a rented station wagon filled with pre-cooked breakfast and lunch, which he would dish out to the actors and crew members on set during the breaks. A map was tucked under his arm by the weary but good-natured wife who always had a friendly blush in her cheeks. Then it was up to Harry to sort things out from there. He customarily turned up on set by six or seven in the morning, usually at a location in upstate New York or northern New Jersey. Those drives were often difficult, and they made him sweat. Attempting to read a map in traffic or deciphering scribbled directions while crossing a bridge or in inclement weather was always a challenge.

One particular morning he got word he didn't have to venture out of the city. He was thrilled to learn that all he had to do was hail a cab to shift the moveable feast to a soundstage on 47th Street.

Harry arrived before everyone else and occupied his time by throwing stones at a mailbox. In the distance he saw a small fellow, walking much taller than his true height, drawing closer. Harry could tell the man was incredibly fit.

A beaming Jack LaLanne, probably in his 60s at the time, introduced himself to Harry. No limo, no entourage, simply Mr. Jack LaLanne on his own, clad in his signature dark jumpsuit. The day's shoot was a fitness commercial and Mr. LaLanne was the talent. He and Harry amiably passed the time on the crumbling sidewalk waiting for the soundstage to open. Their easy gab quickly turned to fitness. Mr. LaLanne sized up young Harry and asked him how many pushups he thought he could do.

"Gee, I don't know. It's kind of early for pushups, isn't it, Mr. LaLanne?"

"It's never too early for pushups," was the encouraging response.

"Well, I don't know, maybe I can do forty."

"Why don't you give it a whirl, young man," Mr. LaLanne said smiling.

Harry surprised himself by doing one hundred pushups under the tutelage of his mentor, this giddy, muscular gnome. Mr. LaLanne took pride in the young man's accomplishment, and Harry remembered spending a splendid day with the charming and uncomplicated gentleman.

Harry's woolgathering was interrupted when a pain in his right hip began to outrank the effectiveness of his mind. More shooting pains coming from different places encouraged him to pay attention to his reality and ease his plodding pace to a near standstill. His gait was beginning to resemble that of the 285-pound Bartolo Colon's jog around a different kind of park. Local sportswriters mused that Colon, the veteran New York Mets pitcher, recorded the slowest time rounding the bases in Major League history after hitting an unlikely home run. It was his first career home run and would likely be his last. Harry was certainly giving the big man a run for his money.

Harry heard some chatter and peered over his shoulder. Those two young women, maybe late 30s, obviously athletic, determined by their conditioning and physical appearance – they were coming up on him again, about to lap him. Harry should have felt embarrassment but coming off his Jack LaLanne reminiscence and having nearly completed his third go-around the reservoir, he was encouraged by his inaugural run, despite the inconveniences. If his body would cooperate, he would build on this, he thought.

As the women passed on his right, Harry picked up on a familiar scent; the air around him was thick with a lilac aroma. The first time the women passed him, Harry was lost in a previous reverie. Harry quickly flashed to the notion of the mysterious woman. The woman who rescued him in the storm. A similar scent filled his kitchen the morning of his groggy awakening. Much to the dismay of his barking hip, Harry picked up his pace and caught up to the women.

"Excuse me," he said breathlessly, "Is that a lilac scent I'm picking up?"

The instant the drunken-sounding words came out of his mouth, he knew he would find himself in hot water. The serious-looking one – she looked angry prior to his interruption – now turned and glared at him.

"Really? That's the best you can do? A man of your age. Please."

"I apologize, what I meant to ask was…"

And she quickened her pace, leaving him behind. Her running partner, turning back to Harry and then backpedaling, shrugged her shoulders and mouthed the words *I'm sorry*.

Five minutes later, Harry, with his hand on his smarting hip, approached a circle of spectators gossiping around the unflappable Great Dane who hadn't moved an inch since Harry last saw her.

"How irresponsible. How could someone abandon a dog?"

"The dog has a tag. Let's report the owner," said another.

Harry approached the blathering group from behind and proclaimed, "Lolly, *klaatu barada nikto*." Dialogue uttered by actress Patricia Neal when she attempted to unlock the imposing robot bodyguard, Gort, in the film *The Day the Earth Stood Still*.

Harry challenged himself to remember…screenplay written by Edmund H. North, from a story by Harry Bates. He felt good about remembering, giving credit where credit was due. And now he was free to enjoy the sight of Lolly coming to life much like Gort. She parted the crowd of fussbudgets and loped to Harry's side. Of course, Lolly knew nothing about *klaatu barada nikto* – she was simply responding to the announcement of her name. Harry had played this game before, enjoying the expressions on the faces of people he decided were a day late and a dollar short.

"You know, you should never leave a dog alone for that long." It was the angry-faced runner who decided Harry had tossed a Molotov cocktail one-liner at her. She caught up to Harry as he and Lolly were walking away. Surprisingly, she found herself having to quicken her stride to keep up with them. Her running mate, who looked mortified, was attempting to tug on her friend's sleeve, encouraging her to beg off. But she kept on whiffing at every attempt, and the angry bird was already at Harry's heels.

"I'm talking to you, sir," the unfriendly one demanded his attention.

Harry took a breath and stopped dead in his tracks. "Yes, what can I do for you?"

"Are you aware of how irresponsible you are?"

"I have a notion you're going to explain."

"You put the people of this park at risk, and you jeopardized the health of your dog by abandoning…"

She wasn't certain of Lolly's sex, and proceeded to do an awkward inspection, changing her position several times to get a better look at the dog's plumbing.

"Her," Harry said.

"Her!" She said it as if it accompanied a karate kick.

"Would you like to pet her?" Harry said.

Before she could answer, the woman's partner joined them and tugged gently on her friend's arm.

"Come on, Claire, stop it now. Let's go." She turned to Harry, "I'm sorry for my friend, she hasn't taken her polite-pills this morning," she said frowning at her friend.

"Please don't apologize for me, Brenda. He's an arrogant jerk and a masher."

"A masher? I haven't heard that one in a long time," Harry said raising an eyebrow.

"You've been called out before? Why am I not surprised?"

"I'm interested in language; masher, it's an old-time expression for a misogynist. I am not a masher. I *am* a man of a certain age as you noted. Didn't we go to high school together?"

Brenda made an oh-boy face and watched the woman bristle.

Harry continued. "I've lived long enough on this planet to understand my responsibilities. Many days I fall short. So far, I'm doing okay today. I'm sorry my behavior has inconvenienced you. For that, I blame myself."

Harry and Lolly walked off leaving the grousing woman in their wake. Her friend skipped to Harry's side as he and Lolly continued on their path to freedom.

"Hey, I wanted to say the lilac thing was right on the money. It's this cheap perfume she buys at the gift shop in town. You know, the one owned by that statuesque woman who is as polite as my friend Claire."

"Oh, I know the place. Emma's Gift Shop, thank you." Harry made a face he hoped his new friend did not notice.

Emma again. The woman did have a reputation. It was an odd pairing: his lovely and beautiful wife Felicity and the bombastic Emma. The two of them running around town, sharing cocktails and chuckles. Pondering it very quickly, Harry realized Felicity must have brought out the best in Emma. Felicity brought out the best in everyone.

Harry stopped walking and watched Lolly nuzzle the stranger named Brenda, who was all too happy to reciprocate.

"How old is she?"

"I couldn't in good conscience tell you the lady's age."

"She is beautiful."

"Yeah, she's good."

Harry took an instant to check out the woman who was focusing her affection on Lolly. Yes, probably late 30s, fit; with clear, soft skin. The scent coming from her was not as sweet as the fragrance coming from her friend, the sourpuss. It was much softer, a gentle field blend of fragrant flowers. *Subtle, a more grown-up choice*, Harry thought. He liked it. This woman, Brenda, was cheerful and appealing, but clearly too young for him to be giving her the once-over. He admonished himself silently. He felt his cheeks flush when Brenda noticed his surveillance. She smiled softly.

Harry spoke first. "Uh, I'm sorry about what I said to your friend. I know I'm much older than you, er…her, surely. I wanted to needle her a little bit. It was rude."

"Why are you apologizing to me? And I don't mean you should apologize to her."

"You seem like a nice person. I'm not usually rude to women."

"She deserved it. By the way, my name is Brenda Streeter."

She held out her hand and Harry took it. She had a good solid grip.

"Harry Kavanagh. The pleasure is all mine."

"Well, Harry, maybe I'll see you around," she said, punctuated by another smile.

"Uh, huh," was all he could say.

Harry was a little out of sorts, nervous. He may have smiled back at her. He unsuccessfully attempted to play back the last seconds in his mind. Harry was beginning to hope he had returned her smile. He wasn't certain. *What just happened? Was she flirting with me or vice versa?*

Brenda Streeter jogged back to her simmering friend. Harry walked on. Once out of sight, he clutched his throbbing hip and began to limp. Harry was feeling discombobulated. His day began with a heated run-in with the cop. Out of the blue he finds himself attracted to another woman. *Another woman.* First the ER doctor and now this younger woman, all in a very short time span. He was feeling alive, yet guilty, and then there was the physical pain. The thoughts of his inevitable rematch with Emma capped off his disorientation.

"This is what happens when I step out in the world, Lolly."

Day-fishermen, working on their family's dinner – many of them were leaning against the stone wall of the reservoir, watching their lines in the cloudy water. One of them, a Hispanic man, noticed Harry's pronounced limp and the obvious expression of misery on his face. The man reached into his cooler and grabbed a chunk of ice.

"Mister?"

Harry turned his aching hip in the direction of the man's voice. The fisherman tossed him the ice. He gestured for Harry to apply it to his hip.

"Oh, my goodness. Thank you, my friend."

Harry Kavanagh's new friend was named Eduardo and he was pleased to be of assistance. Harry rested against the stone parapet and applied the ice to his hip. The two men struck up a friendly conversation as they watched the sun burn through the mist.

Chapter Nine

The door flung open and Harry limped into the kitchen, his posture reminiscent of the Hunchback of Notre Dame. Lolly calmly followed him. For some reason, Harry clicked on the TV remote and fled into the bathroom. There was no way he was taking the stairs. Not until his body apologized to him. The tradeoff? The downstairs bathroom was claustrophobic, and water sometimes leaked from the shower onto the tiled floor. Harry's goal was simple and immediate: get some hot water flowing onto his body. He stepped clumsily into the narrow fortress; shucking his clothing like a transitioning Clark Kent entering a phone booth. Then came the beginning of a long shower. Harry was under water for nearly the entire episode of *The Rifleman*, which could be heard on the TV in the kitchen.

The water felt good, but Harry's hip continued to lecture him.

As Harry washed his hair for the third time, his thoughts became a jumble again. His mind was bubbling about Jake at Parris Island. He thought of the bright-eyed woman named Brenda, whom he was certain he would never see again. Doctor Armstrong from the ER – *that was her name* – and the hypertensive cop and the dope's bout with his taillight. Harry's attention segued into what he should have for dinner because that's the way his mind was operating. He was all over the place. Harry considered cooking the Largemouth Bass Eduardo gifted him as he left Silver Lake Park. Harry cursed himself when he remembered that he left the fish in the backseat of his car. He would have to retrieve that sooner than later.

Harry cleared the clutter from his head and began singing "Beyond the Sea." He even sounded lousy in the shower and he knew it.

"I never cease to amaze myself," he said sarcastically.

That song played on the juke box nearly every time they entered the Broome Street Bar in SoHo. "Beyond the Sea" was their song. Everyone knew it. When they were young, Felicity and Harry lived in a closet-sized studio apartment on Broome Street near the entrance of the Holland Tunnel. The Broome Street Bar was a stone's throw away and their oasis. The bar was knee-deep in dime-store philosophers, ruffians, undercover celebs, and artists of all makes and models. In those days, Harry and Felicity barely made the rent, yet they managed to get a cold beer and a burger served in pita whenever there was a need. There always seemed to be a need. Whenever their bar mates saw their approach through the large rectangular window, there would be a mad dash to jumpstart the juke. By the time they entered the place, Bobby Darin would already be serenading them. Harry thought he heard their song on the night of the storm. It must have been a delusion. The shower head sputtered when Harry turned off the faucet. When Harry's feet hit the wet tile floor outside the shower, he upended and fell.

"Oh, hell!"

Harry heard comedian Billy Crystal's voice doing a Howard Cosell impression, "Down goes Kavanagh! Down goes Kavanagh! Down goes Kavanagh!"

After the shower, Harry had a notion to keep his body moving. Take an easy walk, maybe. He wanted to work out the bugs. When he stepped out onto the front porch, he became distracted by a pile of mail. Harry's aching body surrendered onto the porch steps. His posture sprang upright when he found a letter from Jake. He tore it open as Lolly kept an eye on him from behind the front door. When she began to huff and puff, Harry reached back and opened the door. She sat beside him and leaned all over him as he tore open the letter.

Dear Pops,

Yes, you can imagine there are days when I wake up hating my life. I think about sleeping late and eating potato chips in bed. I'm happy with my decision and I know this decision will be a catalyst for my next big adventure. Things are tough here, but I wouldn't want it any other way.

We did this thing the other day called the confidence course. It's a challenge, climbing, running, carrying heavy weight, and as Yul Brynner says forever in that silly movie, "et cetera, et cetera, et cetera." I know I just made you proud. A kid from my generation who remembers an old-time actor. A really dated movie, by the way. Good upbringing, I guess. Most of the guys here think movies began with Spiderman. I actually enjoyed myself during the obstacle course exercise. The confidence course. I tried not to smile. If anyone sees you smile here, you're a dead man.

I came into this thing in better physical shape than most of the guys and I'm benefiting from it right now. I sleep like a log. I don't even dream, just pass out. Hope you're going easy on yourself. I want to hear that you're thinking of going back to work. Give Lolly a big hug for me. Love you, Pops, stay frosty. Reporting from this godforsaken island – Jake out.

What an unexpected pick-me-up, Harry thought. *Jake is taking care of me and he doesn't even know it.*

"These sentiments from a kid who couldn't find his sneakers two years ago. Do you hear what I'm saying, Lolly? And now he's a recruit in the Marines satisfied with his accomplishments. Kids, they'll blow your mind if you don't stunt them."

As one of Harry's public-school teachers, Mrs. Harris, used to say, "All good things." Harry smiled and nudged Lolly with his shoulder. *All good things to you, my son*, was his thought.

During his walk with Lolly, Harry's hip ached, and his ass hurt from his surprising bathroom flop. He knew he must have looked like a horse's ass. Falling wasn't funny at the time. Envisioning his slip an hour later, well yeah, the episode *was* comical. He began to cackle. The tendonitis in his elbows began to harmonize, the direct result of his pushup experiment. Notwithstanding his preoccupation with his clogged emotions and his persistent inertia, Harry was feeling connected to the world. The exercise, as grueling as it was, the glow of little Charlie Perkins, the insouciant paperboy, the generosity of the fisherman named Eduardo, and the letter from Jake made Harry feel buoyant.

Harry's head leaned backward, and he began to laugh like he hadn't laughed in years. It was a cleansing. A joyful release of metastasized grief. Out of the corner of his eye, he saw the odd expression on the face of his neighbor, Arnold Fleck, gaping at him as he drove by slowly in his car.

Harry felt a buzzing in his pocket. It was his cell – probably a reminder that he had missed an appointment. Harry was in the habit of muting his phone because he couldn't stand any of the ringtone options. It was a text. Harry retrieved the message and made a sound that sounded like a laugh. Lolly looked up at him and yawned. It was a message was from Will: *Hiya Pops, wanted to let you know I'm in love. Gonna hit the library. Ciao.*

"Oh, boy, now there's real trouble ahead," Harry said aloud. Lolly looked him over, expressionless.

Fifteen minutes later, Lolly slowly sat her elongated body outside a storefront. Harry stepped into the newest coffee shop in town, a place called The Splendid Cup. He had visited two or three times before and came away disappointed. The place was on the way to Emma Kendall's shop. She raved about this java hut; maybe Harry was missing something. At five dollars a pop for a small cup of coffee, the brim should spout rainbows. A cup from her favorite niche would be an appropriate peace offering. More importantly, there was Harry's interest in lilac-scented perfume worn by the person who pulled him out of the drink. And did his laundry. There was that.

When Harry walked into the coffee shop, he thought he saw the young barista's shoulders swoon. He was wearing a T-shirt that said Zoo York. Harry didn't recognize him, per se, but apparently, he was familiar to the barista. Harry tentatively stepped up to the counter.

"Yes, sir. I know, you'd like your coffee hot."

"Okay. Is that so hard to do?" Harry said, pocketing his smile.

"As I've explained to you in the past, we have to be vigilant."

"We've met before?"

"Yes, we're old friends," he said in a mocking tone. "You always complain about the temperature of our coffee."

"And vigilant you say?" He didn't mean to, but he sounded like a British commander in an old war movie.

"We don't want to scald ourselves, do we? The coffee is as hot as the safety standards allow."

"Vigilant, it's a striking word, but does it really apply here? Did you have your *Watch-on-the-Rhine Crispies* this morning?"

"Whatever, sir."

"Whatever, already? My goodness. You're the reason good people need strong coffee."

"Okay, sir, what…"

"May I politely explain how I prefer my coffee?"

"That is your right, however, as I've explained, in terms of temperature, there are safety standards."

"I'd like a hot cup of coffee. You're not going to need a hazmat suit."

"You're amusing, sir. Raising the already appropriate temperature thing, though. No can do."

Harry kept his voice low until this point. His impatience was reflected in his elevation in tone.

"We're all New Yorkers here. We take a lot of crap on a daily basis. Sometimes all we want is a cup of a hot coffee without a lecture. You get me, Waldo?" *Waldo*, it was a stupid-sounding moniker. Harry sometimes used it when he was angry, to punctuate or give balance to a sentence and as a replacement for the many profane words fighting to come out of his mouth.

The customers in the shop stopped fingering their newspapers and mobile devices. They became attentive to the live episode playing out before them. The barista pressed both hands on the countertop and leaned closer to Harry.

"Our coffee is hot!"

Harry turned and walked away. He heard the barista's melodramatic sigh followed by his utterance of "freak." His way of saying, don't let the door hit you on the way out. Harry stopped dead in the doorway. He pinched the bridge of his nose with his fingers. He turned and glared at the young man who was fluttering about, pretend-busying himself. Harry waited patiently. The barista tried to ignore Harry's presence, but he was drawn to Harry's glare. The customers were rapt. It became so quiet that Harry became aware of the sounds of someone on CNN announcing breaking news. *How much breaking news can you have in one day?* Harry thought.

Harry thought, *What am I supposed to do? Punch this nincompoop in the snout over a stinking cup of coffee?* He shrugged the idea out of his mind and hopped out of the shop, nearly colliding with a group of real estate agents spilling out of their office next door.

"Oh, I'm very sorry," Harry said.

"No problem," said the smiling woman in the lead.

Harry said conspiratorially, "A mice infestation." Harry fiddled his fingers articulating that little creatures were scurrying across the floor.

"Really? That must be new," she said making a sour face.

Her twisted expression became contagious. The other agents grimaced in their own unique way. The lead agent herded her team away from the coffee shop. The smile on Harry's face grew.

Harry took Lolly home and jumped into his car. He couldn't imagine meeting Emma Kendall without coffee. Good, strong, hot coffee. Harry found himself standing inside her gift shop a few minutes later. The gift shop was located on Forest Avenue, a street with barely a tree in sight. Harry hadn't thought about what he would say to Emma, or how he would explain his interest in the lilac perfume. He arrived armed with two cups of coffee purchased at one of his favorite delicatessens, Manoscalpo's. Good-tasting hot stuff had for a third of the price peddled by the not-so-splendid place Harry had sabotaged.

The inside of the gift shop was supposed to be staged as a cozy cottage. After his cursory looksee, Harry was reminded, much like Emma's personality, the place was ostentatious and scattered; a little uncomfortable to navigate.

"Well, hello there, Harry." The sound of the booming voice belonged to the stooped figure slowly unfurling in the stock room. Emma Kendall's shape was blooming until she reached her full contour. She was dressed in a tight-fitting black dress with high heels, elevating her already imposing figure nearer to the water-stained drop ceiling.

"Did you bring me coffee? Did you? How sweet," she said wiggling out of the back room. As she drew closer to Harry, a look of concern washed over her face. "Oh, Harry. You have a little black and blue there," she said pointing in the vicinity of his head.

"Oh, I fell in the storm the other night. Turns out I have a minor something or other."

"Poor baby. A concussion?" she asked, emphasizing the word concussion. She took the coffee from Harry and looked at him with such sympathy, it made Harry squirm.

"This isn't from The Splendid Cup?" The look of sympathy quickly faded.

"No, Manoscalpo's," he said.

She put her nose to the coffee. Her sympathetic look returned.

"You're looking at me like I'm a puppy being sent to a kill-shelter."

"I feel badly for you. That's all."

"Well, thank you for your concern. How's the coffee?" He watched her sip from the Styrofoam cup leaving a clown-like red lipstick signature on the rim.

"It's a beautiful thing, Harry," she said pretending through her teeth. *Danke schoen.* "It was very kind of you to drop by after my performance."

Harry smiled. He wasn't sure how to respond.

Jaycee Singletary was across the street at an untidy strip mall, standing outside a store that tendered newspapers and loosies. Singletary was "reading" one of the local papers. This pretend game allowed him to keep an eye on the gift shop. There were three newspapers that covered the area. Two of them did a more than acceptable job writing restaurant reviews, announcing community events, and reporting on local stories. The newspaper Singletary was manhandling was not his favorite. The attempts at good writing – hard news – dramatized the paper's astounding lack of depth, nuance, and brainpower. This was Singletary's opinion.

Singletary watched a Bullmastiff discard what may have been the previous night's potluck on the ground beside a parked vehicle. The dog's caretaker, an elderly man looked stricken. He wasn't prepared to collect the dog's impulsive deposit. Singletary ambled into the parking lot and offered the man his newspaper. On the front page was the face of one of the borough's councilman giddily endorsing a former reality TV celebrity for president.

"Thank you," the older man said.

"You're very welcome," Singletary smiled.

When the older man realized the front-page photo would be ground zero for the dog's detritus, he hesitated.

"Thank you again," he said slowly bending, looking conflicted.

"Strong community relations make the world go around," Singletary said as he ambled off, referring to his own act of kindness.

The man looked confused, but didn't comment since he had a big job ahead of him. Singletary heard the man grumble a word under his breath. It was an expression Singletary would find a place for.

Singletary meandered across the street so he could get a better look at Harry Kavanagh speaking to the woman inside the gift shop. He was familiar with the shop. He knew who Emma Kendall was. There was something about her, something familiar that tugged away at him. Singletary let this pass, so he could focus his thoughts on Mr. Kavanagh.

Harry Kavanagh – he was perhaps a man on the losing side of life. The opinion was easy for Singletary to dispute, since the reportage came from the dry-mouthed coward Corbin Reece, who inadvertently spilled his guts to Singletary over too many Jameson's Irish Whisky at a musty pub in Manhattan. Reece played a role in Kavanagh's misery. He was coerced into participating in the coverup that was Felicity Kavanagh's murder. Reece was an easy target. His story was so perverse the details managed to make Singletary's stomach tingle with nausea. *No small feat*, Singleton thought, solemnly shaking his head.

Reece was ordered to make Felicity Kavanagh's death appear like a drowning accident induced by alcohol. If he didn't comply, his extracurricular activities would be exposed, or even worse, as Reece explained through sloppy drunken tears, he would be chopped up and stuffed in a suitcase. His body parts tossed into the Kill Van Kull, the polluted tidal strait separating Staten Island from Bayonne, New Jersey. Reece knew who he was dealing with and he had no doubt that his resistance could mean the end of his days, one way or the other.

Why was Felicity Kavanagh murdered? Who was the puppeteer? This was something Singletary had never gotten around to. He wasn't interested in going that route back then. Although a man of great confidence, Singletary knew casting a wider net now could set in motion a slew of unpredictable challenges. Perhaps that's why he left behind Reece's cellphone and laptop. He wasn't sure. During his time with Reece, he was interested in getting at the core of his darkness, so he could methodically siphon his life's savings.

Singletary tried to put it aside, however, he remained concerned with Corbin's proclamation of hidden journals, which could potentially spoil his freedom.

Reece felt compelled to reach out to Kavanagh. Singletary witnessed Reece's clumsy attempt to make contact with Kavanagh from his darkened niche at the restaurant hours before his deadly leap. Singletary feared that Harry Kavanagh was in someone's line of fire. But he couldn't quite work out *why* Kavanagh was in jeopardy. If Kavanagh knew something – if Reece passed along information to him, revealing his wife's murderer – or if Kavanagh came across something on his own, wouldn't he be spending time with detectives or the district attorney rather than this uncouth divorcee?

Singletary felt like he cheated himself for not taking the time to get the entire story from Reece when he had the chance. Information is power; it leads to negotiation. *This is what happens when you go the easy route*, Singletary thought, chastising himself.

Four years after his wife's death, if Kavanagh was still in the dark, why go after him? Maybe they thought Kavanagh caught of whiff of something. And now, years later, if anything happened to Mr. Kavanagh, no one would make the connection. If the deed was done cleanly, no one would suspect anything. *Harry Kavanagh might well be on the losing side of life*, Singletary thought. He certainly has lost a lot. But he was still on his feet. As far as Singletary could tell, Harry Kavanagh was sober, dressing himself in the morning, maintaining his home and some semblance of his life. Singletary respected that in the man. Without knowing him, Singletary decided he was attracted to Kavanagh's unforeseen journey.

Being the curious and vain person he was, Singletary decided to extend his stay in New York City's mostly forgotten borough. He chose to be an attentive audience member for the time being. If he deemed action was required on his part, he would consider diving into the *mishegoss*. That was the Yiddish word he heard the old man utter in frustration as he attempted to clean up his dog's pile with the pages of the *Richmond County Register*. Mishegoss. Singletary would in fact do a swan dive into the mess if need be.

Inside the gift shop, Harry spilled too much info by his own estimation. He told Emma he was helped inside his house by a woman he couldn't identify. He knew this definitively: the unidentified woman wore lilac perfume. As it turned out, Emma sold the perfume in her shop.

"If I didn't know any better, I'd say you stopped by to buy a gift for your new girlfriend."

"I stopped by to bring you coffee. And I'm trying to locate the person who helped me."

Emma looked a little curious, but did not follow up; instead, she reached for a small bottle of perfume on a display counter and showed it to him. She sprayed the mist into the air all around Harry.

"That's the one," he said, as he stepped out of the center of the cloud.

"This is a fairly common perfume, meaning you can purchase it just about anywhere. I have a few customers who like it, but none of them seem to be the Wonder Woman type."

Harry thought back to Brenda Streeter's running partner. She was fit enough, but she certainly didn't possess the temperament.

"Well, I knew it was a long shot. I was looking for someplace to start."

"How do you know I wasn't the one who rescued you?"

"Because your handwriting doesn't match the card." He didn't want to remind her she had the scrawl of an arthritic 88-year-old.

"You received a love note to boot? Well, I'm just glad you're okay, Harry."

"Thank you, Emma," he said, kicking himself for mentioning the note.

"And as far as we are concerned, I'm good. We're good, right, Harry?"

"You're fine," and then he said lightheartedly, "Me, not so much. You know, I've been hit in the head."

"There is a statute of limitation on that excuse, my dear friend," she said.

"Oh, really?"

"Yes, there is. And I'll let you know when your time is up."

Harry exited the shop sensing his dignity was still intact. But he was bothered. He remained completely in the dark. He sighed, life was not like a detective story where all the pieces of the puzzle fall conveniently into place. Harry reached a dead end. Unlike the events during the course of an entertainment, this sign seemed to be impassable. As Harry departed, he rubbed shoulders with Jaycee Singletary as both men filled the doorway at the same time.

"Oh, excuse me, sir," Singletary said politely.

"My mistake, excuse me," Harry said, heading out.

Singletary stepped further into the shop and watched Emma return the perfume to the display counter. Singletary noticed she had a wry smile on her face. Singletary could smell the lingering bouquet in the air. Harry Kavanagh's appearance in the shop suddenly made sense to Singletary. Emma was taken by surprise when she saw the stranger staring at her.

"Well, hello, handsome. What can I do for you?"

Chapter Ten

It was the time of the year when darkness fell early and quickly. Harry had no use for watches or time-keeping since he seemed to be on a never-ending sabbatical. Harry had no routine to speak of. When it grew dark, Harry usually figured it was time for supper. But Harry didn't want to stand over the stove, and he sure as hell wasn't going to try out another restaurant this soon. He liked his sand on the beach not on his entrée. He decided to freeze Eduardo's Largemouth Bass and took the easy way out by making himself some hardboiled eggs compliments of one of his neighbors, Kurt Simmons, who lived two blocks away. Simmons, a Verizon employee, had been out on strike for a while. A week ago, Harry made the Simmons family a lasagna with organic ingredients. It was Harry's way of showing support. The company was attempting to cap employee pensions, cut benefits, and outsource work. Nearly forty-thousand workers were on strike along the East Coast from Massachusetts to Virginia, and there seemed to be no end in sight. Simmons dropped off the two dozen eggs with a note thanking Harry for the gesture. The eggs were from the chickens the Simmons family tended to in their very own backyard.

"There's nothing sexy about raising chickens. The poop, the flies, my backyard is a total disaster, but the eggs are great," Simmons told him.

Shaolin eggs, Harry thought. Harry's mouth was jam-packed with the exalted remains of his third hardboiled egg. He gathered the outdated newspapers dropped off by young Charlie Perkins. When he leaned over to recycle them, he noticed the headline reporting Corbin Reece's suicide.

"What?" he said doing a spit-take. A fountain of egg whites flew across the room.

Lolly poked her head up sharply at the sound of Harry's voice. After a beat, she dropped her head across her legs and relaxed.

"Oh, my god. I saw you the other day," Harry said. Then he thought about Reece's hungry look at him, his high sign.

Was Reece's final glance at Harry really a signal to contact him? He was throwing the idea around and around.

"Was it real or did I make it up?" Harry asked Lolly. Lolly was no help at all and Harry couldn't decide on the spot. Harry read further and was astonished to discover the suicide occurred hours after he encountered Reece outside the restaurant.

The headline was bold; the article succinct; nothing remotely personal was reported about the man. You could learn nothing other than his occupation: Staten Island Chief Medical Examiner. No comments of sorrow from friends, co-workers, or loved ones.

"The wake is..." Harry reached for a pair of cheaters he had lying around and read in smaller print the date and time of the service.

"It's right now, over in less than an hour!"

Lolly watched him rush out of the house.

The van der Donk Funeral Home Emporium was not an emporium at all. Not any longer. It was the borough's oldest funeral home and closest to the waterfront. It was founded by a Dutch family who settled in the 1600s. As the story goes, the tag "emporium" was frequently rambled during the prohibition era. The addendum was usually punctuated with a snort and a mischievous side-long glance. During the prohibition era, the funeral home was also a speakeasy – a place where oystermen, smugglers, and washed-up dockside pugilists drank beer and rum, and when there was nothing else, they swilled wood alcohol. The alternative was not only convenient for the owners of the van der Donk Funeral Home Emporium to have on the menu, it turned out to be profitable. When some of the men kicked the bucket from their bout with the horrid stuff, their bodies didn't have far to travel. During that time, the place was also a renowned gambling joint, and if you asked politely, were in possession of your front teeth, and the recipient of a bath within a week, you stood a good chance of procuring the services of a young lady for the purpose of a good "conversation." The cost became more prohibitive the longer the "repartee" lasted.

Presently, the proprietors of van der Donk were solely in the dead body business. The business was thought to be owned by partners who offered nothing more than a cut-rate bereavement experience.

Harry pulled up outside the funeral home and got out of his car. He heard a soft click when his car door closed, suggesting to him it was much too quiet on the street.

The van der Donk was dimly lit on the inside and seedy-looking outside. Harry eyed the place like a murder suspect in a police lineup. As far as Harry could remember, the old structure always looked this suspicious. Harry turned his head slowly in the direction of the old man's bar next door where a barfly was urinating into a planter filled with cigarette butts.

A week after Felicity's death, Harry temporarily shipped off his boys to relatives living in greener pastures, who vowed to love and comfort them in ways Harry was incapable of. Harry impulsively stopped into the crummy bar. Harry's objective was simple: drink himself into oblivion. Among the company of distressed strangers, Harry had thrown back seven double shots of Wild Turkey and awoke the next morning to find the genial porter mopping the floor around him, mindful not to disturb him. The porter told Harry the regulars weren't sure if he were dead or alive. The debate continued while they dragged his body through the parking lot. A special delivery was in the works. They saw it as an act of good will; of course, a few bets were made. As the men were about to deliver him to the doorstep of the dead body shop, Harry had the good sense to vomit all over himself, erasing all thoughts of rigor mortis. The winners cheered; the losers bought drinks. All in all, it wasn't one of Harry's proudest moments.

The funeral home smelled much like the saloon as Harry remembered it. Harry hoped the musty, damp notes in the air would become less noticeable the longer he stayed. The rugs were worn out, and the wood paneling buckled over herniations trapped inside the walls. Harry stood alone in the grim-looking foyer waiting to be directed to a room occupied by mourners. The place was eerily still.

In a pocket-sized office, a man wearing a white shirt with perspiration stains inside his collar was at a desk hypnotized by a reality housewife entertainment program. Curvaceous women were brawling in a kitchen, tearing each other's hair out. The man had an ashen complexion and the dull expression of a small woodland animal. He inspected Harry Kavanagh, who was as poised as possible, standing inside the narrow doorway.

"Yes, what?" The man lowered the volume on the television.

"Good evening."

"Okay, hello."

"Corbin Reece?"

"There's one viewing room. You'll figure it out."

Harry nodded. He overlooked his host's rudeness as he backed out of the doorway.

The viewing room was empty; the casket closed. There were no flowers, no mass cards or notes of sympathy; no signboard or placard with the mention of one Corbin Reece. There were unoccupied folding chairs lined-up into two crooked rows of eight. There was a cardboard portrait of President Ronald Reagan on one wall and on the opposite side, a worn tapestry of Pope Paul VI stared right through Harry. Harry squirmed where he stood.

Harry heard the sounds of loud voices, unfriendly blather. He backpedaled lightly into the hallway and saw the figures of two men. They were shoulder-to-shoulder; squeezing themselves into the office, berating the unseen little man who was captive in his own cage. Without getting a good look at their faces, Harry figured the men were maybe in their mid-to-late 30s. They were husky. Their clothing looked to be inexpensive, right off the rack. They were wearing identical trench-coats; ill-fitting dark trousers with glossy black shoes. Hastily purchased attire for a particular purpose, Harry deduced. Harry stepped back and hid as the men marched out of the funeral home.

The funeral home man held his head in his hands. Then, as if a cartoon light bulb went on over his head, he tore open a desk drawer only to discover an empty pack of Marlboro Lights.

"Shit. Screw it all to hell," he spat.

The man put his head in his hands again and didn't budge until he felt the presence of someone hovering.

"What, are you going to give me the business too?" He looked like he was about to cry.

"No, I'm not. It's not my style," Harry said.

"Well, what the hell do you want then?"

"What they wanted to know."

The man looked up at Harry with a pleading expression. "Look it, I sit in this ass-smelling chair four nights a week. I bring in a liverwurst sandwich. One of those bastards stomped on it like it was a spark in a forest," he pointed to the roadkill on the floor. "Liverwurst, I take mine with mayonnaise for God's sakes because that's the way I damn well like it. And I take a lot of crap for that too, you know? I smoke half a pack of cigarettes a shift and I cap off my very cheerful evening with a visit next door where I can afford to have a few shots from the speed rack…"

"What did they want?" Harry tried to sound firm.

"They wanted to know who paid for the guy's party. The guy in the box."

"All right. And what did you tell them?"

"I didn't tell 'em nothing. I don't know. I just sit here."

"Is there someone I could ask?"

"You wanna pit yourself between my bosses, you go right ahead, pal." He lowered his voice. "The one guy is a Pitbull and on the other side, there's some old-time mob muscle. Me? I just wanna eat liverwurst and wake up in the morning in my own bed, not in a box like your friend, if you get my meaning?"

The man put his head down on the desk and closed his eyes. He was done talking. Harry felt badly for the little man. His night was done in. He had no cigarettes. His nerves were frayed, and his beloved liverwurst sandwich had a heal imprint on it. It meant he wouldn't be getting his mayonnaise fix. Harry dropped two twenties on his desk and departed.

Harry left the place with his eyes fixed on the grimy tavern next door. He felt guilty about his binge following the death of his wife. His guilt grew worse as he opened the door to his car and slipped inside. This time around, Harry didn't pick up the night sounds amid the quiet nor did he notice the shadows that would pursue him.

How could I send my boys away? This was the question gripping his heart. Faced with the truth, Harry knew he felt sorrier for himself than he did for his sons. Harry always thought himself a good person. Harry never had any use for religion, but as he slipped his keys into the ignition, he realized he was a selfish man. For the first time in his life, he recognized what others have: he was a sinner.

Harry decided to do some quick work on his phone before driving off. The tendonitis in his elbow began to yip after only a moment's internet search. Fifteen minutes later, Harry pulled up outside Reece's abandoned domicile. The streetlight was broken. The narrow cobblestone avenue was shadowy and still. Many of the other brick buildings and smaller homes looked abandoned, and or at least in need of serious resuscitation. Harry was aware big development was on its way. Life support had been withdrawn. The block looked like it was on an assisted-suicide program. A swath of this once middle-class neighborhood was on the skids. Outside money, promises, and backroom deals influenced local public servants. The entire area was about to be re-zoned. Conversations and cocktails around the buffet tables were conspiratorial and ongoing. In a year's time, a high rise would occupy the very spot promising a questionable slice of a waterfront view marketed as nothing short of breathtaking.

The windows of Reece's building were boarded-up and spray-painted in the shape of a rectangle with an X stabbing through its heart. Harry recognized the mark; it meant the structure had been condemned. He was about to turn off the ignition when he saw the heavy lock on the front door.

Of course, what was I thinking? This is not going to be easy. He sat back and thought for a second. He decided to drive around the corner to look for another way inside.

The rear view of the building was much more striking, Harry thought. It reminded him of a post-apocalyptic collage. The backyard was a dumping ground for crumbling bricks, old mattresses, disembodied furniture, and piles of tires. Harry parked at a dead end abutting the backyard of Corbin Reece's building.

As Harry was making his way over the uneven surface of what was essentially a junkyard, he was careful not to twist an ankle or stumble into a pit of debris.

What am I doing here? Am I that lonely and hard up that I have to invent an adventure for myself? Corbin Reece's pathetic look in my direction could have meant absolutely nothing. Did he want to tell me something about Felicity? Who the hell knows? He was intoxicated. Sloppy drunk. Maybe he wanted to borrow money. Or maybe he wanted to talk sports. Was any New York team on a winning streak? No, of course not, forget about that idea.

It was obvious to Harry that Reece had become a slip-and-fall drunk. He'd seen his act firsthand. He appeared as if he had nothing else going on in his life other than a profound hopelessness that strangled him like a tightly cinched necktie. The rigors of his profession or his lonely life or both had taken a sorry toll.

The yard was pitch-black and cemetery-quiet. Harry took this into consideration and was about to abandon his frivolous investigation when he discerned there were shadows wavering behind him. This motivated Harry to push ahead, taking quicker, clumsier steps, if only to avoid the threat, real or imagined.

Harry didn't feel like an intrepid hero following a hunch. That kind of intuition was reserved for the gumshoe in old movies. Harry didn't feel like an investigator; he felt silly, out of his league. He felt like a horse's ass. He conjured the expression every other day and recognized it as another remark thrown around the Sunday table by his grandfather and uncles.

In any event, Harry felt like a frightened middle-aged man stumbling in the darkness. More movement. Harry thought the shadows were taunting him – playing a *red-light-green-light-one-two-three* kid's game – drawing closer to him each time he reluctantly double-checked. There were well-documented drug issues in the neighborhood, but it was late; Harry couldn't imagine many fleet-of-foot heroin addicts prancing after him under the cloak of darkness. Harry's breathing quickened as he fumbled for a tiny flashlight he remembered to remove from his glove compartment. He depressed the button at the tip of the handle producing a narrow beam of light revealing practically nothing at all. As far as he could tell, there was no one on his tail. He allowed himself to breathe easier.

The rotting back door of the building was flimsily chained. It would allow Harry to slide inside the building. The twinge of optimism Harry experienced was a fool's game. It encouraged him to attempt something that was perhaps very dangerous. Harry looked over his shoulder before shimmying inside the dark, odorous edifice.

Harry stumbled on the uneven steps. His flashlight was more helpful in the tight confines of the condemned space than it had been outside in the expanse of darkness.

The first four apartments he investigated were barren. No furniture, only junk; no signs of life, nothing. There was one last apartment to inspect on the top floor. Harry nudged the door open with his toe. A spartan living space. Reece's apartment, Harry nodded to himself. Given the decrepit condition of the building, Harry could not fathom how someone would be allowed to occupy the space. Harry tried the light switch without any expectations and moved on, his quivering light leading the way. The place was austere. There were some healthy-sounding flies buzzing around in the kitchen. They were feasting on rancid leftovers abandoned in the trash beneath the sink.

Harry stood three feet inside the flat when he heard the floorboards in the hallway groan. He whirled around and gasped like a frightened child. Looming in the doorway, glaring at his less-than-radiant flashlight beam, were dark unkempt eyebrows, a strong nose, and a solidly tensed jaw. The entirety of those facial features was scowling down at him from a higher angle. Next to that face was another face, the same face, similarly heated. Harry knew in a flash they were the inquisitive boys; the authors of the emporium shakedown. Identical twins, the liverwurst sandwich slayers, and this time they were here for him, Harry reasoned amid the many other scrambling thoughts running amok inside his head.

One of men was wielding something in his hand. Harry couldn't make sense of it. The angrier face swatted Harry in the face with it. Harry felt his nose pop, his body's momentum landing him against the foyer wall. He could feel the skin directly below his left eye begin to swell. As the young men began to argue, Harry realized he had been assaulted with a shoe. A very large shoe. Harry was hit again. He was hammered down to one knee. From his low vantage point, Harry watched his stalkers grunt and groan as they put their shoes back on. The stocky boys had silently stalked Harry in their socks until they were on top of him. Until it was too late for Harry to take evasive action. Harry struggled to get to his feet and was shoved against the wall. He tasted the warm current of his own blood pouring from his nostrils.

"Why are you paying your respects to a man like Reece?"

"I, uh…" Harry could barely speak.

"Are you a friend of his?" Harry couldn't determine if it was the same voice. The interrogation continued with both men hovering over him. Harry could smell their cheap cologne and nervous perspiration. He saw mouths moving in the shadows, spitting out accusations he couldn't distinguish because of his disorientation. They became frustrated when Harry couldn't answer their questions. He tried to rise again. He was smacked with an open hand. Harry's already tender ear began to reverberate with pain; he fell hard on his haunches. The brothers continued to argue with one another. Then they crouched beside his face. Their questions came quickly, and they were concise. Two of the same faces, although one of them appeared conflicted. Harry was hoping for a split. Perhaps one of them was the good cop. Harry hoped for some relief.

"You were the only one to show up all day. The only person!"

"What kind of man are you? Are you a player in his club?" asked by the one with the conflicted expression. Harry sensed his rage wasn't genuine. It was an act to satisfy his enraged brother.

"I thought he was trying to tell me something and a few hours later he was dead," Harry said realizing his statement may have put him in deeper jeopardy.

The angrier of the two hooligans stomped his feet and began to pace; struggling to make a decision. His brother extended a hand to Harry and began to yank him to his feet. Harry believed he saw his face soften. When the angry man whirled ready to pounce, the "good brother," against his better judgment and to save face, grimaced and then punched Harry in the face. Harry went down hard. Harry felt nauseated. He tried to look around the apartment, for a way out but his surroundings became even dimmer. Harry fell into a weary state of semi-conscious that gave way to an uncomfortable sleep.

Chapter Eleven

"Does your face hurt?" There was a beat, then came the response Harry heard throughout his entire childhood, "It's killing me!"

The unraveling sounds of laughter reverberated. A mad scientist's cackle, like the screams performed by actors so long dead their kids were probably dead too. This was kind of incessant racket Harry was trying to fend off.

"I must be losing my mind. Where am I?"

The din of the maniacal laughter subsided, and Harry was able to jar himself to a bleary state of consciousness.

Harry's entire body ached. *Let the inventory begin*, his inner voice reluctantly proclaimed. His sore hip, his burning ear, his throbbing nose – his entire face for that matter. Dried blood was caked above his lips and on his chin. His impulse was to vomit; he fancied it an encouraging sign.

"The last time I yearned to puke was when I was in college," he said aloud in a dried-up voice. "That very first grain alcohol party at Moravian College…ooh. Look how far I've stumbled since Corbin Reece kissed the floor at that lousy restaurant."

Harry's stomach moaned. His notion of vomiting was a fine idea. He sarcastically recognized it as an early highlight to his day. His fleeting nausea didn't prevent him from aching for one of his pancakes, although in his current state he couldn't imagine summoning the strength to stand over the stove.

"Oh, Christ. How long have I been here? It must be morning."

With all that had transpired, Harry was thinking about Lolly and then his thoughts meandered to his kitchen floor. No one wants to be welcomed home by a steaming Sphinx-like stockpile mounted alongside the breakfast nook. The thought of poor Lolly holding it in all night long consumed Harry more than his own circumstances. Harry decided it was about time to think about pulling himself together and making his escape. Lolly was long overdue for a walk.

Harry's surroundings were dim, but there was hope. The darkness was evaporating before his tired eyes. Harry got to his knees and realized he was encased in a closet. The door was open. Perhaps he crawled there on his own or maybe those two-tons-of-fun, the brawny, bushy-browed brothers, hung him out to dry. As he struggled to get to his feet, distant and undistinguishable sounds reached his ears. They were muted, persistent, nagging, resembling a toy-like symphony that Harry could not make out. Noises and cadences resembling the bleeping, chirping melody of an ice cream truck maybe, but then again, not quite.

Harry stood, outstretching his arms, supporting himself inside the claustrophobic vault. He heard yelling. Hoarse-sounding voices, bellowing orders; whistles that were strident, possibly familiar, resembling cat calls. But again, Harry wasn't certain what he was hearing. Then silence. No noise, no toy-tinkering melody bleeping about. Harry looked up sharply and the pain in his neck sang an excruciating aria. His newest distraction came from above. An unseen peril resounding with the reverberation of a powerful engine, and it was chugging nearer. The devil's locomotive on a collision course with a human being trapped by the fragility of his own mind and body.

Fluorescent-jacketed workers with hard hats were moping in the backyard of Corbin Reece's building. Although every one of their mornings kicked off at this early time, they seemed to be barely awake, as if it were their first day back after drinking with the boys. They stood well back from the dilapidated building, receding to the edge of the property line, barely summoning the initiative to sip their coffee. They were waiting to be shouted at by their boss.

Joe Tedesco, the supervisor, was so morbidly obese, his fluorescent vest didn't stand a chance of closing over his big-section. He turned his head slightly to the left as Robert Devine sidled up to him carrying a cup of coffee in one hand and a bacon, egg, and cheese sandwich in the other.

"Bacon, egg, and cheese. The national sammie of the island," he said smiling at Devine.

"It's too early," Devine snapped.

"What, you didn't bring nothing extra for the boys?"

"Sorry man, all I could manage was to get your shit-bag-of-a company this tit job. A national sandwich? We're living in this fetid petri dish called a borough. You're a fucking moron."

"Screw you and top of the morning to you, Bobby. How come someone as lazy as you needed a ringside seat?" Tedesco responded with a certain amount of mirth.

"You're awfully chipper today. What, did you find a secret drawer filled with Caramello bars?" Devine exhaled, as he set his feet firmly in the dirt. "You know me, Joey boy. Just making sure what needs to get done gets done. It's in my job description." Devine cradled the sandwich in his hand just above the level of his breast.

Joe Tedesco looked at him and snorted.

"Hell, Bobby, you're holding your sandwich like it's the baby Jesus and you're getting ready to walk the tightrope over the Niagara Falls. Have you ever been in love with something you didn't wanna eat?"

"Hey, that's funny. Standing beside you I look like Chuck Norris."

"I got digestive issues, none of which are my own doing," Tedesco said, buffing his enormous belly with his palm.

Devine twisted his head from right to left then bobbed his chin until he was able to reach the breakfast sandwich with his mouth. He took a big bite and appeared to swallow without chewing. He bit off the plastic top on his coffee and spat it out. He slurped the hot coffee and immediately began to retch.

"Wrong pipe, holy mother of God," he gasped, dropping the cup of coffee, splattering both his and Tedesco's trousers. The men scattered clumsily, glaring like the other was to blame.

"Don't look at me that way. That's the way you used to play right field when we were kids. What the hell, Bobby, you're a human kamikaze pilot. Your Indian name is Bobby Iron Glove; we used to call you Bobby No-Hands, remember?"

"Do you ever listen to the stupid words that come out of our mouth? That was the perfect cup of coffee, goddamn it. But this one was on me. My bad fat Joey," he said, beginning to calm down.

"Will you look at the two of us," Tedesco moaned.

"What are you talking about?"

"Nearly 600 pounds between us, standing in this asshole filled with rubbers and diapers. And now there's coffee stains on my pants where I usually piss myself. You with egg all over your face."

"Eat less and introduce yourself to a dry cleaner. There's one on every block. What do you want from me?"

"How the mighty have fallen, hey, Bobby?"

"You sound like you've been reading books, Joey. Why would you do that? Guys like you, you're meant to take up space and stroke out, that's all. The end. Don't think so much or the little brain between your legs might actually wake up, and God knows you wouldn't know what to do with that."

"Thanks, Bobby, you always know the right words," Tedesco said stepping away from Devine, stung for the last time. The bigger man's feelings were hurt. He nodded to one of his guys and was handed a hard hat and a vest. He threw them at Devine, knocking the sandwich out of his hand and onto the rubble.

"What did you do that for? I was just saying," Devine sputtered.

"I'm just saying, put them on or get off my job site," Tedesco said scowling at him.

Harry took a timorous step out of the closet and the ceiling exploded, showering rubble and grit on him. The roar of a powerful engine revved up again and Harry's eyes widened in terror.

"Hey, there's someone in here! Hey, stop," he yelled looking up, noticing blue sky where the view didn't exist seconds earlier.

Harry trembled, taking in the gaping hole above his head, disbelief splashing over his consciousness. He shook painful flecks of dirt from his eyes. *It looks like a nice day outside*, the thought was an absurd one, but that's what came into his head. Harry shook the grime and debris from his body like a wet dog shaking off water after a dip in a lake. Harry looked up again, expecting to awaken from this nightmare. The sky was cloudless; no signs of tiny birds prancing from limb to limb, fluting their morning melodies.

Harry's heart nearly stopped when he saw the hydraulic arm of a demolition excavator swing into view above the makeshift skylight. Harry opened his mouth, but before he could cry out, the bucket swooped down and lopped off another slice of the building. Harry screamed words, profane words he never thought himself capable of uttering.

He dashed from the closet as a section of the wall exploded and disintegrated into a mound of rubble. Harry was knocked to his knees. A worn-out canvas bag was birthed from a hiding place deep inside the crumbling wall. Harry scrambled to his feet with the canvas bag tangled under his right wrist. The bag went along with him as he made a mad dash for the quivering hallway. As he ran down the staircase, Harry heard Jake's little voice in his head.

"Excavator truck, back loader, front loader, dump truck, bobcat..."

Harry clambered down the quivering steps. Amid the chaos, his little son's voice gave him something to focus on as the walls were crumbling behind him. Jake was obsessed with all kinds of construction trucks and would often recite his repertoire without any encouragement.

"Fabiance!" The little boy's repetitious exclamation bewildered his parents for a time until Felicity figured it out. Fire truck plus ambulance equals fabiance. Just about that time the FDNY had established their own fleet of ambulances – their markings were similar to the traditional fire engines and trucks. Through a little boy's eyes, this new fleet of Fire Department ambulances was articulated as fabiance.

"What a smart boy." It was Felicity's amused voice singing in Harry's ear. *I'm not going to allow this memory to be squandered by my ruination; this is not a good day to die*, Harry thought as his body continued to careen down the narrow staircase disappearing behind him.

Arnold Fleck could not believe it. His toes were nearly touching the cement floor of Harry Kavanagh's basement. *I'm inside the bastard's house, finally!*

Fleck's face was beet-red. His shirt was crimped near his chest. The basement wall was scraping his paunch as he awkwardly lowered himself.

Harry burst out of the same door he had entered the previous night. He emerged covered in grime, and his face was bruised and bloodied. He was wild-eyed and feral-looking; the handles of the canvas bag were tangled around one of his elbows. The fluorescent-jacketed men who were about finished cleaning the crud from their fatigued eyes and begrudgingly waking up to their day all yelled in astonishment. Big men crying out like frightened kittens. Caught in the grip of real life, these many big men responded by stutter-stepping, spinning around in place and jumping about: a jittery, comical group, unable to respond appropriately in the moment. The men who managed to stop off at the deli beforehand were in for bigger trouble. Sandwiches were dropped and trampled; streams of coffee were sling-shot from Styrofoam cups in surprise.

Fleck knelt over in pain, rubbing his bruised stomach. He tried to catch his breath and calm his nerves. *I wish that damn dog would stop barking*, he prayed. Kavanagh's Great Dane was above him in the kitchen, fully aware there was an intruder inside the house. Fleck spotted Harry Kavanagh leaving the house the day before and noted his car never returned. After years of anxiety and sleeplessness, Fleck decided to take a chance. He turned around and faced the dimly-lit room stacked with cases of wine from that woman's wine shop. He heard the basement door rattle at the top of the stairs. The Great Dane was pushing against the door with her giant paws. Fleck scampered to the bottom of the stairs and shot a glance upward, terrified. He saw the basement door straining, clattering at the behest of the giant dog's strength.

"If that dog manages to open the door, I'm a dead man," he whispered.

Fleck took a quick look around. "This was a mistake," he exhaled. "It's not here. I'm trapped in the goddamn basement. What was I thinking? I need to get by that damn dog and that's not happening today," he murmured as his entire body trembled.

Fleck cursed his stupidity. The incessant barking and the banging against the door was driving a cold knife through his heart. He covered his ears with his sweaty palms. Fleck saw dust particles diving through ribbons of light, spilling through slits framing the door each time the dog jarred it with nearly 175 pounds of attitude. Fleck felt a warm sensation in his loins. He was peeing himself.

Robert Devine couldn't believe his eyes…Harry Kavanagh? *Is that Kavanagh? What the hell is he doing here?* The thoughts screamed through his head. *And what is he carrying?*

Harry ran through the backyard like a fullback. Head down, stumbling, side-stepping obstacles, taking offbeat angles, but somehow remaining on his feet. The workers bellowed at him, attempting to calm him and slow him down. A few of them reached out to grab him as he ran by, but they were too slow and preposterously uncoordinated. Tedesco was screaming into his walkie-talkie, ordering the man in the excavator to shut everything down.

Harry escaped into his car and the automobile zig-zagged backward, the tires squealing down the street.

When the hydraulic arm stopped slashing above the property, Tedesco looked over at Devine, taking in the frozen look of disbelief on his face. He followed Devine's astonished expression toward the street.

"Bobby? Do you know that guy?" the fat man said, nearly emptying the air out of his lungs before he finished asking the question.

Devine didn't hear a thing; he was trying to figure out the implications of Harry Kavanagh and Corbin Reece floating around in the same universe, other than the obvious connection.

Tedesco turned away from the stupefied Devine and growled at his team, "Now which one of you geniuses inspected the building? I wanna make sure I put my fat foot up the right asshole."

Climbing out of the basement was a different type of challenge altogether. Fleck stacked two cases of wine and once aboard propped his elbows on the sill of the basement window. Just as he was making headway, Harry Kavanagh's car zig-zagged into the driveway coming to a sloppy, bouncing halt. Fleck panicked, falling backward, tumbling off the wine boxes and onto the cement floor. He heard himself cry out. It was the catalyst for a new barking binge from the hound.

Harry slung himself out of the car. The canvas bag fell to the ground near the basement window. The window wasn't closed properly, but Harry didn't catch on. He staggered toward the kitchen door, forgetting about the bag.

Driven by fear, Fleck hoisted himself out of the basement window, cracking the pane with his heel. He closed the window awkwardly and scrambled to his feet, shoveling the canvas bag in his arms. He scooted through Harry's backyard taking the bag with him. He felt his stomach bottom out. He walked quickly and clumsily once his feet found the sidewalk, fleeing away from the house. Fleck realized he couldn't return home without fear of being seen or the threat of Kavanagh's dog barking at him. His knees ached and the bruised skin on his stomach burned.

Harry burst inside his house through the kitchen door. Lolly immediately ran by him, outside and on the hunt.

"Lolly," was all Harry could manage to sputter as he leaned against his kitchen counter, all of his energy completely gone.

Lolly loped outside, her ears on high alert, pointing skyward. She was restless and hopped-up with indignation. She drew a bead on Arnold Fleck nearly a block away, walking hastily toward the center of town. She hesitated; all her movements slowed. For an instant, her anxiety ceased. She abruptly turned away from Fleck and her body followed her gigantic head as she galloped across the street. She ran to Arnold Fleck's house, easily polishing off the front steps. When she reached his door, she defecated enthusiastically.

Harry was trying to work through his exhaustion and disorientation. He doused his head under the sink and ran water all over his head and face. He heard someone enter the kitchen and turned to face the interruption. It was the bewildered-looking Emma Kendall standing in his doorway, holding two Styrofoam cups of coffee.

"Jesus Christ, Harry. What the hell happened?"

Before Harry could answer, Lolly nudged her way by Emma and calmly cantered into the room. She met Harry's open palm and leaned into his body, nudging him affectionately with her head.

Emma set the coffee on the countertop and opened her mouth again. "Harry, Harry, Harreee?"

Harry shook his head, not quite prepared enough to say much more than, "I think I need to go to the hospital." He paused. "Again," he said in a whisper.

Emma Kendall persisted, jabbering questions all the way over on their drive. Harry's coffee sat wedged in the holder between them, unopened and untouched. Emma was steering her car with her left hand while sipping coffee and gesturing with her right. She remained fixated on Harry while unconsciously dripping coffee on her lap on successive maneuvers. She didn't seem to notice, nor did she miss a beat. She didn't take into account Harry wasn't in an answering mood. He remained quiet while she continued speaking.

Harry's hands were folded on his lap and his body silent. He didn't bother to put his seat belt on and the alarm bleeped continuously. He would not confess to his foolhardy and dangerous night's adventure. In his peripheral vision, Harry caught sight of a blurry red lipstick stain on Emma's Styrofoam cup as she gesticulated, nearly crossing into his territory.

Finally, Harry managed to say, "Emma, please?"

Emma's head jerked backward. Her lips pouted. She was clearly insulted. "For fuck's sakes, Harry, put your seatbelt on. That damn alarm is driving me to drink."

Harry looked down at his hands and willed them to move. He secured his seat belt and remained silent.

Chapter Twelve

Emma Kendall had the bright notion of stopping her vehicle in a no-parking zone. The hospital security guard waved a hand at her. She ignored him.

"Get out here, Harry. I'll park in the lot and meet you inside."

It was music to Harry Kavanagh's ears. He slid out wordlessly and planted his feet on the sidewalk. He stared at his dusty New Balance footwear. Black body; the white N staring back at him. He should have worn his orange sneakers, he thought. They were much more comfortable. He felt unsteady on his feet. He replanted his feet and prepared to move ahead despite his exhaustion.

"Harree, coffee," she purred. She wedged his coffee cup from the console and offered it to him with an extended arm. Harry's cloudy interpretation of her offering was she appeared surprisingly timid. His imagination betrayed him further when in his mind's eye he envisioned her as a maiden from the Renaissance with wild curly locks, clad in a bodice peeled back enough to entice any rogue. She was offering herself to him. Her pouting lips begging him, "Take me, please?" But within her plea was also the subliminal warning: take me or else. Or else I will cut you up and make a sandwich out of you. Harry shook the nonsense out of his head. He decided not to judge Emma harshly. He was beaten up and sleep deprived. She was good enough to drive him to the hospital. He didn't have many friends to speak of. His expression softened and after a long pause he said to her, "Thanks for the ride."

Emma laughed at his vulnerability.

"Okay. Listen, Harry, you better get inside quickly. You're acting like a zombie from Mr. Roger's neighborhood."

"I don't get the reference, but now's not the time," he said.

"No context, darling. Just words, one after the other forming a sentence. That's the way it goes. Don't think too hard or your toes might curl up."

He waved her off gently without accepting the coffee. He noted that it came from The Splendid Cup. He pointed himself toward the main entrance. Harry glanced at the security guard who was scowling in Emma's direction.

"Do I look like a man who needs a lukewarm cup of coffee?" Harry said to him wearily.

The security guard spied Harry's bruised face. "You need something, Frankenstein." He said it with levity. "Don't worry, they'll put you back together," he said nodding at Harry.

Harry trudged through the revolving door wide enough to shepherd fifteen patients. He heard the security guard barking at Emma, "Now lady, you can't leave the car there. Don't you even think about it. Move it or lose it. That's what I said, MOVE it or LOSE it!"

Harry filled out paperwork at the ER reception desk. The receptionist recognized Harry. She made a face he didn't see. Harry slid the paperwork back to the receptionist and turned off his brain. He couldn't take in what her lips were saying to him, but he figured she was inviting him to sit in the waiting room.

Harry sat wearily in a corner seat. He noticed the same guy, the Kit Kat-inhaler; he was back too. This time he was eating two of those candy bars at a time, like a sandwich. *A diabetes sandwich*, Harry thought. The man washed it down with a Red Bull. He was standing very close to one of the television screens dramatizing a landlord/tenant dispute on a courtroom reality program.

"Why do they always side with the landlord? The dude has other responsibilities. Maybe he had to pay off his ex-wife? The man should wait for the rent. He can afford it. It comes when it comes. That's it. We gotta lick this shit in the butt."

Harry's head rose from his chest, reacting as if he'd been given a hot foot. "What did you say?"

"Brother, you okay? You look like you danced with Mike Tyson?"

"That expression you used?" Harry's mood was worsening. His temples were galloping.

"Expression, espresso, Tyrell Biggs, let's call the whole thing off," he said in a familiar singsong but mocking tone. "What's your problem, Humpty?"

"My problem *is* the expression goes, nip in the bud. Nip something in the bud, nip it in the bud," Harry said through clenched teeth.

"Oh, I really thought it was nip it in the butt, but who cares? Nip it in the butt. Lick it in the butt. That's more optimistic, depending on who your date is, am I right?"

"My current dilemma is I'm in a public space and I find your ignorance profoundly offensive," Harry replied.

"Listen, little man, I'd beat you with my left hand, but it looks like your fairy godmother did all the work for me," the man said with a snort. He swiveled his shoulders back to the television.

Harry sprung from his chair like a marionette. Little white clusters were popping before him, blocking his vision. He narrowed his eyes until the clusters vanished. He began to make his way toward the man with surprisingly bad intentions on his mind. Harry was having trouble breathing. His face was swelling around his nose, and he was forced to breathe through his mouth. But it didn't stop him from making his move.

The man whirled around wearing a smirk. When he saw the tight expression on Harry's face, he backpedaled, closeting his leer. Harry looked like an asthmatic bull on the charge. The man pressed himself against the wall, hunching underneath the mounted television. There was nowhere else to go.

Harry had no strategy. He wanted only to smite the ignoramus. He didn't care about consequences nor did he take into consideration the man was a much larger version of himself. He'd been knocked around enough for one day and he felt humiliated. It didn't help that he was dazed and angry. It seemed like poetic justice to Harry that the little man should inflict pain on someone else for a change. As he neared his target, a body intervened, sliding in between. Harry knew this person. It was Shelby Martin.

Shelby was wearing beige trousers and a cotton knit shirt with the name of the hospital embroidered on it. Pinned on the collar was a button with a smiling face with the words, "How can I help?"

Shelby was a person who created discomfort for some of the conservative-leaning people in the neighborhood. Harry didn't know whether Shelby was a man transitioning into a female or actually, if he was transitioning at all. He never gave it much thought. He'd always maintained a casual and cordial, hello-and-good-morning, rapport with Shelby.

Harry met Shelby Martin at the local greenmarket located in a crumbling asphalt parking lot beside a methadone clinic. As far as Harry knew, Shelby moved to Staten Island several years ago. Harry recalled Shelby had previously explained to him that he identified as male. Shelby currently worked part-time at the hospital gift shop. And as Harry came to his senses, he was grateful for Shelby's magical appearance.

Shelby rested his hand gently on Harry's chest. It was clear to Shelby that Harry was not in his right mind. He spoke softly. "Mr. Kavanagh, why don't you take a seat? Allow me to punctuate this run-on sentence."

Shelby was referring to the jabbering brute. Harry acknowledged Shelby through exhausted eyes.

Harry said, "Thank you, Shelby. And please call me Harry."

Harry took a few tentative steps backward and collapsed into a different seat. The man recovering beneath the television took some measured breaths. He tried to act casual as he pushed himself off the wall; his swagger was on hold. He sized up Shelby through blinking eyes, inspecting the odd-looking man crowned with a woman's wig, wearing a thin layer of lipstick, but otherwise no other makeup.

The brute's lips were pursed, about to utter something he perceived to be witty, but would in fact be offensive. He was interrupted before he could say something stupid by Shelby's abrupt gesture toward the security guards at the end of the hallway. Both security guards weighed well over 300 pounds. Their arms seemed too short for their bodies. When they walked, their legs slid without the benefit of their knees bending. They looked like giant Claymation figures slowly ice skating toward the waiting room.

The man tried to play to the room. "Who are you supposed to be, Robin Hood?"

Shelby didn't answer him and when the security guards arrived, Shelby said to them, "Gentlemen, really, if I see this man in this waiting room again, I'm going to ask you to collect his rent."

To Shelby, the suddenly insulted brute asked, "Hey, who are you? Who do you think you are?" Then pleading his case to the security guards, "Who is this thing to kick me out? It's my day off and I'm catching up on my shows. My TV is broken."

Following Shelby's orders without question, the security guards corralled the man and led him down the corridor. On his reluctant walk toward the exit, the man made certain everyone heard his farewell words. "Faggot," he spewed.

Harry watched on from his seat; he was impressed. Shelby, the gift-shop-worker; the man with a soothing voice wearing a woman's wig and lipstick must have earned a great deal of respect in the workplace. The security guards reacted to his measured tones without hesitation. Harry wondered what other fires Shelby had snuffed out along the way to command this impressive level of deference.

Harry made a move to get up, but Shelby put a compassionate hand on his arm.

"Don't even attempt it. Relax until you're called."

"Thank you for that. I lost what little I have left of my mind."

"What happened?"

"You mean just now or my new look?" Harry responded.

Shelby made a circle with his finger, meaning *your face*.

"Well, it's a long story or should I say a story that is still unravelling. Trouble seems to find me."

"Shouldn't you have called the police? It's obvious you didn't bump into your refrigerator in the middle of the night."

"There's so much I have to figure out first," Harry said unevenly.

Their conversation was interrupted by the sounds of big Emma Kendall coming their way.

"There you are, Harry," she announced. Translation: mama's here; everyone else step aside.

"I have to get back to the gift shop. Take care of yourself, Harry," Shelby said abruptly.

"Thank you, Shelby."

Shelby made a quick turn, avoiding Emma's inspection as she landed in front of Harry. She followed Shelby with her eyes as he walked off. A knowing smile crossed her face.

"Your new girlfriend? Someone has to teach him to walk like he means it."

"I don't think that's a very nice thing to say, although I'm not sure I know what you mean."

"You're confused about a lot of things, aren't you, Harry?"

Emma casually flashed a disgusted expression his way. There was no attempt at concealment. Her face read as if she stepped onto a pile of dog poo and blamed Harry for her misstep. Harry's impulse was to laugh at her, at that face. He was running out of patience, but he held himself in check. He was about to temper his comments when she spoke.

"Oy, Lordy, why didn't you tell me I spilled coffee all over myself? I'll be right back. I have to venture to the ladies," she said brightly, as if admiring roses. Emma smiled at him and shook her hips in the direction of the restroom.

Harry shook his head. *What the hell did Felicity see in this woman?* A question he'd asked himself several times.

After tiresome questioning and evaluations at the hands of the hospital staff in the triage area, Harry was eventually acknowledged by Dr. Armstrong entering the area. Harry slid off the examining table as the gum-chewing nurse exited the room. Dr. Armstrong greeted him with a stoic look, all business, which was rather disappointing for Harry.

"Get back on the table, unless you have somewhere else to go."

"Oh, okay," he said feeling scolded. He wiggled back onto the table.

"Your brain CT looks fine…"

"Tell that to my brain. It's going to have a hard time believing you," Harry interrupted.

"Your CT facial bones show a small left lateral orbital fracture. The muscle does not appear to be impinged," she hesitated, waiting for him to respond.

When he remained quiet, she said, "You're out of witty remarks already?" A hint of a smile showed up on her face.

Harry took a peek at her while she was preoccupied with her notes. Harry noticed how penetrating blue and distinctive-looking her eyes were. Then she looked directly at him. They were tired eyes but striking nonetheless. Those eyes were suddenly staring at Harry, and he began to squirm in his seat. He was unaccustomed to such scrutiny from a dazzling origin.

"My boys tell me I'm corny," he said looking away from her – trying to avoid her hypnotic glare. "Occasionally I have the sense to reign it in. Apparently, I left you – the audience – wanting more, so to speak," he said it with his head down, the words emanating through his weary smile.

He peeked up at her again while she glanced at her notes, tucking her slight smile so deep inside it was as if it never existed. All work and no play again, and her tone backed it up.

"Lots of ice and Ibuprofen for you. You might want to follow-up with a neurologist. Just to make sure. You still have a concussion."

"Do you like coffee?" Harry asked abruptly.

She put her clipboard under her arm and looked at him, mildly annoyed. Harry had surely been knocked around some; he was feeling a little dopey. He gave himself permission to go for it. He wasn't the improvising type. Quite the opposite, but he found Dr. Armstrong interesting, attractive. She possessed a confident, sure-footed presence. And those eyes. Perhaps on any other day he would have hesitated, looked away and when he turned back she would be gone. Too late. Like a boy at the seventh-grade dance, finally pulling the confidence up from his toes to ask for a dance five minutes before the end of the party. If he'd run into her at the supermarket, perhaps he wouldn't have had the confidence to clumsily pad the conversation. Presently, that wasn't the case. She was a captive audience. He was reminded of her behavior the first time they met. Her odd reaction to him: her abrupt departure. She had something she wanted to say to him and he decided he was going to guide her there. The fact that he didn't feel particularly charming nor did he look like Cary Grant in *North by Northwest* didn't concern him in the least. The dopey, dazed feelings he was experiencing in the wake of his escape from the building collapse were offering him a false sense of confidence he was comfortable using to his advantage.

As he was woolgathering, his mouth moved without his permission and he said to her in a dreamy sort of way, "And who wouldn't want to have some of that music in their life?" He was referring to those eyes, her eyes, and the pleasure of her company.

"Excuse me?"

"Would you like to get a cup of coffee with me?" He said it without hesitation, ignoring the emphatic surprise in her previous response. "Just coffee. Fresh, hot coffee," he said.

She took a breath and considered his proposal. Harry was confident things were going to go his way.

"I heard there's a new place on the avenue?" She folded her arms and looked him over, mildly amused.

"Yes, The Splendid Cup," he said smiling. He wasn't going to say a negative thing about the place. He didn't want to stop the momentum.

"You know, now that I think of it, one of the nurses heard they're having rodent issues."

"Word gets around fast," Harry whispered to himself. "There are other places," he said brightly.

"Mr. Kavanagh…"

"Harry, please."

"Harry, I've been meaning to apologize to you for the way I acted…" She weighed what she was going to say next, "…the first time you came into my ER looking like a mugging victim." Her smile was in full bloom. She pulled back, immediately trying to conceal it. She was obviously conflicted, but it was clear to Harry she was fighting a losing battle.

"About my sudden departure. There's something I'd like to share with you." She said this in a lower, more serious tone of voice.

"You don't have to sugarcoat it. I was a mess," he said.

"Well, yes, you were, you are, but that's not what I was going to say."

She exhaled. She was opening a door she thought perhaps she should have left closed.

"I recommend you take a few more days off," she snapped. "No leaping from tall buildings in a single bound or whatever else it is you've been doing." She paused. "I don't want to know what you're doing…"

"Apparently, the world's been carrying a grudge," he responded. "But was there was something else? I interrupted you."

"Keep your face out of harm's way," she said moving toward the exit.

"Wait. That wasn't what you wanted to say."

"No, it wasn't." She clutched the door knob firmly.

"So, no climbing trees?" He knew he was losing her.

"Enough banter for today," she said tersely. She spied her watch. "I'm going to move on," she said definitively. "Perhaps we'll finish this up at another time."

"I opened my big mouth and I dissuaded you from telling me something."

"This should be a conversation over a meal. Find me when you're up to it," she said, void of any trace of invitation in her voice. She left the room quickly, her lab coat sweeping behind her like Vader's cape. Harry heard her frustrated exhalation from where he was sitting.

Harry sat motionless on the table. He began swinging his feet like a fidgeting boy waiting for a parent to pick him up after school.

"Whoopee," he whispered to himself with no evidence of enthusiasm. "I have a date."

A few moments later, outside in the hallway, Harry spied Emma Kendall having a stern conversation with a concession machine, ultimately kicking it until her Doritos were coaxed free. Harry stepped back out of her view. He pulled over one of the security guards. He convinced the guard with a little help from his friend Andrew Jackson to explain to Emma that he would be held for further tests and she should go home. Harry waited in the men's room for fifteen minutes until he figured the coast was clear. In that time, he counted at least six men using the urinal and not one of them washed their hands.

Outside the hospital's entrance, Harry walked directly to the taxicab stand and hailed his ride. The cab pulled up and Harry slung his humbled body inside. Emma Kendall stood and watched the cab leave from behind a large potted bush filled with cigarette butts and other trash. She was not wearing a happy face.

On his drive home, Harry determined it was time to make a list. With Felicity on the planet busy running her shop and he occupied with teaching and committee work, lists had come in handy. He and Felicity were co-running a thriving household then. Their boys, those gangly, growing boys on the verge of muscles and mustaches, were a vibrant presence in the household. The boys needed lots of checks written for various extracurricular exploits and they needed rides to just about everywhere. There was never a dull moment. Thank goodness for the list.

Then Felicity died, and everything went quiet. Four years later, Harry's sons are on the next leg of their journey. Jake's socks are provided for and Will is at college, smitten. But something is brewing on the home front. Uncertainty and menace are in the air. Harry's humdrum life has taken an unexpected turn. Harry decided it was time to take some action. He needed to sort things out. He had to make a list.

Chapter Thirteen

Emma Kendall was sitting at the counter of her local diner having the Big Boy Special. It was a mound of scrambled eggs and too many home fries. She lifted her eyes and watched the waitress flipping through the newspaper while speaking to a girlfriend on her cellphone. Emma looked at her empty coffee cup and said, "Customers, what customers?"

With her cellphone practically attached to her ear, the waitress reached for the coffee pot and refilled Emma's cup without looking at her.

"Why is it called the Big Boy Special? Why not the Big Girl Special or the Successful Woman Special?"

"Really?" the waitress said to her, finally making eye contact.

"Yeah, really," Emma said with a smile, although she didn't mean it.

Emma went back to tackling her breakfast while the waitress resumed her conversation. Emma heard her ask her friend on the other end of the line, "Would you say my body is banging or curvaceous?"

Emma raised her eyes again and discreetly gave the young woman's physique a good looking over. Emma mulled it over. Maybe she was 28. The waitress' question prompted Emma to consider herself. Emma shoved her plate away and fingered the package of Sweet'N Low. She tore open the packet, noticing two sanitation men seated at the end of the counter. They were taking turns checking her out.

Emma lifted her chin with pride as she daintily sipped her coffee. Emma considered herself to be the embodiment of sensuality. She'd never see 28 or even 38 ever again, and it distressed her. The garbage men, as Emma was slow to figure out, were not ogling her after all. The men, who were old enough to have adult children of their own, were devouring the sight of the ingénue poured into the waitress's outfit. Emma let some wrinkled dollars flutter out of her purse. She paraded out of the diner in a huff. No one seemed to take notice.

On the same morning when one of the local New York City newspapers (not the *Times*) mimicked a *People* magazine interview with actress Julianne Hough talking about her preference for her curvaceous 28-year-old-body verses her 19-year-old-banging body, State Senator Irene Roth was stealing some time for herself. Her tears would not be noticed, which was why she wasn't concerned about crying in public.

Tears or perspiration? No one could tell the difference since Roth was on the treadmill at her local gym. Roth was working hard to recover some semblance of her former curves. The imperfections in her body were a minor concern compared to her bigger life entanglements. She continued to suffer every passing day since the death of Felicity Kavanagh. A split-second decision contradicted everything she stood for. It changed the tone of her life forever. Roth's mind did not wander as one's mind is apt to during a methodical workout. She purposely directed herself back to her childhood. She remembered being a determined child. She took great pride in the fact that she was a fighter then. How did she end up being so ravenous for unceasing affirmation?

She recalled her pre-teen experiences, those "special" Wednesday evenings at St. Thomas. She and the neighborhood boys would sit low in their seats in a classroom amid the darkened hallways of the Catholic school building. Twitchy Father Teagan was ordained to teach them the Catechism of the Catholic Church. Teagan instead preferred to rant about his favorite subjects: lewdness and masturbation.

Some evenings he expanded the lecture to lewdness, masturbation, and shame. Lewdness, masturbation, and shame at your service. Young Roth thought it sounded like a late-night commercial. Some kind of law firm. During the oration, Teagan's sleepy-lidded eyes washed over the boys as if they were toasted almond ice-cream bars ready to be licked. The priest's raving didn't always go over as well as he thought. The boys snickered and made fun of him behind his back as he skulked around the classroom. They mimicked his many twitches, his spouting ear hair and joked about the cologne he bathed in. There was strength in numbers in the classroom. Once Father Teagan possessed a boy one-on-one in his private office, things would take on a darker tone. There would be no laughter. Father Teagan was a seasoned pedophile.

Assisting Father Teagan in the classroom each Wednesday was 12-year-old Corbin Reece, who sat away from the smaller boys, with his head bowed throughout the lecture. Reece was responsible for handing out mimeographed sheets of paper that held scripture or other words that supported Father Teagan's sweaty lectures. Reece was the senior altar boy, branded as the priest's favorite, but not anyone else's favorite. Irene Roth felt sorry for Reece; she heard rumors of how the good father *ruined* the boys.

Irene had heard one of the boys whisper to another, "He ruined me. Has he ruined you yet?"

Corbin Reece was an emotionless boy. Irene saw no inner light within him fighting to break through. He looked like he was adrift. She was convinced he had been ruined, over and over again. She was never permitted to ponder the fate of Corbin Reece for too long. In the classroom where the pedophile priest honed in on the boys, virtually ignoring her, she was often left to reflect on the violence in her own life.

The reward for putting up with the cleric for one solid hour in the classroom was two hours of basketball time in the church gymnasium, "unmolested." On the treadmill with tear stains blotting her cheeks, Irene Roth chuckled sarcastically at her addendum…*unmolested.*

Corbin Reece never made it to the gym. After the classroom lecture, with one hand on the shoulder of a doe-eyed classmate of his choosing, Reece would deliver the next sacrifice to a private office. Parents had no clue, no idea of the lifetime scars the cleric inflicted on their innocents. Father Teagan was operating during the golden age of pedophilia. In those days, no one reported anything about anyone. It wasn't done. In fact, if a child returned home, and reported a priest or a teacher had struck them, the parents would respond by cracking them twice over, for angering a revered disciplinarian and embarrassing the family.

Roth eventually earned a basketball scholarship from Lafayette College. But it was those early years in the St. Thomas gym where she developed her skills, outplaying and outsmarting the boys on and off the court every single week. During breaks, one or two of the boys would invade the girls' bathroom under the guise of jocular antics and try to cop a feel. Roth became so accustomed to their misadventures that she'd often lie in wait for them. She broke one boy's nose (explained as a basketball injury) and often kicked and punched her attackers in the most vulnerable place. Her response didn't prevent the boys from invading her space, so she continued to fight back. She'd return to the court angered and exhilarated and outplay them. The priest would sexually assault and humiliate the boys and they in turn would strike back by preying on their own victim. It was a horrific dance. The pattern made sense to the young girl.

Irene Roth had a compulsion to push herself physically, to work out her demons: striking back at the boys, beating them at their own game. She would return home and on occasion recount her on-the-court victories to her father. As was his nature, he would inspect every inch of her with his bloodshot eyes while attached to his threadbare upholstered living room chair. Sometimes Irene would notice what she interpreted as a blush of pride painting his pallid face. Her father, Herman Roth, was an otherwise sadistic man. One moment praising his daughter for besting the boys; the next demeaning her intelligence, her physical appearance, or blaming her for the short-lived life of her mother whom he nicknamed the Sainted Wino.

Irene Roth clearly understood the reasons why her reprisals were essential. It was harrowing to be pawed over, touched in places she hadn't explored herself, slandered and then discarded. Perhaps some girls would have crumbled right there (and rightfully so), but young Irene was energized by the adrenaline her body summoned to retaliate.

What was wrong with these boys? Who raised them this way? Why would they think my body was their personal tray of hors d'oeuvres?

She hated the priest for indoctrinating them; she hated their parents like she hated her own father, for their profound failure to provide love and safety.

Later on, after her energy faded, the 12-year-old would crumble in solitude, often in her bedroom with the door locked. Irene Roth understood why it was necessary to earn a scholarship and desert her only parent. She knew why she put up with so much violence on Wednesday evenings. Horrible experiences came in a bigger package at home. Time spent outside the reach of her father was time well spent. The trials of her youth crafted her into a resilient adult. There were only two people, two men in her life, she could never navigate. Men whom she could never work around or please. One way or another, she would often find herself pleading for their unconditional love, much to her own shame. Two men whom she could never hurt back – not for a lack of trying. They held a spell over her. They were her kryptonite. One of those men was Herman Roth, her abusive father, and the other one was calling her on her cell.

Roth was plugged into her cellphone. She secured her slippery ear plug sliding around her perspiring ear drum. She disregarded the television monitors. They were reporting a forest fire and a tornado ravaging different parts of the country, an annoyed New Jersey Governor Chris Christie being questioned by reporters, a steady diet of anorexic-looking models parading on a runway, and a professional athlete over-celebrating some kind of a score.

"I heard about your opposition to the City Council bill," she said to Thaddeus Calendar.

"Oh, good morning to you," he sounded off sarcastically. "It's a foolish bill."

"The bill is not going to be overturned and you're going to piss off a lot of people," she said a little too loudly.

The eyes of one of the yoga instructors admonished Roth. *When was the last time you ate a sandwich, you skinny bitch?* Roth gave the middle finger to her see-through spine when she floated by. Roth was suspicious of anyone who never said *umm* when they put something delicious in their mouth. Something savory; something food related, she reminded herself. *How do these women exist on dry toast and spring water?*

"A couple of your gravy-tie-stained friends are making it seem like it's a tax on the middle and lower classes and that's bullshit," Roth said.

"The media has already dubbed this thing the plastic bag tax. I had nothing to do with that."

"Oh, really? Because of your whining behind the scenes."

"You know me well enough to know I don't whine."

"Whales are washing up dead all over the world's beaches, and they have one thing in common: their stomachs are filled with plastic bags."

"Are you really trying to sell me a bill of dead whales?" He sounded as if he was preoccupied.

"People care more about whales than you think. They care more about them than they care about your re-election or mine."

"If you force people to spend money for a plastic bag for their groceries, then you, my lady, will garner plenty of opposition from the simple folk. Perhaps some of your dandruff falls onto my shoulders because we've been allied in the past. We need to be on the same page."

"You've had no difficulty separating yourself from me lately, politically or otherwise."

Roth wiped away a fat bead of sweat that fell into her left eye. She didn't want to speak to him any longer, however, there was a lot on her mind, and their conversations had become fewer and farther apart lately. She softened her tone a bit.

"Sounds like you had more than your share of coffee, Thad."

"Been up since four-thirty, ran three miles, and I'm as sharp as ever. How about you? How many doughnuts have you eaten?"

"I should hang up, but we need to speak about this church thing."

"Suddenly, think I'm fonder of whales," he said.

"You need to pressure the governor and his people about extending the statute of limitations for reporting sexual abuse." It was a test she knew he was going to fail, but she tried it anyway.

"You want to take on the Catholic Church and Albany? Your guilt hasn't derailed your ambitions, but it hasn't made you any smarter either."

Roth felt her blood boil; she responded to him in a hissing whisper. "Don't you ever say that to me again, do you understand? My guilt is private. It's the one thing I own that you are not privy to. Do you understand me?"

"Sounds like someone hasn't had their coffee." His tone was softer, but not apologetic.

"Right now, the church and Albany are vulnerable. People are sick of this stuff. Vile and disgusting men preying on children since the dawn of time. I'm going to be on the right side of this."

"You are on the right side of it. No one will blame you for trying. Say the correct things publicly as I do. You'll fight the good fight, but the odds will be against you. So, when we lose the compromise, we can emote on the news and say we tried. But something is better than nothing. It's a win–win."

"People have suffered, are suffering."

"We're not speaking about vulnerable children recounting nightmares; we're hearing from middle-aged people who look as broken down and as desperate as the accused. I'm certain some of these people are making up stories for a payday. Remember, the church is our friend."

What Calendar didn't know was Roth was in secret discussions with his eminence Michael Cardinal Murphy of New York to create a new independent reconciliation and compensation program for children who had been abused at the hands of Catholic priests and diocese employees over the years. She knew the cardinal from her early church-going days. Her route was an end-around, and if she succeeded, the victims she advocated for would benefit. She wasn't concerned about setting Calendar off or hurting his feelings. He had no feelings. She didn't care about what the governor's response might be. He was a gifted orator, an empty suit who was often slow to take on the church in such matters. But she thought pressuring Calendar and by association the governor was a good plan B in case her old friend Cardinal Murphy decided to ditch her or rewrite her program.

All those Wednesdays ago, young Irene Roth reported Father Teagan to the parish boss, the then *Monsignor* Murphy. Irene was worried the monsignor would brand her a liar and worse – drag her home and interrogate her in front of her volatile father. The subsequent mental and physical beatings would have been relentless. But it didn't go that way at all.

After one of Teagan's sweaty lectures, Irene shuffled into the gym and realized there would be no after-game for her. She suspected all the players had finally been ruined. Which meant there was no way to strike back at her tormentors. Many of the boys stopped attending altogether, obviously convincing their dull-witted parents that they'd prefer to stay home and study their math. Toward the end, the boys who showed up were lethargic, uninspired; not interested in competing.

Disappointed, but mostly angered, Irene chose to skip catechism and interrupted the monsignor at the rectory while he was enjoying a good pipe and passable brandy gifted by a parishioner. She had never met the monsignor before. His eyes appeared kind for an imposing, big-shouldered man. Irene, the skeptic, noted a softness about him. He invited Irene to join him in his private office. She looked down at her feet, hesitating – knowing full well the potential dangers that could be lying in wait. The monsignor's teeth were a brilliant white and his smile comforted her. She hesitated until she felt the palm of his hand on the small of her back. She was swept into his inner sanctum.

Inside the darkened office, she became aware of her own halting breath. Her nostrils were struck by the aromas of stale tobacco, moth balls, and a Lysol product. The stranger listened intently; he whispered somberly to a young priest who was acting as his secretary and confidant. Irene told them what she'd heard from the boys. She couldn't hear the sound of her own voice, but her mind assured her that she was speaking words. She became fixated by the senior priest's meaty hands and his large knuckles, which appeared to be swollen. She followed the direction of his hand as he raised the brandy snifter and put it aside for later. Irene recounted the sobbing sounds from behind Teagan's door. Expressions remained dispassionate. Within a week, Teagan completely disappeared from the landscape. Roth never learned if he was fired or sent off to a secreted place where degenerate priests were allowed to live out their days. Roth maintained an off-the-books working relationship with the man who would eventually become the Archbishop of New York. She could never quite decide if the grand gentleman was an ally or an adversary. She never tipped her hand and neither did he. Over the years, Roth used her relationship with his eminence to accomplish some measure of good.

Another reason for bringing this issue to light with Calendar was because she yearned for him to do the right thing. For once. He had no feelings, yet she hoped for a scintilla of evidence that he may possess a shred of decency. She knew she was fooling herself. She was an addict and he was her drug of choice. She knew better than anyone what Thaddeus Calendar was capable of.

Was sitting down with the archbishop a transparent attempt to redeem herself? If so, she didn't feel redeemed. Besides, she was bitterly disappointed with the limitations of the original conversations. Her proposal extended the statute of limitations. She was banking on her relationship with the top priest. It still wasn't a great deal, but it was better than no deal. She felt she couldn't press the archbishop any further. Calendar was correct in one regard: you can't take on the Catholic Church and expect a clean win. The guidelines for review and compensation didn't look back over the amount of years Roth wanted. That meant many victims seeking justice would not attain closure or receive compensation. Yet Roth knew the plan would be hailed as a success by Albany and the church. Calendar would be left out in the cold having received no credit for no work done. Calendar was not in the business of being a third wheel. He would be furious once the plan went public. Calendar continued to sermonize into her earbud. She decided she'd heard enough.

"Stop orating. The sound of your voice could put a herd of cattle to sleep."

"That's a little harsh," he said in a calm, smooth tone.

"Hang up."

"You sound a little out of breath. Are you pleasuring yourself, darling?"

"I'm in public, you ninny," she said.

"Even better. By the way, you are saucy this morning."

"You were born in Brooklyn, Thad. Don't give me that saucy shit."

"So, let me remind you that you will never speak to me this way again, privately or in public," Calendar fumed.

"Oh, really, are we ever going to be together in public or in private? We're supposed to be working together on a number of initiatives," she reminded him.

"In public? Oh, absolutely darling, but not today, no."

"Why not today?" Her eyes were searching for the water fountain. Her throat was dry, and she was done with him.

"In private is another story. I'm inside your apartment. And I'm waiting for you."

She knew she was going to betray herself before the pathetic mealy-mouthed words came spilling out of her mouth, "I've lost nearly 6 pounds."

There was a pause and when he answered, while there was little enthusiasm behind his words, they were enough for her. "Wonderful. Be here in ten minutes. No later."

Irene Roth steered herself off the treadmill while it was still in operation. She headed for the exit as if she was under the spell of a vampire. She hated herself more than ever.

Arnold Fleck spent the last few days pouring over the journals he discovered in the canvas bag secreted from Harry Kavanagh's driveway. More than good reading – he thought they were inspirational. It provided him with a blueprint for his future. The words between the pages added up to the lecherous and filthy adventures of a bitter man. Fleck was enraptured by it. The author's name wasn't assigned to the work; however, his history of misdeeds was clearly articulated between the mildewed pages. The man was a monster, a serial molester; he had been since he was a boy. He was victimized by a priest, and subsequently guided into the life by this mentor. While the author danced around the idea that he may have dimmed the hearts and minds of his wards over the years, he never once sincerely apologized for his deeds. And when there was a hint of clarification, he saw his behavior as guiding the youngsters through a rite of passage. In his estimation, he went before them as others had traveled amid the shadows before his time. It wasn't the Disney way; it *was* the real way of life. No one was immune. The author was embittered by those who took advantage of him. He became a pawn, under the direction of others. Made to do things under duress to shield his character and protect his livelihood. He would do anything to safeguard his vulnerability and ultimately his freedom. He was pressured to cover up the murder of Harry Kavanagh's wife, Felicity, who unbeknownst to the writer, was the woman at the core of Arnold Fleck's anxieties since her death.

There were a few puppeteers mentioned in the writing, but there was one name Fleck recognized; whom he thought would be the weakest link. Fleck's practice was on life-support. He certainly couldn't understand the reasons why; however, it was clear to his patients, particularly his female patients. Fleck was a boundary-less person, and some found him to be downright creepy. He was down to one staff member. There were occasions when he was forced to answer his own phone. But now he saw a clear path, to an easier life; to an early retirement. It was his chance, and he was going to take full advantage of it. Fleck didn't feel remorse for Felicity Kavanagh, her prickly husband, or their snotty boys. He was nearly free, and he breathed easier than he had in years. He could rake in a substantial amount of money very quickly and take a vacation. By the time the dolt Kavanagh discovered the object of his anxiety located somewhere in his own house, Fleck would be long gone, drinking a tall rum cocktail in an exotic place through a silly straw.

The author wrote extensively about his coverup role in Felicity Kavanagh's death as it pertained to his occupation. He was the Chief Medical Examiner. After five seconds of research on the internet, Fleck learned the author's name was Corbin Reece. He also learned Reece was very dead. It didn't matter. Fleck had already chosen his soft target and he was very much alive.

Chapter Fourteen

Harry Kavanagh knew he had to don his thinking cap, but he decided not to fight his exhaustion. He took the good doctor's advice. He allowed his brain to turn to mush and gave in to some quality shut eye. He dozed for days in a pair of pajamas his wife gave him a week before she died. He'd awaken in those pajamas and subsequently wash and iron them while listening to WBGO, one of the longest-running non-commercial jazz radio stations in the country. He remembered the look on Felicity's smiling face when she presented the pajamas to him. He smiled where he stood recalling the memory. The pajamas were much too big for him now, but he wore them anyway.

His mind was quieting; he was beginning to feel relaxed. Each morning, he marveled at the changing colors of the facial bruises staring back at him from the glass framed in the kitchen cabinets. He didn't have the courage to look at the mirror. Harry slipped back into those pajamas while they were still warm. For four days, he and Lolly barely left the house save for some essential duties. He watched black and white movies, cooked a Pappardelle Bolognese for himself, wrote letters to his boys and regained some strength. Strength was particularly on his mind – the fact that he didn't have any.

Included in Harry's morning regiment was time set aside to stretch, something he hadn't done much of in recent years. He would attempt this while "curling" too many cups of coffee.

Harry switched from WBGO to YouTube where he rediscovered a video of a young tenor in the 1980s, José Carreras, belting out an aria. In his pajamas, in his favorite room, the kitchen, Harry basked in the melodious and powerful voice of a man he had always admired.

Carreras was Harry's favorite dramatic tenor. He was often the forgotten one amid the giants, Luciano Pavarotti and Placido Domingo. By the time Carreras teamed with Pavarotti and Domingo to perform those historic concerts, he had already battled leukemia, having had to go through grueling chemotherapy. Harry considered Carreras' early performances of the aria "Nessun Dorma" to be as thrilling if not more so than his ballyhooed contemporaries. Listening to Carreras inspired Harry. After an hour of the swashbuckling sounds of the tenor, Harry imagined he felt like a champ:

comprised of the prowess of Michael Jordan and the zip of Zorro rolled into one long-lasting Cuban cigar. Harry knew it was a convoluted thought, but it meant he was feeling good. Before he knew it, he began to croon as only he could. Not exactly on pitch, but he didn't care.

"Take my hand, I'm a stranger in paradise," he sang, dancing around the kitchen, leading his partner, which was one of Felicity's coffee mugs. Michelle Obama's face smiled back at him.

When Harry deemed himself fit enough to head out into the world, he spent the next week running and consequently walking at Silver Lake Park, doing an increasing number of pushups each time, testing his body – attempting to build some backbone. He signed himself up for the accelerated program in his mind, foolishly ignoring the risks. He felt like he was proceeding like a brash teenager, which was clearly not his style, but at least he wasn't worried about getting acne. His body shuddered when he tested it beyond its limits. Much like the very first used Volvo 240 DL Wagon he and Felicity once owned. Every time the speedometer hit 58, the old wagon buckled like a starship being sucked into a black hole.

Harry pushed aside the pain and soreness. At the end of each workout, he would encounter Lolly, untethered; sitting patiently, waiting beside the same park bench. On Harry's approach, Lolly would slowly wheel her head toward him. His lips mumbled curse words she'd heard before but could not interpret. Harry caressed the top of Lolly's head. It gave her permission to lean into him. They traipsed toward the final grassy incline leading to the car parked on the avenue. At no time during his workouts did Harry worry about paying bills or think about the annoying Arnold Fleck or the bombastic Emma Kendall. The context of the park offered no reminders of the young woman he had hoped to run into, Brenda Streeter. Nor did his mind wander to the discovery of Dr. Armstrong's striking blue eyes. He was only thinking about making his list and building strength because he thought it might come in handy as he limped forward into uncharted territory.

Harry pulled into his driveway and turned off the ignition. He hesitated for some seconds as his eyes seemed to be thinking, trying to recall something locked somewhere inside his mental hard drive. Harry flashed back to the crumbling building – running outside and narrowly escaping. He shuddered in the driver's seat and took hold of himself. He closed his eyes. His eyelids fluttered. In his mind's eye, he heard men shouting. He remembered driving home in a near stupor; in probably some state of shock. There was something else. Something inside his cranium he couldn't dig out. He looked around the inside of the car searching for something. He wasn't sure what he was looking for.

"What? What? What can't I remember?" He mock-pounded his head with his hands.

He scanned his forearms and noticed his hair was standing on end. After a long beat, he turned to Lolly, made a funny face at her and shrugged. He could not recall the canvas bag that was tangled around his elbows. He climbed out of the car slowly and stiffly.

"Oh, Lolly girl. Here it comes now. Right on schedule. Payback for my stupidity. Mucho pain."

Lolly followed him as he limped toward the kitchen door. He couldn't decide what part of his body was more deserving of a bouquet of flowers and a box of chocolates. A car pulled up curbside. Harry saw young Charlie waving from the passenger side of his father's car.

"Hey, Mr. Kavanagh?"

"Hello, Charlie," Harry said brightly, offering a flinching smile. When he raised his arm to wave, he felt a sharp pain in his side.

"You okay, Mr. Kavanagh? You look like you have a bad headache or ate broccoli or something."

"It was the broccoli. Oh, no Charlie, I'm fine," he waved to Charlie's father with the other hand.

"I wanted to remind you the assembly is today. I'm the cowbell player, remember?"

Harry had forgotten he agreed to go to Charlie's school to pinch hit for his father. Harry smiled and said, "Of course I remember."

"Thank you," Charlie's father mouthed those grateful words and shot Harry a bigger thumbs up than the last time.

Harry nodded and smiled, deciding this time not to wave at all.

"See you, Lolly girl," Charlie sang in a celebratory tone as they drove off.

Harry was a get-there-early-kind-of-a-guy, always has been. That was never Felicity's style. Their departure and subsequent arrival contrasts fell somewhere in between a slight inconvenience and a ticking time bomb for them both. Their impulses represented them at their core. Typically, Harry liked to play it safe while Felicity could potentially tiptoe along the edge of a parapet blindfolded five minutes before an appointment without a care in the world. Whenever they were heading out as a family, it wasn't uncommon for Harry, Jake, and Will to wait in the car for fifteen minutes before Felicity would emerge. During their stay, the little boys would grumble and inevitably one of them would say, "You have to say something to her, Pops."

"Yeah, that's not a good idea," Harry responded between clenched teeth. "When she comes outside, please tell her how beautiful she looks. And mean it. Don't patronize her." Although, he completely understood they would be patronizing her. And if she caught on (it was a fifty-fifty chance) then Harry would catch a skillful, and protracted, lecture that would make his brain freeze over.

"Pops, why *are* we in such a hurry to get to the salami table anyway?" Jake said one day, nearly tossing their universe into a tailspin.

"You mean, why are we early for the appetizers?"

"Yeah. But yeah, Pops, why?" Will's tiniest of voices weighed in on the question of the ages.

"You know, boys. It's one of the mysteries of life." Harry said it in the rich, melodious fatherly voice that could still captivate them, especially at night when he made up bedtime stories. The boys were still at that age then when they'd believe almost anything their father told them. But in truth, Harry knew their squirming was rooted in his impatience.

"Hello, my handsome men," Felicity said beaming as she entered the car. She was usually beaming. As the boys talked over each other, fumbling to compliment her, Felicity looked at Harry with that crooked smile of hers and said, "I don't know why you boys sit in the car for fifteen minutes when we could all walk out of the house together?"

The boys looked at each other unable to come up with the right answer. Harry smiled and bowed his head obligingly. Harry had given up attempting to explain his shaky hypothesis that this leaving-early thing was somehow linked to the male DNA. Felicity leaned over and kissed Harry on the cheek, leaving her mark. She reached into the backseat and squeezed the hands and ankles of her little men.

"You're off the hook this time, Mister Man," she said to Harry. "We're off to the salami table. Right, Jake?"

"Right, Mom," little Jake barked.

And quoting Will when he was just a toddler, Felicity said, "Let's broom away." Translation: Let's hit it. I'm ready to go now. Consequently, the happy family drove off and arrived at their destination early enough to bear witness to the naked salami table being dressed.

So, being in the habit of arriving someplace before the lights are turned on, Harry, true to form, was sitting in an aisle seat in the empty public-school auditorium forty-five minutes before the assembly was due to commence. The janitor, who was dry-mopping underneath Harry's raised feet, looked at him as if he had stolen his bag of Doritos.

Harry smiled at Charlie when he entered with the other kids in the band. Charlie hesitated when he reached Harry's seat. The boy leaned in and whispered, but not skillfully enough, "Mr. Kavanagh, I heard my mother say she has someone she wants you to date. A friend of hers who has really big…"

Harry cringed as Charlie struggled to recall the rest of it. "A big personality, I think." Harry smiled, and Charlie skipped down the aisle, catching up to other children proceeding on stage for their last-minute rehearsal. Another early bird, a teacher who was sitting nearby marking papers, inspected Harry with upturned eyebrows. Harry could not determine if she was a friend or foe.

"Oh, apparently he's my matchmaker," Harry said grinning. He unconsciously twirled the wedding band on his finger.

Without a word, the teacher lowered her chin into the homework, using her chest as a shelf for the papers she had already finished scoring.

Harry reached for the journal he had brought along for the ride and began scribbling. It seemed like a fortnight before he heard the sound of the cowbell, but each time he did, between those long intervals, he looked up from his notes and gave Charlie a big smile. After his workout, he'd spent forty minutes with an icepack on the various continents of his body. So, Harry was still not able to wave efficiently. But Little Charlie was none the wiser, and blushed and soaked up Harry's recognition like a sponge.

Harry was very pleased he ran into Charlie and his father outside his house. He would frequently attend one thing or another for his boys when they were small. He remembered this one particular outing.

It was Will's fifth-grade assembly. In those days, it seemed like someone was always graduating from something. After Will's assembly, the little boy announced to his parents that he wanted to speak to his friend Julia, to express his deep and devoted love for her. He didn't exactly say it in those words, but that was the gist of it.

"Well, honey, why don't you begin with happy graduation?" Felicity suggested tenderly, as she knelt before him; sneaking a peak at Harry that read – *I just can't*. Little Will considered his mother's words and said, "Okay, Mom. Good idea."

Harry missed those days terribly. He missed his wife's infectious smile; their boys' insouciance. Jake was at Parris Island – talk about the loss of innocence. He missed everything about his old life aside from his fat clothes. He forced himself out of his reverie. This was neither the time nor the place to grieve. He was here for Charlie. Harry was grateful for the little man's kinship and was happy to be in the audience for him.

Harry looked down and inspected his journal. It was a Family Dollar special, however, it was obvious to Harry there was nothing special about it. It was cheaply bound with a black cover containing mostly blank pages. Save one. Harry purchased it hastily with the intention of initiating a list. He spent a few minutes after his hot shower and subsequent icepack treatment doodling in the journal, drawing caricatures of political figures in the news. While he was waiting in the auditorium, he scribbled the following notes on that same page:

Medical examiner Corbin Reece gives me a little high sign.
Wants to talk to me?
Nearly drown in front of my own house. Accident? (P.S. – take swimming lessons?)
Mysterious woman with lilac perfume rescues me?
Reece commits suicide.
No one attends wake.
Anonymous payer foots bill at funeral home.
Attacked by the liverwurst twins at Reece's apartment.
They hate Reece.
What is going on?
All things connected to Felicity's death?
What do you think...hmm?
What to do next?

Harry was considering his notes when the principal, Mr. Diaz, entered the auditorium. He was a trim man in his 40s wearing a nicely-tailored suit. The folded assembly program was pinched between his fingers. He began tapping it nervously against his thigh. He motioned with a come-hither finger to the band teacher. The band teacher, an energetic sort in his mid-20s with Einstein-styled hair, bounded off the stage and seemingly reached the principal's side in an instant. Not because he was a bootlicker, Harry deduced, but because he was loaded with youth and athleticism.

"What's up? I'd like to get a few more minutes of rehearsal time in."

"What's up is the title of the song you're about to perform for our parents." He pointed to the program. The band teacher shrugged, not foreseeing a controversy.

"What's the problem? Did someone misspell your name?" The kid thought it was a cute gibe, but he immediately stowed his attitude when the principal's dark eyebrows formed a frown. Mr. Diaz jabbed the program with a stiffer finger.

"Holiday Hoedown!" he responded in an anxious whisper that was not particularly quiet.

"I don't get it," the young teacher shrugged.

"Hoedown, hoe, hoe. The word hoedown. *Hoe.* There can be no hoes in our performance." He was forced to compose himself.

Classes of students began filing into the auditorium. Some of the teachers and their classroom aides gave the stressed-out principal an odd look as they passed him by. The band teacher ran his fingers across his lips and looked down. He was trying to mask his incredulity.

"Mr. Diaz, the word means dance or celebration," he commented, staring down at his black St. Laurent high-top sneakers, which cost $262 (he knew because he checked online), gifted to him by one of the substitute paraprofessionals who was vying to become his girlfriend. The fact he was wearing the high tops on a day she was scheduled to attend the concert meant he had made up his mind to commit. In fact, he regretted accepting the sneakers in the first place. *Where did she come up with that kind of money on her salary? And now, how am I expected to reciprocate?* The young teacher's mind was suddenly spinning.

"Do you have another song you can substitute?"

The band teacher looked up. He looked a little uncomfortable for journeying into his personal life.

"I was paying attention to you," he said.

Diaz looked confused and said, "I didn't infer you weren't listening to me."

"Oh," the young man said apologetically. Then he made some sounds in his throat before he responded articulately with, "This is the only song we have besides the national anthem, which we open with. We've been rehearsing for a month."

"That's it. We're changing the name of the song to Holiday Celebration. I'll have some of the secretaries white this out and handwrite the change."

"But the name of the song is Holiday Hoedown," the young teacher gently protested.

Harry adeptly reached over and slipped the program from the principal's grasp. Mr. Diaz shot a questioning look in Harry's direction.

"Excuse me?"

Harry didn't respond immediately as he was perusing the program. After he was satisfied, he rose from his seat and pointed inside the program.

"Mr. Diaz," he said drolly, "I'm afraid you've got greater challenges here."

The band teacher drew himself beside Harry, and he and the principal followed the path of Harry's finger.

"As it turns out, not only do you have another Ho, but you have a Wang in here too. Students David Ho and Timothy Wang. Presents quite a challenge, don't you agree?"

The principal took a step back, exhaling through his nostrils.

"Since you're retitling the song, I suppose you could rename the boys David and Timothy Holiday Celebration. You'd have a lot of whiting out and rewriting ahead of you. And what about their parents? I suspect they wouldn't be too pleased with the name change."

"You're not funny. And you're not helping, sir," Mr. Diaz said snapping at Harry. Diaz turned on his heels and left the auditorium in defeat. The teacher with the shelf who had been marking papers nodded over at Harry with an expression of approval. She was on his team after all, which prompted Harry to bow his head like a nobleman.

"Sir, thank you very much. That was an outstanding performance and a great help," the band teacher said, giving Harry a handshake so firm Harry thought he heard one of his knuckles pop.

"You're very welcome," Harry said, fighting the impulse to shake the misery out of his hand. The swashbuckling band teacher bounded back to his students.

"Okay, boys and girls, let's do this *thang*, shall we?"

The auditorium was filling with noisy children. Their harried teachers and aides were mostly unsuccessful at squelching their enthusiasm. By the time the program was about to begin, Harry was ready for something stronger than a cup of black coffee. Harry couldn't believe it, but his mind travelled back to the infamous pint of bourbon that had destroyed a full-night's sleep. He shook off the memory.

The morning's festivities began with a slew of lifeless speeches by the administration, with seemingly no end in sight. Harry thought he would lose his marbles. Poetry readings from the upper grades spirited him a bit. This was followed by tiny feet parading artwork across the stage. The cheerful clothesline of finger-paintings brought Harry to the edge of his seat. Harry's favorite part of the morning: the energetic band teacher conducting the hoedown song, punctuated by Charlie's perfectly timed cowbell.

Harry applauded alongside the parents of David Ho and Timothy Wang. Harry forgot himself, stepped into the center aisle and waved to Charlie. To Harry's surprise, there was only a twinge here and there. Nothing worth writing to the doctor about. And the little man Charlie radiated and took a perfect bow. Harry's face felt warm. He was beaming. All things considered, Harry Kavanagh couldn't have been happier.

A few minutes later as Harry exited the crowded auditorium, he noticed some commotion ahead. It was not the exaggerated public-school chaos caused by Twinkied-up children being herded by the dreaded Morlocks. This was something else. There was a lot of yelling. Adults versus adults. Harry couldn't make any sense of it. He stopped about twenty feet from the bathrooms, and watched as Mr. Diaz was imploring the uniform security guard who Harry decided looked familiar.

Standing patiently before them with his head bowed was Shelby Martin, looking as if he were waiting his turn at the guillotine. He was wearing his signature wig, slight line of lipstick and was clad in beige khakis. Harry took a few measured steps closer. Platoons of children marching from the auditorium were inadvertently nudging him on their way back to their classrooms.

Harry took the gentle shoving like a gentleman and did not flinch or complain. The teachers and school aides leading the parade were transfixed by the red-faced Diaz. As it is with a roadside accident, their curiosity quickly waned once the flow of traffic pushed them further ahead.

With no fanfare, Shelby turned quietly from the scene of the accident and exited, looking very embarrassed. He brushed by Harry without saying a word. Something pricked up Harry's senses, but the message was slow to reach the command center in his brain. By the time Harry figured it out, Shelby was gone. Harry refocused his attention on the brouhaha. Diaz pointed at the man whose nameplate read Lynch.

"I'm making an official complaint to your supervisor, Mr. Lynch," Diaz said. He stormed away for the second time that morning.

"Go the fuck ahead," Lynch said it like a man who instantly knew he was in over his head. "I guess I'll have a sit down with my union rep then."

As Harry approached, the identity of the man, Lynch, became clearer to him: he was the man from the hospital waiting room. The loudmouth whom Shelby skillfully ordered off the premises.

"Hello. I saw him chewing you out. Are you all right?" Harry said in a sympathetic tone.

"Yeah," Lynch said, steaming.

"What happened?"

"That little faggot, it's his, *it's* fault."

"The man wearing the wig?"

"Yeah, the guy who dresses like a bitch. You know that thing works at a hospital. Who would want that around sick people and around children? How about in a church?"

"How about a church?" Harry responded feigning innocence.

"I know most people would agree with me. Miss Thing doesn't belong in no church either."

"You mean his appearance is offensive to whom, God? Zeus?"

"The whole motherfucking deal, yeah. Shit yeah."

Harry scratched his chin and said, "I see what you mean."

"I bet you do. You're a godly thinker like myself."

131

A godly thinker? Harry kept it close to the vest. "And so what happened?" Harry said, encouraging him to spill.

"He wanted to use the little boys' room. That's how it all started. Can you imagine that?"

"And you couldn't let him do that," Harry said shaking his head with more feigned understanding.

"Hell no. And I couldn't let him use the ladies either 'cause maybe he does have a dick. Or maybe he doesn't. Either way it's not right. I have to do my job. What would Jesus do?" Lynch said pushing out his words.

Harry noticed the hall had emptied.

"Well, how would you know?"

"How would I know what?"

"If he was a male or she was a female?"

"My point exactly."

"Well, maybe you should have checked."

"What?" Lynch said slowly, suddenly looking like a dazed insect. One that was swatted, but not yet squashed.

"Instead of shoving your hands down your pants, probably your hourly pastime, maybe you should have done a more thorough investigation of the suspect," Harry said, his voice wavering.

Harry was not happy with the string of words he linked together. He blamed this on his emerging anger. He closed his eyes and shook his head, castigating himself. His indignation had lain dormant for many years – in fact, for most of his life. Felicity had always made life easy for him; shielding him while she made the difficult decisions and took on most of the confrontations life handed out. Since his wife's passing, Harry was becoming aware he presented one way, however, a darker side of himself was closer to the brim than he realized. His torment and humiliation stemming from his molestation never allowed him to truly sleep peacefully. These feelings of humiliation and victimization clogged his veins, stunting him; he was sometimes quick to anger and slow to cool off. Felicity knew this about the man. And because of her awareness and deep love for him she created a safe haven, sheltering Harry whenever she was able, by keeping him far away from significant crises.

Lynch's face went through a series of contortions as he monitored the map of discomfort on Harry's face. Harry was searching for a way out of the labyrinthine traps set in his mind. Lynch cursed under his breath and was about to walk away from Harry when a stunning look of recollection hardened on his face.

"You!" he hissed like an over-emoting actor portraying a villain in a mega-movie. "The prick from the hospital." His eyes narrowed, and his tobacco-stained teeth were locked down tightly.

"Yeah, you win. You got me," Harry said, wearing a phony penitence on his sleeves.

"So, I get it now. I insulted your faggot wife and you wanna be a wise guy." Lynch looked Harry up and down with an expression of utter disgust. "Man, you're like a faggot vine of poison ivy with a scoop of dipshit on top. That's what you are." Lynch spat out some more of his trademark killer breath.

"I don't even know where to begin with that analogy, you odious moron," Harry said quietly.

Harry thought it was the perfect time to fulfill an ambition of his. He thought he would have saved the *Glass-Key* move for the loud-mouth Robert Devine, employee of State Senator Irene Roth. Given the special circumstances Harry currently found himself in, he knew his time was now. His anger subsided once he finalized his decision. He felt downright giddy inside.

"What the fuck are you smiling at?" The dopey-faced security guard looked insulted.

Harry bent his right leg at the knee and swung the toe of his brand-new Oxford, purchased at where else? – Harry's Shoes on the Upper West Side of Manhattan – and he thrust the point of his Italian shoe leather forward, making direct contact with Lynch's shin. The response was immediate. Without making a sound, save for a yip of corrosive air shooting from his lungs, Lynch creaked forward at the waist. Harry straightened him up by his shoulder, applying very little pressure. It was about as easy as manipulating a marionette. He put his palm on Lynch's chest and without saying a word, he shoved him into the bathroom. Lynch tipped over a garbage pail on his way to docking the one side of his face on the hard black-and-white-tiled floor. Lynch groaned and painstakingly probed his cheek with a finger, trying to assess the damage. He swayed onto his back cursing the condition of his uniform shirt, which was wet with a mixture of urine and water from the trickling privy. Lynch stared incredulously at the undercarriage of the trough. His one eye was immediately dripped on.

Harry turned away without saying a word. He felt his lip quiver. Once the deed was done, he became an immediate nervous wreck. His brow was moist, and his heart was galloping. His left eye twitched without his endorsement. He was aware of his own movements because he heard his hollow-sounding footsteps echoing in the empty hallway. Harry turned a corner and drew near the security desk beside the exit. He nodded without expression to Lynch's partner, the drowsy security officer sitting at a displaced first-grader's desk.

The Lynch guy was worse than a jerk, but Harry was riddled with guilt. He was fully expecting to be arrested and sentenced to life imprisonment in a public-school bathroom complete with clogged toilets and sweating urinals.

Harry tilted his chin down at the security officer. She did not look up. She slid the log book toward the edge of the desk without lifting her eyes. Harry folded himself at the waist and signed himself out using the name Don Diego de la Vega, the fictional name of the man whose alter ego is Zorro, one of Harry's favorite childhood idols. Harry placed the pen down, stood erect and exited. The sound of the door closing echoed in the abandoned hallway. The security officer's eyelashes fluttered with sudden life.

"Oh, my."

She put a hand on her chest, trying to calm herself. Her shoe squeaked on the recently waxed floor when she shifted her weight in the tiny sacrificial chair. She was reading a passed-around copy of *Fifty Shades of Grey*. She was scarcely aware of Harry Kavanagh's presence and his departure.

Harry walked off some of his nervousness once he got outside. He suddenly found himself veering into the middle of the street. He put his palms out, resembling a military man demanding a driver to halt at a checkpoint. Shelby's 1974 mint-conditioned yellow Ford Pinto station wagon slowed to a stop and Harry leaned into the driver's side.

He said to Shelby, "Of course you know you're driving one of the most dangerous cars ever made by the American auto industry?"

During it's time on earth, the infamous Ford Pinto easily developed a reputation as having a poor safety rating given its propensity for the fuel tank to explode on rear-end impacts.

"According to my therapists over the years, this is my way of living on the edge," Shelby said dryly, without looking at him. "I'm a very conservative driver."

"With an obvious death wish. What about the other guy?"

"I'm always keenly aware of the other guy."

"Why don't you stop by the house for some coffee?" Harry asked.

"I operate it locally and barely fill the gas tank," he said, looking at Harry.

"I'm aware you're a very responsible person. I'm not really looking for an explanation. Coffee?"

Shelby looked at him with an expression he couldn't conceal. "Thank you. I need a restroom. Can you provide your address?"

"Let's stop the charade. You know where I live," Harry said as he stepped back onto the curb.

He watched Shelby drive off. His adrenalin boost was long gone. Harry studied the tremor in his hands. The street was silent and vacant. Only the distant sounds of children milling in classrooms, teachers orating, and the din of the abrasive-sounding school bells could be heard. Harry straightened; he felt his feet firmly planted on the sidewalk. He took few calming breaths. He felt a gentle wind breeze past his ear. A peaceful expression gave way to a confused look on his face.

"Now, where did I park my car?" he said aloud. "I don't have a clue."

Chapter Fifteen

Harry entered the kitchen and heard the toilet flush in the half bath off the laundry room. Shelby emerged and nodded sheepishly at Harry.

"You left the door open and since we're old friends," he said, referring to Lolly as she ambled over and nudged her nose against his leg. "Since we're old friends, she decided not to eat me."

"Her name is Lolly," Harry said stoically.

"It's a pleasure to be formally introduced," Shelby said, stroking the big dog's head.

Harry moved to the stove where he immediately began fussing with a coffee pot.

"I rarely use public restrooms as you might imagine, however, I was feeling a little indisposed this morning. I should have known better."

"Do you have someone at the school?"

"I experienced a little bit of an anxiety episode coming on and I required the emergency services of their facility. It was very foolish of me."

Harry turned away from the stove. "I want to thank you. You probably saved my life. I've been thinking about the impact my death would have had on my sons. Especially with what they've already been through." He completed his sentiments in a tone so soft his words were barely audible. "With losing their mother. Thank you."

"How did you figure it out?" Shelby responded in a quiet, inquisitive tone.

"In the school hallway…it was your cologne."

"My lilac-scented perfume."

"Yes. You weren't wearing it at the hospital. Where did you purchase it by the way?"

"Locally. I'm unscented when I work. You stand out at the hospital if you smell good. Given that I already come with pre-existing baggage, I endeavor to keep a low profile. As preposterous as that may sound."

"Removing Lynch from the waiting room so handily – is that your definition of keeping a low profile?"

"He wasn't a patient and he was offensive. The entire episode was quickly forgotten."

"Not by Lynch."

"Well, perhaps that's something he should discuss with his therapist."

"By the way, you have excellent penmanship. Where are you from originally?"

The coffee pot began to issue vague sounds that promised percolation. Harry lowered the flame on the stove. Shelby looked out of the kitchen window and gestured to the curbside water basin.

"I was driving home the night of the storm. He was big. Clubbed you with a thick branch and ran off when he saw my headlights."

"And here I thought it was an accident."

"I didn't get a look at his face. Getting you out of the frigid water was the priority."

"Well, I'm very grateful you know how to prioritize."

"What's going on in your life, Harry?"

Harry glanced over at the percolating Corning Ware coffee pot, and then with a sweep of his hand he offered Shelby a seat at the kitchen table. When Shelby sat down Lolly lowered herself onto one of his feet. Shelby rested a hand on Lolly's neck.

"Well, it sounds crazy. Like I'm living in some kind of movie."

"Genre?"

"Not exactly a comedy," Harry responded.

"Given the fact that someone tried to shorten your life, my impulse is to go with whatever your instincts are telling you."

Harry sat wearily across from Shelby. Lolly moved over to Harry's side and leaned against his leg.

"Four years ago, my wife died in an automobile accident. She was drinking, they said. Drunk driving. That's what the report said. I couldn't believe it. She drowned when her car went off the road."

It sounded odd to him, his retelling. The sound of his own voice was businesslike. He wanted to get through the explanation quickly. Harry swallowed with difficulty. Shelby noticed his eyes glaze over. Harry's vitality quickly deserted him. He was beginning to experience the full weight of his bereavement. This heaviness was all too familiar. Harry spoke very slowly and carefully, almost sounding like a stroke victim.

"She didn't drink every day. On a rare occasion she could lose count of the number of cocktails she had…Look, she was a responsible person who had one goddamn bad night. Jesus, it's not fair. She was everything…"

Shelby reached across the table and briefly gripped Harry's wrist. Harry's shoulders rose and fell. His eyes fluttered closed; then he opened them. He nodded and redistributed his weight in the chair.

"Thank you," he said softly. "Then, I don't know, a week, ten days, two weeks ago, the chief medical examiner tried to get my attention at a restaurant."

"Did you have a conversation?" No answer. "Harry?" Shelby said in a sympathetic tone.

Harry looked at Shelby with a sudden sense of urgency, like a recuperating amnesiac with new information he was compelled to share. Harry pushed himself from the chair and Shelby watched him pace.

"No, he was three sheets to the wind. A mess. He smelled of cigarettes and booze. I wasn't interested in speaking with him. In hindsight it was a bloody mistake." Harry sat down heavily and exhaled.

"Because you were hoping he'd give something?" Shelby studied the clouded look on Harry's face.

Harry was quickly becoming detached again, losing himself in a trance. Shelby arose from the table and turned off the stove. He poured two cups of coffee and deposited them onto the table, loudly, purposely, to startle Harry back to consciousness. He brought over spoons, the milk, and the sugar. Harry looked at him, suddenly enlivening and with more awareness.

Harry said with a wan smile, "You know where everything is."

"Lolly showed me around. You know." Shelby slid back into his seat.

"You asked me a question?" Harry said watching the steam rise from his coffee.

"Was it a mistake, not talking to the medical examiner?"

"Yes. Because he committed suicide that night. He wanted to unburden himself. That's my feeling."

"Is that right? It makes sense."

"He wanted to tell me something. And then…" Harry sipped his coffee; his eyes opening wider. "And then, Jesus. No one admitted to paying for his wake. I was attacked by a couple of guys with very large feet. Behemoths compared to me, who seemed to have a beef with the dead man."

"Have a beef, there's an expression. I haven't heard that old one since my last Edward G. Robinson movie."

"These days I'm feeling old. So, I guess I talk old." Another weary smile. "But I would have thought you would've been more impressed by the word behemoth," Harry said.

"What are your plans? What are you going to do about this?"

"I have some ideas. I'd like my body to heal before someone else decides my face needs a tune up."

"Harry," Shelby shifted his glance downward. "Forgive me. I didn't report what I saw to the police. A person with my eccentricities. They would have laughed at me."

138

"Please, Shelby. You saved my life."

They drank coffee contemplatively, in silence. After a few moments, Shelby slid out from behind the table.

"Be very careful, Harry." Harry nodded and Lolly followed Shelby to the kitchen door. "And Harry, if you need me, I'm not as genteel as I appear to be."

"You've already proven it, Shelby, thank you."

Shelby patted Lolly's bowed head and departed. Harry pushed himself away from the table and addressed Lolly as brightly as he was able, "What do you say, Lolly? Walk or nap?"

Lolly looked at him plainly. "I think it's time for a nap. That's what I think," Harry said, starting out of the kitchen. Remembering the door was previously left unlocked, he did an about-face and locked the kitchen door. Harry ran his hands through his hair. After a beat, he walked out of the room with Lolly at his heels.

It was not unlike any other day for Robert Devine except he was sitting at a larger desk. He made the move on his own. It raised a lot eyebrows among the staff.

"Get over it," Devine belched in the direction of his office mates.

The state senator's chief of staff, Nando Ricci, was in a coma and not expected to live. His wife reported he collapsed face down into a tray of cannolis moments after his morning jog to Pasticceria Aldo, his favorite bakery. Nando Ricci was a genial man known for his kindness and generosity. As a routine, he would pick up dozens of newspapers and deliver them to the doorsteps of his elderly neighbors. Every Monday night, he purchased twenty pizzas from nearby pizza parlors, because he wanted to support as many small businesses in the community as possible, and he would have them delivered to a homeless shelter. He nicknamed Monday night *abeetza* (pizza) *night*, because everyone deserved a little kindness and *abeetz* on a Monday.

Behind the scenes, Devine was Irene Roth's agitator and sometime (without her knowledge) her clandestine thug. Nando was her goodwill man, her Boy Scout, and he played the role sincerely and to the hilt.

Devine gambled that Roth would approve of his initiative. So, he moved himself and his clutter one desk over, to Nando's larger and distinctly neater desk. He'd earned it. So he thought. He protected her in big and small ways. And then there was that really big one, that life-changing save. She could never forget that. They were joined together forever. Like a dysfunctional family. So, his move was no gamble after all, Devine concluded. He could do nothing wrong. It was impossible for him to make a mistake. What a feeling. He was glad Ricci was out on his back. Devine was never a Nando Ricci fan. He despised the lectures Nando dished out on every subject known to man:

You're a grown man, you need to wear an undershirt.
If you're a guest at someone's house for dinner, spend at least thirty dollars on wine or dessert.
If you think you need a shower, you do.
If your cologne smells like candy, you're an amateur.
Before every meeting, make sure there is nothing caught between your teeth.
Never wear a baseball cap backwards, it's uncouth. Never wear a baseball cap.

A new Boy Scout was needed, but the appointee wouldn't be announced until after Nando Ricci's name appeared misspelled in the *Richmond County Register*'s obituary column. Robert Devine didn't expect to be named the next chief of staff. As long as his contributions were appreciated, and he got to sit behind the larger desk, the title meant nothing to him.

Devine lined up two large halves of a mozzarella, sun-dried tomatoes, and prosciutto hero on Nando's desk beside two large cups of coffee and a deli tub of rice pudding. A late lunch, or a snack; he wasn't sure how to categorize his impromptu picnic. He couldn't decide on a plan of attack either – dessert first? He was about to make an important decision when State Senator Irene Roth returned from a meeting. She stopped in front of Nando Ricci's desk and glared at Devine. He froze as he was reaching for a cup of coffee.

"It's okay, right?" He said it in a small voice.

"Really? Are you fucking kidding me? Get back to your own desk and stay there."

A few faces spied over their afternoon assignments and smirked at Devine's undressing. Roth headed into her office and closed the door behind her. Devine cleared his throat and began moving his haul back to his former site. That's when his phone rang. He leaned over the desk and answered the phone.

"Hello, State Senator Roth's office, Bobby Devine speaking."

The calm and collected voice on the other end of the line belonged to Arnold Fleck, reaching out from his recently purchased burner phone. Fleck began reading the narrative from one of Corbin Reece's lost-and-then-found journals. Fleck's comb-over became unwieldy as he strolled along the windy strip of beachfront beneath the Verrazano Bridge. The echoes of the automobiles from above provided a compelling white noise. Fleck smiled to himself as he read. He was enjoying the bright sunlight and the brisk air. He was confident and feeling completely free. A most unusual deportment for a man like him.

Devine's eyes widened as recognizable sins were read back to him by an unrecognizable yet extremely confident voice. Devine plopped down at his desk. And then there was a pause. The story resumed with the following announcement: "If you don't want me to call this office again, I suggest you provide your cell number."

Devine obliged, in a voice that sounded childlike. Devine looked around, worried. But no one was watching him. All the rabid beavers, as he called his colleagues, they were busying themselves at their tidy desks. He was all alone. He exhaled.

"The next time I call we're going to discuss my retirement plan. Have I made myself clear?"

Devine looked around the room again and nodded unconsciously.

"I said, have I made myself clear?"

"Y-Yes, sure thing," Devine sputtered. Beads of perspiration came out to play above his lip.

"And that's all I have to say about that for now. I'll be in touch. Ciao."

The phone line went dead. *And that's all I have to say about that for now*, Devine repeated the words in his head.

Devine was sweating, but he felt a chill throughout his body. He rose from his seat and marched out of the office. He strode down a hallway, his thighs chaffing as entered the bathroom. He stood in there anxiously. Devine's mind was racing. A guy resembling Harry Kavanagh bursts out of Corbin Reece's demolished building, and not too long after he's being squeezed for money. Devine splashed water on his face and considered his options. There was only one call to make.

"Yeah, that's what I'll do," he said looking into the mirror.

"What did you say?"

The janitor had entered while Devine's thoughts were ping-ponging.

"Nothing. I said nothing. Where are the paper towels?" Devine asked gruffly, holding up his wet hands like a mad scientist about to be fitted with surgical gloves.

"You usually wipe your hands on your pants. Stick with what you know," the janitor said turning his back on Devine.

Jaycee Singletary shadowed Harry Kavanagh from his house. He was a man true to his word. Once he decided to keep an eye on Harry, he could find no compelling reason to redirect his attention. Singletary was in fact in attendance at the public school. He was masked in the crowded corridor and a front-row witness to the public row that had taken place outside the boys' bathroom. He heard the profane words spoken by the school security officer. Jaycee Singletary was a true believer of handing out a cup of reckoning now and then, because no good person deserved to be browbeaten. Singletary regarded himself an equalizer and his personal intervention was ultimately decided by the risk factor. Jaycee Singletary quickly determined that making a pizza delivery to the security officer Lynch, whose first name was Jimmy, fell into the low-risk category. He decided on pepperoni.

Jaycee Singletary was on the trail. He found himself at a pop-up gallery space in a warehouse near the waterfront. He was carrying a pizza box. He observed the congregation milling around the gallery from outside a doorway on a narrow iron landing. In the mix were reverse-mortgage-ready boomers, tattooed bikers, bank executives, and other local posers. This was a private affair. No press permitted; no nosey Parkers. Singletary was halted outside the doorway by a paw belonging to a goliath crammed into a tuxedo.

"I'm not on the list?" Singletary asked politely. "Are you sure?"

The man was three inches taller than Singletary and when he spoke, the words went over Singletary's head.

"This is an inside gig. None can pass without the writ." His words hung heavy in the air.

Singletary knew the brute was doing his job.

"That's groovy," Singletary said, dosing him with his own brand of mischief. "How about this?" Singletary asked. "Pizza delivery?"

"Nice try bro. No writ, no pass."

"I appreciate your work ethic and your brevity. I confess I am a big fan of Mr. Lupa," he said beaming through his fib.

Singletary shifted his weight without causing a response from the gatekeeper. He peered into the gallery space and saw Louie Lupa surrounded by sycophants, one of whom was Jimmy Lynch.

Louie Lupa was the star attraction of the clandestine opening. Singletary recalled Lupa as a controversial figure. Remembering last year's *mishegoos*, Singletary accessed the word again, because it seemed to fit and it was fast becoming a favorite of his. Last year's mess began when Lupa unveiled his *Santa Can't Really Black* series of paintings and sculptures depicting black Santa Clauses.

Painted on clay were the faces of long-gone African American actors, Lincoln Theodore Monroe Andrew Perry, otherwise known as *Stepin Fetchit*, and Willie Best. Willie Best's character was referred to as *Sleep n' Eat*. Lupa's racist response was his comeback to an African American family-run toy company in Detroit whose emergence onto the national scene resulted from their successful Black Santa toy sales. Their prosperity ruffled the Brooklyn-born bigot. One could not be lazy, illiterate, or simpleminded and be Santa Claus was Lupa's point, meaning Santa can only be Caucasian.

Using the images of the actors who played these stereotypically inferior characters got Lupa fired from his day job as a janitorial aide in a urologist's office. The internet responses were not in Mr. Lupa's favor. He was immediately reviled. Soon after, however, something else happened, something terribly disturbing and revealing: he became celebrated in some suburbs. His work began to sell, admittedly succeeding beyond his wildest wet dreams. Singletary recalled watching Lupa interviewed on a local TV segment. Lupa bragged about purchasing a condo in the US Virgin Islands as a result of his newfound success.

The mealy-mouthed Lupa, who resembled a ferret, said to the young blonde reporter who appeared to be fighting back a gag reflex, "Yeah, I just bought a *gondo* in St. Thomas."

Off the record, the reporter chided him, "*Stink*, *Stank*, and *Stunk* would be your children's names, if you were ever allowed to have test tube babies."

"What's this year's excitement?" Singletary said from his spot outside the doorway, and without looking up at the big body.

"Jesus is white," was the deadpanned response.

"How appropriate for a man of Mr. Lupa's acuity," Singletary said. "Oh, yes, I see them now."

Singletary observed twelve crosses about six feet high and four feet wide comprised of old railroad pilings. Each cross had a sculpture affixed at the peak. Bright white faces painted on the sculptures depicted Lupa's fantasy of an Aryan Messiah.

"The man is making a living, not earning one," Singletary offered.

"Uh, um."

"I suppose I'm still not getting in?"

"Have no writ?"

"No writ for me, brother." Singletary shrugged, sounding upbeat nonetheless.

When the big man tilted his chin downward, he saw...nothing. Jaycee Singletary, the gentleman that he was, had quietly taken his leave.

Later that evening, Louie Lupa was celebrated at a home in the exclusive Todt Hill section. It was a secretive affair hosted by flamboyant attorney Joseph Bacci. The rotund lawyer was a church-donating conservative who fervently believed in Lupa's work. After dinner, Bacci, whom the media loved to call "Joey Kisses," was eager to see the new work in solitude, away from critics and do-gooders.

Lupa, Bacci, and the chauffeur, previously known as the giant gatekeeper, entered the gallery space. Lupa and Bacci were under the influence of a few too many shots of Limoncello. The two men shared crude remarks about female reporters and boasted about their sexual conquests. Bacci spat phlegm into an ashtray while Lupa tried to pick his nose with his knuckle. All three men were smoking Cuban cigars.

When Lupa flipped on the lights, Bacci's cigar fell out of his mouth. Lupa nearly gagged on his stogie while the giant calmly removed his cigar from his mouth and grinned. He couldn't help himself. Mounted like a corpulent white Jesus on one of Lupa's crosses was a sobbing Jimmy Lynch. He was blindfolded with one of his socks, bound with twine and gagged with his own urine-stained underwear. He was completely naked. The other sock was loosely slipped over his limp genitalia. The word *ignorant* was scrawled across his sagging chest in black marker.

Chapter Sixteen

Spilling Felicity's fate to Shelby the day before made Harry feel despondent and sluggish. As he rose from bed, he felt like he needed a pick-me-up and decided on a shower – not your typical soap-on-a-rope-comforting-middle-aged-man shower, but an energizing cold shower. Not usually a part of his repertoire, if ever. A few seconds into the experiment, Harry was hopping up and down as much as his body would allow and he bellowed some high-pitched undecipherable jabber, trying to convince himself his bright idea was not meant to be a suicide mission. He did feel invigorated though and danced out of the shower humming a tooth-rattling rendition of "Beyond the Sea." He considered making this cold dip a part of his new routine, maybe.

He graduated to his bedroom with actual words coming out his mouth. Much to his surprise, he found himself singing a respectable version of "Mack the Knife." Harry had things to do, things he needed and wanted to do. An idea came to him. He decided to kill two birds with one stone.

"That's exactly what I'm going to do, Lolly." He was so excited he could have easily said, eureka!

The big dog watched him from the doorway. She took a few loping steps into the room. She circled seven or eight times before she stretched out on the floor beside Harry's bed. Lolly batted her eyelashes and then closed up shop in favor of some much-needed shuteye. Harry dressed quickly.

But Harry's confidence did not tag along for the ride. He showed up outside the restaurant questioning his bright idea. The Mid-Island Marina encompassed several family-run restaurants that dotted the shoreline. In Bocca al Lupo was the only eyesore and unfortunately it was Harry's destination. The worst establishment on the best block so to speak. In Bocca al Lupo was an old houseboat converted into an Italian restaurant. Harry entered the main dining area from the street. He noticed the tiny observation deck at the stern, an open-air dining area when the weather cooperated. The deck was currently off limits.

The inside was narrow, dimly presented and empty. Harry selected a two-top a few feet away from a large fish tank. The surviving fish looked like hostages, gasping and desperate to slip Harry a note pleading for a rescue plan.

The waiter, a somber, dark-haired man with a narrow frame approached taking slow mincing steps. He was wearing a short black tie and a white shirt emitting an odor of perspiration evidenced by the uncomfortable twitch of Harry's nose. He discarded a menu in front of Harry without saying a word.

"I'll be joined by another," Harry said.

"I'm wiping down the other menus with Windex."

"Okay, cleaning is good," Harry agreed, although he couldn't find evidence of significant cleaning going on by the looks of his surroundings.

"There's nothing that says delicious like the smell of Windex on my menu." He said it with his tongue in his cheek.

The waiter responded with a blank expression, "You can share the menu. Sharing is delicious too." He filled two glasses from a scarred plastic water pitcher and walked off.

"Thank you," Harry said to the man's back.

Sharing is delicious too. An interesting comeback; it reminded Harry to never underestimate people. The pungent fellow had a sense of humor.

While Harry was deciding if he should have a go with the glass of cloudy water, he noticed movement in the fish tank. It wasn't one of the hostages flagging for help; it was a reflection. A real live person was sauntering toward his table. There was a coordinated and graceful moving of arms and hips going on. Pleasingly buoyant. *Sauntering indeed*, Harry thought.

Emily Armstrong sat before Harry had the opportunity to stand and greet her properly. Emily Armstrong's hair, untethered, was long and healthy-looking. Harry knew little about these things, but he guessed her hair had been blown out. He learned the jargon from his wife. She came home one evening looking simply gorgeous and Harry complimented her.

"Oh, I had my hair blown out," Felicity said, twirling herself around him impishly, gloriously.

"Doctor Armstrong," Harry sputtered, his eyes refocusing on the present.

"Oh, Harry. Emily, please. You already have two strikes against you," she said looking around the place. "But will the bread be delivered warm or cold, hmm? That's the big question."

"I do have some good news, Emily." He said her name awkwardly and without a great deal of confidence. "The water is wet. Cloudy and wet."

"Like tomorrow's forecast. Yes, and it looks like there are particles swimming in your glass."

Harry's forehead wrinkled as he leaned in to take a closer look. His inspection was interrupted by the waiter who delivered a basket of bread wrapped in a cloth napkin. As he stepped away, they immediately reached for it, their hands inadvertently touching.

"Warm bread *is* good," she said smiling. "You have a stay of execution."

"I think he used the napkin to wipe down the menus. Windex is his best friend."

"Don't let it throw you. I think we're still ahead of the game," she offered.

Emily Armstrong didn't look like Dr. Armstrong at all. And since she'd already held his interest as Dr. Armstrong, Harry felt like he was getting in way over his head with Emily Armstrong.

Dr. Armstrong off duty was Emily Armstrong. Her stunning blue eyes and all her other good parts were packaged nicely in jeans, high boots, and a waist-level leather jacket. Harry mused that she looked like a model from the pages of *Wonder Woman Magazine*, if there were such a thing. He decided that she could chop wood, write a novel, and fly a rocket into deep space without breaking a sweat. Surely Felicity was capable of all that and possibly more. Harry was on his own here with a perfect stranger; the newness of it all made him feel like he was bound to make a mistake. He found himself as Joseph Campbell often spoke about…in unfamiliar territory. But he was as smitten as a grieving man could be.

Harry had allocated his morning and the top of afternoon to track down Dr. Armstrong. Emily Armstrong – he liked the way it sounded. He considered visiting Shelby to ask if he knew her; if he could put them in touch, but he quickly realized how immature the approach was. Harry was thirty years out of high school. So, Harry took a chance, and drove over to the hospital and found Doctor Armstrong holding up a long line in the cafeteria. She was tapping a finger to her cheek trying to make a decision. Harry turned to a young intern at the end of the line who looked like he hadn't slept since the day he was born.

"What do you suppose she's doing?" Harry asked the yawning man.

"Trying to decide between the spoiled egg salad or the rancid tuna sandwich."

Emily Armstrong was surprised to see Harry. She appeared to be exasperated at first. Harry knew there was something she wasn't telling him. He used this to his advantage. Fresh off his stimulating shower, he decided to pay her a visit. And this wasn't all about her holding back. Harry thought it was time he got out and enjoyed the company of an accomplished woman. After shifting her weight several times, Emily Armstrong agreed to an early dinner.

Emily Armstrong said with a bit of levity, "It's obvious you don't get out much."

"I blame myself," he said shrugging. His finger found a hole in the checkered table cloth. Harry winced as he took a closer look around the restaurant. There was an exposed light bulb dangling over the bar. The wall calendar posted a previous month – possibly a previous year. Harry chose not to look any closer.

"I'm very sorry about this place. Especially after the lunch you had to endure. We can go somewhere else."

His date fluttered a hand in the air, dismissing his comment. "The restaurant's name, by the way, the translation is 'the wolf's mouth,' but the expression in Italian literally means good luck."

"Probably not a good idea to wish your patrons good luck before they dig into a dish of calamari," he said breaking off a small piece of bread.

The waiter was halfway to their table when Emily Armstrong said, "We'll start with an order of calamari and two Manhattans, up and sweet with Maker's Mark."

"Jack Daniels," the waiter said.

"That will do," she said.

The waiter turned on his soft heels and left them alone. Harry looked at her with a questionable expression.

"I suppose you do drink?"

"Sometimes when my mouth is open," was his quick reply. "It's convenient." He didn't know what he was saying. He was nervous.

"You chose the place. We should take it on." She made a funny face that included a smile.

"All right," he said. "I like the way you think."

She chuckled. "Have you read the Yelp reviews?"

"I didn't get that far." Harry was feeling guilty again. There was a method to his madness, but he couldn't explain it to her. The place was a bad move. He should have done his own dirty work and taken her to a respectable place.

"One of the reviews said something like, it's the kind of place where the waiter throws food at you and sometimes you have to duck. There was another one that mentioned it's not the kind of place where you eat and run. When you see the place, you should just run for it, or something like that."

Harry knew he was wearing a grin the entire time she was speaking. He was quite pleasantly surprised by her sense of humor. Her demeanor was completely different outside the hospital setting. The drinks arrived. They clinked glasses and sipped at the same time. They noticed the waiter was standing in the wings awaiting their opinion.

Harry sensing the importance of the moment said, "Did you make these?"

The waiter bowed slightly. Emily sipped her cocktail without breaking eye contact with the waiter.

"Very good," Emily offered. To Harry she said, "At least we know they can make a good drink."

The waiter took a few steps backward, nearly stumbling before righting himself and moving off.

"I was surprised to see you this afternoon," Emily said.

"Well, certainly without injury," Harry replied.

"Without a flesh wound or head wound. Yes. I'm pleased you stopped by." Then she looked at his face the way a doctor would. "And it looks like you're healing nicely."

"Well, I believe I promised to veer safely away from anything resembling a head-on collision."

"I want to cut right to it Harry. I'm usually very good at being direct, especially in the context of my profession, but…" she hesitated.

Harry wasn't sure what to expect. Was she working herself up to asking him to the prom? Or did she want to know what his favorite color was? His astrological sign, perhaps? In any case, while she was hesitating, he decided he would be ready for her: *Yes, I'll go to the prom with you. Hamilton Blue. Virgo.*

Emily looked away from him. She brushed one of her long fingers against her lower eyelash. She redirected her cerulean blue eyes, aiming them directly into Harry's line of fire. She was going to tell him something serious. Harry didn't know if he was ready for it. *Uh oh, here it comes*, he thought.

"I was at the meeting with your wife. Your wife Felicity." She uttered the name with her eyes closed. "Her last meeting. It was an empowerment gathering for professional women in the community. It was nearly the end of Women's History Month and someone must have tapped some idiot on the shoulder and said, *You'd better hurry up and do something*. It was organized by the borough president's staff. He arrived at the meeting with his lap dog, explaining that he was the son of a woman and he married a woman; in his mind this qualified him to lead the discussion. After about ten minutes of speaking nonsense, he wished us luck in our professional lives and left. Cold hors d'oeuvres and warm chardonnay followed. Your wife was particularly appalled by the wine selection."

"Okay," Harry set his drink on the table. *Now what?* he thought.

"I followed the story. According to the reports, Felicity was found to be legally drunk, the major factor leading to her car accident."

"Drunk driving. That is correct." Harry felt the heat on his face.

Sensing his growing irritation, she said, "I'm not judging Felicity."

Harry's vision narrowed. He felt a migraine coming on and it was not the song he wanted to hear. It was reminiscent of the migraines he experienced after Felicity's sudden and absolute demise. He didn't come to this lousy restaurant to go over Felicity's last night on earth. Certainly not over cocktails. He barely made it through his discussion with Shelby.

"Sometimes Felicity overdid it," he said it softly, out of the side of his mouth. He was conscience-stricken. To hear the words spilling out of his mouth, he felt like he was betraying her. He should have said nothing.

"The thing I've been wanting to tell you. What I've been wanting to tell you since…is this," Emily Armstrong paused and took a deep sip of her drink. She wiped the lipstick stain off the rim of the glass with her pinky.

"Ironic, here I am drinking this down like lemonade and…" she frowned, reprimanding herself.

Harry heard enough. He was aware he was about to sabotage their whole thing, but he couldn't help himself. His heart began to race. He wanted Felicity's name erased from the playbook.

"Emily, I suppose I asked you to dinner to hear you say something like, 'I endured a lousy marriage, my job is rigorous and it's time to get out into the world again.' And then I would explain how difficult it's been for me dealing with my grief. I suppose I have to move on too. Then we'd find something to laugh about over a little cappuccino. I'd introduce you to my dog. Then we'd plan to go to the theater without inviting Lolly – that's my dog's name."

She sat at attention in her chair. "Well, that's rather presumptuous of you, Harry. Why would you speculate about my marital status?"

"Well, why else would you agree to a lunch or dinner date or whatever this is?"

"A date? Is this what this is?"

"An early dinner date, er…a meeting?"

"I've been wanting to tell you something. When you showed up today, you made it easier for me."

Harry felt his face burning with embarrassment. He certainly wasn't going to search for a wedding band on her finger. And here he thought he was on a first date of sorts. What an idiot. He couldn't look at her.

"I came here out of respect for your wife. I thought there was something you should know. Granted, it has taken me a long time to work up to this. But when I saw you in the ER…" She started to rise. Harry put an uncomfortable hand on her wrist and then realized how inappropriate it was. Before he could retreat, she pulled her hand away and remained seated.

"Emily, I'm sorry, what did you want to tell me?"

She looked away from him before deciding to proceed. She took a few measured breaths and continued, "Your wife wasn't drinking. I spent the evening with her. She seemed determined to see something through. I don't remember what it was. But she was drinking sparkling water."

"Did you go to the police?" It sounded like an accusation although Harry didn't mean it to be.

"You're damn right I did. Any other questions?"

Before he could gather his thoughts, she rose and marched out of the restaurant. Harry sat there frozen. He felt like a horse's ass for presuming Emily Armstrong would have any interest in him, a formerly sedentary fat man who was nothing now but a frail sedentary man. But he remained angry with her for waiting four years to share her account of things.

If Felicity wasn't driving under the influence...Corbin Reece tries to get to me – then he commits suicide. Harry's mind was trying to work things out.

The calamari arrived, but it wasn't delivered by the waiter, but by the owner Nicky Sotto. He was about 60, impressively shouldered, and his hands were as large as a baseball glove. He wore a 1970s' patterned sports coat that actor James Garner might have worn in the old television show *The Rockford Files.*

Sotto observed Harry and with a smirk he said, "Women – you can't live with them and you can't shoot them, or can you?" Nearly six decades in his new country and he held onto the Italian accent he inherited from his parents.

"What are you going to do?" Harry shrugged; he realized quickly Sotto was the reason he came to the crappy place. He put away his sad face and played along. It was the plan from the beginning.

Sotto gestured to the waiter who tiptoed over with two shots of Limoncello. He placed them on the table. Harry made a gesture and Sotto sat down in Emily Armstrong's abandoned seat.

Harry's cursory research led him to the restaurant. Building Department Records showed that the van der Donk Funeral Home Emporium and In Bocca al Lupo were owned by one Nicky Sotto. If Sotto had a partner as the sad man at the funeral home mentioned, there was no record of him. A few more seconds of research told Harry that Nicky "No Doz" Sotto had lived his life in and around the mob. He was arrested several times on assault charges and had spent time in jail. He was an enforcer in his youth. The moniker "No Doz" was earned according to reporters covering his trials – he enjoyed testifying on his own behalf. He would talk the courtroom into a stupor, ultimately amusing the jury, and frustrating the opposing counsel. But you needed No Doz because Nicky Sotto could talk until you fell asleep. He never gave any of his bosses up and was a well-liked player on the team.

Sotto slid the shot of Limoncello in front of Harry with one of his knuckles. "Get the taste of her right out of your mind."

"Right out of my mind. Uh, okay," Harry said. He took a sip. "Thank you."

"I can see you need a good woman." Sotto snorted something deep into his throat and then tossed the Limoncello back like he was a gun-for-hire at the old saloon.

"Well, you can see how my date went."

"I gotta place, full service. Private, very private. For a moderate price, complete satisfaction."

"A what kind of place?"

"A relaxation place, for the man."

"And then I get to go home alone afterward. That's the real kick, right?"

"You got it. You're your own man. Who feels better than you?"

"Is it a union shop?" Harry thought he was being amusing, but Sotto's lips did not move.

"I'm offering you something for a man, you're making fun?" he said as he pinched one of his eyebrows between his thumb and index finger.

"Oh, no. I'm sorry. I would be a fool to mess with a man with your shoulders. And your hands. I've never seen catcher's mitts like those. Why would I want to incite you? I say stupid things sometimes."

"Tough work makes a man tough," he looked over his guest's hands until Harry held them up for a full inspection.

"I'm a lightweight. I try to use my brain, when it works. Speaking of your place, do you own a quaint funeral parlor on the North Shore?"

There must be something with the seat across from him, Harry thought, because like Emily Armstrong, Sotto suddenly shifted his weight and his demeanor darkened.

"The place is busted," Sotto growled.

"Busted?"

"I have to throw a coat of paint on the walls."

"Yeah, but you might disturb the fleas." Harry laughed; Sotto did not.

"And who wants to know?"

"Well, I'm the one asking the question. So, I guess I want to know." Harry was losing patience with Sotto. There was nothing much about the man to like. Harry wanted to get out of there quickly, without getting hurt and with some helpful information if possible.

"A friend of mine was laid out there. I was told that his going-away party was paid for by an anonymous benefactor."

"So, so what? That's good."

"I'm a friend of the family. They want to be able to thank someone properly."

"Business is business."

"What does that mean?"

"It means, it's none of your business. It's my business."

"Nicky, come on…"

"You know my name now too?"

Thinking quickly, Harry said, "Everybody knows you, Nicky."

"Nobody like you knows me."

"I want to be able to tell the family something. What about your partner?"

"My partner, eh? My partner left the business. Tell the family of yours they should be grateful and say to them business is business."

"Business is business, yeah okay," Harry said whining; losing patience.

"You don't know much, do you, my nosy, nosy friend?"

"I understand the pitfalls of living a provincial life."

"You're a stupid man," Sotto huffed.

"I know that if I lifted weights and put steroids on my peanut butter and Nutella sandwich, I'd feel like less of a man than you think I am right now. I know if I stuck my finger into your ear and felt the mushy part of your brain, you'd continue to say dopey things, which makes you an even bigger horse's ass than me. Who's stupid now? How am I doing, Nicholas?"

Harry couldn't prevent the train from coming off the tracks. Sotto disgusted him. He was a thug, and now he was in the business of selling women. Selling them out for the price of a happy ending. The entire time Harry was on his rant, he watched Sotto's face flinch, pinch, and tighten. It encouraged him to continue flicking him with his words.

When Harry finally sat back and took a breath, the aging bully exploded. He pounded a fist on the table. The drinks tipped over. The calamari bounced on the floor.

The words burst out of his mouth, his accent full blown. "You cann'a talk'a to me like'a I'ma man in'a cheap'a suit."

"Forgive me if I'm wrong, but I think I just did. Business is business, my friend." Harry rose from his seat.

"You come in here and insult me like this. Where do you think you're going?"

Harry saw a reflection in the fish tank. This was no seductive echo, not this time around. There were two goons, big ones, plodding around in the background – waiting for Sotto's high sign. Harry had a feeling they weren't busboys. They were broader than the liverwurst twins and they were blocking Harry's path to the outside world. Virile-looking 30-somethings with trimmed eyebrows and muscles on top of more muscles. Harry noticed one of the fish had died and was floating at the top of the tank. Harry took it as an omen, and knew he had to figure a way to get himself out of the mess he stupidly put himself in.

Harry pointed to the fish tank. "By the way, one of your appetizers just got eighty-sixed."

"Shame. How about I name it after you? In your memory. What do people call you?"

"I get called a lot of things."

"You're funny now. Later, no. Maybe I should call you the dead fishy man. I'd start praying. Prayer is gonna be the *theme* of the day. See, I know words too. Theme. How's that?"

"I wouldn't be too impressed with yourself. It's a small word. And about your suggestion? The name doesn't roll off the tongue. I'll pay my check when I return from the little hoodlum's room, okay, Nicky?"

"Yes, you will pay," Sotto said with a contemptuous smile.

Harry rose from his seat and casually followed the restroom sign to the stairway circling downward. Harry hurried down the stairs the instant he was out of Sotto's view. His smartass mouth put him in deep trouble. He was keenly aware of the certainty of seeing Dr. Emily Armstrong sooner than expected, but in the ER, all broken up into human jigsaw puzzle pieces. And that was the best-case scenario.

He found himself in a lower-level hallway blathering, "Business is business, all's fair in love and war, first things first, I'm a marked man."

He broke out into a cold sweat. He was hyped-up. Claustrophobia and fear of bodily trauma were front and center.

The hallway resembled the constricted confines of a submarine. Harry rushed into the restroom. He slammed the door and threw the tiny lock behind him. *It couldn't keep a Smurf or a small boy with the runs at bay*, Harry's inner voice screamed. He exhaled with relief when he saw the window. It was a small window, but Harry was hopeful. With a little luck, maybe he could avoid being heaved into a six-foot-deep ditch. He stepped onto the sink and wiggled through, tearing his shirt. He bought the damn shirt at the Gentlemen's Warehouse for $79. It was a crappy shirt and like most of their inventory, overpriced and generally poorly made.

"Don't ever shop there again, Harry," Harry said as he lowered himself onto the catwalk below deck. His hip screamed in pain, but he kept his mouth shut. The catwalk led him to a parking area to the left of the restaurant's main entrance.

As Harry climbed into his car, he could see the back of one the goons guarding the entrance from the inside. He heard the other one screaming for help. His body was lodged in the tiny window. The inside goon finally figured it out. He bolted through the front door and ran after Harry's car. He was stiff and awkward; it looked like his joints needed oiling. He didn't stand a chance of catching Harry. Nonetheless, Harry was in a full-blown panic. "Holy crap," Harry said to himself. His trembling hands strangled the wheel as he drove away.

"Holy, holy, bloody fucking hell," he spat out. Collecting himself, he said apologizing, "Pardon my vernacular."

Chapter Seventeen

Harry awoke the next morning in a tangle of blankets. His bedding betrayed him, and he wasn't thrilled about it. It was too early for human interaction. Darkness was still sitting outside his window ledge. Not that Harry was so eager for human interaction after the previous day's journey into stupidity.

It was early; he knew he wouldn't be able to go back to sleep. He'd have to do something. Do something about something. Do something about this Felicity business. And Harry was certain he couldn't do anything before coffee.

Harry heard himself groan. He thought he sounded like a humpback whale vocalizing during breeding season. Harry had the misfortune of catching a whiff of his breath. Truly cringe-worthy. Maybe the song he was singing was pleading with him to brush his teeth.

Harry covered his mouth with one hand. His shoulders swooned but they were not relaxed. His body felt miserable all over. Uncle Sebastian would say it this way: *miz-a-bull.* Harry kicked off the blankets with his heels. His hip pinged; his back was as stiff as an ironing board. Another rotten night's sleep. Sights and sounds of the apoplectic Nicky Sotto were beating inside his head throughout the night.

"You cann'a talk'a to me like'a I'ma man in'a cheap'a suit."

Harry's nightmare played over and over again like a needle stuck on vinyl. Harry thought it was a telling response. It revealed Sotto's insecurities, relating to his family's experiences as immigrants in their new country. Harry rolled around searching for pencil and pad. Maybe Sotto's sentiment was something he could use if he ever decided to write something other than a shopping list. He quickly gave up on the idea and stumbled toward the shower. He wanted to forget all about Nicky Sotto.

Harry ran the cold water, but immediately changed his tune, "The hell with this."

By the time Harry emerged from the hot shower, his fingertips were so wrinkled he wasn't sure if he could manage the most basic pancake roll. He plodded downstairs and drank a tall glass of water he was "cultivating" in the fridge. Cultivating: the act of placing a tall glass of water into the refrigerator at night. In the morning the water would be chilled to Harry's liking. That's how Felicity described this dotty habit of Harry's. Felicity often discovered several glasses of water cultivating in the fridge. This either amused or annoyed her depending on the kind of fires she was putting out behind Harry's back.

Harry toasted a framed photograph of Felicity and said, "I blame myself, my love." A tear quickly sat on his lower left eyelid. He immediately thought of an interview with Vice President Joe Biden who recalled a story about grief. Decades ago, a former governor of New Jersey explained to him, one day the memory of a lost one would bring on a smile as quickly as it did a tear. Harry wasn't really there yet. Not with any consistency.

Harry drank down his cultivated water and felt somewhat refreshed. He noticed his shriveled fingertips had bounced back. He was trying to decide if he was hungry when he realized Lolly was nowhere in sight. She usually emerged to greet him in the morning. Harry walked over to the laundry room. Lolly was sound asleep atop her padding of many blankets. Harry noted the gray in her muzzle and admitted for the first time the big girl was getting older. She was 5 years old. Harry knew these majestic dogs didn't have the lifespan of a turtle. Harry got down on his knees and stroked Lolly's face until one of her bloodshot eyes opened.

"Good morning, girl. I know it's early, but what do you say we get a little easy exercise this morning?"

A half an hour later when Harry reached for the knob, he realized the kitchen door was unlocked. Harry shook his head confusedly. *I must be losing my mind, forgetting to lock the door at night*, he thought. Five minutes later, Harry and his best girl Lolly were taking a leisurely walk through the woods at Clove Lakes Park. Harry forgot about his mental lapse while Lolly was showing absolutely no interest in the darting squirrels. The morning sun was rising through the thinning forest. The leaves had changed color while some had fallen away completely. Some of the naked branches looked like sickly arms reaching toward the sky in an act of desperation.

Harry turned up his collar after a gust of wind caught him by surprise. Lolly was off leash and slow to keep up. She kept peering over her shoulder. She wanted to be somewhere else. Harry was concerned about her lethargy.

They finally reached the dog run. There were no signs of the obnoxious Bobby Devine or Emma Kendall. Harry hadn't heard from Emma, and he was more than okay with that. He was feeling the need for distance; a chasm-sized length would do just fine. Harry was, after all, familiar and reasonably comfortable with his solitude. Certainly he could stand pat for a while longer, he thought. His discomfort with Emma's forwardness, his ineptitude around

Emily Armstrong, and his chance meeting with the younger Brenda Streeter whom he'd boyishly hoped he'd run into by accident was all the evidence he needed: he was not ready for prime time.

Harry took a few moments to go through a series of light stretches. He decided on a spot and got down on the leaf-covered soil and did three sets of twenty pushups. He was feeling stronger. Not so limber, but dare he put it out there, he was awake. This was particularly encouraging after a sleepless night.

The smaller dogs turned up and bounded around Lolly, happily sniffing, encouraging her to frolic. Harry wasn't paying much attention because his thoughts wandered back to Emily Armstrong. He shook his head bitterly. Yesterday's meeting was a disaster. He owed her an apology. He checked his watch. It was still very early. He had a notion how he could make things right. At least he should try.

"Let's go, Lolly."

He spotted her about twenty yards away, making her way back through the woods, the way they came. Even the little dogs had given up on her.

"Lolly?"

She continued bobbing ahead without interruption. Harry jogged after her. "Hey, where are you going, girl? Wait up for your old man!"

Big Bobby Devine stood there without a clue or a plan. His empty stomach growled. He didn't have breakfast, and he was starving. He hadn't swilled coffee or devoured his typical meal that included a bacon, egg and cheese on a roll, and an everything bagel with a double schmear (which doesn't make it a schmear at all) of cream cheese laced with jalapenos. He was following an impulse and shot out of the house as quickly as a man his size could. An impulse driven by panic. There were strange things happening around him. The weight of this baggage could possibly descend and suffocate him. That's the way he looked at it. Danger, exposure, the end. He wore his fear like a fetid cloak.

He'd gotten up twice in the middle of the night to take a shower. The aroma of his own nervous perspiration made him dizzy. He was compelled to follow this impulse. This sudden idea of his meant checking up on Harry Kavanagh. Devine was so clouded he didn't realize that his appearance outside Kavanagh's house could jeopardize everything. And yet there he was, in broad daylight standing across the street from the man's house with barely an idea in his head. He buttoned the top button on his overcoat and suddenly felt the need to pee. He shook out one of his legs hoping to stifle the impulse.

As far as Devine knew, some crazy motherfucker covered in debris hotfooted it from Corbin Reece's building as it was turning into mush. The escapee appeared to be doing a dance with a canvas bag. Devine feared he understood the value of the bag's contents: it was a prize retrieved from Reece's nest. It contained the narrative read back to him over the phone. Was that runner Harry Kavanagh? Devine wasn't sure anymore. He couldn't recall the make or model of the car the man fled in. It was some kind of older car. Or was it? The entire episode was a blur. It was a shock to see the man launching himself from the site. Soon after the incident, Devine received the shakedown call. The mystery man didn't sound like the son-of-a-bitch Kavanagh.

And then talking to himself in a feeble voice, Devine said, "And I haven't been able to piss straight ever since."

Devine was angry, but his ire couldn't suppress the jitters. He was perspiring in places he'd never thought possible. He wouldn't enjoy taking two showers a day. Taking off and putting on his clothing was an Olympic event. He would exhaust himself. He was in trouble. It was obvious – he and the dumb-as-a-rock Heastie missed something when they searched Reece's apartment. And now Devine was captive to a dead man's voice. A bedtime story from hell.

Devine stood on the sidewalk outside Arnold Fleck's house. He observed Harry Kavanagh's house from across the street. He had no idea what to do next. That's when Arnold Fleck came two-stepping out of his house whistling a happy tune. His doughy body was zipped up tightly, secreted inside his recently purchased gym attire. The local gym was a new haunt. Fleck learned the schedules of a few women he liked to binge watch. He'd accomplish this while taking a leisurely stroll on the treadmill. Unlike Devine, Fleck had a plan, albeit one rooted in his narcissistic fantasy. In his mind, he would be coming into a great deal of money. Fleck was convinced that after a few expensive dinners and his swallowing an M&M's-sized bag of Viagra, one or two of his new gym buddies would consent to having sex with him. It made perfect sense to Fleck.

"Good morning," Fleck blurted to Devine. "Are you the new paperboy?" Fleck said, thinking he was funny.

Devine nearly jumped out of his skin. He settled down and nodded to the middle-aged man. Fleck had a body like Harvey Weinstein. He wore an early version of Rudy Giuliani's comb-over atop his head. Fleck fiddled with those stray hairs. Devine anxiously circled the spot he was standing on because he couldn't think of anything better to do. Fleck was about to climb into his car, but the uncomfortable-looking big man was still riveted to the sidewalk. Devine dug into his pocket and rearranged his scrotum. He began cleaning the wax out of his ear with one of his thick fingers. Fleck recognized Devine's attraction to the house across the street. The house belonging to his nemesis, Harry Kavanagh.

"Maybe I can help you with something?"

"Oh, Mr. Harry Kavanagh..." Devine muttered, fumbling. He couldn't believe he said the name out loud.

"That's the guy you want," Fleck said, stabbing his middle finger in the air, then pointing it at Harry Kavanagh's house.

"Oh, okay," Devine said clearing his throat.

"Is he in any trouble? It would make all my dreams come true."

"Really? Why's that?"

"Maybe you're his doctor and you've come to give the bastard his annual prostate exam with the rusted arm of a backhoe."

"Excuse me?"

"He is a giant asshole, after all."

"Really?"

"Yeah, really. Maybe you're with the IRS. That would make me happy too."

"No, I'm, uh, with the police."

"Even better. Is he in any trouble?"

"Well, yes, trouble. Probably, maybe, but I'm not at liberty to say." *Not at liberty to say* – what a dumb-ass thing to say, he thought. Devine's breathing quickened. He lifted the perspiration under his eyes with his index fingers.

"He's a little prick with a big attitude. Terrible neighbor, lousy disposition; nobody likes him. His wife was the neighborhood drunk."

Devine flinched at the mention of Kavanagh's wife. He was relieved to leave her memory behind when he noticed his shoelace was untied. He thought he could muster the flexibility to bend and tie the shoelace. Generally speaking, he couldn't bend his body on any given day. Devine made the command decision: leave it alone. He nodded again to Fleck and walked off awkwardly with one-foot sliding inside his flopping Oxford.

Fleck observed Devine with curiosity. He was amused by his ineptitude. "Well, if there's anything I can do?"

No response from Devine.

"Ciao. Then that's all I have to say about that for now."

Devine lifted his chins. He turned back to Fleck with renewed vigor. "What did you say?"

"And that's all I have to say for now. Ciao."

And then it came to him. Devine abruptly stood erect, pulling his shoulders back; he couldn't prevent a childish smile from emerging. That's because *the voice* – it was familiar. He was face-to-face with the man on the other end of the shakedown call. It didn't make much sense at the moment. He was willing to overlook the minutia. He struck gold. The only thing that mattered.

Fleck dropped his car keys and while bending, he noted the big man was watching him. Staring at him; sizing him up. Fleck's stubby fingers fumbled with his keys as he squirmed into his car. He couldn't quite describe it in words, the peculiar way Devine was observing him. A third party might describe Devine as a kidnapper who had discovered his mark.

Devine kicked off his loose shoe and watched it sail into the middle of the street. He signaled for a touchdown with his arms. He walked away clumsily, but obviously relieved.

"What the hell was that?" Fleck exhaled.

Fleck backed his car out of the driveway in jerky movements. With the sneer of a madman, he drove over the fat man's shoe in the middle of the imaginary end zone.

Harry arrived at the hospital during the shift change. He parked on the street rather than deal with the hassle of the labyrinthine parking lot. Harry cracked two windows and left Lolly in charge inside the car. She yawned and struggled to sit tall in the passenger seat. Harry jogged across the street. As he approached the main entrance, he spotted Dr. Emily Armstrong heading in for a day's work.

"Eureka," he said, but not loud enough for anyone to hear. "Dr. Armstrong…Emily, please wait."

When Emily Armstrong turned around, Harry Kavanagh stopped dead in his tracks. She had a contusion beneath her right eye.

"What ha…?"

Emily Armstrong wore absolutely no makeup. Her skin looked pale and her eyes were busy recounting some recent dread. Her eyes were filling with water, but given her demeanor, Harry knew they weren't tears. She was angry. Very angry. She swallowed; pointed a finger much too close to his face.

She was surprised by her response. She took one step backward, to collect herself. Her words were calculated and spoken quietly: "It should have been very clear to me from the beginning that you were toxic."

She closed her lips tightly and bowed her head. She considered criticizing him further. Instead, she turned her back and walked away.

"What are you talking about?" Harry blurted.

He was stricken by her accusation. She continued without turning back. He shook off his distress and took a few quick steps in pursuit. He was closing in at her heels.

"You mean someone I know did this to you?"

"It was a warning," she said tight-lipped, without turning her head.

Harry was about to follow her inside, but the familiar security guard stepped directly into his path. His casual good nature was absent.

"Not today, not tomorrow, not any day," he said.

Harry understood the message. The guard assumed Harry was responsible for the bruise on the doctor's face. Harry wasn't in the mood to clear his name. He swiveled away from the man's glare and retreated. One foot after the other suddenly seemed to be a challenge. Harry was trying to make sense of what just happened. His breathing quickened. He pinched his temples with his fingers as he anticipated a migraine was about to make an unscheduled visit.

"And don't come back to this hospital unless you're in a coma. Otherwise I'll put you in one."

He didn't hear the man's threatening words spilling behind his back. There was a hollow-sounding clamor brewing in his head. Like the winds of a newly born Nor'easter. In addition, a simple beat, beat was beginning to emerge. This racket between his ears was posing a threat. Harry couldn't focus. He was in a fog. Harry ignored the horn of the hot dog vendor; his truck swerved to avoid him. The hubbub inside Harry's braincase ceased when he reached the other side of the street.

"Nicky Sotto," Harry said, seething. His temples began to pulsate with authority.

Nicky Sotto liked to arrive early to his barely-seaworthy restaurant. Mornings were tranquil. Even he grew tired of hearing his gravelly voice, ordering the idiots around. When he wasn't threatening to have someone worked over, he was operating his off-the-books massage parlor business, or his busted funeral parlor. So, he enjoyed his alone time. This meant spending time in the kitchen, his kitchen. All by himself. His grandmother and mother never allowed him to step foot in their kitchens. He would catch a beating if he was discovered. His grandmother's wooden spoon was as dangerous as a crowbar in someone else's hand. She swatted him so many times he had nightmares about the old battle-axe. Since his mother and nonna were long gone, he enjoyed the freedom to shuffle around in his own kitchen, to make a little something for himself whenever he wanted. There was nothing like kissing the rim of the espresso cup. Savoring the first taste without being threatened by an old *facciabrutt* (ugly face) swinging a piece of wood at your head. From his kitchen, Nicky Sotto would usually go to the office to select what bills to pay and which vendors to stiff.

Sotto was bent over the stove deep-frying little balls of dough that would emerge as Zeppoles. He was wearing a sleeveless T-shirt. He and his tribe would matter-of-factly call this a wife-beater. He was humming something or another. As things stood at the moment, he couldn't complain. Life was quiet.

Harry pulled up to In Bocca al Lupo. The street out front was empty save for a lime-green tinted 1972 Cadillac Coupe Deville. The car was in mint condition. It was something Harry didn't notice on his first visit. His mind was on other things. Harry was certain this was Sotto's little baby. *So, Sotto is here*, Harry thought. By the looks of things, he was alone.

Harry stepped out of his car. The calming sounds of lapping water and baying seagulls went completely unnoticed. Harry let Lolly out of the car and led her to the restaurant's entrance.

"Stay here, girl. Don't let anyone by you," he said firmly. He felt badly about his tone and gave her a quick pat on her head. Harry placed her there for backup, just in case. Lolly hedged, taking approximately fifteen seconds to sit firmly and comfortably. Her big body blocked the entrance. She guarded her spot like a drowsy sentinel. Anyone approaching would have to deal with her was Harry's idea. Harry peered back at Lolly as he descended the catwalk. Lolly still appeared to be a little loopy. Harry reset his mind on the task at hand and moved ahead. He counted on getting inside through the bathroom window. The element of surprise would be his only advantage.

Nicky Sotto put a zeppole in his mouth. His head tipped joyously from left to right. He did a little dance as the dough sprinkled with powdered sugar cooled inside his mouth. His happiness was brief. He turned his smiling face away from the stove. The smile was suddenly wiped clean from the surface of his big round face.

"Huh?" he said wide-eyed, his mouth full, and then a muffled, "Ooh, ouch!" The Zeppole burned his tongue. More importantly, a cast iron skillet was rocketing toward him.

Blood splatter shot from his nostrils. The career ruffian toppled backward like any number of Mike Tyson's victims. He hit the floor hard. Hot dough shot from his mouth. Blood was leaking onto his salt-and-pepper chest hair sprouting from the top of his formerly pristine wife-beater. The shattered man steadied himself on his stomach with his elbows. His vision was blurry. He thought he saw a pair of orange sneakers walking out of the kitchen. Sotto heard himself curse his mother and grandmother. Then he passed out.

Lolly's tail began to thump against the wooden deck when she saw Harry rising from the catwalk. Harry was relieved to see that his sidekick was a little more animated. He hugged her long neck as they walked side-by-side toward the car. Harry inspected his hands. Not a tremor to be seen.

Fifteen minutes later, as Harry drove through the North Shore area, he noticed he was manhandling the steering wheel with Sotto's blood specks on the sleeve of his jacket. The problem at hand was the jacket didn't belong to him. It was Jake's and it was one of Harry's favorite things to shrug into when he was in a hurry. A few years ago, one of Harry's arms wouldn't have made it through to the sleeve. He was that overweight. But now, it was a piece of cake, so to speak. It was a simple green field jacket with a *Ghostbuster*'s patch sewn on the right shoulder. Sewn on by you know who. Whenever he wore the jacket, he felt closer to his wife and to his older boy who was toiling at Parris Island.

"You must be going through hell, Jake," Harry said to himself. "Stay frosty."

Harry shut out the approaching memory of Felicity sewing on the patch. He considered turning the car around in favor of Manoscalpo's Deli, but the decision would take him out of his way. Harry's morning had already been complete. He was suddenly weary. He required coffee and some convenience. He wasn't going to get his wish.

Harry was scanning the area trying to decide on any one of the third-rate delis in the neighborhood. Out of the corner of his eye he spotted his least favorite set of twins. Those big boys who roughed him up inside Corbin Reece's flat. They were convening across the street. They were dressed in the same bargain-basement garb. Harry pulled the car over sharply and looked over at Lolly.

"Jesus Christ. What now, Lolly?" Harry exhaled.

Lolly didn't say anything. Harry felt the weight of her head in the crook of his elbow. Lolly fidgeted until Harry began rubbing her head and nose.

Harry observed the two as they chatted. Their duds appeared to be as wrinkled and tired-looking as the men themselves. Harry was able to distinguish the "nicer" hoodlum by the doughy expression on his face. That brother entered the deli that had a St. Pauli Girl advertisement in the window, complete with a shapely blonde clad in a German beer-hall outfit, and a robust magic-marker moustache. Harry's boys used to call this store the skelly deli. Jake once told him, "The only thing you can get in there is a bag of stale chips and an air-born virus."

Harry smiled to himself. He returned his attention to his dog. He thought about taking Lolly with him for backup but changed his mind when she yawned in his face.

"You stay here and relax. I'm going to handle this on my own." Lolly nodded a lazy gaze at him that Harry interpreted as a look of skepticism.

"If only I had some good quality kitchenware on hand. Well, if things don't go in my favor, at least I have decent health insurance."

Harry stepped out of the car. It was barely nine in the morning and Harry Kavanagh was on the move again. This time he was focusing on the liverwurst boys. It made sense to Harry to start with the hard case because the nasty boy was out in the open and accessible. Harry leaned against his car questioning himself, as any sane person might. Some truths are indisputable. The sedentary, pasty-faced college professor and occasional writer, who once lived a quiet, unremarkable life – he wasn't around this morning. Perhaps the old Harry was evolving into something else. By this time of the morning four years ago, Harry would be twisting himself out of bed, tangled in sweaty bedsheets, wearing only one sock, groggy; stubbornly attempting to squeeze into trousers that were a size too small for him.

Harry had shed the weight; the bereavement diet. He was attempting to exercise for the first time in years. He was coming to terms with the violence around him. He possessed the common sense to be fearful, yet the ruckus was becoming as commonplace as the accusations of fake news hurled by idiots. Harry Kavanagh had reached a new level and there was no such thing as turning back at this stage in the game. The fact that he was tired carried little weight. He was going to do what he was going to do.

Harry pushed himself off his car door and started across the street. Yes, he thought it was wise to confront the meaner brother first. Cut off the head of the snake sort of thing. Harry shrugged off the pain in his hip. His mind was so cluttered with thoughts of what he should do when he reached his target that he didn't notice he was walking with a pronounced limp.

These boys humiliated him once before. Harry's unexpected thrill of slinging the very large skillet into Sotto's nose had nourished him with enough confidence to carry him across the street.

Harry reached the other side of the street with the mean one in his crosshairs. Harry walked past the smiling German beer girl without giving her the time of day. The narrative below her shapely figure read: *If you like a Girl that has a deep golden color, distinctive full-bodied taste and 'hoppy' aroma, then the Lager is for you*. Harry had no time for silly posters, pretty girls with moustaches, or lousy beer.

Harry neared the alley dividing the buildings. He took a second to observe the young man from behind as he hunched over to light a cigarette. Harry watched him wander deeper into the alley where a dumpster sat.

The meaner-looking one, his name was George Anastasopoulos. He and his brother, Arsenios were originally from Canada where their families settled after arriving from Greece. They currently resided in upstate New York where they were employed at their Uncle Mike's diner. Their lives weren't very sexy. They cooked, bussed tables, and occasionally cleaned up chunks of vomit, compliments of the late-night college crowd. The young men also held on to a secret. It consumed and tortured them both. It compelled them to travel to Staten Island, the forgotten borough, to plead with the powers that be.

George innocently swung around and blew cigarette smoke from his lungs. His head twitched in surprise when he saw Harry entering the alley.

"What, no hello?" Harry said stifling a yawn. It ruined his attempt to appear in control.

The man-child flung away his cigarette in anger and puffed out his chest. "What do you want?"

"Let me see if I can get this straight. Now you're the sensitive one?"

"I don't like surprises."

"Funny words coming out of your mouth. By the way, you should know I might have died where you and your handsome brother last left me."

He spat air from his mouth, annoyed. "Died? What are you talking about? I hit you with a shoe."

"Apparently, the place was scheduled for demolition the following morning. I happened to be sleeping off your smack down when it began raining bricks."

George's thoughts were discombobulated; his answer verified it. "Well, we said what we had to say and now that's over. You lived."

"You said what? All I heard were the sounds of my face being used like a paddleball," Harry said.

Ten feet separated them. The kid attempted to leave the alley, but Harry stepped into his path. Harry could feel his heart racing. The younger man tried smoothing out his wrinkled coat as he considered his options. He bit down on his lip and arrived at a solution. He looked confident.

Harry read the slower-witted man perfectly. "I know what you're thinking," Harry said. "You're thinking, he's not so imposing. And you might be right. You, and the other half of your dopey brain, already jammed me up once before."

"Yeah, sounds about right."

"When you humiliate someone the way you did, it leaves a stain. There's only one way to get rid of it. If you want to come for seconds, you'd be helping us both out. This time I'm the one who's mad, and I see fear in your blurry eyes."

"You talk funny, sir."

"Sir? Then there is hope," Harry said. His laugh came with an exhalation, releasing some of his stress.

The sneer on George's face disappeared. His eyes opened wider. "Is that blood on your jacket?"

"I've had a busy morning." Harry could see the doubts clouding the mind of his antagonist.

"What?"

"Do you want to have a conversation, or are you up for something else?"

"My brother will be back in a minute," he said minus the brashness.

Arsenios turned the corner with his arms filled with Hostess Suzy Qs, several orange sodas, and bags of chips.

"Hey man, I got a diabetic's level of sugar here to go along with some chips," he said with his eyes peering into the brown paper bag. He looked up and observed the standoff. He looked bewildered. "What's going on here, sir?"

Harry smiled. "Another sir. Boy, do I feel a lot better. Okay, it's confirmed."

"What do you want?" The brothers said simultaneously, and then they glared at one another.

Harry shook his head, disapprovingly. He pointed to the junk food. "You're both going to have a stroke before lunch. Let's go to my place. I'll put on some coffee and make omelets."

The boys looked at each other with empty expressions.

"Let's keep our shoes on, shall we? I'm exhausted. I don't feel like fighting all of a sudden, do you?"

Harry walked past Arsenios and exited the alley. Harry turned back to them and said firmly, "Come on, let's go."

After seconds of indecisiveness, the boys took slow, awkward steps, following Harry.

"Throw that garbage out," they heard Harry say, with his back to them. Arsenios under-handed the junk to George. George juggled the mess in his arms, before shoveling it into the dumpster.

Chapter Eighteen

The news had broken. The state senator's harried aides were busy taking phone calls throughout the morning. Reporters from the city's newspapers and television networks were outside the office waiting for a statement from her. The local newspaper reporters had yet to arrive, having yet to put to bed less time-sensitive pieces such as *Child-Friendly Orthodontists*, or *The Island's Best Pizza Crust.*

The big news – the real news – the only news worth reporting was the cardinal of New York City held a morning press conference announcing a program to compensate people abused by the clergy. The announcement was met with surprise. Up until the morning's announcement, the Catholic Church seemed reticent to place themselves in a position to be sued by hundreds, possibly thousands, of people claiming to be victims. During his meeting with the press, the cardinal named State Senator Irene Roth as a friend of the Catholic Church and as someone who assisted him in shaping the parameters of the program. He went further, stating that he knew Senator Roth believed in transparency and justice and closure for the victims.

Irene Roth sat quietly behind her desk as her phone rang off the hook. She ignored the knocking on her door. She sat motionless with her hands folded on her desk. She could hear her employees scurrying outside her office. She was staring at her 20-pound ornament that had been a fixture on her desk for years. A block of solid molded glass resembling a fish tank. Inside were the frozen figures of six happy-looking, brightly orange-colored fish. Roth's mother purchased it at Abraham & Straus in downtown Manhattan in 1965. It cost nearly sixty dollars, more than she was making in an entire month as a part-time secretary at a lumber yard. Roth would always check in with the fish whenever she needed a pick-me-up. It reminded her of her mother and the happy-go-lucky fish always made her smile. But that was then. Before her life changed forever. Irene Roth knew her sentimental block of glass had been soiled with Felicity Kavanagh's blood. It had been wiped, but not cleanly, not professionally. You couldn't see the blood with the naked eye; however, Roth knew any third-rate police lab would discover the blood trace in seconds. She should have removed the glass from her office, but every time she reached for it, she became breathless, experiencing pangs of guilt and remorse. And so, it stayed, as a not-so-friendly reminder that she was complicit in a coverup.

Roth decided to pick up the ringing phone. Her movements were slow and trance-like. It was Thaddeus Calendar. He was irate. He called Roth a glory seeker and a political hack. Rage resonated in every syllable. He proceeded to hurl so many profanities at her she couldn't keep up. Roth moved the phone away from her ear and let it curse the room.

Calendar took a breath, then continued, "Not only did you make me look like an asshole with my constituents, but the governor's office called me this morning. Apparently, they were working on their own fucking plan that he was going to let me in on, but cardinal blowhard, the dick-sucker himself, with help from you know who, made everyone else look like a fucking doodling hair bag." He stopped to take another gulp of air. Roth heard him cursing at one of his aides. And then back into the phone, he said, "Oh, and a message from Albany, you can forget about their support. You screwed them. How are going to afford your fancy gym membership now, you glory-seeking see you next Tuesday?"

She said calmly, "Ever the wordsmith, Thad."

"Next time you order a slice of pizza from a serial masturbator picking his nose across the counter, he's going to say to his friends, 'You know who that fat bitch is? She used to be somebody.'"

"Yeah, I know, I used to be a contender. Nice going, senator. As original as always."

Irene Roth hung up on him without saying another word. She looked across at the little orange fish just beyond her reach and she smiled with her mouth. Her eyes, however, were unmoving and somber.

George Anastasopoulos inhaled two omelets without saying a word. He pushed away from the table and sequestered himself in Harry's living room. Without removing his rumpled coat or his shoes, he huddled on the couch and closed his eyes. Lolly followed him inside and watched as he mumbled to himself and passed out in a matter of seconds.

In the kitchen, Arsenios was finally able to speak freely, even though his brother had issued a warning before his departure. "I'm crashing for ten and then we have to make the bus," is what George said to his brother with a deep scowl dug into his face. Arsenios knew what he meant: don't say a fucking thing.

Harry moved gingerly around the kitchen. Gently cleaning up and puttering with little movements as to prevent any distractions. He poured Arsenios more coffee, but the refill sat untouched. Arsenios' head sank deeper into his chest. Harry had a lot of questions, but he wanted the answers to come from the young man without too much prodding. Harry wanted to gain his trust. He waited patiently on Arsenios as George's oversized heels were digging into his brand-new couch cushions in the other room. As if waking from hibernation, Arsenios lifted his head, looking more alert. He pushed the cup of coffee away. Harry sat down across from him and folded his hands.

"Truly sorry for assaulting you. Truly. We thought you were a friend of Reece's; that would make you a terrible person."

Harry took a breath and said nothing.

"We had an appointment with the state senator today, but it was postponed." Arsenios began to retreat inside himself. His head began to droop again.

"What was the interest in Corbin Reece? I have to ask."

"Interest?" he snorted, "It's an ugly story, Mr. Kavanagh. I don't think I can share it. I'm ashamed, deeply ashamed." And then he said in quieter tone, "We both are."

"Arsenios, I believe Reece was going to share information with me regarding the death of my wife. At least that's what I think was going to happen. He jumped out of a window before I could learn anything."

"Death of your...Oh, I see. I'm sorry." He took the time to take in the framed photographs of the Kavanaghs placed around the room.

Harry nodded without taking his eyes off him. "I wouldn't be prying if I didn't think it was necessary. And it is necessary, Arsenios. I believe my wife's death was not an accident."

Arsenios got up slowly and went to the sink. He poured himself a glass of water and set it aside. Lolly returned from the living room and pushed her head into the young man's hip. Arsenios patted her head. He spoke without looking at Harry.

"When we were kids, our parents sent us to a sleepaway camp. When we were young. So young. A priest, a Father Teagan, he was responsible for running the place. One of the camp counselors was Corbin Reece. He and this priest worked as a team."

Harry walked over, lifted the glass of water, and placed it in Arsenios's hand.

"There's been a lot written in the newspapers lately. I know where this is going. Please don't feel obligated to say any more about it."

Arsenios slugged the water back quickly. He gagged a little and then looked at Harry through moist, regretful eyes.

"My brother and I never spoke about those horrible moments until recently. All these years and never, we never talked about it. Those names were erased from our memories. Maybe it was self-defense. Last year, George blurted out their names during a nightmare. Then had a nervous breakdown. And after George recovered..." he said unconvincingly. His voice was drifting away.

Harry needed to keep the ball rolling and said, "You decided to track them down?"

Arsenios nodded as a tear dripped out of his left eye. "Teagan died years ago, but Corbin Reece was the chief medical examiner here."

"Why go to Senator Roth?"

"The deputy mayor of our town, she's a good friend. Someone we grew up with. The only person who knew our story, until now." He cleared his throat. "She heard through the grapevine that Senator Roth was an advocate."

"You went to her for help?"

"Yes, we did."

"And did she help you?"

"She told us she was working on a plan that would compensate children who were abused by priests or church employees. She was one of a few taking the initiative."

"You were going to speak with her about the priest and Corbin Reece?"

"Yes, we go through the Staten Island newspapers every day online, and after we read about his suicide, we came down here, but..."

"Whatever you want to say is okay."

"It took a lot to get George to travel. He's fragile. And I apologize again, sir. I'm sure you weren't thinking either one of us were fragile when we were assaulting you." He sucked the last drop of water from the glass. He carefully placed the glass down on the marble countertop.

"The irony is, the plan won't help us. It's not aggressive or comprehensive enough. We heard it outlined on the morning news. The statute of limitations for us has expired. The crimes committed against us happened long ago. We were just little kids."

"That doesn't necessarily mean you won't have legal recourse," Harry offered.

"Both men are dead. Teagan is long dead."

"People who do these horrible things, they don't do it once. Many more people will come forward. Your reportage will be corroborated dozens of times over."

"Maybe you're right, Mr. Kavanagh, but we're both tired now. I should get my brother home. We have to help our Uncle Mike run his business."

"I'd be happy to drive you to Port Authority."

"No, thank you. You've been very kind. We've come this far on our own."

"Yes, you have. You should be proud of your efforts." Harry swallowed and closed his eyes tightly. When he opened his eyes, he saw Arsenios observing him closely.

"What's wrong, Mr. Kavanagh?"

"Only my wife knew what I'm about to share with you." He moved back to the table and sat.

Arsenios shifted his weight so his back was leaning against the countertop. He watched and waited for Harry to continue.

"I was molested by a family member, multiple times. For years," Harry said.

Arsenios's body language became more rigid. He looked helpless. He took a few steps forward and stopped. He was incapable of saying anything. Harry put his hand up, gesturing, it's okay. Harry continued speaking, some restrained bitterness seeping from his voice.

"These unconscionable crimes. Don't let them define you. My wife was my life preserver. She gave me the freedom to make mistakes. She covered for me, comforted me, encouraged me. She preserved my sanity. And now that she's gone, I understand these episodes, these horrible deeds, they make me weak and they make me strong. This thing that happened to you and your brother, while you cannot erase it, surviving, fighting – dealing with it – it can make you stronger. Don't close your eyes to it, Arsenios."

George appeared at the doorway, observing them through probing, bloodshot eyes. "What's going on here?" His demanding tone made Lolly look sharply in his direction.

"Lolly, relax," Harry ordered. "You don't want her mad at you, George."

Harry looked from George to Arsenios. "You two have each other. Discover ways to deal with your pain and take care of yourselves."

"Hey," George interrupted, keeping a wary eye on the dog. "What did I say?"

Arsenios poked a scolding finger in his brother's direction. "Please, just shut up, George," Arsenios responded quietly, but firmly. He turned back to Harry and in a softer voice, "What about you, Mr. Kavanagh, what will you do now?"

A bone-tired smile slid across Harry's face. "Do you mean, can I take my own advice?"

"I mean about your wife?"

"I'm a late bloomer. I'm working on it."

"I'm very sorry about your loss, Mr. Kavanagh," Arsenios said.

Harry and Arsenios gazed in George's direction when they heard him clear his throat.

"Thank you for breakfast," George said. His expression was softer. It was nearly childlike. The anger and tension were completely washed from his facial features. "Thank you again, sir."

Chapter Nineteen

Sebastian (Sebe) Brazzano was in his 80s. He was propped in a beach chair in front of Montalbano's Bakery on the corner of Avenue U and West 7th Street in Gravesend, Brooklyn. He was clad in a sweatshirt dabbed with old paint stains. A blanket was wrapped around his legs and there was a worn-out Brooklyn Dodger's baseball cap tilted atop his shaved head.

Montalbano's Bakery was a family-run business now operated by old man Montalbano, who was born in America after his parents came over from Italy. Next door to the bakery was a Korean grocery.

Sebastian Brazzano lived around the corner on West 6th Street, in the house he was born in, in January 1932. A square of cement real estate between the bakery and the grocery, that was his spot. He and his beach chair laid claim to it decades ago. He got to survey his stomping grounds, tell old stories over and over again to his neighbors and friends. On occasion, old man Montalbano would shuffle out of his bakery and stuff a warm cruller in Sebe's pocket while he was holding court.

Sebe was partaking in a little verbal sparring with his spry neighbor, the Korean grocer who was not as old as he was. Sebe put a hand up like a don in a mafia movie and the give-and-take ceased. As Sebe began his oration, the other man seemed all too happy to be able to concentrate on his task at hand. He was arranging an array of colorful fruits and vegetables in storefront bins, displaying an impressive show of dexterity and speed for a man his age.

"Hey, if I told you this one before stop me. But if you wanna be my friend for life, you won't stop me. Because maybe this time I'll add something you never heard before. Maybe it has a different flavor. Different flavors are good. Maybe the story, it's true, maybe I'm telling a fib, or maybe it's the way it happened. Whatever happens, I'm gonna reel you in like a big fish. Yeah, okay?"

"Yeah, okay," was the quick response. The man bowed slightly and smiled without looking at Sebe. "Maybe you say whatever you want, and I pretend it matters much," he deadpanned.

"You got me there, Yoo Jin," Sebe, the first old man said.

Yoo Jin looked over at him and smiled. "What, no Eugene today?"

"How long have we known each other?"

"Many years too long."

"That means we're almost ready for the box. You know the box?"

"I can't die. I have children."

"Your kids are in their fifties."

"Someday when they grow up, then I can sleep in the box all I want."

"I'm feeling old today," Sebe lamented. "Not as old as old man Montalbano."

Yoo Jin interrupted his thoughts. "He's a teenager compared to you."

"Oh, well, I'm sorry. Sometimes you wanna pass things along, but then you think maybe your time is running out."

"Don't be sorry about anything my friend. Live for today."

"You can call me Sebastian from here on. No Sebe, no more. Sebe…okay? I will pay you back the same respect, the respect you deserve. You will be Yoo Jin forever."

"That is my name, but nicknames are earned. They are a sign of friendship." Yoo Jin looked over at his friend who seemed uncharacteristically stalled. "I have always felt your respect, even when you murder my name on purpose or by accident."

"Sometimes language ain't pretty, you know?" Sebe Brazzano smiled and then he couldn't help himself. He laughed. It was a raspy laugh. The release was just what the doctor ordered. It was a good laugh all right; it made him feel much better. He patted his chest until the rumblings of his compromised respiratory parts subsided.

"So then, I'm telling you this story. Okay?"

"Hurry. I'm almost finished here. Then I have to take my children to finger-painting," he said, enjoying his joke.

Sebe told him the story of his stickball days on West 6th Street and Avenue U in the 1940s. On Sundays, the mob would knock on doors on West 6th Street and give the order for everyone to move their cars "or else." Sebe, who was only twelve or fourteen at the time, was often paired with returning servicemen in their early-to-mid-20s. A stick ball team was comprised of four players: a pitcher (who doubled as the first baseman), a third baseman, a second baseman, and an outfielder. Sebe was the outfielder and an extraordinary ballplayer. He later went on to become a star player at Lafayette High School, then with the Brooklyn Royals, a storied sandlot team. He ended up in the Pittsburgh Pirates organization and came up a few years before the great Roberto Clemente. Sebe was on his way to becoming a major leaguer when he broke both legs thwarting an armed robbery outside a motel the Triple A Team was staying at. It took him nearly a year of rehabilitation to get his legs strong again. But he would never roam anyone's outfield again. With his baseball career over and a citizen's arrest already under his belt, he did the next best thing: he became a policeman.

"So," Sebe continued. "The mob would take bets on these games. It was like a tournament and it went on all day, all day. Thousands of dollars would pass hands and you know what my reward for winning was?"

"Yes," said Yoo Jin. "Six pennies and pretzel."

"Oh, yeah. And if I was lucky, one of the guys would buy me a chocolate egg cream soda."

"Yes."

"What, I told you this before?"

"Yes, and when you play the outfield, the ball would travel from West 6th Street, go over the buildings onto Avenue U too." He made a gesture toward the avenue where the street began to rise.

"Yeah, yeah. And as the only outfielder, I would have to track it down like DiMaggio, except Joe had it easier. I would run and run and had no idea whether or not a bus was gonna murdalize me as it came down from over the hill. Dead to rights I would 'a been. There were many times when it was close."

"Then you would have never lived to tell me the story, so many times," Yoo Jin said with a smile.

"Did I ever tell you the one about the old Madison Square Garden? How I snuck in and how I met Humphrey Bogart?"

Yoo Jin stood upright and did some gentle stretches. "That story? Let me think, oh yes. Forty-seven times last week alone," he said, straightening the cap on Sebe's head.

"Hey kid, you're sitting in my seat," Sebe said, doing a pretty good Bogie imitation. "And I told you about his hat, right?"

Sebe's friend nodded and said, "And one day the story will have the ending you have written for yourself."

"I hope so," Sebe said quietly, and he watched Yoo Jin enter his store. "Yeah, I hope so, but I may be running outta time."

Harry tossed and turned throughout the night. He felt terribly for the Anastasopoulos twins. Not much of a sleeper even with a clear head, Harry had those sad men on his mind. He sat up in bed and turned on the television. To make matters worse, he caught an early-morning breaking report: a news story was unfolding – approximately sixty athletes, girls and young women, some of them Olympic hopefuls, had come forward to accuse an Olympic team doctor of molestation. The abuse occurred over a period of years when the young athletes were away from home, while training or rehabbing at a USA

Olympic facility or at Michigan State University. The abuse spanned a period of nearly twenty years.

"What the hell is wrong with people," Harry spat out.

He ran his hands through his hair. He was sickened by the details. He knew in situations like these, the numbers would grow. Many more women would come forward. He couldn't watch anymore. He pointed the remote, but inadvertently changed the channel to one of those TV stations that cater to viewers his age. During a commercial break, Harry almost purchased a pillow that seemed to be the cure-all for just about everything, from male pattern baldness to chronic halitosis. Harry came to his senses in the nick of time. He had already dug into his trousers on the floor and pulled out his credit card. He was ready to pull the trigger. He wanted the night to be his friend; he wanted to sleep better.

Harry was fully prepared to make a purchase he would certainly regret later on. He flung the credit card out of his room for good measure. He watched it sail into the hallway. It was well out of his reach. Crisis averted. For now. Harry decided he would sleep better knowing he couldn't purchase the lousy pillow from the pie-faced salesman begging for his business.

Harry often reached for his credit card whenever he became hypnotized by an infomercial. He purchased the peanut butter maker that produced a feces-colored spackle, the ice cream maker that made ooze and the inverted umbrella that flew better than a kite. If Felicity picked up the droning sound of the TV from another room, she would often shout at Harry, with a certain amount of amusement in her tone, "Get away from the TV!" or "For the love of God, put your credit card down!"

Harry shrugged himself free from his reverie when he heard the television theme by Lalo Schifrin playing over the end credits of the show he used to watch when he was a kid. He was certain private eye Joe Mannix saved the day while he was daydreaming.

Harry felt compelled to get out early and begin his day with a flourish. He looked around for Lolly. She was nowhere in sight. She had obviously made the decision not to climb the stairs. Harry snapped off the TV and bounded toward the bathroom. Experiencing immediate stiffness in his lower back and a twinge in his hip, his eagerness and pace slowed considerably. He moved the curtains aside above the toilet; it was still dark outside. No surprise there. He turned on the faucet and slid under the hot shower.

After a second or two, Harry jumped – *What the hell am I doing?* He was still wearing pajamas. He didn't move immediately. His hand–eye coordination had been dulled by twenty years of inactivity. He was incapable of moving anywhere fast. Harry languished under the waterfall for a good ten seconds. His pajamas were completely soaked.

After drying off and changing, Harry found Lolly dozing beside the dryer. She looked up at him with a one bloodshot eye. He turned on the dryer. The heat and the vibrations sent her fast asleep.

The sun was coming up as Harry lumbered into the diner. He was feeling a little worked-over. His limp returned. The pain stayed with him until he sat at a two-top that hadn't been bussed. The place was packed and noisy; people were fluttering around him. Apparently, he wasn't the only morning person in town. A group of gray-haired husbands, retired he guessed, were bursting with tall tales and humorous stories about their wives. A small side of turkey bacon or maybe some oatmeal and then most of the crew would trek over to the mall for twenty loops around the Apple store.

Harry's eyes and ears followed the activity around him. He wondered about his own future for a second. Was this what he had to look forward to? He hated the mall.

Harry peeked longingly into the empty coffee cup left behind by the previous insomniac. Sitting at a table that wasn't cleared was a classic no-no. Harry lived on the planet long enough to know he had committed a crime somewhere between a misdemeanor and a murder. He would sincerely apologize to the busboy or busgirl and then be very polite and patient. The coffee pot would eventually return and so would his pulse.

Harry thought he heard his advice to Arsenios Anastasopoulos echoing inside the abandoned coffee cup. Harry was still in his own world, dinged-up and sluggish. Of course, he wasn't in his right mind. A conclusion Harry came to on his own very quickly. But his advice was sincere; Harry hoped the twins would take care of themselves. Now, if he could only take his own advice and be kinder to himself. Harry acknowledged he was a work in progress. He hoped it didn't show too much. Felicity wasn't around to ease his pain. The brothers had each other. If they could realize that, perhaps they could turn a corner. That was Harry's wish for them. Harry picked up a half-eaten piece of rye toast. He considered it, but it was as hard as a shingle. He dropped it on the plate.

Thinking back to that horrible news story, Harry said aloud, "What the hell?"

"Don't know, sweetie. If I had all the answers, that cutie Justin Bieber would be serving me eggs," one of the waitresses on the move blurted out.

Two busboys came over and cleaned Harry's table in a jiffy. Harry apologized for his impatience. The Mexican youths smiled politely and headed off to rescue the next diner. That same waitress returned with a pot of coffee, a menu and a million-dollar smile. Harry watched her pour.

So, Harry was squatting at this diner, where he'd been several times before, trying to jump-start his day. Harry surveyed the landscape with curiosity. The staff represented America's latest wave of immigrants under siege: Mexicans and Haitians. The entire floor staff appeared to be in their late teens, or early 20s. They were a happy staff, working diligently with a comfortable flow. The waitresses were caught up on the lingo; Harry heard them refer to their customers as *hon* and *sweetie*.

The Polish matriarch behind the register, she was the owner, and another story completely. She was about Harry's age with big eyes and even bigger hair. From what Harry remembered about her, she wasn't born around the corner, but if you let her tell her story, she'd tell you she'd been around the block. Florrie had a habit of flirting with Harry whenever he cashed out. Harry stopped at the diner on purpose. He wanted to be around friendly people. Even though Florrie made Harry a bit nervous, she was no Emma Kendall. He wanted to be someplace where people knew him by name. On this particular morning, hon and sweetie were close enough.

After eating an embarrassingly large breakfast that didn't include turkey bacon or kale or anything organic, more coffee was poured. The waitress twisted her agile body around the two-top and made a skillful getaway with the steaming coffee pot.

"How's that, hon?" She said it with her back to Harry as she was already off to her next destination.

Harry threw back his fourth cup of coffee like it was a tall glass of ice tea. Where had the time gone? He rose from the table feeling bloated and guilty. He thought about taking his orange sneakers for a loop-around at the mall. His plate looked so clean he wondered if it would go into the dishwasher or simply be reused. The coffee-generated pulse in his temples was beating close to the danger marker. As he walked toward the front of the restaurant, he prepared himself.

"Well, hello there, dearie. You look handsome today," Florrie said as Harry approached the cash register. And of course, then there was *dearie*. The waitresses wouldn't take that one on. Dearie belonged to Florrie.

"Thank you, Florrie," Harry said with a reddish hue in his cheeks. "You look as bright and as lovely as ever." He smiled back at Florrie.

Today was a big day. He was going to have a sit down with his Uncle Sebastian. Sebe Brazzano was a lot of things. He'd been a New York City cop for nearly thirty years back in the day. A copper in the days when President Gerald Ford unceremoniously told New Yorkers he wasn't going to bail them out. It was a time when every day looked like bad weather; when every nook of the city was dangerous and mysterious.

Harry trusted his uncle like "nobody's business." An expression he learned from the Brazzano side of his family. "Not for nothing but," as Sebe often said – *that* was another one of those prized expressions. A saying that expressed either the importance or the lack of importance of the status quo. Not for nothing but – in this case the preface emphasized the importance of the moment. Not for nothing but, the men were going to go over Harry's list and decide whether or not Harry was out of his mind or out of his league. So this was very important.

Was there enough floating around to believe Felicity's death was something other than the result of too much lousy chardonnay? Uncle Sebe spoke plainly. He would let Harry know.

Florrie's big eyes swallowed Harry whole. She was waiting on him. Not that she minded. She liked to tease him. Harry couldn't find his credit card, and he was flustered. He remembered flinging it out of his bedroom. Harry finally surrendered some wrinkled cash. Florrie gave Harry his change along with a big smile.

Harry visited the little diner for validation. Florrie gave him a big wave goodbye through the window. Harry got a dose of what the doctor ordered, plus more caffeine than he could handle.

"Uncle Sebe, here I come. For better or worse," Harry said as he climbed into his car.

Chapter Twenty

By the time Harry showed up at the corner of Avenue U and West 7th Street, Sebe Brazzano had already taken his first nap of the day in his beach chair. Old man Montalbano waddled out of the bakery and handed Sebe a cup of espresso.

"Thank you, Frankie boy, who's better than you?" He bowed his head out of respect.

Montalbano saw Harry's approach and asked, "Hey kid, you wanna one?"

Harry thought Frank Montalbano's accent resembled Nicky Sotto's. "No, thank you, Mr. Montalbano. I've had too much high-test today."

Montalbano checked Sebe's proud expression and agreed with him, "Yeah, he looks good, no?" The old baker re-entered his shop clicking his tongue in admiration.

"You look good. You lost more weight. You look like you been working out." Sebe said.

"A few pushups here and there."

"Siddown kid. But you look tired though. Tired in the eyes." Sebe took a sip of the espresso and rested the cup atop an empty apple crate acting as a side table. "Lemme see what you got?"

Harry took a deep breath and unfolded a piece of paper he withdrew from his pocket. His uncle took it in his quaking hand. Harry grabbed a crate from the front of the grocery store and sat on it.

"Are you okay?" Harry asked noticing his shaking hand.

"Me? Solid as a barge," he pronounced.

Harry chuckled, "Solid as a barge?" He rearranged the blanket across his uncle's lap.

"Ain't a barge solid?"

"Okay, yes."

"You give up too easy. Good, I rest my case then. Lemme see some cheaters," Sebe said extending the other hand.

"Cheaters?"

"C'mon, Harry, you know what I mean. Gimme a pair of something I can read with, will you?"

Harry reached inside his jacket and pulled out a magnifying glass. "I was ready for you," he said handing it to Sebe.

Sebe made a face as he examined the magnifying glass. "You set me up. You're a wise guy, but this is much better than glasses." He looked over Harry's latest list.

Medical examiner Corbin Reece gives me a little high sign.
Wants to talk to me?
Nearly drown in front of my own house. No accident.
Mysterious woman with lilac perfume saves me?
Reece (medical examiner) commits suicide.
No one attends wake.
Anonymous payer foots bill at funeral home.
Nicky Sotto, not talking.
Attacked by the liverwurst twins at Reece's apartment.
They hate Reece. (Okay, got this figured out).
What is going on?
Emily Armstrong is assaulted. (Nicky Sotto).
What's going on?
Something to do with Felicity's death?
Reece connection, maybe. Emily's attack. I'm clueless.
What do you think? (Meaning me).
What to do next?
I don't know.
Uncle Sebe?

Harry watched his uncle go over the list. Harry had some answers already. Those answers led to a dead end. The Anastasopoulos boys were not trying to get to Harry; they were trying to secure a meeting with the state senator, hoping for some justice. The "woman" who rescued him from drowning in his own zip code was Shelby Martin. Harry did believe Corbin Reece wanted to reveal something to him. Someone did attack him outside his house perhaps believing Reece had passed along information or was about to. Something bothersome yet oddly in his favor clattered around inside Harry's brain: maybe Reece was murdered? That would mean something too. It would add a little zip to his list. He could put that one in his *one-for-me* column. His mind was firing with encouragement and doubt. He hadn't even bothered to tell his uncle about Reece's "career" as a child molester. He wasn't certain it was relevant. It might just get in Sebe's way. Harry feared it would clutter his uncle's mind and weaken his argument.

As Harry watched the old man consider the information in front of him, he was struck by a screwy thought: the attack on Emily Armstrong, what if it *wasn't* Nicky Sotto or one of his cronies? Harry didn't get a straight answer. She never did say who assaulted her. This would strengthen his argument. Harry considered that Sotto looked shocked when he was attacked. *But who wouldn't be shocked by a runaway skillet?*

Harry ran it through his mind from the beginning. Someone kills Reece, or he commits suicide before he has a chance to say something. Believing Harry has some information or evidence pertaining to Felicity's death, he is clubbed outside his house. The attack did not grant the anticipated results, so Emily Armstrong is assaulted, a warning meant for him – to leave things alone. As Harry was thinking this through, he was tapping on his temple with his index finger. Harry felt Sebe's hand rest on his wrist. His uncle's hand was surprisingly warm.

"Relax, okay. Relax, kid."

"Okay, what do you think?"

"I think, why would this Reece guy reach out to you?"

"Exactly."

"Wait, wait. Relax. Relax. This is your impression, correct?"

"Yes. He made a little high sign like in the old movies. He wanted to talk."

"Like in the old movies," he repeated, making a dubious sound with his mouth. "I love the old movies too, but…" Sebe's voice trailed off, and then the old man yawned. "Pardon me," he said.

Harry looked down, feeling foolish. Sebe tapped Harry's wrist firmly with one of his arthritic fingers, demanding his attention.

"There's no reason for this guy to wanna talk to you?"

"No, not really, no. Certainly not after four years."

"You're not friends, enemies, neighbors? You're nothing to each other, right?"

"Right. Nothing."

"And what you're saying is, the only thing he could tell you is something about Felicity's passing? Something fishy?"

"That's what I've been obsessing about."

"All right."

"All right what?"

"Do what you have to do."

"What does that mean? I mean, Uncle Sebe, I know what it means, but what are you telling me?"

Sebe took a deep breath and he began to cough. Harry drew closer to him. Sebe warned him away with a sturdy stop sign: his open palm. The rise in his chest calmed and he began to speak.

"Listen, you were lazy in your marriage. I'm sorry to tell you. You allowed Felicity to do everything for you and she did. With great love and asking for nothing in return, right? She's gone now, and you have this feeling, maybe it's nothing, maybe it's something, but you want to do this for her. So…"

Harry was stung by his uncle's words. Harry had no idea how transparently lazy he must have been. There was nothing he could say to defend himself. Uncle Sebe was right.

"So?"

"You should go ahead, play Mister Detective, eh. Even if you're wrong, your heart says you wanna do something for her. There's nothing wrong with not being lazy for your wife. Even now."

"It wasn't the ringing endorsement I was hoping for. Of course, you're right. Where do I start?"

"Talk to people who were at that last meeting she was at."

"That was years ago."

"Do the work. Track them down."

There was something else Harry wanted to tell his uncle.

"Dr. Emily Armstrong," he said.

"What is that, a new show on CBS? She carry a gun?"

"The friend of mine on the list. I'm thinking it was a warning for me. She was at a community meeting Felicity attended. She was roughed up the other day after we had lunch together. She swears Felicity was sober the night she died."

"You got three things: the high sign from the dead guy, the attack outside your house, and okay, this woman's story now. Oh, and her being mugged. Well, that's something, no? That's four things."

"So, what you're saying is, I'm not losing my mind?"

"I'm saying yes. I mean, no. Listen, I'm telling you, this stuff may be something. And go through Felicity's emails, the last few months especially."

"I completely forgot about her emails."

"Well, you're no detective, not yet," he said with a wan smile.

"That's the most obvious start. It didn't cross my mind."

"You need to do something else."

"What's that?"

"Check in with your precinct. Talk to the commander and some of the cops who were at the scene."

"They may think I'm a nut."

"Nobody likes to be told they missed something, especially cops. But this way, everything is on the books, out in the open. In case anyone complains about you nosing around, the cops will put two and two together and remember, it was the nut with the conspiracy theory. May save you a rough time down the road."

"They're not going to listen to me. Sounds like a waste of my time."

"Everybody knew Felicity in the neighborhood; sometimes a no switches into a maybe. Sometimes it shakes the whole thing up and sometimes nothing matters. But you don't know nothing until you do the work."

Sebe looked tired; Harry rose as Sebe handed the slip of paper back to him. Sebe slid the magnifying glass into his pocket. "I'm keeping this, wise guy."

"Sure. Thanks, Unc," Harry said.

Sebe's eyes peered from under his weary lids and looked Harry over with a mixture of sadness and pride.

"If this turns out to be true, if someone harmed our beautiful girl, you get the coward. You nail that bastard, but good. You hear me?"

Harry nodded.

"And remember, if there's one guilty guy out there, then there are the rest of them. The low guy on the totem pole always gives up the next bad guy and so on, and before you know it, everybody is hung out to dry. Criminals are only smart in the movies. In real life, they're a bunch of dumb mooks. They're dumber than dirt."

Harry shook his head at that last bit of wisdom.

"There's no loyalty among villains, thieves, and scoundrels. They're not part of some union. They don't look out for each other," Sebe said.

Seconds after his declaration, Sebastian Brazzano's chin slowly dipped toward his chest. He quickly fell into a deep sleep. Harry made certain the blanket was tucked in. He caught Yoo Jin's eye behind his storefront window. Yoo Jin gestured that he would take care of Sebe. Harry smiled softly, thanking him.

Chapter Twenty-One

Harry Kavanagh couldn't sleep, yet again. He despised himself because he was watching more television than usual, and not the kind he enjoyed. He held his ground, bleary-eyed, watching TV ads for skin-tightening cream, one for the elimination of a double chin; the other to get rid of pillow-shaped bags under the eyes. There were exercise products, reverse mortgage ads, and insurance commercials for people over the age of fifty. By 4 a.m., Harry had seen more of Alex Trebek than he cared to. And after sharing part of his overnight with Oprah, whom he greatly admired, he grew tired of her familiar singsong aria.

"We get it, Oprah. *You love bread*," he said observing what he hoped was a glimmer of the rising sun outside his bedroom window.

He popped off the television and padded down the stairs. As he descended the steps, he did a cursory search for his errant credit card. He scratched his head and yawned. No luck. He shuffled through the hallway, checking in on Lolly in the laundry room, asleep atop her bunched-up blankets. Harry made it to the kitchen sink and filled the percolator with water. He fiddled with it over the stove and looked back at Lolly.

"Morning, my good girl." She didn't budge.

Harry opened the refrigerator and squinted into the harsh light. There was a deli container of olives stuffed with blue cheese, for the martini he promised himself a month ago, a dented half-gallon of milk, a few eggs (hatched by the backyard chickens), and some weepy spinach destined for the compost. Harry turned his back on the fridge and hovered over a stack of mail on the countertop. He flipped through the pile without reading. Harry was restless. He wanted the day to begin before its time.

"Let the game come to you." He'd heard sports commentators say it many times before. Let things flow naturally. Don't force anything. Everything will slow down, and opportunities will present themselves. It was good advice for stepping onto the court or into the batter's box, but in real life? Does it apply when you think your wife was murdered?

"I'll let you know," Harry said to himself without inflection.

It was Sunday. The day after his meeting with his uncle. Was this to be his first working day as a private eye? Harry tried to take his own temperature.

Things wouldn't come to him unless he was an active protagonist. Harry's body twitched. It was an awkward shiver. He attempted to cover the spastic move by outstretching his arms, to limber up. He startled himself when his fingers banged against the coffee pot.

"Ouch," he said. "Damnit."

Lolly poked her head up from a deep slumber. Her eyes were red and droopy-looking. She took an instant to consider Harry's clumsiness, and then she went back to sleep.

"I have to get out of the house," Harry said massaging his fingers.

An hour later, Harry was reluctantly jogging around the Silver Lake Reservoir. There was a clammy layer of mist in the air. He ran down his body's inventory. No signals of desperation were emanating from his hip or knees. Harry's mind began to wander.

He accessed memories of a younger Felicity at the beach, laughing while chasing after her two little men, Will and Jake. It reminded Harry he hadn't gotten a letter from Jake in a spell. His training was rigorous and the demand for sleep rightfully came first. Writing a letter to his father was not on the table. Harry wasn't offended. He knew the kid was under a lot of pressure from all angles at the godforsaken island. Harry remembered Jake was on a complete news blackout. The boy was fortunate. He didn't have to deal with the brutal political campaign playing out from every seam. Harry knew Jake was gearing up for something the Marines called the Crucible. The Crucible, the last challenge a recruit must go through to become a Marine. It's an exhaustive physical, mental, and even a moral challenge, which serves as the climactic training experience. The Crucible happens over more than a 50-hour span. The test includes food and sleep deprivation and over 45 miles of marching whereby the recruits are being presented with many strategic challenges. Harry hadn't heard from Will either. He was in love the last time he was heard from. Harry snapped out of it when someone called his name. He looked up and saw Eduardo waving to him with a cheerful smile on his face.

Harry waved back, "Hello Eduardo!"

"How was the...?" Eduardo held up a Largemouth Bass he had just caught, still on his line.

"Soon," Harry said. "For a special occasion."

Harry jogged past Eduardo. He felt guilty about not cooking up the Bass. He should have paid the man the proper respect by feasting on the gift.

This way of thinking was Harry's ball and chain. Harry's childhood bared glimmers of light that helped him make it through. As an adult, he perpetually felt like he was wearing a soaking wet overcoat. His immune system wasn't immune to much. Because he was reminded of the horrible things men do to children, Harry could access shame or guilt in an instant. The smallest thing could set him back. Something as insignificant as not cooking something given to him by a friend riddled him with guilt. Harry almost always felt stunted. There were days when he couldn't follow the advice he'd given the Greek boys. Harry considered his uncle's words, "lazy in your marriage." Harry wondered if he had been lazy throughout his life. A lazy husband and father, a lazy writer, a lazy pancake-maker, and a lazy college professor?

Harry recalled a meeting he had with his graduate school thesis advisor, writer Venable Herman. The old professor was a sensitive man who thrived on getting to know his students. Harry steered clear of Professor Herman whenever he had an opportunity. Harry, being an intensely private soul, did not want to be "psychoanalyzed by a stranger," he confessed to his classmates.

But Venable Herman wore the grad student down, emerging from his office, strategically lingering around the community coffee maker where Harry would eventually show himself. After a lot of trepidation, Harry presented the professor with an innocuous screenplay he had been working on. The script was entitled *Probie School*; it was the story of a privileged and *lazy* (there's that word again) kid whose father tricks him into becoming a New York City firefighter, to prove his manhood and to win back his trust fund. There had been studio interest in Harry's script at the time, but the interest quickly waned. Harry was fairly confident his silly little script was safe enough to present to the old master. The master would swiftly dismiss the script for the insouciant work it was, and Harry could go on drinking tepid coffee without looking over his shoulder. Things did not turn out that way.

Harry sat down in Herman's office and pensively watched as the teacher began fiddling with the pages. When Herman finally lifted his eyes and looked at Harry, he began to sob. Harry was incredulous.

"But Venable," Harry pleaded, "It's a comedy. You're supposed to laugh."

Years later, Harry told the story at Herman's memorial service and everyone was tearfully amused.

That *was* Venable, he heard mourners mumbling. Harry had the realization then: Venable Herman saw through his charade – right through the pages of the lightweight tale. Harry's story was not so silly after all. The professor understood the comedic confusion dramatized by Harry's lethargic protagonist was representative of Harry's real-life pain. Harry grew to love the old man, and the teacher respected the limits Harry put on their relationship. Much of their time together was spent speaking about superficial things, but Harry knew he was being played. Harry felt safe around Venable Herman, and that said a lot. The only other person Harry truly felt safe around was his beloved wife.

As Harry walked back to his car, he saw a young man running through the park with his Labrador. An athletic young man with his frolicking dog. A picture-postcard moment, yet Harry managed to make it about himself. Harry was feeling his age. Before he managed to completely bathe himself in self-doubt all over again, he shivered himself out of his reverie. It was as if someone doused him with a version of the ice bucket challenge, without the exhilaration. Harry was indeed steadying himself for an inevitable impact. He was gearing up for his own Crucible. There would be no room for indecision or self-doubt.

"If this turns out to be true, if someone harmed our beautiful girl, you get the coward. You nail that bastard, but good. You hear me?" his uncle told him.

This was Harry's challenge – starting now, in earnest on everyone else's lazy Sunday. He exhaled some cold air from his lungs.

When he returned home, Harry stepped around the big girl as he dropped in a quick load of laundry. Harry slid into the kitchen and leaned over the countertop. He opened his laptop and poured himself some coffee. Researching back four years, Harry couldn't find any information about the borough president's symposium. Harry tried to come up with the names of the women in Felicity's circle – women who would have accepted the borough president's invitation. Women in business, women active in civic associations and volunteerism, those were the types. Harry pulled a pad from a drawer and began scribbling. It wasn't long before he came up with nearly ten names. He was proud of himself. Many of the women were friends or acquaintances of Felicity's. He still had some of their phone numbers.

Harry spent the next half an hour calling women he had rarely spoken with since his wife's wake. No one seemed interested in answering questions about Felicity's frame of mind nor did they want to speculate about how many drinks she had four years ago. Harry was astonished by their lack of curiosity and sincerity; some of them were peculiarly dismissive. They wanted to get on with their Sunday. If there was a silver lining, Harry knew Emma Kendall wasn't with Felicity on her last night on the planet. At least he didn't have to deal with her unpredictable personality. Emma was having a very public row that final day, evicting her husband Michael Little, whom she described as a "passive aggressive little prick," from their house. Emma ended up in the ER the same evening Felicity drowned. After she booted her husband, Emma spent the rest of the day drinking Bombay Sapphire out of a soup bowl.

Emma confessed months later, "I came down with an aggravating dose of alcohol poisoning."

It was quickly becoming later in the afternoon, but Harry wasn't ready to throw in the towel. Lolly slid in beside him, partially leaning against his body;

seemingly staring through the kitchen drawers beneath the countertop with her x-ray vision. Lost in one of her typical doggie trances.

"Go back to bed, you," Harry said patting her head.

Lolly turned without fanfare, plodding back to the laundry room. Harry picked up his pad and went over his accounting of the women who sipped room-temperature chardonnay. Harry winced, and a new thought opened his eyes.

"What about our friend Irene Roth? Our friendly neighborhood state senator. Was she there? Maybe she knows something. What do you think, Lolly?"

When Lolly didn't respond to his query, Harry searched his cell. He didn't have Roth's number, and her office was closed. In any event, he knew calling her office would be a mistake. His chances of getting Robert Devine on the line was a strong probability. He didn't want to give Devine anything, not one clue; not an iota of information. He had to speak to Roth personally. He knew where she lived compliments of the *Richmond County Register*'s series of articles entitled *Meet Your Elected Officials*, which ran some months before. Harry could barely remember yesterday, but Roth's address stuck out in his mind for some reason. He chuckled, recalling he read the newspaper article seconds before he repurposed it as a drop cloth. Harry departed through the kitchen door forgetting to tie the laces on his orange sneakers.

Seventeen minutes later, Harry found himself in an upscale neighborhood. The locality was beautified by age-old trees, expensive homes, and narrow and twisting landscaped roads. The ten-foot-high security gate at 57 Button Nook Road was open. Harry pulled into the long driveway leading to the front door of Irene Roth's French Colonial home. Roth's home was modest and charming. Some of the tree limbs on the edge of her property were misshapen. As if they were turning their backs on the newer development outside her property line.

Harry pulled up a few feet behind some type of eccentric-looking sports car. Harry was no car maven, but he could tell this one cost a fair amount of money. It reminded him of something Will had asked him when he was small. Always the observant one, little Will noticed a balding middle-aged man diving a convertible and turned to his father while the family was driving together.

"Hey, Pops, how come old men always have nice cars?"

He remembers Felicity chiming in, "Maybe they're trying to compensate for something?"

Letting the comment pass, Will asked, "What kind of cars do ladies buy when they're old, Mom?"

"First of all, your mother will never be old. Besides, someone as smart as your mother would never want a new car. She'd spend her money wisely."

"I would travel the world with my family," Felicity said.

"How'd I do?" Harry tilted his head. Felicity reached over to peck him on the cheek.

"I like your father very much, boys," Felicity said beaming.

Harry considered the irony in his breezy response to his little sons, "Your mother will never be old."

Those words echoed as his left foot stepped out of the car. Harry's right foot followed. He lifted his chin to see a man posing in the open doorway of Roth's home. The man was middle-aged, in good shape, wearing an ironed white shirt with an open collar. He sipped something from a short glass, presumably scotch, Harry thought.

"Before you take another step, you should tie those silly laces and get back into your car," said Thaddeus Calendar. It was a threat sung in a light-hearted tone.

"I'm looking for Irene Roth. My name is Harry Kavanagh."

Calendar's eyes blinked unnaturally. He stood a little taller as he breathed in Harry's name for a long beat. As Harry was about to say something, Calendar wagged a finger at him.

"Mr. Kavanagh, today is Sunday and you're on private property. Do you have something against football?"

"Well, the front gate was open and..."

"If my fly's down, it's not necessarily an invitation to perform fellatio. Although, there are worse ideas."

Harry recognized the man from the front pages of the tabloid newspapers. Harry wasn't a big fan of easily-imparted profanity. And he wasn't a big fan of sexual harassment, barroom fights, grandstanding, and bullying constituents. Without missing a beat, Harry cut him off before he could continue.

"A philosophy you endorse at staff meetings?"

"The man with the yellow sneakers has wit. Who would have guessed?"

"The sneakers are orange, Senator Calendar. Now, please let my state senator know I'm here?"

"Any business you have to conduct with Senator Roth can be done at her office during normal business hours, Monday through Friday."

"My visit is personal in nature. Here's my other problem and you're probably aware of it. One is required to get a flea dip after passing by her gatekeeper, Bobby Devine."

"And let me guess, you haven't had your shots yet?"

"I'm suggesting he hasn't had his," Harry responded.

"That's very good," Calendar said shaking his head. His smile widened, exposing his ostentatiously capped bright white teeth that looked like a row of Chiclets.

"So long, Mr. Kavanagh."

Harry backed into his driver's seat and started the car. Calendar gave Harry a pompous *toodle-oo* wave of his hand.

"By the way, your zipper *is* down." And Harry pointed.

Calendar looked down twisting his glass, inadvertently spilling his libation onto his trousers.

"I blame myself, senator. I had no expectation you'd fall for that seventh-grade gag."

Calendar flung his empty glass at the car and it smashed against the driver's-side door. Harry winced as splintered bits of glass peppered his face.

"What the hell is wrong with you?" Harry shouted.

"Get off this property or I'll call the police," Calendar growled.

"That'll go over very well. You're intoxicated, and you look like you forgot to wear your diaper."

"Get the fuck out of here," he said taking an unsteady step forward.

Harry backed up his car slowly under the inspection of the rosy-colored nose belonging to Thaddeus Calendar. As Calendar turned to re-enter Roth's house, Harry sprung the car forward and banged into the sports car, damaging the fender.

"So sorry," Harry said as he sped away from the apoplectic man, last seen twisting with rage in Harry's rearview mirror.

Arnold Fleck sucked down the last of his two-thousand-calories-worth of a milkshake, that he convinced himself was a smoothie. He belched loudly and confidently. He was sitting comfortably in a plastic armchair in the center of the mall's food court. He outstretched his arms, admiring the chaos around him. There was a table occupied by elderly Italian men passionately arguing about a bocce match. Two young brothers sitting behind Fleck were wrestling for a slice of pizza before their harried mother could open the box. Nearby, a caboodle of raucous teenagers were poking fun at one another while eating disco fries with their fingers. A chattering church group of men and women were knitting the same scarf. A celebratory posse of high school cheerleaders commandeered six or seven tables as they boasted about their football team's big win.

Robert Devine, clad in his office attire, oddly capping it off with a tight-fitting hoodie, pulled out a chair and sat down across from Arnold Fleck.

"You look like Friar Tuck."

Devine removed the hood without saying a word.

"Okay, Bobby boy. Lemme see it," Fleck said gloating.

Devine raised a designer cotton shopping bag made in the UK and placed it on the table. It had the black and white image of the sultry Italian actress Claudia Cardinale on it.

"Beautiful. Claudia Cardinale. Do you know how many nocturnal emissions I had over her when I was a kid?"

"Spare me the nostalgic journey of your jizz."

"You're cranky. What, you haven't had your third lunch yet?"

Devine began to push himself away from the table.

"Next week," Fleck ordered.

"What do you mean, next week?" Devine said lowering his voice. "There is no more next week."

"You can shout your displeasure from the rooftops, Bobby. All around us people are fighting over calamari," Fleck said. He waved a finger at him and continued. "No one ever wants your opinion, am I right? That's why you're here. You do as you're told."

"You had your Sophia Loren bag, then the Gina Lollobrigida drop, now Claudia what's-her-name? We agreed on three drops," Devine said. His anxiety was blooming.

"I know you've never read a book, but you know how this goes in the movies. Besides, I'm in love with this company. It reminds me of what beautiful women used to look like," Fleck said stroking the shopping bag.

"You'd better be careful," Devine said raising his voice more than he intended to.

"I told you. You have nothing to worry about. The woman over there, wearing her pajamas in public, feeding her diabetic kids waffles with whipped cream and chocolate syrup, she doesn't give a shit about you."

"There will be no more deliveries. We agreed. Three times. Ten thousand dollars each."

"Thirty thousand dollars, really? Only the appetizer. Next week I'm going in a different direction. I want something a little finer, elegant, more satisfying. I want Audrey Hepburn. And to be consistent, I'm going to choose a number that will really fill me up. Make it happen, Bobby. Say, fifty thousand."

Fleck peeked inside Claudia Cardinale to confirm the money was accounted for. He rose and walked away from the sulking Devine, sitting lower in his plastic chair. Devine nodded and shot a subtle wave to someone on the other side of the food court.

Arnold Fleck was so preoccupied clutching his beloved shopping bag he wasn't aware that he and Claudia were about to be shadowed.

"Right. Just like in the movies," Devine said under his breath. It wasn't said in a sinister fashion or with any sense of satisfaction. It was a prediction. Devine looked nauseated. He couldn't see a clean way out of this mess. Something was going to stick, and that meant trouble. Devine had another prediction. Arnold Fleck's future much like his own looked bleak.

Devine spat impulsively at Fleck's back, "Who the hell is Audrey Hepburn?"

Without turning around, Fleck said, "You're such a loser."

Chapter Twenty-Two

Harry entered his kitchen only to find Lolly staring at him expectantly. Her tail was thumping enthusiastically against the refrigerator.

Harry knelt beside her and stroked her ears. "What's up with you? Do you know something I don't, huh? Did you eat Arnold and Fleck?"

Harry looked up at the sight of his handsome son stepping into the room with a wide smile on his face. Harry sprang to his feet and threw his arms around Will.

"What are you doing here?" Harry said joyously.

"I had a few days and we thought we'd drive down state for a home-cooked meal."

Harry squeezed him tighter.

"Pops, you're gonna crush me if you squeeze me any tighter. Hey, you been working out, old man?"

Harry extended his arms, holding Will by the shoulders, taking him in.

"You look great, Will. I'm so happy to see you. Christ, you're tall. When did that happen?"

"I've got you by at least three inches, old man."

"Yeah, but how?"

"We're going in opposite directions, Pops."

"You got it right," Harry said exhaling. Turning back to Lolly he said, "You were in on the surprise, weren't you, girl?"

As the son inspected his father, his expression shifted to a look of skepticism.

"What's wrong?" Harry asked.

"Pops, you have glass in your hair. Shards of glass in your pompadour."

"Funny, wise guy. I do not have a pompadour."

"You have little cuts on your cheek and you smell like a bucket of scotch," Will found himself saying, incredulously.

"You're a comedian," Harry said without a care in the world.

"What happened?"

"A drunk threw his drink at me. Typical lazy Sunday in the Shaolin."

"Oh, listen to you," Will said laughing. "In the Shaolin? Really? Are you okay though? What happened?"

Harry nodded and then his ears pricked up at the hum of movement in the other room. Harry looked at Will with a questioning expression.

"Did you say *we*?"

"But, Pops, what *did* happen to you?"

"Not a big deal. Let it go, okay?"

Julie pranced gracefully into the room wearing a warm smile. She looked like she was about to take a curtain call.

"Hello, Mr. Kavanagh, My name is Julie. I'm very pleased to meet you."

Delighted by her entrance, Harry moved Will aside and drew the young woman in for a warm embrace. Will and Julie exchanged amused facial shrugs over Harry's shoulder. Harry pulled back, feeling embarrassed by his unbridled enthusiasm.

"Julie is my…" Will stammered.

"You can say it, Will. Go ahead. Mr. Kavanagh, I'm his girlfriend."

"Well, okay everyone," Harry said. "Listen you two, please forgive my enthusiasm."

"And your cologne," Will added.

"And the fact that I smell like a bucket of scotch, but I'm so happy to see you, Will. I'm thrilled you're here too, Julie. I apologize for the hug. Forgive me if I crossed any lines."

"We don't hug much in my family. I'm open to more hugs in the future, Mr. Kavanagh."

"Good then. I don't get much company. I feel like I'm rambling, sorry."

Harry unexpectedly felt a wave of grief wash over him. He prayed it would pass quickly. He steadied himself against the refrigerator. Julie rested the back of her hand over her mouth, trying to hold her own emotions in check. It was difficult to see their host struggle with his feelings. Will gave his father a good-natured slap on the shoulder. Harry pushed himself off the fridge. His demeanor brightened.

"I'm good. All right everybody. What do you say Julie, I get cleaned up and later on I take you two out for dinner? There's this place at 83rd and Amsterdam on the Upper West Side called Fred's. Fred was a Black Labrador raised by the owner and so when you enter the restaurant there's hundreds of pictures of other people's dogs there. I have a picture of Lolly framed in there. And by the way the food is great."

"Pops, take a breath," Will said.

"Really rambling. Sorry, kids."

Will said, "That's a ways to go to for dinner, Pops. And we've already been in the car a long time."

"Oh, that's an awesome idea, Mr. Kavanagh, but Will tells me you make a killer carbonara," Julie said eagerly.

Harry was taken with Julie's enthusiasm. He said, with a glint in his eye, "Well, I haven't made much carbonara since I was a fat man. But that's a good idea."

"Yeah, and we're a little beat, Pops. It was a long drive," Will added.

"I'd love to cook for you if that's what you want."

Harry's cellphone buzzed on the countertop. He recognized the caller and let the phone shimmy across the marble.

"Aren't you going to get it?"

"It's your mother's friend, Emma Kendall. I'm going to let it go," Harry said.

"Friend?" Will made a face. "Mom thought she was a psycho," Will added off-handedly, rummaging a cabinet looking for snacks.

"Your mother didn't socialize with psychos. She's eccentric, maybe."

"How come there are no snacks in the snack cabinet?"

"Because you and your rotten brother aren't around," was Harry's response, already leaving Emma Kendall behind.

"There's nothing like your carbonara. Why don't you give us a shopping list while you wash that scotch right out of your hair?" Will winked at Harry, impressed with himself.

"I got it, Nellie Forbush. Sounds like a plan. Sure," Harry said grinning.

When the kids returned later in the day, the kitchen was already filling up with the savory aroma of onions Harry was sautéing. Harry was tooling around in the kitchen. His hair was wet and combed back. He looked relaxed. The muscular musical tones of José Carreras were coming from the Bose.

"Wow, it sure doesn't smell like the college cafeteria," Will said.

"That's because it smells amazing in here," Julie said.

"Black peppercorns, heavy cream, a hunk of Pecorino Romano and pancetta, right?" Harry said, looking up from his onions.

"Check and check," Will responded.

"Can I do anything, Mr. Kavanagh?"

"No, Julie. Why don't you two relax and I'll shout when we're close."

"We'll take Lolly for a stroll around the neighborhood," Will said.

At the sound of her voice, Lolly rose slowly, working the kinks out of her old-girl's body.

"Oh, geez," Harry said to himself.

"What's wrong, Pops?"

"I should have sautéed the pancetta first, then sautéed the onions in the love juice left behind by the pancetta. It's been a while."

"I'm sure it's going to work out," Will said reassuring him. "See you in a little while, Pops."

"Have fun," Harry said digging through the groceries. He watched the kids corral Lolly and head out the door.

They ate in the dining room with the lights dimmed accompanied by the jazz vibrations courtesy of WBGO. Harry loved that the kids were enjoying their food. He never thought he'd see Will so comfortable in his own skin with a young woman.

"Will, you've come a long way since your fifth-grade graduation," Harry joked.

"Oh, can you stop?"

"What?" Julie nudged Will with an elbow.

Harry realized he may have said too much and decided he didn't want to embarrass Will.

"It's nothing. I'm enjoying your company, both of you. And you two seem to be enjoying one another. It's a nice thing to see."

"This is you stopping?" Will pleaded with his father.

Julie playfully elbowed Will. He rose from the table shooting a mock-angry glare in his father's direction.

"Julie and I will clean up and you can watch *The Maltese Falcon* or some other movie as old as you are."

"That's not nice," Julie said, rising to help clear the dishes.

"He reminds me every chance he gets that I'm getting older," he said to Julie. To Will, he sang "But sorry, kiddo, some things are even older than I am, *The Maltese Falcon* being one of them."

Harry retired into the living room. He moved to the credenza and opened a drawer. He stared at his wife's laptop. He tapped it gently, then ran his finger across the top, marking a path through a fine layer of dust. He removed the laptop and carried it to the couch. Harry opened it and found a ticket left behind on the keyboard. It was a ticket to see Jackson Browne at their local venue, the grand St. George Theater. It was the last event they attended together, days before Felicity's death.

Felicity was disappointed because Browne, who appeared with performers Sara and Sean Watkins from Nickel Creek, focused his acoustic performance on his lesser known tunes – the ones that rarely made it on stage during his heyday. Harry recalled Browne commending the community for loving the theater back to life, or something like that. Harry never forgot that comment.

That's exactly who Felicity was, she was someone who could love anything back to life.

It seemed like they switched personalities that night. While Felicity was frustrated by Browne's musical choices, Harry thoroughly enjoyed the evening. Harry was put under a meditative spell. Browne's gentle, soulful performance permitted him to recall all the people he had loved in his life, and the hopes he had for he and his wife and for his children. He was looking forward to spending the rest of his life with the woman whose hand rested inside his.

Harry turned on the laptop and it didn't budge. Not a twinge, an electrical itch, grunt, noise or hint that it was ever going to return to life.

"Of course, Jesus" Harry said.

Just like his wife, the computer had been silent for years. Harry rustled through a drawer and found the charger amid a junkyard of pencils and other scraps. He plugged it in and returned to the couch. He heard the kids in the room behind him loading the dishwasher. What glorious sounds, he thought. The echoes of activity and laughter. And he liked the idea he wasn't the one loading the dishwasher. In Harry's opinion, the most dreaded job on the planet. He sat back and closed his eyes.

Nearly two hours later, Harry opened his eyes and noticed shadowy reflections bouncing off the living room walls. It took him a few seconds to realize Bogie was grimacing his way through the final moments of *The Maltese Falcon*. Harry sat straighter when he noticed Julie, clad in pajamas and a robe was sitting on the floor in front of the television. Lolly was cuddled up beside her like they were the oldest of friends.

"Oh, hello, Mr. Kavanagh. I hope you don't mind. I've never seen this movie before."

"Not at all," Harry said repressing a yawn. "Where's Will?"

"He's asleep in the guest room," she said turning back to Bogie.

Harry smiled to himself. Julie wanted him to know they were sleeping in separate bedrooms. He hadn't gotten that far. They figured it out on their own without forcing him into making an awkward proclamation. They were young, the both of them, and whatever they did upstate was their business but in Harry's house, well, he was the parent. Harry stopped his mind from overworking. He was old-fashioned. They made it easier for him and he was relieved.

"The, uh, stuff that dreams are made of," Spade said to Detective Tom Polhaus.

Harry and Julie watched Sam Spade take the bird from Polhaus and walk into the hallway. The fabulous Warner Brother's soundtrack climbed dramatically as the elevator doors closed on the distraught face of Miss Wonderly.

"And Sam Spade out," Harry heard Julie say as she hopped to her feet. She stroked Lolly's face and looked at Harry, pensively.

"I never saw a Humphrey Bogart movie before. He was a little guy who talked big. But he could back it up. You believe every word coming out of his mouth. It was enjoyable. Well, goodnight, Mr. Kavanagh. Thank you for dinner and for the movie."

Harry smiled, "My pleasure." Harry watched her take on the stairs two at a time. After a long yawn, his eyes fell on Felicity's laptop. The green light told him the device was charged. He reached for it, reluctantly.

"But I'm not so convinced I'm fully charged and ready to go," he said thoughtfully. Harry scanned emails leading up to the days before his wife's forever departure. A few exchanges between friends; mostly reminders about the borough president's gathering. The women who were eager to attend with Felicity were the same ones who had no time to speak to Harry.

He found a draft Felicity was working on for a community newsletter. He nodded intermittently as he read through it.

Making Businesses Work on Main Street USA

Who opens a small business in a storefront that had a long history of failed businesses on a street where there's no parking just days after a hurricane? I did! And while there are many challenges of being a stakeholder in our neighborhood, I love owning a business here!

Being the owner of Felicity's Boutique Wine is my dream job. I get to create my own homey work environment, share my passion for hospitality with my neighbors, many of whom have become my friends, and elevate the image and expectations of what tourists, fellow New Yorkers, and even other Staten Islanders perceive about my neighborhood. Let's face it, a woman-run, boutique wine shop with a focus on organic and traditional wines run by an educated, progressive, native Staten Islander flies in the face of the mobbed-up characters the media is comfortable assuming Staten Islanders to be. Some of our fellow Staten Islanders have questioned the safety and economic viability of our own Main Streets and I am happy that I have changed perceptions enough to become a retail destination for many customers from all over the island in addition to our loyal core of North Shore locals.

But there is a dire need (and plenty of room!) for more complementing small businesses in order to make our Main Streets really bustle! In order to do that, a long hard look needs to be given to parking, street safety, and perception around our neighborhood.

Changing the culture of parking entitlements from city agencies so that customers can park easily and stroll safely is essential to the economic health of current businesses as well as the ability to attract new small businesses. Daytime parking congestion prevents businesses from thriving and deters new businesses from considering the location as viable. Parking abuses and congestion is the number one economic challenge to my business. It appears to me that it is easier to predict the success of the larger neighborhood endeavors than the riskier business of opening a small business in our neighborhood. There is infrastructure and support for these large projects, which small businesses currently lack.

When parking and walking safety is on par with other successful Staten Island mainstays like…

Harry couldn't read on. He sighed. Felicity was constantly speaking out against parking entitlements and abuses in their burgeoning neighborhood. A seemingly never-ending supply of phony placards were gifted to city agencies: police, postal workers, court officers, probation officers, even members of the District Attorney's office, who in turn doled them out to relatives and friends who parked locally and hopped onto the ferry heading for the city. Cars commuting into the neighborhood flaunting dashboard placards were granted free parking for life. The cars squatted all day long, blocking anyone willing to feed the meter. It was a challenge to frequent Felicity's shop, the bank, post office, etc. Felicity engaged an NBC reporter, one of those guys-on-your-side reporters to investigate her complaint. The reporter said on the air, "St. George is the epicenter of illegal parking in New York City." The report ran on three consecutive nightly newscasts and blatantly pointed out how traffic agents and police refused to ticket anyone with a placard. Not a thing changed after the report ran. Free and accessible parking for all eternity continued for everyone except for those people living in the neighborhood.

Felicity was continually ignored or put off while active plans were evolving to accommodate parking for tourists surrounding the commercial development. As far as Harry could recall, Felicity had spoken to local leadership on many occasions without any results.

He remembered Felicity saying once, "The only person who should have a free parking spot is a brain surgeon standing by for an airlifted patient."

Felicity didn't get the opportunity to finish the fight or the article or her life. Who ever thought Felicity's lease would outlive her? Certainly not Harry.

Harry yawned against his will; his last few thoughts put a bitter taste in his mouth. His fingers got caught in a knot in his hair when he tried to scratch his head. Pompadour indeed. He tried to stretch his arms with the laptop balanced on his knees. Harry felt stiff and was about to call it a night when something caught his eye. He opened the next email.

Harry's eyes narrowed. He clenched his teeth. His face froze in a deeply angry frown. His face appeared as if it was rearing back for an animated eruption. Harry's impression of himself was his eyeballs were filling with a cartoon's version of a rising tide of boiling liquid. He imagined if he would scream, he might mimic the worst three seconds of William Shatner's acting career: *"Khan! Khan!"* Harry's anguished cry, what would it be? It came to him quickly. *"Arnold and Fleck!"* Didn't sound right. Or would he simply select the Shatner-esque choice? *"Fleck! Fleck!"*

Harry heard his neck crack. He wanted to scream bloody murder, but instead he found himself flying from his perch.

Harry saw himself from above, an out-of-body experience, lurching through the kitchen door and darting across the street. He knew he was a captive to the signals his brain was sending him. And his brain was instructing him, no – ordering him – to kick the living crap out of his neighbor.

The kitchen door was unceremoniously slapped shut on Lolly's blood-shot expression. She huffed and hopped for a few seconds and began to bark like nobody's business. An ancient-sounding aria that could frighten away a pack of woolly mammoths.

Arnold Fleck was passing through his darkened center hallway when he was distracted by the commotion. That dog's barking from across the street. Fleck was wearing a pair of tighty-whities and a clinging V-neck T-shirt. Clinging, because it was at least one size too small for his frame. His black socks were pulled up high, nearly reaching his knees. His knees were facing the rear of the house; his torso twisted itself toward the front door. One fingertip rested on his lower lip; he unintentionally mimicked a pinup girl from a bygone era caught in the act of surprise. Fleck stared at the man who burst through the front door of his inner sanctum. His fingertip fell off the ledge of his lower lip and he was left agape.

"Do you have a skillet?" Harry Kavanagh asked dully, slightly out of breath, without the evidence of the violence rising within him.

"A what?" Fleck said incredulously.

"A frying pan."

The second time Kavanagh spoke Fleck knew he was in for it. The man was holding something back; he was angrier than hell. Fleck sensed his neighbor was about to blow.

"You wanna make me breakfast for dinner?" He tried to sound neighborly.

Julie and Will stumbled down the stairs when they heard Lolly baying. They spotted the laptop on the floor near the couch, its screen revealing the image that set Harry off on his tirade.

"Oh, that is disgusting," Julie said.

Will and Julie ran across the street in half the time it took Harry. They stood, waiting for the next shoe to fall, several feet behind Harry in the open doorway of Fleck's house. They arrived in time to hear Harry tell Fleck: "No, Arnold and Fleck. I do not want to make you breakfast for dinner with the skillet. I want to break your goddamn nose with it."

Julie rose to the tips of her toes and whispered over Will's shoulder. "I hope he hits him good."

"My father is not the hitting type," he whispered out of the side of his mouth.

"Why don't you take a shot at him?"

"I think I will," Will said taking a step forward.

Before Will could advance, he and Julie watched as Harry followed an impulse. Harry strode determinedly toward his bewildered neighbor, his right-hand slung well back behind him. With an awkward catapult-like motion, his arm shot forward and his fist sped in the direction of Fleck's fleshy face.

Fleck turned slightly, bracing for the impact. Harry landed his punch underneath Fleck's left eye. Fleck flopped, and Harry stood over him, breathing erratically. Harry hovered as Fleck's flesh began to swell in real time.

"Where is your computer?" Harry bellowed.

"My what?" It was a high-pitched squeal issued from a man who was ready to plead for mercy.

"Your goddamn laptop, Fleck. You know what I mean. Where is it?"

"It's in my dishwasher."

"Don't get cute with me," Harry warned.

"No really, I use it like desk drawers," Fleck let out a long, painful moan. A frightening thought popped into Fleck's head as Harry moved on.

"No, wait!" He rolled over onto his knees and struggled to get to his feet.

Will was on him in a flash. "Stay down, Mr. Fleck, or I'll put you down," Will said.

Fleck looked over at Julie, hoping for some sympathy.

"Sir, I don't have enough middle fingers for you," Julie spat at him.

Harry opened the dishwasher and true to Fleck's words, the racks were used for filing. An assortment of bills and documents were neatly filed in the top rack. There were also stacks of money, lots of money filed neatly inside. Harry was taken aback, but after his initial surprise he saw Fleck's laptop adroitly positioned in the bottom rack. As he reached for it, he noticed something else that gave him pause: the canvas bag. The extra material was folded over itself carefully and sloppily wrapped with duct tape. Harry struggled to remember where he had seen the bag before. He heard Fleck grousing and snatched the laptop.

Harry flung open the basement door and chucked the laptop down the stairs. It wasn't manufactured to survive Harry's ire. The laptop bounced and crashed its way down to its dank resting place.

With tears clouding his vision, Fleck crawled on his knees and watched the shapes of the three of them crossing back to Kavanagh's place. The buoyant teenagers, each holding up their side of Kavanagh. They were supporting the weight of the man as they led him away. Kavanagh's shoulders remained even, his steps slower than theirs. He appeared as if he were in a trance.

"I hope you have a fucking stroke, Harry and Kavanagh." Fleck's defiance was said in a vicious low tone.

Still on his knees, Fleck crawled to the entrance and nudged the front door shut with his shoulder. He rolled over onto his back. Tears leaked from the corners of his eyes.

"I'm finally free."

Fleck clapped his hands and started to laugh. He rolled around like a mutt shaking off water after a bath. Indeed, the thing he had been worrying about for years was out in the open. And as far as Fleck was concerned, it was behind him now. The fetid odors given off by a garbage truck – even that stench dissipates over time. The cost was a punch in the face and the price of a new laptop. Easy peasy. Fleck was giddy. Now, with all his cards out on the table he could move forward. He would continue to change the rules of the game by collecting a "pension" from his new best friends, Devine and company. For his added pleasure, he would do some traveling; take off-the-beaten-path vacations where he would happily pay for sex with young women and with girls whose lives were hopeless.

"I'm free, I'm free, I'm free. I am free." he sang as his face continued to blow up.

Chapter Twenty-Three

Will's father was in a dark mood. He wasn't interested in being slapped on the back for slugging Arnold Fleck. Harry was tight-lipped; anguished. Without making much eye contact Harry apologized to the kids for losing his temper. They didn't seem to mind his behavior. In fact, they were invigorated by it. But Harry was sick to his stomach. He went up the stairs to bed. Lolly looked like she didn't want to take on the steps, but after some consideration she decided Harry could use the company. She hop-limped after him.

The kids watched Harry's departure with admiration and concern.

"Your father knows that even though he destroyed the laptop, the image is still there, right?"

"He made his point. He's probably not thinking beyond it," Will answered quietly.

Will Kavanagh and his new girlfriend Julie never made it to their respective bedrooms. They were so charged up by Harry's takedown of the neighborhood pervert, they chattered the night away on the living room couch until they reluctantly drifted off to sleep.

The following morning, Harry descended the steps showered and dressed. Lagging behind was his slower-moving and ever-faithful companion, Lolly. Their descent awakened the embarrassed teenagers from a night's sleep tangled in each other's arms.

Arnold Fleck was in Harry's rearview mirror. His dose of the heebie jeebies was washed away the instant Harry hit the shower.

"C'mon, you Muppets. How about some breakfast?" He immediately decided he wouldn't say *breakfast* around them anymore because Emma Kendall spoiled the word for him.

Emma had said to Harry, "Let's agree, when you're ready, you'll take me up on my *breakfast offer?*" Meaning a roll in the hay with her and the gorilla suit. The ordeal would qualify as a threesome. Harry was having enough trouble rolling in and out of bed on his own. He didn't want any company. He certainly didn't want Emma's company in that way.

"Pancakes in ten minutes." It sounded like a marching order although Harry didn't mean it to.

"Thank you. Good morning, Mr. Kavanagh," Julie said, pushing hair away from her face with her palms. "That sounds like a generous offer. I'll be down in a minute."

Julie could not prevent a formidable yawn from escaping, which drew a high-arching eyebrow from Will. Suddenly embarrassed, Julie covered her mouth and shot up the stairs. Harry caught Will staring at him.

"Since when did you become such a bad ass?"

"I like pancakes."

"You know what I mean, Pops. One minute you're combing your hair with glass and the next you're slugging the president of the neighborhood watch."

"Nothing about last night to your brother. Make myself clear?" Harry said pointing a finger at him.

"Yeah, I suppose. But he'd get such a kick out of it. The old man going rogue."

"Please, Will, okay?" Harry pleaded, softening his tone. "He's got more important things to think about than worrying about his old man losing his marbles."

"Losing his marbles? Who says stuff like that?" Will rose from the couch and followed Harry into the kitchen. "You gonna be okay, Pops?"

"I will be after some coffee." Harry put his arm around Will's waist.

"Jesus, I just cannot believe how tall you are."

"Really? We're back to how tall I am? We danced this dance already."

"We danced this dance already? Who says stuff like that?" Harry joked. Then more seriously, he reminded Will, "You heard what I said, yes?"

"Yeah, Pops. Nothing about this to Jake."

Barely an hour later, Harry was saying goodbye to the couple as Julie's car backed out of the driveway. Harry waved with his left hand.

"Make good choices," he shouted with a chortle erupting from his throat. Felicity used to say it to the boys after she patted their heads and shoved their behinds into the public-school hallways. As the boys got older, the send-off became a running joke.

Julie removed one hand from the steering wheel and blew Harry a kiss, which made him blush.

"You're killing me, old man," Will shouted at him as they drove away.

Harry walked out of the medical building three hours later. His midnight bout with Fleck earned him a broken pinkie. He had something called a boxer's fracture. His pinkie was put in a splint. His right hand was wrapped as was a portion of his forearm. He received instructions to see an orthopedic within a week at which point he would probably be informed he'd heal in 8–12 weeks.

Harry did not go to *his* hospital. He made the decision to go to an urgent care center located at the other end of the island. Felicity used to call this neighborhood the ass-end of the island for no particular reason Harry could figure other than it was far away. Harry thought it wise to cap his "frequent flyer" visits to the local sick bay because he didn't want to run into Dr. Emily Armstrong.

Jaycee Singletary observed Harry Kavanagh leaving his house in the morning. Being an observant fellow, he noticed Kavanagh was favoring his right hand. Singletary wasn't prepared to follow him because he was on foot. Singletary noticed a woman driving slowly down the street. It was the Kendall woman from the ghastly gift shop. She appeared to be waiting for Harry Kavanagh's car to put some distance between them before making her final approach.

Harry Kavanagh drove off. Singletary observed Emma Kendall park her car beside Kavanagh's house. Singletary had decided to keep an eye on Harry Kavanagh. While Singletary was missing some specifics, he suspected who was responsible for the death of Felicity Kavanagh from his "heart-to-heart" with the deceased medical examiner, Corbin Reece. Singletary considered revealing what he knew, however, he was concerned about getting caught up in a web that would cost him his freedom. He wrestled with this while shadowing Kavanagh. He hadn't come up with a satisfactory solution. In the meantime, he was somewhat satisfied with being Kavanagh's clandestine bodyguard. It was the best service he could provide, and it was better than nothing. But what if something happened to Kavanagh on Singletary's downtime? Singletary shook his head without realizing it.

Emma Kendall's appearance was an interesting development. From what Singletary could see, Kavanagh and the gift-shop woman had a strained relationship. He was adept at reading body language, and Kavanagh seemed uncomfortable around her. Singletary shared innocent small talk with the woman the last time he made a purchase at her cluttered shop. It was the same day he rubbed shoulders with the unsuspecting Harry Kavanagh. Singletary recalled Kendall's flirtatious manner, yet she couldn't hide her displeasure directed toward Kavanagh. The woman seemed somewhat disturbed by Kavanagh's appearance. She wanted something from him that he wasn't able to provide. Not that he'd been in the situation himself, but Singletary understood why Kavanagh would squirm in her presence.

Singletary studied her intently. She was a tall woman, weighing somewhere between 160–170 pounds. Her stature was strong; evenly portioned, shapely. She was flamboyant, that's it – the adjective Singletary settled on. Her hairstyle and makeup displayed confidence, perhaps overconfidence, and her curves were more voluptuous than Singletary remembered. She fancied herself a sensual creature. Her amble down the path to Kavanagh's door was a three-act play in motion. He wondered if she was aware she was being watched, or if her walk was business as usual. Singletary could smell her perfume from a distance of fifty feet. Too sweet, not complex; not a three-act play. He involuntarily tugged on his ear when he observed Kendall remove a key from her purse. She entered Kavanagh's house as if she were the one paying the mortgage.

Jaycee Singletary heard the *whoop, whoop* elicited by the police cruiser crawling up beside him. Singletary silently berated himself. The thick-necked cop with the name tag Heastie stuck his head out of the window. Singletary knew the name. He was one of the "fucking jerkoffs" the formerly living and breathing Corbin Reece blabbed about with bitterness. Heastie was on the team.

Well, how about that? Singletary thought to himself after he digested the cop's name. *I wonder what he's after? And right outside Harry Kavanagh's house? Certainly not a coincidence.*

"What are you doing here, cowboy?"

"Excuse me, officer?"

"This ain't Broke Bear Mountain Lane. Know what I mean?"

"Not certain what you're referring to, sir?" Singletary knew the cop was referring to the movie *Brokeback Mountain*. Heastie's self-satisfied sneer was accusing him of being a homosexual interloper.

"You have identification?"

"Our little dog got loose. I was out searching for her. She does that sometimes. Little Swoosie."

"Identification."

"Oh, goodness. I ventured outside without a wallet. I live right over there." Singletary pointed over his shoulder to one of the houses behind him.

"What kind of dog is it?" Heastie asked, burping up his breakfast.

"A little dog."

"No one cares about little dogs."

"What about Swoosie?"

"Police business. Now go home, get outta here."

"Oh, okay, certainly, officer. I'm sure she'll show up."

The cop car chaperoned Singletary toward a house he hazily indicated. Heastie watched as Singletary opened the front door and entered a house belonging to someone else.

Singletary stood in the foyer. The woman padding around in the kitchen poured a hot cup of coffee and placed it on the table. A morning TV news show was blaring as she was puttering.

"Honey, is that you? Hot coffee on the table, hon!" She yelled to the ceiling.

Singletary found himself looking down at a small white dog. He knelt and stroked the dog. The dog rolled over and stretched contentedly.

The woman of the house disappeared into the pantry. Singletary walked silently down the hallway and entered the kitchen. He lifted the coffee from the table. He exited silently through a back door spilling out into the unraked backyard.

The husband, dressed like a teller, walked down the stairs looking for his cup of coffee.

"Coffee?"

"It's on the table, silly," came his wife's sing-song response.

But the kitchen table was a barren desert. The husband pleaded with urgency, "Cough-feee, where?"

His wife marched out of the pantry ready to scold him. But she stopped in her tracks and stared at the kitchen table, dumbfounded.

Irene Roth looked up from behind her desk and searched the pained face of Robert Devine. He looked constipated. He minced closer to her desk. In the most absentminded way, he was about to rest his hand on her sculpted fish tank.

"Do not put your hands on that!"

"Umm, okay. Sorry."

"What the hell do you want? And why do you look like someone's force fed you a box of stale Bubba Burgers?"

"It's just that…"

"It's what? I'm not your priest. I'm not accepting confessions."

"Nothing then," he said with a hollow look in his eyes. He had a ketchup stain on his lapel, and his shirt was buttoned incorrectly. He looked sloppier than usual. Devine exited the office taking uncertain steps. His shoes exhaled a squeaking sound when he planted one flat foot in front of the other.

Roth instinctively knew something was building. She believed Devine's mood was driven by fear. There was something in play that she wasn't privy to. She knew Harry Kavanagh paid a visit to her home. As it is her habit to review each day's security camera footage, she noted Kavanagh's arrival, observing his exchange with Thaddeus Calendar, who himself showed up unannounced. Calendar took off before Roth arrived home. He had himself a drunken fit, breaking a vase and spilling scotch all over her living room furniture and floors. *Forget about asking the dope to give me back the spare key.* The following day, Roth hired a company to change the locks – every single lock on her property – including the security panel at the front gate. She was out of the loop. Something was about to happen, and she wanted to get out in front of it. It was time she thought about herself for a change. She wanted her life to be something else.

Irene Roth opened her desk drawer and removed a pristine pair of white gloves. She slipped into the gloves and lifted the fish tank into a heavy-duty shopping bag. She swiveled out of her chair and exited her office carrying the reinforced bag.

Harry Kavanagh wasn't thrilled about meeting Deputy Commander David West. The word around the neighborhood: he was a hot head. Harry was following the advice of his uncle. Harry wasn't going to reveal his amateurish attempts at detective work. He wanted to glean information and make an important request. He made his request over the phone but didn't come away with an answer. After several more calls to the precinct and brief email exchanges with the commander himself the meeting was set.

Harry was ushered into the commander's office by a uniformed officer who closed the door behind him. Harry was greeted by the smile of the precinct's leader, Commander David West. To Harry's left was Officer Brenda Streeter, standing ill at ease. After his initial surprise, he played it straight, pretending they had never met, which was exactly the way she played it. Officer Streeter was clad in the department's more casual uniform, capped off with the distinctive light-blue windbreaker worn by the community affairs police officers.

The commander put his hand out, but Harry waved his injury in surrender.

"What happened to your hand?"

"Oh, I punched my neighbor. Broke my pinkie," Harry's voice trailed off as he landed on a small leather couch facing the commander's desk. "I don't know why I said that, sorry," Harry offered. He was surprisingly nervous.

"Did I hear you correctly?"

"Uh, yes," Harry said clearing his throat. "My neighbor and I don't spend the holidays together."

Officer Streeter raised an eyebrow. She watched the commander's frown lines deepen.

"You don't seem to be the type to roust your neighbors." He sounded like a Dodge City lawman.

Harry picked up on that.

"I reckon I was the type on that particular day, sheriff," he said. After a thoughtful beat, Harry offered another apology. "I'm very sorry. I possibly had too much coffee today."

"Mr. Kavanagh, this is Officer Brenda Streeter. She's one of our community affairs officers," he said sitting behind a desk that appeared much too large for his frame.

"With all due respect, why is Officer Streeter joining us today?" Harry asked.

"Well-I-thought," the man said hesitating, primarily because his decisions are never questioned. "I believe this to be a community issue. Officer Streeter works in community affairs."

"I'm here to discuss the passing of my wife, Felicity Kavanagh, who met her unfortunate end in this community. This matter, however, is not a community issue," Harry said, his face reddening. "It's a deeply personal issue."

"I'm curious about the situation with your hand," the commander said ignoring Harry's comments.

"Why did you assault your neighbor?"

"Assault?" Harry felt blindsided by the incrimination and didn't appreciate being sidetracked. He exhaled, deciding it would be beneficial to play nice.

"The good Doctor Fleck emailed a picture of his genitals to my wife a few days before she died. I just discovered it."

"The good Doctor Fleck?"

"My neighbor, Arnold and Fleck, uh, that's what I call him." Harry shook his head bitterly. He was so used to saying the name that way. "Read his online reviews. They'll make you laugh until you cry."

"And no charges were filed?"

"I didn't think I could file for something like that. I threw his laptop down his basement steps." *I should keep my mouth shut*, Harry thought.

"You knocked him on his ass, and you destroyed his personal property?" the commander queried.

Harry caught up quickly; he knew what he was in for and so he said, "In a manner of speaking, yes. Yes, I did." He felt his heart beating inside his shirt.

"It's curious your neighbor the good doctor not filing charges against you."

"I don't find it curious at all. Did you forget the part about his sending a picture of his genitals to my wife?"

Harry turned to Streeter who remained expressionless. Harry's shoulders slumped. He said to her, "You see, officer, this is how it is. I'm here to discuss a deeply personal matter. I've come for assistance, and your commander comes off the rails in the most distracting and unhelpful way." Harry turned back to West. "Do you think you'll be able to stay on topic?"

"All right, Harry, whatever you say. You pay my salary, right?" It sounded like an affront.

"Let's start again. What can I do you out of?" the commander said glancing at his watch.

Harry looked over at Streeter. She wasn't going anywhere. He was forced to spill in her presence.

"We exchanged emails about my wife." Harry took a deep breath.

"Your wife, yes. We were nearly friends once. She enjoyed a good adult beverage that one. What a royal pain in the ass."

"Jesus Christ. What's wrong with you? You're slandering my dead wife as I sit here."

"My comments were meant in the kindest way possible."

Harry's cheeks reddened. He spoke to West without blinking. "Feel free to show me the disrespect or contempt you think I deserve. Your comments intended to mar the memory of my wife will not be tolerated…by me."

Brenda Streeter bit her lower lip and observed the men in silent amazement.

"And let's cut the bullshit. My wife was not nearly ever your goddamn friend. Pardon my vernacular."

"Now, you see here, Officer Streeter, I invite a community member into my house and he immediately displays a lack of appreciation. But that's okay. We protect and serve those who don't give a crap about the dangerous work we do. It's all part of the job," West lectured.

"Officer Streeter, my wife owned a business not far from here. I'm sure you passed her wine shop a thousand times…" Harry continued before she could respond. The entire time his gaze was locked on Commander West's look of contempt. "She had a problem on her street."

"Your wife had problems with everyone and everything," the commander chortled.

"Your commander pops out parking placards for his friends and family like they were breath mints."

"Oh, really, why would I do that? What would I have to gain?"

"Maybe they give you the impression that you're a much taller man."

The commander threw up his arms and made a face appealing to Streeter. She stared without meeting his eyes.

"You're like your wife," he said, turning back to Harry. "A malcontent, a complainer, a do-gooder."

"Parking placards used illegally," Harry continued. "His family members and compadres from the ass-end of the island (Felicity's comment was a stab – he finally got it), they park in our neighborhood every day. Their cars squatting for the entire work day in a commercial area. Every day, five days a week. Everyone else, if they can find a spot, they have to feed the meter, but not the members on the commander's team. They park here for free, hop onto the ferry, go to work, shop or perhaps go see *The Phantom of the Opera* for the tenth time. It makes life difficult for shop owners to do business because there's no place for locals to park…and spend their money. This entitlement kills our neighborhood businesses. Felicity complained to your boss, but nothing changed. This is the way he serves his community."

The commander absently twisted the watch on his wrist and said, "You didn't want to take up all my valuable time speaking about parking, did you?"

"You know why I'm here. So let's get to it."

West folded his hands on his desk and straightened up in his chair.

"Okay, you say our deceased medical examiner wanted to speak to you, but he didn't? What's that supposed to mean?"

"He didn't follow through because he dove out of a window."

"And you say a woman at some party says your wife wasn't drinking? The ME report says she was loaded."

"It was not a party, it was…" he stopped to gather himself. "The witness is a medical doctor who spoke to your detectives."

"And you want me to have the body exhumed? Because you believe there was some kind of foul play?"

"Yes. And I was attacked outside my house. I believe it's connected."

"Well, that doesn't surprise me. You're not a very good neighbor, are you? Can you identify the person who attacked you?"

"No, I, uh…"

"Well, any witnesses then?"

Yes, there was a witness. My camera-shy friend, Shelby.

"No."

"Two experienced detectives signed off on this: one is retired, one deceased. I respected them both."

"May I speak to the retired detective?"

"No, you may not. There's no compelling reason to investigate further. Your wife had one too many drinks. I'm sorry for your loss," he said standing up behind his desk.

"You could have told me this over the phone, or during our email exchanges," Harry said through clenched teeth.

"I wanted Officer Streeter to meet you."

"You wanted to make an example of me. You wanted to show off."

"Officer Streeter was recently transferred here. I wanted to show her how we do things around here." He turned slightly but did not directly address her. "And this is Harry Kavanagh. So-called writer. About twenty-five years ago, he had a series of Off-Off-Broadway runs. I don't think you'd call them hits. Tiny theaters with the smell of urine in the aisles. What did you make on those stinkers, a buck and a quarter each? *Murder in the Kitchen, Murder in the Attic,* and *Murder in the Basement.*"

"*Murder in the Cellar,*" Harry said correcting him, his bitterness mounting.

"One of those stinkers was made into a shitty movie that tanked. And so, we have a deceased community pest who knew her way around the liquor cabinet and her husband here, a writer of low-rent mysteries who imagines mayhem in every corner of his life. He sees a coverup in everything, including his wife's accident. Which by all accounts was a DUI gone worse than usual. A teaching moment I could not pass up," West said through smiling eyes.

Harry rose, disgusted by the commander's lack of decency. He barely had the time to string together another thought when West rounded his desk and got directly into his face.

"If you make more plans around your dinner table, I wanna know about it. Don't do anything halfcocked. You might injure someone in the community. And I'll encourage your next victim to file charges."

"Dinner table?" Harry said, his eyes blinking.

"Leave the police work to the professionals, or I'll be so far up your ass you won't need to scratch the itch in the back of your throat."

Harry stared at him for a long second. "You're a despicable person, you really are. I didn't know what to expect, but I certainly didn't expect to see your ignorance on full display."

"Get some reality therapy and move on with your life," was the commander's response. "Consider it free advice. You're welcome."

Harry said, "By the way, how long have you been working with the I'll-be-so-far-up-your-ass line? Is it the song you sing to new cops? The line you're thinking will be remembered for generations? You think they're impressed by someone like you? A caricature? A wisp of a man? A tiny bubble like yourself? They're asking themselves, who's the mashed potato with lips who tries to talk tough? You're a bad actor. You're no Humphrey Bogart. They laugh at you over beers and shots at the end of the day. The quip's not bad, but since you can't back it up, it makes you look smaller than a lawn ornament. How's that for a line – smaller than a lawn ornament?"

Harry was still talking to himself a block from the precinct when he heard someone calling his name. He turned and saw Brenda Streeter jogging after him.

"Hey," she said.

"Hey," he answered, curious to find out what was coming next.

"Look Harry, I'm going to make it short and sweet. I'm 38, and I've been in a lot of shitty relationships mostly with other cops..."

It sounded like the preface Harry was expecting from Emily Armstrong with the exception of – mostly with other cops. Harry sat down on a bench and took a breath. Harry thought Brenda Streeter was studying him like he was a high-school shop project that unexpectantly turned out okay.

"So, would you like to go out for dinner?" It was the only thing he could think of.

She laughed at him. "I can eat on my own time. I want you to come to my apartment. I want us to take off our clothes and have a few laughs."

"Officer?"

"Really?"

"Ah, Brenda, right? Sorry."

"Yeah, that's more like it, Brenda," she said with a bite.

"Brenda, if I take off my clothes, you *will* have more than a few laughs."

"You're funny, and you need a break," she said trying to convince him.

"I'm a little confused."

"It's obvious you haven't been with a woman in a while. You're a genuinely amusing man. You make me smile."

Harry was doubtful. What is it with women suddenly wanting him? First it was Emma and now this young cop. He didn't know what to say.

"I've never been accused of making anyone laugh."

"I know quality when I see it."

"What about those relationship mistakes? You didn't see quality then?"

"They *were* mistakes." She paused. "Look, I really dug the way you stood up to West. Nobody talks to him that way. I was busting a gut, trying not to lose it. You used your words, man. You're a man with a vocabulary and a smartass to boot. Phew, you're making me wet, Harry."

"Oh, geez, perhaps you're simplifying things," he responded apprehensively.

"Yes, of course I am. I don't have much time. I have to get back."

"I don't know, Brenda," Harry said.

He was attracted to her. Yet he was feeling apprehensive and convinced himself the timing wasn't right. And there was the age difference.

"I'm twelve years older than you. You're out of my league, and I'm out of my mind on some days."

"I am not a kid," she said pointing a finger at him. "The age thing is not a big deal. And I am not out of your league. Your wife was a solid citizen and she selected you. Every woman wants that kind of guarantee."

"You mean, I've been vetted?"

"Expertly vetted."

"I think I'm still raw."

"All right, Harry," she said taking his good hand. "When you're feeling up to it, give me a shot at wearing you out. It'll do us both some good. What do you say?"

"I want to say that you're a very nice woman."

"My grandmother is a nice woman. She sews the holes in her nylons. In her nylons! You're breaking my heart, Harry. You really are. I have to go," she said exasperated.

"Timing's not right, is what I want to say, but I think there's more."

"Find me when you come up for air."

"I'm in the middle of something. I have work to do."

He wasn't sure if he was referring to conquering bereavement mountain or getting definitive answers to Felicity's death. He settled on both.

"You loved your wife. It was a beautiful thing, but there's a time to exhale. You're killing me, Harry Kavanagh. You really are," she said shaking her head.

"I've heard that before."

"In the meantime, stop punching the hell out of yourself." She turned her back and jogged in the direction of the precinct.

Chapter Twenty-Four

The streetlight outside the Kavanagh house was flickering. The narrow street cloaked in a descending fog looked like the cover of a noir book jacket.

Harry Kavanagh decided to take Officer Streeter's advice: he was going to stop punching the hell out of himself. For the time being. He knocked around the kitchen and poured himself a cup of tea with his left hand. He wanted to calm his nerves, so it was an herbal-tea nightcap for him. He snapped on TCM and reached for an Advil he dug off a shelf. Harry's right hand was throbbing. He chided himself for not making an appointment with an orthopedic.

Tomorrow's another day, he thought. *Foreign Correspondent*, one of Hitchcock's earlier films starring Joel McCrea, was being introduced by TCM host, Ben Mankiewicz. Harry was about to get cozy when he noticed Lolly's bowl was untouched. He looked over and saw her sleeping in her spot. Lolly opened a bloodshot eye and stared back at Harry. Her tail thumped weakly against the dryer. Harry knelt beside her and stroked her head.

"What's the matter, girl? Not hungry?"

The dog's tail thumped with more enthusiasm.

"If it's any consolation, you and I will grow old together. What do you say?"

Harry straightened and returned to the kitchen. He dimmed the lights to set the mood. He was about to watch the movie when he spotted something outside. Harry opened the kitchen door and stepped into the damp night air. He saw an outline of a car parked beneath the flickering street light. The windows were fogged. He was about to take another step when he felt Lolly's presence behind him. She was gingerly pushing the kibble around with her nose. Harry looked over his shoulder and smiled.

"That's my big girl," he said stepping inside the house.

Bobby Devine was sitting in the passenger seat. He was urinating into a pickle jar. He watched Kavanagh close his door.

"The only family vacation we ever had. My parents drove us to Florida and my father refused to stop for the bathroom, so me and my brothers had to pee in a jar," Devine said tightening the lid on the jar. "Wasn't such a bad idea."

"Your piss smells like hippie beer," said Officer Heastie, the man in the driver's seat. Heastie was out of uniform, comically concealed in a dark hoodie.

"The worst part of the trip was having to hear that Cher song *Half-Breed* over and over and over again. My father played that cassette tape until it caught on fire. Goddamn it, the man loved Cher. How much longer?"

"Your father was a fruitcake. It's still early. I want the dumbass to be dopier than usual before we take him."

"What do you mean, we?"

"What do you think, you're along for the ride? To piss in a bottle and reminisce about your father's lame taste in music while I do all the fucking dirty work?"

"I'm your sidekick. That means I don't do anything. I'm here in case."

"In case of what?"

"In case you figure out how to spell reminisce and your brain matter explodes all over the fucking windows."

Heastie was about to protest further when his face wrinkled into a look of disgust. "What the fuck?"

"What's the matter?" Devine said. He tried to follow Heastie's glance.

Heastie stepped out of the car.

"Wait. You there. What are you doing?" Devine hissed at him.

Heastie was greeted by Jaycee Singletary. Singletary was walking "his dog." He greeted the thick-necked cop with a smile.

"Well, hello, officer. Sharp-looking hoodie. Good evening." Heastie glared at him with a look of stone-cold suspicion.

"Can you say hello to the good officer, Swoosie?" Singletary said to the dog. The words were barely out of his mouth when Heastie short-punched him in his side. It was a quick and a powerful blow forcing Singletary to double-over. The little dog sized-up the cop and showed its tiny teeth in protest.

"Police business is none of my business. I understand officer."

He could scarcely get the words out. Heastie watched the odd man stutter-step away, clutching his side. Singletary turned back to him and straightened up, putting aside for the moment his pain from the assault.

"If I were you officer, I would remove the hoodie. You might falsely arrest yourself or shoot yourself in the back."

Heastie thought the man was leering at him. Heastie took one step toward him, seething. The car window zipped down. Devine leaned over.

"Hey, get back in here," Devine pleaded with him, failing to be discreet.

Heastie jumped back into the car cursing under his breath.

"What the hell is wrong with you?" Devine asked.

Heastie didn't respond, he watched Singletary enter his house with the rat-sized dog.

Singletary entered the darkened foyer, shutting the front door softly. He doubled-over, rubbing his side. The little dog hopped around his ankles, sympathetically.

"I'll be okay, little one," he whispered. Singletary removed the dog's leash. "You're a good little girl. It was lovely to make your acquaintance again. Go to bed now."

As Singletary moved toward the kitchen, he saw TV shadows flickering through a bedroom doorway, and spilling out into the second-floor landing. Singletary opened a narrow door and entered the basement landing. He closed the door behind him and quietly descended the steps. The little dog obeyed him. She waddled over to her bed and cuddled up inside.

"Honey, I think I hear something downstairs," came a voice from the second floor.

"It's nothing. The dog would be barking like crazy," the woman of the house responded.

Fifteen minutes later, Singletary emerged from the basement holding a tool bag. He opened the refrigerator and took a bite out of a left-over hunk of lamb. He exited through the back door.

Heastie turned to a dozing Devine. "All right, let's go. We make it quick. You take back what belongs to us. Watch me scare the shit out of this amateur."

"Fear of God. Nothing more," Devine yawned.

"What about the Kavanagh guy?"

"What about him? Nothing."

"We're here. We should pay him a visit too."

"And do what, give him a lecture? What's wrong with you? For now, we let sleeping dogs lie."

"I still say we should beat the shit out of two fucked-up birds with one stone," Heastie spat out.

"You're an idiot. You don't know what you're talking about."

"You don't sound like no sidekick. You're supposed to support me," Heastie whined. "He showed up at what's-her-name's house the other day."

"So, the fuck what? You're not following orders. And besides, listen – I said *I thought* it was Kavanagh coming out of Reece's place. I must have been wrong because if he had the journals, we'd all be getting it up the ass by now. This fucker has what we want."

"Then what's he doing showing up at her house?"

"The guy hasn't been laid in years. What do you want from me?"

"You haven't gotten laid since the '90s. I don't see you showing up there," Heastie laughed.

Heastie started to get out of the car. Devine grabbed him by the sleeve.

"What, already?"

"We get what we need, remember? Fear of God, you moron, nothing more," Devine warned. He pulled out two pairs of surgical gloves and handed a pair to Heastie.

"Oh, thanks," he responded cordially.

Devine shook his head. He was filled with nothing but worries.

Harry awoke more than halfway through *Foreign Correspondent*. He ran his fingers through his hair and yawned. He rose from the recliner and stretched. Harry moved to the kitchen door and noticed the car was gone. He ran water in the sink thinking about his next move. Harry was done with the bastard David West.

"Sorry, Uncle Sebe. You were wrong about putting everything on the books."

Harry decided he would try to speak with Irene Roth again. He grabbed a glass of cultivated water from the frig and drank. The window above the kitchen sink overlooked the driveway. Harry noticed the overhead light was on inside his car.

"Oh, crap," he said on his way outside.

Harry pulled the handle with the intention of shutting the door properly. He noticed groceries on the passenger seat.

"I must be losing my mind."

He reached across the front seat and tugged on a plastic bag filled with fruit. When he shut the car door, a family of oranges spilled from the bag. He became hypnotized, staring at the oranges rolling around his feet. He struggled to pull a memory from behind a locked door inside his head.

The sound of an explosion blared inside Harry's mind.

Harry pressed his body against the car. He held his head in his hands, momentarily frightened. He saw himself bursting through an imploding building. He remembered something wrapped around one of his elbows; flapping around as he fled. In the backyard of Corbin Reece's building, he shot past a phalanx of slow-footed men, all of them a blur. Harry remembered slinging himself out of his car. The thing tangled around his elbow. It fell to the ground in front of the basement window. Harry knelt beside the window and pushed it open. *A cracked pane?* "Don't get sidetracked. The hell with the window. What was I carrying? What did I leave behind? Come on, come on, come on," Harry pleaded with himself, still holding his head in his hands. It came to him suddenly; it was a canvas bag. The bag regurgitated from the crumbling walls of Reece's closet.

Harry's arms fell to his sides. "Holy moly," he said to himself. "Holy Mother of God and her entire Mahjong team!"

Harry was aware he was speaking gibberish. He was astounded, feeling anxious. Jabbering seemed a good way to release some anxiety.

Harry realized where he had seen the canvas bag. The muscles he had barely developed, they were tensing. He could feel his entire body tightening. All of this was leading to another rendezvous with the hapless Arnold and Fleck. It made perfect sense to Harry now.

Neighbor Fleck's house was dark. There was nothing unusual about it. It was very late. Harry stood outside his neighbor's front door. He was reminding himself he had acted in ways, done things recently, he never thought he was capable of: confronting people verbally and physically, and then there was the Nicky Sotto episode. He stood in the darkness; trying to figure out if he was in control of himself. Harry took his own temperature and decided he was neither calm nor out of his mind. He was driven to find answers. He forgave himself on the spot for anything he may do moving forward.

Harry was about to move on, but he stopped mid-step. The darkness reminded him of the horrors of his childhood. He was conjuring feelings of failure and deep shame. The evil uncle. He crucified Harry for years. He was inside Harry's head, mocking his weaknesses. Harry looked down. His right foot was six inches off the ground. A middle-aged birdman, a crane losing its balance. Harry placed his right foot securely on the ground.

Harry observed his reflection in the pane of the storm door, provided by the muted nightlight. All the exasperation and violence he had worked up for Arnold Fleck disappeared. He thought his reflection looked weak and his body frail. His right hand was wrapped, and his posture weary and stooped. Harry straightened up as he reached for the doorknob. He felt an electric-like stab in his troublesome hip. His hand throbbed.

"Chrissakes," he said in a bitter whisper.

He peeked over his shoulder and saw the shape of Lolly's face keeping tabs on him through the pane on his kitchen door. He turned his attention back to Fleck's front door, and this time he twisted the knob with his left hand. The door was locked. A strong gust of wind momentarily blinded Harry. He scampered down the front steps and hurried around to the side door.

The storm door was flapping under the influence of the same prolonged gust. Harry wiped his eyes with his sleeve and re-tied his robe. He held onto the flopping storm door with his left hand to make the noise stop. He gingerly twisted the doorknob with his injured hand. The door opened easily, and Harry stepped up into Fleck's shadowy kitchen. He secured the rattling storm door by closing it quietly but firmly behind him.

It was dark and still inside the room. Harry had seen too many old movies and written enough mediocre scenarios to realize something was amiss. Fleck didn't respond to the alarm provided by his rattling door. He must be dead drunk or plainly dead.

Harry waited for his eyesight to adjust to the darkness. He moved deeper inside. His hearing was pretty good, and yet he could hear nothing, not a thing, nothing until...

Harry tilted his ear slightly to one side. He thought he was picking up the beat of a ticking clock. *Maybe it's the clock above the stove*, he thought.

"No, can't be. Who has a ticking clock over their stove these days?" Harry whispered to himself.

Harry took a breath. He sensed he was standing taller. He was following his instincts, and he trespassed to get closer to the truth.

Harry's eyes were adjusting. He could discern objects strewn around the place. Drawers were spilled open, throw rugs overturned; artwork and frames were on the floor in a series of reckless piles.

"Yep, I know how this movie's going to end," Harry whispered. "Everyone is going to die." The words were filled with doom, but the sound of his own voice calmed him.

One of Harry's investigative toes nudged several pieces of glass belonging to a shattered mirror. He stepped carefully. Harry heard it more clearly than before. It might as well have been a gong. Harry realized the ticking sounds were coming from a wristwatch. Signaling a useless SOS through the silence.

I'm going on tock, Harry thought. *Tick, Tick, and tock*...Because it's the way he thinks. This lack of rhythm is what makes him such a lousy dancer.

Harry looked down on *tock*, and his expectation was confirmed: the body of Arnold Fleck was face up on the floor.

Harry didn't have to strain to see Fleck's dead eyes were staring at the ceiling. He knelt beside the body. Harry didn't see noticeable wounds: gun shots, stabbing marks, or any other obvious signs of trauma. Fleck was surprised, browbeaten and terrified by someone until his heart checked out, Harry concluded.

Harry pushed off the floor with his left hand and stood erect. He had no prayers for Fleck. The pain in his right hand and hip became less of a nuisance. His body and mind were still. Harry tilted his head in the direction of the kitchen. He allowed his chin to lead him there.

Harry clearly knew what his next move should be. He moved cleanly over to the dishwasher and opened it. As he expected, the intruder or intruders had no way of knowing Fleck operated his dishwasher like a filing cabinet and safe. Everything was the same, neat, untouched. Harry saw the line-up of bills and paperwork, and the efficiently filed packs of cash. His eyes landed on what he came for: the canvas bag.

Harry tucked the bag under his arm and abandoned Fleck's house. He strode beneath the flickering light devoid of emotion. As Harry approached his house, Lolly stepped away from the door, making way for her solemn friend. Harry decided to take a quick shower, change into proper clothes, and prepare himself for an overnighter. Was he going to call David West, the thin-skinned top cop and tip him off? Not likely.

Chapter Twenty-Five

Officer Heastie's ungainly feet flapped toward the entrance of his hastily-built condo. His nest was located smack in the middle of the other townhouses. He nudged his eyes with his knuckles. He saw the figure of a deliveryman through the rectangular-shaped frosted window outlined in the front door.

"Okay, wait a minute. Jesus Christ," he said, not happy at being called away from his couch. He reached into his sweatpants and removed a ball of lint as he opened the door. The deliveryman presented Heastie with a pizza box.

"How much do I owe you?" The cop let out a sloppy yawn. "Wait a minute. I didn't order pizza. What time is it?"

Jaycee Singletary stood flawlessly erect inches from Heastie's clouded expression. He smiled and said, "You know, my uncle Elijah Cook asks himself this question all the time."

"What? Where do I know you from?"

"The question he asks himself all the time is this...What really happened up there on Choctaw Ridge?"

"Hey, this pizza is cold."

"Who doesn't like a slice of cold pizza every once and a while?"

"What?"

"Uncle Elijah believed the spirit of Billy Joe McAllister lived on in some of us. Inspiring us to dedicate our lives to stand up against hate. On occasion, we must bring to bear the hand of violence in the face of unconscious cruelty."

"You're the skelly dog walker? What the hell?"

Heastie's eyes noticed a twitch in Singletary's right arm. His hand was holding ten inches of good old American-made plumbing. Old yet certainly substantial enough to inflict considerable damage to say, the human body. Heastie's human body.

Before the mixed-up cop could shake the cobwebs from his brain, Singletary cuffed him in the mouth with the pipe. Heastie made an ugly sound and slipped backward into a stupor, unconsciously handing the pizza back to Singletary.

Singletary stepped inside and gently closed the door behind him. Heastie was writhing in a growing streamlet of his own blood. Singletary set the pizza down, removed cloth and duct tape from his backpack. He stuffed the wide-eyed cop's mouth with the cloth and taped it shut. Wielding the pipe, he proceeded to break Heastie's arms, taking a time out for a few bites of cold but delicious Staten Island pizza.

Inside Swoosie's house, the husband and wife were stumbling around in the basement with a dim flashlight. They were bundled in heavy robes. Swoosie was looking down at them from the landing; wagging her tail.

"I can't understand it," the husband said. "I just had this thing serviced. There's no reason for the heat to go off."

"Where are the light bulbs?" she asked, looking around. "Hello darkness my old friend," she clucked.

"There's nothing funny about this," her man moaned.

The flashlight beam landed on the heater. A pipe was missing. The disconnected areas were expertly capped off.

"I don't get this," the husband said looking completely bewildered.

Nearly next door, Harry Kavanagh felt empty inside. His emotions air-lifted from his body. He had stood over the corpse of his flabby neighbor and recovered what he expected to be evidence in a crime. The crime of his lifetime. Harry would never look at a dishwasher the same way. And the car loitering outside? The car was gone now – probably driven off by Arnold Fleck's chaperone to the other side. Harry had no feelings about Fleck's demise, except to conclude he would probably not get an invite inside the grounds beyond the pearly gates. It didn't matter that Fleck's wake would resemble Corbin Reece's send-off. An empty room filled with plastic chairs. The only thing that mattered was Harry's objective. Find out what really happened to his wife, and inflict some well-deserved pain if it were called for.

Harry finished his quick shower, his body having hungrily soaked up the bursts of hot water pounding against him. He wanted to maintain a clear head and his purpose. He tried to hold off approaching memories of his wife: a flashback of their last words. Permission not granted.

She had probably sashayed like Betty Davis heading toward the door, leaving for her meeting. "She you later, hon," she said.

"Okay, Headly." He called her that sometimes. He wasn't sure why. It was a silly nickname. Neither one of them could recall its origin.

She kissed him on the shoulder while he was puttering over the stove. "Don't hunch," she said.

"Okay," he hummed. He didn't bother to turn around.

And then she was gone. Forever gone.

Harry donned dark clothing. Yes, clandestine plans could unfold. Blending into the shadows would be to his advantage. Truth be told, he dressed for his wife. Felicity always remarked that he looked sharp in dark clothing. He was overweight in those days. At that weight, Harry thought he looked like a lumpy arm chair wearing a toga.

"Even a fire hydrant is handsome in a black turtleneck," he remembered telling her.

Harry wanted to be driven by the rage he knew he could summon; not memories that could make him soft. And so, he said to his deceased wife in an even tone, "I'll talk to you later, Felicity."

He stepped outside into the darkness with the curious Lolly in tow. Harry tossed the canvas bag into the backseat. He never got the taillight fixed. He hoped it wouldn't present a problem. They climbed inside and drove away, slowly and inconspicuously. Harry had homework to do.

Harry hadn't returned to Felicity's shop in years. He kept paying the rent, and so the landlord never complained. The doors remained closed for business. Harry knew it was only a matter of time before big development would reach the shop. The landlord, who owned half the block, would eventually try to invalidate the lease in favor of a new hotel no one wanted. It was happening all over the neighborhood.

Harry entered the dark place and headed straight for the rear of the shop. He sidestepped ethereal cobwebs and lifted a trap door. He took a step down and flipped a light switch to his left. Since big dogs and cellar steps are not a good match, Harry carefully guided Lolly to the lower level.

The windowless cellar was dry and cobweb-free. Felicity's office, intermittently occupied for reviewing invoices and writing checks. There was a simple wooden desk, the corresponding chair, and a leather couch Harry napped on while Felicity orchestrated lively wine tastings above his head. Harry stood motionless in the center of the room. Lolly, led by her nose, poked around the place for a comfortable place to land. Lolly considered the choices: a hard cellar floor or an inviting leather couch. She looked over to Harry for his permission, but his back was facing her. Harry pulled up the chair and sat behind the desk. He tore away the duct tape strangling his find, and he removed a journal from the canvas bag. There were others inside. He took a deep breath and opened to the first page. Lolly made her decision and jumped onto the couch. She watched Harry read until she dozed off.

It didn't take long for Harry to realize what a depraved person Corbin Reece was. His manifesto was a rationale for his life as a child molester. Reece himself had been victimized, and so he believed he had no other option but to follow the path carved for him. He believed he was ordained by his education and his learned appetites. Reece compared his years of indoctrination to college semesters. Each period of abuse was followed by a more intense and rigorous stretch of violence. The priest, Father Teagan, simultaneously victimized him, and then instructed him how to be a successful predator. On several occasions, Harry was forced to look away from the page. He needed to come up for air. The stench coming off the pages was nauseating. He thought about the struggling Greek boys, Arsenios and George. Those young men (they were young to Harry), brothers who had suffered so much at the hands of the vile co-conspirators.

Harry was yanked back to memories of his own young life; the horrors he experienced at the hands of his uncle, a man married to one of his father's younger sisters. That old wooden shed, originally an outhouse, and the smell of bleached wood and dry heat.

The images of his uncle's brow looking down at him, burning through the timeworn window pane, discovering his hiding spot. The door opening, Harry's youthful face sunlit to the point of temporary blindness; his uncle grabbing him by the shoulders, pinching them; eliciting a silent scream. The sound of the door closing. The light, secreted away, almost always made him pass out. It meant his worst fears were about to be confirmed. Private time for a predator; pure hell for young Harry.

The hypnotic stillness gripping Harry fell away. He pounded on the desk in a rage. Lolly awakened with a start and hopped off the couch. She placed her face in Harry's lap.

"I'm sorry, girl. I'm sorry, I'm sorry, I'm sorry," he said, his quiet sobs disappearing inside himself. He stroked her and directed her back to the couch.

"It's okay. Go back to sleep," Harry said steadying himself.

Lolly awoke hours later and looked up from her perch. She yawned and stretched. Harry's head was on the desk; he was dead asleep. Three journals were splayed before him. The canvas bag deflated at his feet.

Whispers of the names Roth, Heastie, Devine, Reece, Calendar, like wind chimes tinkled through the corridors of Harry's dream. In his mind's eye, Harry saw himself floating through a corridor. Felicity's lips drew closer to his ear each time he hovered near an unmarked door. He could feel her warmth; smell her soft-smelling delicious perfume. Each time a door wafted open, Felicity whispered to him, "Roth, Heastie, Devine, Reece, Calendar."

Lolly looked up sharply. Her majestic ears shot to attention. She began to bark a deep, resonating woof. She leapt off the couch and marched to the cellar steps.

Harry lifted his head and wiped the moisture from his mouth with his wrist. "What is it, girl?"

Harry was groggy and considered lowering his head, but Lolly wouldn't allow it. She began to huff and hop up and down, demanding Harry's attention. Harry pushed away from the desk. He trusted his girl. He knew something was terribly wrong.

Harry froze when he heard bottles breaking from above. *Bottles breaking or are they exploding?* Harry ran past Lolly, and before he could open the trap door, he knew what he was in for. He could smell the fire.

When Harry put his shoulder to the trap door, an immediate flood of dark smoke shot into his face and lungs. He tumbled down the stairs trying to catch his breath.

"Arggh!"

His twisted hip was cursing him; his right hand re-injured. Lolly continued to bark, urgently nudging Harry to his feet with her long face. Harry shook off the shock of the fall and scrambled to his feet. Harry thought he had some time.

"Smoke rises, smoke rises," he repeated.

But as he steadied himself another nightmare presented itself. Harry looked up. The wooden ceiling was blackening at a rapid pace. It was an old structure, more than a century old. Toxic black smoke began to creep through age-old gaps in the ceiling. Harry backpedaled toward the desk, hypnotized by the action unfolding above his head. Then without warning, a portion of the ceiling spilled open.

Aisles of shelving stocked with varietals from all over the world came raining down into the cellar. Dozens of cases of wine fell all around them; exploding like depth charges. Harry fumbled, tripped and danced crazily around the chaos. Hunching like Bela Lugosi's Dracula, he shielded himself with an imaginary cape in an attempt to avoid debris and embers. The cellar was enveloped in a turbulent cacophony: sizzling hot beams; exploding wine bottles; crashing debris.

Harry had a fleeting inane thought: he wished for a lifeline in the form of tenor José Carreras, if he would only sing an aria into Harry's ear. The powerful notes could perhaps shield him from the sounds of the bedlam closing in on him. But it was no good; Harry couldn't successfully summon Carreras, and he couldn't hear himself think.

Harry climbed over a fallen beam. He heard Lolly barking amid the din. He saw her standing on a bottom step near the Bilco doors at the far reaches of the cellar. Harry's mind cleared quickly. There was another way out.

Harry rushed to the desk and swept the journals under his arm. He met Lolly at the Bilco doors. The handle gave when he twisted it, but the doors did not open.

"For effin' sake," he shouted.

Harry could tell something was lodged between the door handles on the other side. Lolly howled with desperation. Harry kept on pounding against the door panels with his shoulder until they burst open. Lolly reached the outside first. Harry stumbled out behind her, not surprised by what he saw. An old wooden shovel had been slipped between the grips. It was at Harry's feet in two pieces.

"Good thing the shovel was as old as me," he gasped. He patted Lolly sloppily with his one good hand.

"You saved my life, kiddo. It seems to be going around." He wanted to smile, but his entire body was tingling.

Harry and Lolly limped toward the car. "Come on, beautiful. Let's get the hell out of here before the constabulary arrives."

Harry and Lolly pulled away from the scene when they heard the clamor of the fire department. Harry decided it was too risky to return home. Arnold and Fleck was dead, colder than before, and Felicity's shop would eventually burn to the ground.

"There is no such thing as an accident," he heard Felicity say.

It was something she said when one of the boys kicked a soccer ball through a window or dropped a peanut butter sandwich on the carpet. In Harry's case, someone was up to no good, out to get him. Yes, it would be flat out stupid to return home. There would be questions, misunderstandings, interruptions, and delays. Nope, Harry wouldn't stand for that.

The instant Harry drove away he could feel himself fighting off sleep. Those names – Roth, Heastie, Devine, Reece, Calendar – were inscribed on his weary mind like skywriting.

According to Reece's journals, his wife's accident was a part of a coverup. Harry learned who murdered his wife. And for what? For nothing, he concluded. For no reason at all.

Harry's heart ached for his wife; his eyes filled with tears. She loved everything about him, the good and the not-so-good. He *was* a lazy husband; he had taken her for granted. He wished he could hold her one more time and take a playful nibble out of one of her hips, his favorite part of her delicious body.

Harry's head flopped onto his chest and his hands fell by his sides. He could feel the car gliding off to the right, but he wasn't concerned, because he was enjoying the timeless sense of wellbeing. He was effortlessly floating toward his own forever sleep. He saw himself smiling as Felicity's lips gently brushed one of his eyebrows.

"You have to wake up now, Harry. I know you're tired, darling, but this is no time for a nap."

The car was flooded with blinding light coming from the rear. A blaring horn from a trailing big rig startled Harry to an abrupt consciousness. His eyes popped open in time to notice he was heading straight toward a pylon. He righted the car and skidded to a stop on the shoulder, kicking up gravel and roadside debris. Wide-eyed, Harry watched the big rig rumble by, cutting through the mouth of the expanse. Harry looked over his shoulder into the backseat. Lolly was fast asleep.

Harry could sense his knee was leaking fluid. His blood was following the laws of gravity, traveling toward his ankle. Other parts of Harry's body were bawling for attention. Like tiny school-room psychopaths on the verge of tying up their harried teacher. The good news? The slightest bit of good news for Harry Kavanagh, he could handle a bloody knee. *Join the club*, he thought.

"I'll live," he said, checking his reflection in the rearview mirror. "Matter of fact, it looks like you can't kill me."

Harry reached into the glove compartment and removed wipes. They were old and dry. Harry cleaned soot and grime from his face and dug into his ears with a product designed for bringing leather back to life. He stuffed the last wipe through the hole in his pants. He clogged the bloody divot in his knee.

"Jesus Christ," he said, shaking his head softly.

The fire was no accident. He *was* the target, but there was something more to the act. Maybe it was a heinous attempt to strike Felicity from the record books? Was it a last-ditch effort to murder her all over again?

Harry tilted the rearview mirror in his favor. Old Lolly remained motionless in the backseat. More than ever, Harry was grateful for his best friend. Her howls reoriented him, reminding him there was another way out. He was given another chance to set things right. He had all the information he needed to go on the offensive. He only needed keep his heart ticking.

There were lighter highlights in the sky. It wouldn't be long before Staten Islanders started another day with coffee and a sloppy bacon, egg and cheese on a roll. Harry was leaving the place behind in his rearview mirror. A grin creased Harry's face as he crossed over the bridge. He couldn't remember the last time he smiled at the prospect of visiting New Jersey. *When was the last time anyone smiled at the sight of New Jersey?* he thought.

He muttered, "Go figure."

Chapter Twenty-Six

Harry Kavanagh's bloodshot eye popped open. The other lid was stuck, but opened after a few failed attempts. Harry woke up in a motel room in Bayonne, New Jersey. He was on top of the bedding. He couldn't move. He felt pressure against his lower back. He was in a fetal position facing the wall. His mouth was dry, and his impairments pinged with familiar discomfort. His tongue reluctantly explored the grotto inside of his own mouth. He longed for mouthwash. Something with a greenish hue, unlike the color of the blood staining the bedspread. He'd have to leave the person in charge of putting the room back together again a nice tip.

Noises emanating from the adjoining room brought him closer to consciousness. Was a hot-sheet couple having a hurried encounter or was someone suffering from a nasty stomach virus? Harry couldn't tell the difference. He checked his watch. He'd been unconscious for only forty-five minutes. He groaned.

Harry rolled over with difficulty, smacking his dry lips and complaining under his breath. His grumbling ceased when he realized Lolly was stretched out beside him, hogging the bed. The source of the dead weight against his lower back.

"Good morning, girl. Can I borrow your toothbrush?" Harry rolled back to the wall and passed out before Lolly could answer. Lolly yawned.

Back on Staten Island in the Midland Beach area, Jaycee Singletary was brewing espresso in a meticulously clean galley kitchen. He was naked, humming something joyful. The blinds were closed. Splinters of sunlight escaping through in even lines highlighted Singletary's sinewy and scarred torso. Further evidence Singletary's life had known its share of conflict. Highlighted was his newest hallmark: the purplish bruising on his side, compliments of Officer Heastie. If he were to visit Dr. Armstrong, she would diagnose his condition as ecchymosis, because of the particular beautiful shades of blunt force trauma. Singletary had no plans to see a doctor. He knew the routine: aches and pains for at least three days, then a darker purple canvas, followed by an evolution toward more interesting greens and yellows. Singletary found himself in much better condition than Officer Heastie.

The bungalow he occupied was not listed in his name. While it was purchased in the name of Shelby Martin and paid for in cash, it belonged to him just the same.

Singletary dropped an expertly trimmed lemon rind into his espresso. On a countertop beside him sat a gift box housing the borrowed plumping pipe. Enthusiastic words pre-printed on a card said – *All I can say is, thanks*! The card would remain unsigned. Singletary would find the time to make the delivery and reunite with Swoosie. He sipped espresso and smiled at the prospect of seeing the friendly little dog again.

Bobby Devine plodded around his bathroom. His shave, shower, and morning constitutional, in that order, would be the highlight of his morning. The room was renovated by a contractor friend who called himself the king of tiles, or something like that. The bathroom looked like a cross between the Disco Hall of Fame and a mausoleum. Devine was called away from his throne when he received a distress call from an incoherent Heastie.

Heastie sounded drunk. He blubbered that he needed a doctor; he'd had an accident in his house during the night. Devine had no idea he'd find his partner so completely broken, which threw him closer to a nervous breakdown. Devine managed to get Heastie to the emergency room where he had to explain over and over again to the skeptical medical staff that his friend's injuries were the result of a drunken fall down a staircase.

"It's a very steep staircase," he explained to the ER doctor.

"Really? Like the staircase in Rapunzel's tower?" Dr. Emily Armstrong replied to the perspiring Devine.

Outside Harry Kavanagh's house, the police quickly figured out the homeowner and his hound were somewhere in the wind. The smoky musk hanging over the neighborhood came compliments of the overnight blaze at Felicity's Wine Boutique. The suspicious fire and Commander David West's recollection that Harry Kavanagh slugged his neighbor, whose name he couldn't remember, attracted the top cop himself to Kavanagh's address. West signaled detectives to knock on doors and look for the one guy with a shiner. He was someone to have a sit-down with.

West turned his back on the anxious couple who shuffled over from their house several doors away. He was focusing on collecting dirt on the smartass Harry Kavanagh. The harried couple were clad in pajamas and tangled in a shared blanket. They maneuvered themselves into West's line of vision.

He thought they looked like jittery English professors who had put in an all-nighter grading papers. They were imploring him to do something about something. Complaining about an important thing stolen from somewhere. They were talking at the same time and in increasingly high-pitched tones.

West noted the little dog at their feet. It was the yapping breed that often drew his ire. This dog sat politely, however, calmly by everyone's ankles. The corner of West's mouth curled into an unexpected smile as he observed the perfect little lady. He reached for the dog, and it leapt eagerly into his arms. He stroked the dog while the couple continued to object to the sabotage done to their heating system. The commander's eyes narrowed when he observed the movements of one of his detectives outside a house across the street.

"Hey, Colella, whadda' ya got there?"

The strongly-built cop was peering through a side window.

"I think I gotta live one boss. And what I mean is, I think this guy's a stiff."

West handed the dog to the husband and asked firmly, "Who lives in that house?"

The couple stopped blabbing. The wife's bluish lips answered first. "Doctor Fleck's house."

"Oh, the good doctor?" West said raising an eyebrow.

"Oh, no," the wife answered. "Not a good doctor. He has a terrible reputation. You have to read his reviews on the internet. We think he's some kind of a pervert."

"Have you ever met a podiatrist who wasn't a weirdo?" The husband joked, trying to endear himself to the stoic cop.

West stuck two fingers in his mouth and whistled like he was at a ballgame. Other cops, men and women previously unseen, emerged from behind bushes and neighborhood niches. They followed their boss who was parading in the direction of the good dead doctor's personal crime scene.

Singletary's bedroom chamber was not much larger than a corporate cubicle. He opened the only closet in the room. On one side were jeans, cowboy boots and denim shirts; the other side held Shelby Martin's clothing. There were pantsuits and blouses in beige colors, soft blues and lighter brown hues. There were three shirts with the name of the local hospital embroidered on it. The short-sleeve shirts were meticulously ironed and draped on wooden hangers. The shirts were displayed like a superhero's clothing line; one of them was waiting to be selected for active duty.

Singletary carefully selected one of Shelby's hospital shirts from the closet. He had already slipped on the required beige trousers. Women's trousers; this pair had buttons at the hip. He slipped easily into the hospital shirt, which was too wide for his frame. A purposeful fit to mask the hard musculature concealed behind the curtain. He turned to his bureau and removed a woman's wig from the smiling mannequin head staring back at him. "Thanks Sam," he said to the mannequin.

Singletary purloined the mannequin and the wig from the backstage of the Poison Pen Theater Company, which was a ten-minute drive from the bungalow. To make amends for his theft, Singletary attended a few of their subsequent productions. Singletary began to brush out the wig in long easy strokes. He started humming again. Maybe it was something from *Seven Brides for Seven Brothers*. He wasn't certain.

When Singletary donned the wig, his entire body appeared more relaxed. His shoulders softened and his toes, which were clenched atop the thin industrial carpeting, became completely composed. Shelby Martin reached for a lipstick and walked into the bathroom.

It was well after 3 a.m. when Harry heard a heavy pounding on the staircase. He rolled over in bed and reached for Felicity. She wasn't there. He'd fallen asleep with his clothes on.

When Felicity hadn't returned, Harry put out a few calls. Her friends told him she attended the meeting; she was probably out having a late drink with one of the gals. Not too concerned, Harry reached for a paperback that he knew would send him off to sleep.

Jake rushed into the room with tears in his eyes. Will followed closely, sobbing into the back of Jake's T-shirt. They both looked utterly broken. Lolly bounded up the steps, her tail wagging. She didn't know any better. She tried to squeeze herself between the teenagers. Will nudged her away with his hip.

"Pops," Jake choked. "Mom is gone."

"Gone?"

"Mom is passed. She, she died…she's dead."

Harry jumped out of bed and landed awkwardly on his heels.

"Pops, Mom is dead," Jake pleaded as his head fell onto his chest.

Harry took a breath. He gently placed his hands-on Jake's shoulders.

"Jake, listen to me. I hear what you're saying, but it can't be true."

"Mom is dead. The police are in the living room. We heard them talking like we weren't supposed to know yet. They're asking for you. They're not very fucking discreet."

Harry took a breath. "I understand the words you're using, but is there any way you may be mistaken?"

Harry Kavanagh awoke with tears streaming down his cheeks. He checked the time on his cellphone and looked stricken. He leapt out of the motel bed so quickly the pain coming from just about everywhere didn't catch up with him until he reached the bathroom. He felt like he'd been mugged.

After a twenty-second shower and a quick stop to pick up dog food, Harry raced back to his local hospital on Staten Island. He planted his car across the street from the parking lot; away from the security cameras. He sat inside surveilling the hospital's entrance. The car was running. Lolly was splayed in the backseat like the sphinx. Her face disappeared into an open bag of kibble.

Harry surveyed the evidence on the passenger seat. The journals, all three of them somehow intact. He flinched at the arrival of the torso beside his driver's-side window. It was Shelby Martin. Harry fumbled as he lowered his window. He tried to reclaim some decorum.

"Forgive me, I didn't mean to startle you," Shelby said evenly.

"I wanted to speak to you."

"You look awfully depleted, Harry. Did you break something else?"

"I could use a tune-up, but that's not why I'm here," he said impatiently.

Harry scooped the journals and shoveled them to Shelby. Shelby awkwardly accepted them.

"It's about my wife. It's the medical examiner's notes. His diary. His account of what happened. The information contained in the journals will prove Felicity was murdered. It was covered up."

"Oh, my. And why are you giving them to me? I work in a gift shop."

Harry answered him impatiently. "You're more than the sum of your parts. I can see right through you."

"You can?" Shelby said, shifting his weight. "What does that mean?"

"You saved my life for Chrissakes."

"I rescued you from a terrible cold perhaps."

"I have to do this a different way. My way."

"Your confidence in me means a lot. But Harry, I'm just one person." *Well, that's not entirely true*, Shelby thought.

"No, you don't seem to get it. I'm instructing you to keep these safe. Until I need them."

"You're ordering me?" Shelby played at appearing mildly insulted.

Harry massaged his face with the palms of his hands. "I didn't think I was going to have to work this hard. All right, give them back to me then." He put out his hands, but Shelby hesitated.

"All right, Harry, but I want a favor in return."

"You're giving the orders now?"

"It's important to me."

"If something happens to me, send a copy of the journals to the district attorney's office and another copy to the *New York Times*. Send the journals, the originals, and this note to my son Jake at Parris Island. And here's another letter for both my boys."

Harry handed Shelby two sealed envelopes he plucked from the motel.

"Now, what's the favor?"

"I live a private life, Harry," Shelby said. "Very private. When you need the journals back, my name or involvement can never be mentioned."

"I understand. Done." Harry said curtly. He could have said more, at least pretended to sound appreciative, but it wasn't the time for pleasantries. He had to get on the road. And he wasn't in the market for wistful words or thoughtful farewells. He got what he wanted and needed to get the hell out of there.

"I have to go."

"What are you going to do?"

"I'm going to rewrite the ending of Felicity's story," Harry said. He looked straight ahead drove off without another word. From the backseat, Lolly saw Shelby's figure diminishing in the distance.

Shelby got exactly what he wanted. He played his role perfectly. His feigned reluctance secured him the prize: Harry Kavanagh's trust and Corbin Reece's leftovers. He secured the journals under his arm and followed the big dog's face watching him as Harry drove off. He was well aware Harry Kavanagh was a grieving and damaged person. Harry was embarking on the final leg of his journey. It was all about his wife Felicity and nothing else.

Shelby took a second to wish Harry Kavanagh his desired result. The sentiment rang hollow in his mind, and so he said quietly, and with feeling, "Good luck, Harry."

Shelby would spend his time reading. He took a breath and exhaled. Without warning, he began to cough. It was an uncomfortable jag, unexpected and longwinded. When his Uncle Elijah Cook was caught in the throes of a good hack, which young Shelby remembered as something in between emphysema and burnt toast trapped down the wrong pipe, the old man would explain with tears streaming down his cheeks the condition he had was known as the creepin' crud.

"Don't worry about the creepin' crud, boy. It ain't gonna git me. I am blessed and highly favored," he would say to reassure the boy.

Elijah Cook smoked six packs of cigarettes a day. He was a puff away from his last breath at every moment. Shelby didn't have the creepin' crud – perhaps an anxious cough. The memory of his uncle's twisted face while maintaining his good nature brought Shelby to a place of raspy amusement. His uncle was the only shining light in his life, until he met another good man, Harry Kavanagh.

Shelby drove with the journals on his lap. If the specter of Jaycee Singletary showed up in the manifesto, Shelby may be forced to make a decision. Make the journals disappear or deliver on the help he promised his friend? His friend. He liked the sound of it. Singletary had done terrible things to some very bad people – people like Corbin Reece. He wouldn't want any

236

more harm to come to the Kavanagh family. He rooted for Harry to get some kind of closure. The decision was up to Shelby, and he was leaning toward doing the decent thing. It wouldn't be such a tough decision to make. After all, no one had a relationship with Jaycee Singletary except for Corbin Reece.

Singletary was a ghost; his fingerprints did have an arrest record though – under another name. In his youth, he saw a waitress being harassed by a trucker at a Pennsylvania diner. The trucker spat in her face over a lukewarm cup of coffee. The young man who would become Jaycee Singletary and countless others over time busted the trucker up pretty good. Punched him so hard the trucker's teeth ended up protruding from the young man's knuckles. When the law caught up to him, the young man did eight months in the hopper for aggravated assault. It taught the young man a valuable lesson: don't jitterbug around town showing off someone else's teeth. It's much easier to rearrange teeth and bones with pipes and bricks and two-by-fours, as long as it's done in private.

Jaycee Singletary didn't leave fingerprints in Reece's hell hole or in the crying cop's shabby condo. Shelby Martin would be sure to meticulously wipe down Reece's journals after the homework was done. If Jaycee Singletary was outed, Shelby would have to let it stand. Shelby was looking forward to sinking into an inherited comfy chair his uncle would often refer to as his reading chair.

The skies were grayer by the time Harry arrived outside State Senator Irene Roth's Button Nook Road residence. Branches seemed to be hanging lower than before. The thick landscaping, albeit thinning due to the advancing season, amplified a gloomy and mysterious presence, which Harry hadn't picked up on before. He was too busy dodging Thaddeus Calendar's poorly pitched glass of scotch.

"We want a pitcher, not a belly-itcher," Harry said aloud, recalling the sandlot chant of his youth.

He didn't think much of Calendar's pitching arm, which he looked forward to breaking. Slowly and painfully. Harry frowned because Irene Roth's place appeared to be impenetrable. And to make matters worse, the security cameras perched atop the main gate were staring down at him. He twitched in surprise when the front gate coughed open in jerky movements.

Harry crossed the threshold. He drove slowly. His fertile mind was expecting an ambush. Harry checked his rearview mirror. Lolly was alert but didn't appear to have any concerns. Harry's shoulders relaxed, and his fingers eased their grip on the steering wheel. The front door of the house was open. He peeked over his shoulder and watched the security gate inching to a close.

"I've been expecting you," Irene Roth said in an even tone as she stepped into the door frame. She was dressed in yoga clothes dotted with perspiration.

"I was finishing up on my stretching," she said wiping her brow and neck with a small towel. Harry rolled down his window.

"I took a chance. Shouldn't you be at work?"

"I needed a mental health day."

Taking a look around Harry said, "Fond memories."

"Oh, really? How's that?"

"Last time I was here your boyfriend threw a glass of scotch at me."

"He's not an accommodating person. He's not my boyfriend." Irene Roth couldn't hold Harry's inquisitive stare. She looked away for a second to reset herself.

"When I catch up with him, I'm going to have a few things to say."

"Such as?"

"I like my scotch in a stationary glass. You don't want to know the rest."

"All right," she said, her tone still colorless.

"Working out. Of course, if you were a murder victim you wouldn't have that option," he said getting out of the car. He opened the back door and Lolly hopped out of the car. She yawned and stretched without a care. "So, you've been expecting me?" he said, raising his eyebrows.

"Yes," she said. Her body was rigid, but her eyes were alive and keenly focused on Harry.

He chortled. "It sounds ominous. Something Sydney Greenstreet might say."

"Sydney Greenstreet? All right."

"Please don't disappoint me any further."

"I know who Sydney Greenstreet is." She paused. "It could be worse."

"What are you saying?"

"For me I mean. I used to be able fit into his clothes."

Harry said, "Self-pity at worst. Self-deprecation at best. You lost weight. Good for you. Dead wives lose everything. There's really no payoff."

"A state of high anxiety helped with the weight loss," she said absently.

"Not as effective as the despondency diet, trust me."

Harry walked toward the front door. Roth stepped aside, her eyes following him as he entered her house. The dog followed Harry inside. Harry disappeared into her kitchen.

"High anxiety. The despondency thing. We are a pair." His voice was dripping with sarcasm.

Roth heard him running the faucet and then placing a bowl on the floor. She heard the big dog eagerly lapping up the water.

Harry emerged from the kitchen without paying any attention to the well-appointed surroundings: the open floor plan with high ceilings, the baby grand piano, or the huge stone fireplace in the living room. Harry made a face as he attempted to remove the splint sticking to his pinky. He nearly mumbled a profanity and decided to abandon the endeavor for a later time.

Roth closed the front door gently and took tentative steps inside, as if she wasn't sure if she was on the guest list in her own house.

"I have lost weight," she managed to say, her nerves still showing.

"You seem obsessed. You look good. If that's what you're waiting for."

"I'm making small talk because I'm very nervous. Are you going to hurt me?"

"I think you'll be a very desirable person in prison."

"I've always thought of myself as a Miss Congeniality type. Have I undersold myself?"

"I've done things I never thought I was capable of, but I'm not the murdering type."

"I wish I could be certain."

"I think you are, otherwise you would have never let me inside. And yes, I believe you have a superior inferiority complex."

"Perhaps you're right…about everything."

"Now you're trying to flatter me. I could murder a song though. I'd prove it to you, but I don't feel like singing these days."

She took the opportunity to look him over when he reached down to rub his bloody knee. "You look like you've been…" She was searching for the proper ending. "You look like you've been active. How hurt are you?"

"Active?" He looked like he was grinning, but his voice was void of humor. "My entire body has been telling me what a moron I've been. Up until now."

"Up until now?"

"I've been playing catch up. Rather clumsily. I'm not exactly Philip Marlowe."

"You've done pretty well."

"My wife was taken away from her family. It can drive one forward. Go figure." He paused and spoke the following words slowly. "I'm just about ready to hand in my extracurricular assignment to the district attorney."

"You found something belonging to Corbin Reece?"

"And this is why you've been expecting me?"

"I know you've been asking questions. I've known David West's wife for years. She says he's been kicking up one hell of a storm around the house since you demanded your wife's case be reopened."

"Yeah, well, his wife can rest easy. Her husband is not complicit as far as I know."

"No, he's not."

239

"He's lazy. He's a jerk. But you know all this, don't you?"

"Um hmm," she said running a finger across one eyebrow.

"Forgive the lack of tact, but that milksop of yours, Bobby Devine, did he report seeing me running from Reece's place? Because now that I think of it, and it's taken a while for my mind to reset, I think I saw him tripping all over himself."

"Milksop," she said nearly smiling. "For someone so old-fashioned you seem to navigate well in the modern world."

Harry moved slowly and sat down on the piano bench.

"You're in a lot of pain," Roth said.

"The physical pain is a barrel of laughs compared to the rest of it," Harry said quietly.

Lolly came loping out of the kitchen and dug her nose into the bloody hole in Harry's knee. Harry winced and gently nudged her away with an elbow.

"Okay, girl. Get out of there." Lolly looked at him, insulted. She circled four times and curled up into a big ball at his feet.

"Do me a favor? Come in and sit down," Harry gestured to her.

Irene Roth crossed the line into the living room and sat on the arm of the couch facing Harry.

"Yeah, I found something belonging to Corbin Reece. He was a prolific writer. This is what I'm thinking after going through Reece's dirty laundry. You'll fill in the fuzzy spots for me."

"If I'm able." She hesitated and said, "Yes."

"By the way, do you know what the biggest irony is?"

"You're going to explain it," she said.

"It looks like Felicity was murdered over a parking spot."

A look of grief washed over Harry's face. It was an intimate expression. Irene Roth fended off tears. After a few attempts she was finally able to pull her gaze away from Harry's anguish.

It was the only thing she could think of to say when she turned back to him: "Do you want something to drink?"

Gathering himself, Harry said, "So, Felicity went to the borough president's empowerment thing with the express notion of making her presence felt. She had already been to West's office complaining about parking entitlements, the placarded parking fiasco in the neighborhood. She'd been to nearly everyone's office in fact. She'd complain about those placards to anyone who'd listen. Turned out, nobody listened. Cops, firefighters, the guys from the recruiting station, the Building Department's guys, Department of Transportation employees, EPA guys, parole officers, court officers, postal workers, they'd all drop these illegal placards on their dashboards, and then their cars would squat for eight hours. Never moving. And the traffic agents were given orders by David West to never ticket his guys, or the city's guys or any agency guys. Everyone knew you couldn't park in your own neighborhood, and everyone in town knew there was nothing they could do about it. It was killing Felicity's business. Cars just sitting there. No parking for small businesses. Never. She was hoping to get one sympathetic ear that night. But the borough president didn't give her the time of day either. He'd have to plead with Commander West to change the culture. Much too big of an ask. And since everyone knows the police run this town, our fair-haired borough president decided he wasn't going to break a sweat over one chatty grandstander." Harry's mind wandered. He struggled to get back on track.

"Are you sure you don't want anything to drink?"

Harry appeared to rally. "Felicity wanted to speak to you too, but you weren't at the meeting. So, she left."

"My aunt was ill. I was taking care of her," she said quietly.

Harry didn't hear a word she said, and he continued. "On the way to her car, she meets your boyfriend State Senator Thaddeus Calendar from Brooklyn."

"He's not my…"

"How am I doing so far?"

"Yes," she said in a low voice.

"He lures her to your office with the idea of getting your help or his promise that he'd talk to West."

"Yes, that sounds about right," she said barely audible.

"Things go awry. The gentleman misogynist from Brooklyn gets busy with his hands, and Felicity probably gives him what he deserved. They struggle, she stops breathing. The end."

Irene Roth lowered her face into her hands and sobbed.

"He enlists your guy, Devine, and the bulldog cop to place Felicity in the water in her own car. Because of your childhood connection to Reece, which he covers quite thoroughly, and since you're a pretty astute woman, you know all about his appetites. You may have mentioned this to Calendar and he strong-arms Reece to get fancy with his report. Driving under the influence followed by drowning. Nobody questions the head injury because it was attributed to Felicity's final seconds in the car. Signed off on by Reece."

"Part of what you're saying is correct," she said, wiping tears with her forearms.

"There must be cameras all over your office. Does any video evidence remain?"

"Reece wrote about me?" The thought appeared to repulse her.

"He accuses you of tipping off Calendar. Your old Catechism days together."

"I didn't tip off Thad. Someone else must have. There were rumors about Reece, but nobody gave a shit," she paused. "The video footage has been written over a thousand times."

Harry bowed his head. "Did you see the video? Did you see my wife's last seconds on earth?"

"Yes." Her eyes became wide and wetter recalling those final seconds. Harry was thinking about what he wanted to say next.

"But I have evidence – which I will personally turn over to the district attorney," Irene Roth blurted.

"How do I get to Calendar?"

"Mr. Kavanagh, why don't you let justice take its course? It's time for me to tell the authorities everything I know."

"On behalf of my family, I would like to wrap up a few things with Calendar first."

Irene Roth wasn't going to press him. "He has a place, north of here. It's a long drive. He calls it the shed. It's a house in the woods. He originally bought the cabin as a getaway for himself and his family. Now it's a place where he takes women like me. I'll text you the address."

"How do you have my number?"

"I've been wanting to call you for…" She couldn't finish the sentence.

Harry stood up. He felt his joints creaking. He started for the door.

"You're all over the news. The fire at your wife's wine shop. Your neighbor was discovered dead in his house."

"And I have a broken taillight."

"What?"

"Wait. The police have found Fleck already?" He opened the front door and Lolly pranced outside.

"Yes, and they're anxious to have a serious conversation with you."

"Devine and Heastie tried to get their hands the journals, which my good neighbor had stolen from me while I was semi-conscious. Somehow, they figured he had them. Fleck was probably blackmailing them. When Calendar's boys came up empty, they put Fleck to sleep; then they tried to burn me down. Makes sense. Can you try to straighten it out with the police while I make a side trip?"

"That's going to take a lot of explaining and time to unravel. Once I turn over the evidence I've been suppressing, I suppose I'll have credibility issues of my own. And probably not much freedom."

Harry turned his back and headed through the doorway. She followed him outside.

"Wait, take my car." She ran back inside and gripped a set of keys from her aunt's crystal candy dish. She took two steps outside and underhanded them to Harry. He snared them with his injured hand and grimaced.

"Take the older car in the garage. It runs great. The Cordoba."

"The what?" he heard himself ask.

"They won't be looking for you in that."

Harry knew she was giving him a head start. If he was lucky, he would spend some private time with the man who murdered his wife.

Harry looked at his watch and said, "How do I know he'll be at this place? The shed?"

"It's where he goes for privacy. The place is in his wife's name, Lambert. So, he feels safe there. If what you're speculating is true – that Bobby and Heastie paid a visit to your neighbor and royally fucked everything up, which is their signature move, then Thad is losing his fluids right now. He's panicking. He'll eventually show up there to drink a bottle of scotch and tug on his own dick."

Harry gave her a look. "Pardon your vernacular."

"I'm not concerned with my vernacular. Outwardly, the asshole can look as cool as a cucumber, but he's a piece of shit in a crisis. He may throw like a troll, but he's unpredictable and very dangerous. I wouldn't put it past him to run."

"There's no place to hide. Why wouldn't he take his chances with our polluted judicial system? I'm sure there are people in high places who owe him a favor."

"He's a coward at heart. He's got money. He's got maybe seven hundred thousand dollars alone hidden away in a safe underneath the shed. And he's got cash stashed away in a dozen other places. He could his spend his days in Key Largo searching the beaches with a metal detector."

"How can I be certain about you or your evidence? How do I know you're not going to sic Devine and the idiot cop on me the second I leave?"

"You'll like this old-fashioned expression…because the jig is up. And I'm giving you my word. It's the only thing I have left to give."

"You've made mistakes. Don't make any more. I have an impulse to thank you for the help, but I can't. I'm sorry."

"I understand," she said quietly.

Chapter Twenty-Seven

Shelby was sitting in his car in a parking lot. The parking belonged to the beach, located across the street from his bungalow. He was able to look out onto the beach and see the water. He opened his window and took a satisfying breath. The journals were on his lap. Jaycee Singletary's presence was not mentioned anywhere in Reece's writings. Shelby felt slighted, but Singletary was safe. Shelby had a promise to keep to Harry Kavanagh. He'd keep the journals secure until Harry needed them. It was time to step aside and let Harry finish things. Shelby knew Harry was gunning for Thaddeus Calendar. He was suddenly struck with an obvious addendum: *What if Harry is finished off instead?*

Shelby got out of the car and stretched. It became a spastic, angry stretch. He was having an internal argument with himself. He was troubled by the question. Shelby kicked one of his tires in frustration. He'd miscalculated. He became very angry with himself. He should have insisted on accompanying Harry. Harry was an amateur. He stood little chance of coming out of this mess unscathed. Shelby's conscience continued to chew away at him. Harry trusted him. When was the last time someone valued him enough to be a confidant, a friend? If anything happened to Harry, Shelby would never forgive him himself.

Before he knew it, Shelby found himself striding toward the beach. He kicked off his white Apex walking shoes and tugged socks off his ankles without missing a step. He surveyed the shoreline through narrow eyes. There were no lonely widowers walking chubby Labradors, no yoga devotees complaining about their lazy husbands. There was no one there to photograph him with a cellular appendage. The beach was his. Shelby needed to work out his mounting frustration. He needed to come up with a solution.

Shelby removed his wig and every stitch of clothing. Standing on the sand in his birthday suit – *Naked in November*; Shelby thought it sounded like a Johnny Mathis song. He folded everything and placed the tidy bundle under the boardwalk. He wiped the lipstick off with his wrists.

Jaycee Singletary waded into the November surf without a hint of a shiver. He dove under the water, and when he emerged, he swam parallel to the shoreline applying long, cleansing strokes. It didn't take him long to figure out another way to help Harry Kavanagh. His friend Harry Kavanagh.

Harry drove conservatively. It was the wrong time to be stopped by the police. He reached for a pair of Roth's sunglasses he discovered with his foot. He put them on. He opened the glove compartment and found a faded New York Mets cap. He pulled the cap over his eyebrows.

"I'm incognito. How do I look? Sexy?"

Lolly was spread out in the back. She was sniffing the Corinthian leather seats. A jowly yawn emerged. Even Lolly figured out that there was no such thing as Corinthian leather. Harry smiled at her response and yawned himself. He tightened his grip on the steering wheel. He was running on empty. He opened his eyes as wide as he could and noted the dusty dashboard and scattered T.J. Maxx receipts. He set the radio dial to 88.3 FM – nothing but static. *Bummer*, he thought.

Harry guessed the car was a seventies-something Chrysler. A Cordoba, she called it. Roth assured him the car would make it to the shed. He didn't doubt it. The engine sounded like it was on steroids. The vintage luxury coupe ran well and was fast. He was banking on making it to Calendar's hideaway without a hitch. Too bad about the radio.

Harry's head began to bob. He was well beyond drowsy. He viewed the message from Roth and estimated he had a four or five-hour drive ahead of him. He needed a pick-me-up. No sleepovers in Bayonne, or anywhere else this time around. He longed for sleep, but there was no time for it. He wanted to get his mitts on Thaddeus Calendar – preferably around his neck. Harry's veins begged for caffeine, lots and lots of caffeine. He decided to head over to see his friend Al, the owner and operator of his number one place to refuel, Manoscalpo's Deli.

Jimmy Lynch was grousing in the back of the bus. He was heading home from his shift. He put the thermos to his lips, but there was no more vodka. He looked deeply into the dull luster of the window and saw his hollow reflection gazing back at him. His mind was racing with bitter thoughts. So much for having faith in his union rep. Once you start complaining about queers and their bathrooms, you're done in. You are history. His mistake was blabbing big in full view. He should have left bad enough alone and let the little homo piss in any bathroom *it* wanted. He'd been through this over and over again in his mind. It wasn't that he looked forward to his yearly prostate exam, but shit, he was out of a decent paying job with good health-care benefits.

A man in a Santa hoodie was dragging a bag of recyclables toward the exit. He looked perturbed when he passed Jimmy Lynch.

"Hey bro," he said looking down at Lynch. His eyebrows looked like dueling mustaches.

"What do you want?"

"Yeah man. I'm speaking to you. Your cologne smells like kitty litter."

"That's right," Lynch mumbled, looking straight ahead.

"You think you're gonna get any pussy smellin' like cat whiz?"

Jimmy Lynch focused his bloodshot eyes on his critic. "You think you're gonna get laid looking like a diabetic Santa?"

"Diabetic Santa? That's weird. The women, they love my Aqua Velva."

"A woman would have to be blind," Lynch replied.

"Sometimes you have to be blind. Sometimes we both have to be," he said laughing, exiting the bus. "Just trying to help a loser out." He saluted Lynch with his middle finger.

The door closed, and the bus belched onward. Lynch grumbled under his breath. There was a good reason he reeked of kitty litter. His new job involved working at a pet store. His boss was an immigrant from a place Lynch couldn't pronounce. Lynch spent his time mopping floors and cleaning out crates. He was up to his eyeballs in shit. It was the only job he could find.

Lynch shook his head, reviewing his string of miserable luck. He was shoved into a puddle of piss, attacked by a madman after the art opening and tied to one of Louie Lupa's crosses. Lupa was enraged until he saw dollar signs. Lupa took Lynch's picture in all his glory – with the sock hooding his thing. The picture went viral. His old friend Lupa sold beaucoup art while he had to shield himself from a boatload of embarrassment. There was nothing Lynch could do but take the first job he could get. He needed something to hold him over until he could find something else.

The bus stopped at a red light. Jimmy Lynch's lids were heavy, but his thoughts were still stepping on his own feet. He tried tucking those humiliating memories away when he was distracted by the deli sign. He started to ruminate about having breakfast when he got home. He had no bacon, eggs, or cheese in his fridge. His options were limited.

Lynch perked up in his seat when he watched a man pulling up in a car in front of the delicatessen. The man removed a pair of silly sunglasses from under his baseball cap. There was something about this guy. It came to Lynch in a hot flash. It was the prick who assaulted him in the public-school bathroom.

Lynch jumped out of his seat, banging on the exit until the bus driver, cursing under his breath, reluctantly released the rear door.

Al Manoscalpo was a small man with broad shoulders. He was wearing a bleached-white waiter's jacket with a black smock underneath that. He had a thick streak of white running directly through the middle of his mane. Harry often joked that Al Manoscalpo looked like the offspring of a muscular wizard and Cruella de Vil. Al came toddling over to Harry.

"Hey, what the hell? You look terrible."

"And you look like an adjunct from Hogwarts," Harry shot back. Then taking a breath he said, "I'm sorry Al, I need coffee."

"Stop it. You're in trouble."

"You're damn right. I need two coffees, milk, one sugar. Then I'll be on my way."

"You're all over the news. Rosanna Scotto says everyone is looking for you. Why don't you go to the police?"

"Because I need coffee first."

"Then you have to get out of here. Right now."

Harry's eyes were drawn to the newsstand. He read a headline that exposed a high-ranking Vatican official as a serial child molester. Harry's knees buckled. He was disgusted.

"Harry," Al said, grabbing his shoulders; steadying his friend. Harry looked at him strangely, following Al's glance through the storefront window. A police van had arrived and plenty of cops were stepping out.

"The community affairs cops. They stop here every day. I have a recommendation that you avoid them."

Al pointed an elbow toward the rear of the shop.

Harry didn't have to be told twice. "Thank you, Al." Harry headed that way in earnest.

The last of the legs stepping out of the van belonged to Officer Brenda Streeter. She was about to follow the other cops inside Manoscalpo's when she spotted a Great Dane rising from the backseat of a good-looking two-door coupe. The dog began to unfold and stretch like a xenomorph from one of those Ellen Ripley movies. Brenda Streeter recognized the hound.

Harry stumbled out of Manoscalpo's back door and was immediately slammed over the head with a foreign object. Something hard. He was shoved against a dumpster. Harry thought he felt something pop in his back.

Jimmy Lynch nabbed the first potential weapon his hands grabbed in the recyclable bin: an empty tomato can. Harry was disoriented, his temple bruised and scraped.

Jimmy Lynch stood before Harry, hopping up and down, cursing. His lust for violence earned him a laceration on his palm.

It took a few cloudy seconds for Harry to recognize the former public-school security guard.

"What the hell is wrong with you, Waldo?" Harry screamed at Lynch. "What the hell is wrong with people?" Harry said, shaking his head heatedly; referring to the screaming newspaper headline.

"I'm sick and tired of innocent people being preyed upon."

"You think you're innocent? I lost my job," Lynch fumed.

"You lost the job all by yourself."

"Your friend the pixie got me shit-canned."

"People lose their jobs when they behave the way you did."

Harry noticed blood dripping from the inside of one of Lynch's fists. Lynch's chest was rising and falling at an unusually rapid pace. He could smell alcohol on the man's sputtering breath. Lynch found a box cutter in his pocket. Harry predicted Lynch was going to try to make a sandwich out of him.

Lynch said, "I'm gonna slice you into cubes."

"I'm about as beat up as I can be. I can't take on any more hurt," Harry said, stalling for time.

Harry looked down at his left hand and regarded it strangely, as if it didn't belong to him. He was gripping a rolled-up newspaper. He must have absently plucked it while he was parleying with Al Manoscalpo. Lynch took a menacing step toward Harry.

Backpedaling for a quick second or two, Harry said, "Goddamn it. Stop it. Just stop it, Waldo!"

"My name is not fucking Waldo. You son of a bitch, you're gonna need a lot of stitches."

Harry's shoulders brushed against the dumpster. Lynch looked like he was stepping through a curtain of haze as he closed in on Harry. Harry's gaze followed Lynch's eyebrows, dancing like angry musical notes. The man's mouth blistered him with a stream of profanity and hatred. Something strange was happening to Harry. He couldn't hear a thing; nor could he feel any…thing. There was none of the usual pain hindering him, reminding him of his limitations. His body felt cool and relaxed. He wasn't being hampered by stress. His body was preparing to go to battle. His mind compartmentalized all aches and pains and it was homing in on the strengths required to outplay the opponent. Intellect, instincts, and speed were the thoughts breezing into Harry's consciousness.

Harry sensed a smile may have emerged on his face. He noted the change in Lynch's expression.

Lynch's display of hatred gave way to an unanticipated look of vulnerability. The newspaper was passed to Harry's injured hand. He gripped it securely and felt no pain.

Lynch moved in awkwardly, top-heavy like a heavyweight lumbering forward, gasping for breath. Harry sidestepped to his right and raised the newspaper like a nightstick. Lynch found himself in no-man's land, exposed defensively. Harry pelted him with the *Richmond County Register*. Blows to Lynch's ears resulted in sirens blaring inside the man's head. He was stunned silly. He dropped the box cutter. He turned blindly, flailing wildly, only to bash one fist against the dumpster. He yelled out in pain. The churning baton found Lynch's right eye, his nose, and lastly, his lurching head. Harry hammered Lynch until the bigger man collapsed to his knees, gasping for air, his nose a bloody canvas.

"I give up. I give up!"

"That's not enough," Harry screamed. "The next time you decide to take your miserable life out on someone else, stay caged up in your basement in your soiled pajamas. Stuff your hate-mongering face with Mallomars until a case of runaway diabetes blows up your veins."

Lynch looked up at him with a whimpering and confused expression.

Picking up on this, Harry looked at him wide-eyed. "I don't know what the hell I said either," he replied exhaling.

"But I get it. I do. I do. I get it," Lynch pleaded.

Harry wielded the paper again, but when Lynch flinched like an abused puppy, he decided to holster it. Harry scooped up the box cutter and put it in his pocket.

A few minutes later, Harry slumped inside the Cordoba. He was in a fog and hadn't noticed the police van was still outside Manoscalpo's. Lolly leaned her face over Harry's shoulder and began nudging him with her wet nose.

"I'm okay, girl. Thank you. Gimme a second to recalibrate."

"You look like you need more time than that," he heard a voice say.

He turned his head toward the voice of Officer Brenda Streeter who leaned into his window. She gestured toward the newspaper tucked inside Harry's belt like a sword.

"I see you're a fan of one of our local newspapers." Harry didn't answer. "Or you're a make-believe pirate," she said calmly. "Which is it?" She absently scratched her nose with her thumb. "There's blood on the newspaper."

"Not mine," he said, probing the bruise on his head with his fingers. Her facial expression didn't change. He became suddenly keen to the idea that she had the ability to stop his progress. He sobered up quickly.

"Look." He was about to plead his case.

"Tell me about the blood and hurry it up," she said peeking toward the deli entrance.

"I ran out the back door of Al's when your van pulled up and some rummy jumped me in the alley. I hit him with a mediocre dose of journalism."

"A rummy? I really love old movies and dinosaurs too. I'm telling you Harry, I'm an old soul and you're nearly extinct. We're a perfect match."

"Can I go now, please?"

"What did he try to steal, your misery?" Harry shook his head. "If so, you should have handed it over," she said.

"You have no idea what I'm on to here," Harry said sternly.

"All right, all right. Take this, you ingrate." She handed him a tray with two large coffees on it. He received the tray with gratitude.

"From Al." She paused. "I'm taking a big chance here, so don't get yourself killed or commit any crimes against humanity. You might want to eventually stroll in and talk to us about the fire and your dead neighbor. You didn't kill him, did you?"

"No, of course not, and I will stop by and talk," he said. "But not right now."

"And Al says you're gonna like this. The corrugated tray is biodegradable."

"I have to go," he said, carefully placing the tray on the passenger's side.

"Please, be smart, Harry, or it'll put a damper on my pension." She pointed a finger at Lolly. "Keep this charming relic from getting into any more trouble, will ya?" Lolly looked right through her.

Harry nodded a heartfelt thank you to Streeter and drove off.

Several blocks away, Harry rambled past Emma Kendall's gift shop. The door handles were manacled with heavy locks and chains. Official-looking documents were pasted on the storefront window. Emma Kendall's store wasn't just closed – it appeared to be shuttered permanently. Harry didn't notice because he was reaching for one of those coffees.

He took a sip and said, "I feel my body being bathed in love."

He nestled the cup of coffee into the tray and turned on the radio, forgetting it didn't work. For an instant, Harry regretted banging the dashboard with his injured hand. But suddenly the radio began to work.

"Thank you. There really is a God. Can't wait to explain it to the boys."

He meticulously tuned the dial to 88.3 FM and listened to a rendition of the song *At Last*, marred by static.

"My mind is a muddle. I can't tell if that's Etta James or Lou Rawls," he said to Lolly grimacing. "Must have more coffee."

250

His hand trembled as he reached for another sip. The Chrysler owned by Irene Roth headed off island in a northerly direction.

Chapter Twenty-Eight

Irene Roth never left her living room. She hadn't turned the lights on as the afternoon grew darker. She was still clad in her workout clothes. They felt like a damp dish towel wrapped around her body. She passed the time cloaked in shadows, pacing; running scenarios through her mind and rebuking herself. She'd given Harry Kavanagh enough of a head start. She was ready to turn over the evidence. She didn't want to take the chance of being visited by any one of Thaddeus Calendar's cockroaches.

Was he capable of harming her?

She asked herself the question several times over, and her conclusion was the same: yes, of course. He was capable of anything if he sensed the walls were closing in. She was the only player who quit the team. She was Calendar's greatest liability.

Roth was feeling the skies were about to open above her head. She impulsively opened a closet and dug deep into a pair of high boots. She pulled out a pack of Marlboros secreted away for a rainy day. She would have her cigarette, grab her evidence concealed in a crawl space; then she would head to the district attorney's office. Roth estimated she still had enough time to get there before the office closed. The DA was known to be a hard worker, not a clock-watcher. If she was too late, she would redirect to Police Commander David West's house and unburden herself over coffee and Entenmann's with his wife.

She needed the cigarette. She stuck it between her lips and looked for a match. She marched into the kitchen and lit the cigarette over the stove just like her old man used to. She became instantly lightheaded when she inhaled. The second tug was a little smoother. She closed her eyes, relaxing her neck.

With the cigarette burning down between her fingers, Roth did her version of a ballerina's audition. She danced and whirled with extended arms. She couldn't help herself and giggled. And no, she wouldn't mention Kavanagh to the DA or the police. She wanted Harry to have his showdown with the man who murdered his wife. She owed it to the Kavanaghs to present the evidence. She would take what was coming to her.

She kicked something in the darkness. It was her cellphone. She was about to turn on a light but opted to get down on her knees and feel around in the darkness. She wasn't prepared to see her reflection in the picture windows or in the large heart-shaped mirror she purchased in New Mexico. The brief feelings of release quickly abandoned her. The dance was done. She thought about her role in the Felicity Kavanagh affair. Her inaction, her silence; more importantly, her allegiance to a corrupted soul like Thaddeus Calendar, a man who causes irreparable damage to the lives of others. She felt deeply ashamed. She angrily stubbed out the cigarette on her beautifully restored floor and closed herself into a fetal position. She began to cry.

Roth heard a faraway noise she deemed to be inconsequential. But it began to make some sense to her. She reluctantly unfurled until she was on her knees, alert and afraid. Like a meerkat searching the landscape for a predator. She redirected her attention to the entrance. It became clear – someone was jimmying the lock. She froze and held her breath, absolutely terrified.

Thaddeus Calendar cursed and groused the entire ride upstate. He'd gotten word about the disaster at the blackmailer's house. The journals Fleck used to bleed them were not found. Nothing of significance was retrieved. The podiatrist had no balls. His weak body decided to take the easy way out and have a stroke. Without the journals, Calendar fretted his only chance of putting the entire affair to bed was heading toward a dead end.

Calendar had other holes to plug. He sneered at the thought of the surprise he arranged for traitor Irene Roth. Calendar, the former criminal defense lawyer, called in a favor to one of his oldest devotees. Someone whose ass he'd pulled out of the fire on many occasions. He never officially represented Nicky Soto at his trials, but he did a lot of work behind the scenes to soften the blow. And now he required loyalty. He needed a job to be done correctly. He was confident Nicky Sotto's boys would take care of business.

This particular stretch of interstate was dark and seemingly endless. Calendar's eyes widened when he saw glistening snowflakes floating onto his windshield.

"Snow? I love snow," he said with the enthusiasm of a child.

Julie and Will arrived. They decided to escape the dorm-room shuffle and head downstate for a quick overnight. Kicking out their roommates for some private time grew old. The couple agreed it was terribly inconsiderate of them. Julie promised Will they could enjoy the country house without any guilt and without worrying about being interrupted. Her parents were in the middle of a nasty divorce. As far as she could remember, they hadn't visited the house as a family in many years. There would be no guests or joy in Cropseyville unless it came at Julie's invitation. Julie was eager to rebrand the cabin as a happy place and not to mention, a hideaway where she and Will could enjoy hours of intimate time together.

They were each carrying a wrinkled bag of groceries purchased at a sad excuse for a general store. After some mandatory dusting and cleaning up around the cabin, they began kibitzing about how hungry they were. They made a funny kind of a deal to cook dinner with the mystery ingredients each had chosen at the little store. They didn't have too many choices. The shelves were mostly bare. They each scavenged to the best of their creative abilities.

"Moment of truth says my talkative stomach," Will said.

"Let's do this thing," Julie said, looking at him hopefully.

Will clutched his paper grocery bag, looking like the Heisman Trophy figure protecting the football. They spilled their groceries onto the kitchen counter and surveyed the other's handiwork.

"A magnum of mayonnaise?"

"I don't know," Will said. "And what's that? A tube sock?"

"I think it's squash," Julie said giggling.

"You think?"

"Cannoli beans, a can of tuna, mayo, a tube sock, loaf of raisin bread with some mystery green coloring around the edges, string beans, out of season strawberries, Pop Tarts and everyone's favorite, Spam," Julie said in a disappointed tone.

"Hell with it. Let's get some pizza," Will offered without batting an eye.

"We're not in Staten Island anymore," Julie said opening the refrigerator. "You're not going to get a good slice here, and there's nothing in the fridge. Let's go into town for wings and fries. Nobody messes that up."

Harry Kavanagh couldn't help himself. He had to make a stop at one of those rest areas along the interstate. He'd been driving with the heat off and the car windows open. It was the only way he could stay awake. He bellowed Bobby Darin songs in an effort to keep the nose of the Cordoba from veering into a ditch. He wasn't too fond of his crooning, but it didn't seem to bother Lolly. She looked thrilled to be taken along on a highway excursion with the windows down. There were big lights blaring up ahead on the right. Harry slowed down and pulled into the parking area.

Ten minutes later, Harry emerged drinking coffee out of a popcorn-sized cup. He finished off the last of the coffee and watched Lolly do her business on a neatly manicured grass median. Harry felt a twinge of guilt over her placement. He cleaned up with the front page of the *USA Today*, smearing the faces of the Vatican officials accused of child molestation. Harry looked up at the night clouds and noted, "Looks like snow. How about that? I hate snow." He opened the door and Lolly lumbered into the car. Harry slid into the driver's seat and closed his eyes. He didn't plan on it, but he immediately fell deep into the Corinthian leather and fast asleep.

It came to him quickly as he swam in the November surf. He had it worked out in his head before the third stroke. That's what a good swim can do. Jaycee Singletary couldn't track down Harry, but he could do the next best thing: track down State Senator Irene Roth and convince her to go to the authorities. According to Corbin Reece, Roth was tortured by the death of Felicity Kavanagh. She was beholden to Calendar because she was putridly-sick-in-love with him. Roth was a powerful woman who handed in all of her chips in exchange for a rotten sentence with a lecherous soul.

Singletary believed he could convince Roth to do the correct thing without applying too much pressure. The walls were closing in on all of them. The first one to confess to John Q. Law might get a break. Singletary decided to put it on the line for Harry Kavanagh. Shelby Martin was his name on the record. Shelby had identification, a job, a house, and an automobile. Shelby Martin was someone he could go back to if there was a glitch. Jaycee Singletary was the only man for the job.

Singletary walked to 57 Button Nook Road from the Midland Beach residence. It took him nearly two hours. It was dark when he arrived. He knelt and pulled up one of his socks, which had slipped below his ankle. Singletary concealed himself behind the trees outside the range of the security cameras he spotted atop the perimeter gate. Singletary watched two men out in the open, clumsily attempting to pry open the gate with crowbars. The big boys, clad in tight-fitting leather jackets, although he had no way of knowing, were muscle belonging to Nicky Sotto. The hoods from the marina were grunting and complaining until they succeeded in prying the gate open. They disappeared inside Irene Roth's property. Singletary pulled on a pair of gloves, yanked his baseball cap over his eyes, and nimbly shadowed the intruders.

Irene Roth was on her knees, frozen. The front door opened and a fit-and-trim-looking man wearing a baseball cap tipped over his brow stood silhouetted in the entranceway. She could tell he was wearing gloves. He tucked the tiny utensil he used to open the door inside his pocket. He closed the door softly behind him and locked it.

"Please don't be alarmed," came the melodious voice emerging from the stranger.

"Um, that's a nice, but you just broke into my fucking house."

"I see Harry Kavanagh's car outside. Is he here?"

She didn't say anything at first. "Who are you? Want do you want?"

"I was surveilling two men who disabled your front gate. I followed them in."

"You followed them? Where are they?"

"Probably attempting to gain entrance from the rear. I suspect they've been sent by the senator from Brooklyn. To prevent you from providing information should you have the impulse."

"How do I know you're not lying? How do I know you weren't sent by him?"

"How long have you been sitting in the dark?"

"A while," she paused. Then she said indignantly, "Because that's the way I roll."

"Turn on a light."

"What? Why?"

"Turn on a light."

She got to her feet and slapped a wall switch with her palm. Nothing.

"They cut the electricity," Singletary said.

"How do I know you didn't cut the electricity?"

They heard clattering from the rear of the house. The stranger tilted his head. "You're running out of time."

Roth monitored her breath and kept a watchful eye on the man as she walked out of the room.

"Where are you going?" he said.

"The kitchen. I have security monitors in there. They run off a separate generator." She disappeared through a darkened door frame. He followed, taking even strides. When he entered the kitchen, Roth pointed the tip of a large kitchen knife at his neck.

"Now, get out," she said to him, breathing erratically.

When he didn't move, she followed his gaze toward the security monitors. They saw two men forcing the back door with crowbars. She tossed the knife onto the counter.

"Alarm system?"

"It would make too much sense, so no, damaged in the last storm," she said, stepping back from him. "I'm an idiot."

"They don't know that. That you don't have an alarm system. So, they're going to want to finish what they came to do, and quickly."

"How much time do we have? Do you think?"

"Do you have cooking oil?" he asked. She made a face and nodded toward one of the cabinets.

"You plan on sautéing something?" He didn't respond. "Why don't we run out the front door?"

"Where is Harry?"

"I'm Captain-Fucking-Obvious, okay? He's not here," Roth spat out.

"If you succeed in making a run for it now, you're going to have to sleep with one eye open. Then again, there's the chance you don't make it at all."

"So, you're an optimist? Why are you helping me?"

"I'm a good Samaritan," he said emptying a can of cooking oil all over the kitchen floor. "This is what's going to happen. You're going to tell the police…"

"I have to get to the district attorney's office."

Without missing a beat, he said, "You're going to tell them that three men broke in. They began to fight among themselves. One of the men took off, got away…"

"That would be you?"

"You're going to give them a creative description of the third man. He looks a lot like the governor of New Jersey. Do you understand?"

"But what about our night crawlers?"

"Where is Harry Kavanagh?" he asked, avoiding her question.

"He's on his way to shake hands with Thaddeus Calendar. He's on his own."

Roth watched with curiosity as Singletary unplugged the microwave. He gripped the knife Roth surrendered. "You have anything sharper than this?"

She shook her head, no. Then she explained nervously, "I order in a lot. I'm thinking of getting this thing called Blue Apron. They deliver fresh food to your house; you follow their recipe. It would deter me from eating one more chicken parm hero. I should get new knives."

He glanced at her disapprovingly. "You enjoy the sound of your own voice." Then he studied the knife. The nightlight revealed his hardened expression. "It's serrated. It's going to hurt, enough."

"I want to make sure we're on the same page. I am not on the menu, right?"

"No," he deadpanned. He didn't approve of her sarcasm.

More noises from the rear of the house. Roth's eyes widened; she couldn't conceal her fear. She knelt on the floor.

"Thank you, whoever you are," she said sitting cross-legged on the floor just outside the kitchen doorway. "Are you sure I shouldn't just run the hell out of here?"

He ignored her. She curled into a ball, trying to control her nervous breathing. They heard the men cursing and banging around.

Singletary spied her in a way he hadn't done previously.

"I've done questionable things on my journey. Some very bad things…"

"Including what you're about to do?" she asked.

"What I'm about to do, I'm doing for Harry Kavanagh and his family."

"Okay, why the soapbox? For my benefit? I've never been accused of being a good Catholic."

"You're going to pay a price. But there's light at the end of the tunnel. If you can find a way to forgive."

"Forgive?"

"Forgive yourself," he replied.

She considered his words, but before she could respond they heard more splintering.

"Holy shit," Roth hissed. "This is real. They're inside the house."

Nicky Sotto's busboys lumbered down the darkened hallway waving jittery handguns. Roth felt her glutes pressing into the floor. Her left wrist was cocked on one hip for balance. She grabbed a knee with her right hand and dug her fingers in. She thought about praying, but abandoned the idea. Praying had gotten her nowhere.

She didn't know why – maybe a peaceful thought before dying – but her mind traveled back decades when she'd spend lazy afternoons at summer camp. It was a city-funded program, and a respite from her father's darkness. She recalled toddling down a dirt road, holding hands with a delicious-looking teenager, whom she had a little-girl's crush on. Her camp counselor's name was Marigold, and her smile could light up the night sky. She and Marigold would sneak away from the group, pick blueberries, and sing children's songs.

"I want blueberries," she whispered to herself. "I want to sing songs."

The pounding of heavy feet ripped her from her longing.

She gasped, "Is this how my days are going to end?" She heard Singletary cough. A tear fell from of one of her eyes.

The first man skated across the kitchen floor the instant his heels met the cooking oil, crashing against cabinetry and appliances. Singletary was waiting beyond the periphery of the oil slick. He hefted the microwave and bashed the man over the head with it rendering him non compos mentis. Irene Roth cringed at the sound of the man's agonized *umpfs*. His palm blossomed and a handgun with its silencer floated freely from his grasp. The second man took a few wild shots as his body contorted along the slippery floor. Singletary slung the serrated knife at him. He missed his target. Two more gunshots grunted from a silencer. Singletary scooped up the first man's weapon and returned fire. The second man's neck was dotted with dark holes. His lids closed, and he appeared to stop living. Singletary knelt beside Irene Roth, who was sitting in a ball. She was rocking; attempting to medicate her anxiety.

"I'm bleeding," she said.

Singletary folded her yoga pants from the waist and inspected the injury. "He grazed you on the fleshy part of your hip."

"Fuck you," she said with a wan smile.

"Your cellphone?"

"I was kicking it around when you dropped in on me." She pointed to the living room. Singletary scurried over and found her cellphone. He handed it to her.

"How do the security cameras work?"

"They're backed up to an external hard drive in my office, running off the same generator."

"I'm going to require a minute to retrieve the hard drive before I leave. I'm going to need a car."

"My car has a tracking device in case anyone gets curious. Take his car, Kavanagh's car, but ditch it fast. The police are looking for him."

"His keys?"

"I've been shot. I can't think about keys right now."

"You'll be fine. By the way, your perfume is lovely. What is it?"

Roth returned his question with a skeptical look.

Singletary chided himself for taking too long to hot wire Harry Kavanagh's car. Singletary's lips curled upward at the sound of Harry's car turning over. He heard the sirens approaching. The local police were way ahead of schedule. Irene Roth was a local bigshot after all. Singletary knew it was going to be close. He estimated the police would arrive in about twenty seconds. He recalled Roth's comment, "Is this how my days are going to end?" He floored the accelerator.

Thaddeus Calendar's car crawled through the woods on its way to the cabin he called the shed. Weekend warriors had been injured along this trail, falling headlong on their bicycles or stumbling into the four-foot natural trenches on either side. This backway trail was barely wide enough for a single vehicle. A local do-gooder painted *Harm's Way* at the beginning of the trail on a piece of scrap wood. The makeshift signpost was nailed high against a thick tree. The trail spilled into a crushed patch of grass behind Calendar's hideaway. A second artery broke away and descended on a steep decline toward the lake some fifty yards below the house.

Calendar drove cautiously as long-fingered branches clawed the sides of his vehicle. His phone lit up. He lifted it dreamily without looking at the name on the screen.

"Tell me something good." His eyes were hypnotized by the wipers clearing snowflakes from the windshield.

"Well." It was the sound of Irene Roth's voice.

Calendar could hear squawking emergency radios in the background. He closed his eyes for an instant, preparing for more bad news.

"Shall I begin with once upon a time?" Calendar heard her say. He hit the break and the car jolted to a stop. His facial muscles tensed.

"One of the men you sent to my house is in a much better place, and the other one is going to have a microwave phobia for a very long time. If he pulls through."

Calendar stared at the phone, motionless.

"It's an inside joke. You had to be here," Roth quipped. "Oh, and you owe me a new pair of yoga pants. I bled all over them. Unfortunately for you, I didn't bleed out."

He snapped off his cell and screamed; his face reddened, and his eyelids nearly turned inside out.

A quarter of a mile ahead, Harm's Way opened up behind Thaddeus Calendar's place. As Calendar approached, he thought he saw flickering lights inside the cabin.

"What the hell? What the bloody fuck now?" he raged through clamped teeth.

He reached under the dash and pulled out a small, unremarkable-looking revolver. He tucked it behind his back, and exited the car without closing the door. He climbed the back steps and entered the house through the porch door.

The place was cloaked in shadows. Calendar could smell wood burning. The reflection of fireplace flames was climbing the opposite wall. He saw Julie asleep on the couch, her head nesting in the lap of a young man about her age. The young man sat low in his seat. His head was tilted all the way back. He was in a deep sleep.

On the kitchen countertop was a bottle of Jim Beam Honey Bourbon, and the remains of the kids' fast-food binge: two dozen chicken wing bones, napkins stained with hot sauce, and enough leftover blue cheese to spackle a hole in the wall. Julie's backpack and a wallet were beside the wreckage and within Calendar's reach. Calendar carefully went through the boy's wallet. He read the name on the New York State driver's license: William Kavanagh.

Calendar put down the wallet. There was frantic activity going on behind his eyes as he attempted to make sense of the situation. He looked shocked.

"Thad? Jesus Christ!" Julie said, standing at attention, staring directly at her father. She was flat out indignant. Will's head rolled onto his chest as he awoke. "What the hell are you doing here?"

"Well, the last time I checked, I was paying the taxes on this house," Calendar said, trying to keep the mood light.

Will wiped his mouth with his sleeve and stood beside Julie. His stance was slouched in apology and embarrassment.

"Who's your young man?"

"Who's my young man?" she answered, exaggerating his words. "Will is my boyfriend."

Will cringed, preparing himself for her father's ire.

"Will Kavanagh, sir," he said, sounding more like a smaller version of himself. Julie looked at him oddly. Will cleared his throat and shrugged.

"This is Thad, my father. I call him by his first name because I like to pretend he's really just my shitty stepfather. It softens the blow," Julie said folding her arms.

"I am Senator Calendar, obviously Julie's father. Albeit sometimes estranged father. You know, the awkward years are upon us all."

"Yes, sir," Will uttered automatically.

"Yes, the awkward years. The years when your father spends his time sleeping with or harassing every intern in Albany while his wife tearfully plans the family vacation," Julie spat.

Julie stomped around the room collecting their things and placing them by the front door. She underhanded Will his wallet. He snared it chest-high.

"Oh, you two don't have to leave. I'll say my goodbyes and make other plans," Calendar said.

Julie looked at him as if she didn't recognize him. Calendar moved over to Will extending his hand. Julie became aware of a bulge behind her father's waistcoat.

"Gracious, that's quite a grip you have there, young man," he said shaking Will's hand.

"Gracious hell? Who are you pretending to be?" Julie said, preoccupied with the knot.

"Did you say your name was Kavanagh?"

Will pulled his eyes away from Calendar and looked over at Julie when he answered, "Yes, sir." Will noticed Julie was concentrating on something behind her father's back.

"Is your family from Richmond County?"

"Richmond County? Oh, Staten Island. Yes."

"I knew your mother," he said, smiling at Will.

"Really?" Will said, not knowing what else to say.

By the look on her face, Calendar surmised Julie had come to a conclusion. He immediately dropped the charade. His disingenuous smile became a sneer. He marched over to Julie and hit her with a vicious slap to the face. Her body buckled. She reached out with an anguished, hopeless look, flailing; her arm

261

snapped the spindles on a kitchen chair on her way to the floor. Will stood motionless, stunned. His feet were frozen to the cabin floor. Julie began to moan. Will shook free from his temporary shock and looked to make a move on the red-faced Calendar.

"No, no, no," Calendar said, breathlessly wielding his weapon. The young man pulled up sharply.

Will said to Calendar through tight lips, the entire time his worried eyes focusing on his writhing girlfriend, "What is wrong with you?"

"You know, Will, as it turns out I know your father too. The little prick opened up a can of worms that will dramatically change the course of my life. Forever."

Two hours later, Harry Kavanagh quietly pulled up in front of the shed. He got out of the car. He opened the back door, but Lolly was asleep. Her leg muscles twitched involuntarily; her eyelids remained closed for business.

Keeping an eye on the cabin, Harry leaned against the car and square-rooted his way through some stretches. His lower back ached from the long drive. No evidence of a José Carreras aria pulsating through his veins. In his typical self-deprecating way, Harry felt closer to Captain Kangaroo than Captain Ahab.

He didn't taste the sweet flavor of vengeance on his lips. He was bone-weary. He'd spent his reserve energy sticking his head out of an open car window, fighting sleep along the interstate. He journeyed to make a stand, for his wife and his boys, but what now? What he would say or do to the man who murdered his wife? He didn't have a clue. He had gotten this far, he'd figure it out. He'd managed to survive a clubbing and a near drowning, a twin beating, a building collapse, a lousy restaurant, a poorly flung bottle of scotch and an inferno. Did he feel a sense of accomplishment? He didn't know what he was feeling at the moment, except the cold. The dip in temperature took Harry by surprise. He wanted to get inside the hideout and let the game come to him.

Harry pointed himself in the direction the cabin. It appeared nearly dark on the inside. Harry held some hope in his heart. He hoped for stairs; lots of them. Harry fantasized about throwing Calendar down a steep flight of stairs. And once he was through with Calendar, he planned on dropping a hammer on the two miscreants, Devine and the cop Heastie, if Irene Roth failed to do her job.

Once inside, Harry noted the dwindling flames in the fireplace were the only source of light. As his eyes struggled to adjust to the shadows...

"I shit you not. As I live and breathe, all of my dreams have come true." The slurred voice belonged to Thaddeus Calendar.

Harry noted Calendar's shadowy figure slumped in a cozy country chair. Calendar yanked the chain on the standing lamp.

"Let there be light," Calendar announced.

Harry casually sidestepped to the fireplace and removed a poker. "I could say the same," he said estimating the weight of the poker.

"What? Let there be light? I don't think I get you good, sir."

"No, you moron. Meeting you here *is* a dream come true," Harry said in a whisper.

"You're a peg in my prostate." The celebratory tone was missing from Calendar's voice.

Harry spotted a gun sitting in Calendar's lap. He shook his head bitterly, disappointed by his unpreparedness.

"You came to a duel carrying a fireplace accessory. You're a sorry amateur, Kavanagh."

Calendar polished off the bottle of Jim Beam and threw it at Harry. Harry didn't move. The bottle missed him by three feet.

"You're going to have to work on that," Harry said.

"Look at you. You're nothing. You come barging in here dreaming of being a hero. Instead, you're a nelly busboy flitting around; afraid of wetting your pants because the girl at the table gave you a boner."

"You're a creative thinker," Harry said quietly, certain his quip would not improve the situation.

Calendar's fingers found the gun in his lap. He staggered to his feet and leveled the gun using both hands.

"Put down the poker or I'll shoot you right between the legs."

Harry tossed the poker aside without hesitation.

Calendar cackled. "There's a line we never heard in those cowboy movies when we were kids, eh, Harry? Shoot'em between the eyes, yes. Shoot'em right between the legs? Not so much. I am a creative thinker."

"Yes. You're brilliant, of course," Harry deadpanned.

"You have the floor. Isn't this about the time when you make the speech? The one where you tell me how much I've stolen from you, eh?"

"There would be no lessons learned, would there? Why should I waste my breath?"

"You may have a point. If Felicity…"

"Do not say her name," Harry warned. His head was beginning to throb; he could sense his heartbeat ramping up. His anger was on its way up, taking the express elevator.

"Or what? You'll use profanity?"

He waved the gun at Harry like a conductor. Harry took a deep breath.

"If your wife was compliant, we could have had a ménage à trois. Me, giving her what she really needed, and you, changing the sheets."

Calendar's sneer disappeared and his expression darkened. "Out," he said, firmly pointing the gun at Harry.

Harry began to back out the way he came.

"No," Calendar barked. "We're going out the back."

"Whatever you say."

"Yay, damn straight whatever I say. Since you've changed the course of this mighty river," he said looking crazy, pounding his chest. "Since you've forever changed the course of this mighty river – me – I believe there's more I'm required to take from you."

Calendar plucked an oil-stained rag from the tool shack and tossed it to his hostage. Calendar ordered Harry to blindfold himself. He barked directions at Harry as they descended through the thicket. Harry stumbled several times only to have Calendar's encouragement come in the way of a kick to his side. Harry was bruised and battered, his left side embossed with Calendar's shoe prints. His palms were bloodied by several falls. Calendar ordered Harry to stop moving. Harry could sense they'd reached an open area. He could discern light creeping in from beneath the blindfold.

"Take off your veil, you son of a bitch," Calendar ordered.

Harry removed the rag. A burst of light, acting like a shroud, prevented him from seeing the entire picture. There was a silhouetted shape resembling a large fallen tree, no – maybe it's a car. It *is* a car, angled directly in the path of a body of water, a lake. Headlights? No, yes of course; they were blasting. That's where the light was coming from. Harry rubbed his eyes. The visuals were not completely adding up.

"Pops? Are you okay?" The voice sounded anemic.

"Will?" Harry's voice couldn't conceal his anxiety.

Harry hoped he was dreaming. He flashed to a funny text he had written Will a week after he left for college his freshman year:

Already put a hot tub in your room and got a tattoo. Enjoy your independence, read, laugh, be curious; make yourself proud. How's the food? Miss you. Pops.

"Pops?"

Harry wiped his eyes with blood-stained palms. He looked like a deranged raccoon. Julie's car was angled toward the murky drink; the brights were on. The overhead light inside the car revealed Will and Julie. They were trussed in the front seat. Their torsos roped to the seats; their hands and feet were bound. The car was in neutral; the emergency break was the only thing saving the teens from drowning. Will clearly appeared fatigued. Julie's skin was blue. Her face was bruised and swollen. She was shivering. Harry turned wide-eyed to Calendar for an explanation.

Calendar threw up his arms and said, "What? You didn't know our kids were an item? Small world. Now here we are. One big happy family. But alas, there won't be a reunion around the Thanksgiving table. Fuhgettaboutit as we say in Brooklyn," he cackled.

"What are you doing?" Harry was anguished; incredulous.

"I'm going to shave my head and get a spray tan. Then I'm going to spend my time with hookers and Heinekens."

"This isn't 1942. Gliding through a stop sign without ID and you're detained in ten minutes."

"I helped a lot of clients in my day, crafty men; dangerous men who would genuflect before me. New identity, and a new life away from all the bullshit."

"Sounds like a life worth living. You're stupider than I thought. You'll be a liability to everyone you approach. You're poison."

"I have money. Lots of cash. Hidden all over the place. A dozen different places."

"It won't last. It never does. You'll be selling lawn chairs at Walmart before you know it. Turn yourself in. Get what you get. It'll only get worse for you."

Harry knew Calendar was sobering, and he took it as a bad sign. Calendar would become more impatient when he realized his situation offered him no reasonable options. Harry knew he had to keep him preoccupied until he could figure something out.

"What are your plans, Calendar? After tonight's performance?"

Before Calendar could move his lips, Harry wheeled around to Will and barked, "And you Will, for Chrissakes. Twelve years of kung fu and you end up roped like an innocent calf."

Calendar let out a laugh, saying, "Your life for theirs? Or all of your lives, for nothing – just for fun? Who knows? I'll make my decision in about five seconds. To answer your question, those are my immediate thoughts."

"Calendar, your own daughter?" Harry pleaded.

Calendar shrugged. "I never ever remember getting a Father's Day card. Isn't that right, sweetie?"

"Fa-fuck you," Julie spat, her blue lips trembling.

"And I rest my case," her father said. "My family has been dead to me for years."

"Your dishonesty and ugly behavior ka-kills everything you touch," Julie raged.

"Your mother chose the wrong man. C'est la vie, as we say in Bensonhurst."

Harry decided it was now or heaven. His mind was a jumble...*now or heaven?* If he lived through this ordeal, he would remember this mental fart. But living through the ordeal at hand, surviving Calendar, and rescuing the kids was foremost on his mind. He marched directly toward Calendar. Calendar's expression went blank when he saw the determination on Harry's bloodied face.

"Stop where you are," Calendar ordered with a calm confidence. There was no trace of the bourbon in his tone. "Put your hands on your head." Harry obliged, because he had no immediate plans to use his hands. He couldn't remember what he was wearing on his feet. His beloved orange sneakers maybe? No, he didn't think so. It really didn't matter. He would have to go with what he had. He kept walking.

Calendar held the revolver at waist-level and said, "That's better, but stop. Stop!"

Harry stopped less than twelve inches from Calendar's leering expression.

"You're a real wise guy, Kavanagh." There was hatred in his eyes. "You ruined my life."

Harry could smell the bourbon on Calendar's breath. Harry was about to do his thing: the Alan Ladd thing, the kick to Calendar's shin. The move worked so well on Jimmy Lynch outside the boys' bathroom. But Harry was distracted; he was drawn back to Will when he heard his son calling his name. Pleading with him to help them.

Will struggled to get out of the car. He inadvertently depressed the emergency brake with his foot, releasing it; the car began to roll quickly toward the water. In a panic, Will managed to put the break back on, but it didn't matter. The area was too slick, and the car continued to slide forward.

"Will!" Julie shrieked. "We're going to drown!"

Harry looked back at Calendar who lowered his weapon. Calendar watched the car slip into the black water. He was completely hypnotized by the action. Forfeiting the preconceived kick, Harry plowed his palm as hard as he could toward Calendar's beak. He wanted to drive Calendar's nose deep into his skull. He wanted him to sniff his looming death.

Harry's expectation was not a reality. Calendar shook off his reverie and turned away as Harry was about to strike. Harry's blow became an awkward slap. It was however, enough of a jolt for Calendar to lose his grip on the revolver.

The men clutched each other, tying themselves up into a sloppy wrestling heap. They saw glimpses of the dark landscape as they rolled over the damp earth, searching for the upper hand – the errant handgun. Harry saw the car's headlights submerging.

"Pops, we're going under. Please! Hurry!"

Calendar decided to give up on the gun. He wanted Harry to stand by helplessly and watch the drowning. Harry was about to pull free, Calendar clawed at him, preventing him from getting away. The men heard something commanding their immediate attention. A muddled heartbeat or the pounding pulse of a gallop, and it was drawing nearer.

"What the hell is that?" Calendar asked, as if he expected Harry to answer.

Harry didn't disappoint and said to him, "It's the fucking Hound of the Baskervilles to you. Pardon…my…vernacular."

Harry rolled free of Calendar. He stumbled to his feet as the car disappeared into the lake. Harry ran toward the car. Calendar scrambled to his feet. He was keen to pursue, but his instincts implored him to take a peek over his shoulder. An incomprehensible sight burst through the darkness: a giant growling dog, its limbs fully extended in mid-air, with gobs of saliva spritzing into the night. Harry heard a muted cry. It was the air forced from Calendar's lungs as he was set upon by the vengeful Lolly. Without looking back, Harry dove into the frigid blackness.

The car lights were still operating. Harry could see the blurry shapes of his youngest son and his girlfriend struggling wildly with their restraints. Will and Julie exchanged a frenzied look at one another. Somehow there was hope in their eyes. Harry reached into his pocket and pulled out a set of car keys. He let them drop away. He struggled with the ropes. He felt his strength draining rapidly, and he was beginning to panic. He remembered something and dug into his other pocket. He pulled out Jimmy Lynch's box cutter. He cut the ropes binding Will's hands and feet and then placed the box cutter securely into Will's hand. Will knew exactly what to do next. There was more rope to cut.

Harry knew his time was up and he hoped his son's youth and strength would be the ticket to finishing the job – saving himself and Julie. Harry's arms felt heavy, and his legs were numb. All of his injuries cried out now, constricting him further. He couldn't move, and his lungs were about to explode.

The front of the car pitched forward, jarring Harry as it headed deeper into the murk. With his last bit of strength, Harry pushed himself away from the car with his feet. He didn't want to get tangled up with Will and impede his progress.

Harry's head popped through the surface of the lake; he gasped for air. He fought to keep his head above water, but his body was heavy. His arms and legs were not responding. His toe reached the edge of a ledge. He couldn't feel the bottom any longer and he couldn't stay afloat. He took a big breath, and his head submerged into darkness. His last scrambled thought was some kind of inarticulate, guilty, fervent wish for the life of the two teenagers.

Julie emerged from the passenger side and stood atop the sinking car. The water was nearly waist high. She disappeared under the water, reached inside the window and pulled out Will. They struggled to gain their footing on the roof of the submerging auto.

"Where is he?" Julie pleaded, scanning the dark surface of the water.

"He's got to be somewhere over there," Will said pointing, trying to catch his breath. Before he could firmly set his feet, Julie did a perfect dive into the lake. The car sagged and gurgled, sliding deeper into the water. Will balanced himself firmly. He sprang into the water and followed Julie as the car was swallowed whole.

Moments later, they each held onto a fistful of material belonging to Harry's jacket. The teenagers dragged the limp body through the mud. Harry's eyes bulged open and he began retching water and bile.

Harry had a unique perspective. He was on his back staring up at the teens who were dragging him to safety. They appeared invigorated by their escape and subsequent heroics.

Will looked down at Harry and said, "You'll be okay, Pops. We got you."

Harry wasn't certain, but he thought Will winked at him. There were no tears in Will's eyes, no boyish pouting, no signs of grief. Will's adolescent features were gone. His jawline looked like it was etched in stone; his expression read determination. This was the kid who used to sleep with an orange like it was his teddy bear. That funny business was a distant memory. This business was new. Will Kavanagh and his girlfriend Julie Lambert were officially all grown up and in the lifesaving business.

They let Harry down gently. Harry rolled over until his eyes landed on Calendar.

"Watch him," Harry said, in a damaged voice not much louder than a whisper. He waved a trembling finger in Calendar's direction.

"There's a gun out there somewhere."

Calendar was on his knees, muddied, covered in wet leaves; groveling beneath Lolly's incessant growling. Harry tried to speak, but instead he continued to vomit. After his jag was done, Harry gestured to his rescuers to come closer. Julie knelt beside him and Harry spoke in her ear in a ragged, breathless cadence. Julie covered her mouth with her hand. Fat teardrops immediately fell from her eyes.

"What is it Julie? What did he say?" Will pleaded.

"He said," Julie paused, "…he said, that man murdered your mother."

268

Calendar spotted the errant revolver tented beneath a pile of leaves. He crawled toward it. Nice and easy, trying not to arouse the angry hound to new heights. Lolly followed his movements, escorting him. Her large head hovered inches above his.

Harry saw the it first. "Ga-gun!" he belched.

Lolly's growl intensified at the sound of Harry's voice. Calendar's hand slid within a finger's-length of the weapon. He blinked when he saw the tall boy charging him. Calendar estimated he would reach him quickly. His hand stopped quivering when he firmly grasped hold of the revolver.

With his confidence restored, Calendar rolled his torso into position. His sudden movements were enough for Lolly to act. Her jaw clamped down on Calendar's elbow causing him to cry out in pain. A gunshot rang out. The bullet was launched harmlessly into the night's sky. A roundhouse kick shattered Calendar's orbital bone, rendering him limp and unconscious. Will Kavanagh plucked the revolver from the mud, looming over the man who destroyed his family. Harry Kavanagh's body was too weak to celebrate. He was about to grant himself permission to take an unscheduled nap, but the sight of Will standing victoriously over Calendar filled him up with so many emotions.

Harry decided to let himself go. He wasn't worried. He knew he'd eventually have the opportunity to tell Will and Julie how enormously proud he was. He heard their voices above him. He felt warm. He could sense the tears flowing from the corners of his eyes. He found himself falling comfortably into a deep and well-deserved sleep.

Chapter Twenty-Nine

Harry was taken completely by surprise by all the attention. Following the climax of the Thaddeus Calendar affair, he became a person of interest for better or worse. He'd fielded twelve offers to teach at universities across the country, and several publishing houses asked him to write his memoir. Reporters camped outside Harry's home for days. Harry was sleeping lousy, and it was worrisome to see poor Lolly restless and uncomfortable in her own home.

Harry's neighbors emerged from behind closed curtains without offering much in the way of condolences or congratulations. It became abundantly clear to Harry that his neighbors wanted him to skip town, taking with him the traveling media circus his antics had attracted.

Harry was fielding all this minutia at a time when he required quiet moments for reflection. One morning in the midst of the disquietude, he attempted an old-fashioned hook shot with his cellphone. He wanted to be rid of the damn thing. It never stopped ringing or vibrating inside his pocket.

Harry was no Kareem Abdul-Jabbar to begin with. With Harry's timing hampered by nagging injuries, he managed to miss the receptacle by a wide margin. His cell banked off a kitchen cabinet and the screen shattered on the tiled floor. Harry decided it was a hell of a shot after all.

Being a creature of habit, Harry decided on a staycation at his little motel room in Bayonne. Some relative peace and quiet was in order. The certainty of flushing toilets and amorous couples heard through the motel walls filled Harry with a feeling of cockeyed nostalgia. Anything was better than spotting a reporter urinating into a Fanta bottle outside on his front lawn.

Reporters tripped over themselves when they spotted Harry and Lolly sneaking out in the middle of the night. There was shouting, plenty of cursing, and sudden blasts of unsteady camera lights. Harry sped away smiling as the media scurried like stunned bugs.

Harry nodded to Lolly sitting tall in the passenger seat. He had the little boy Will on his mind. With a glint in his eye, Harry said to the big girl, "Let's broom away, shall we? Next stop Bayonne."

In the following days, Harry emailed Will from the library to check in on him. He made his calls the old-fashioned way, from a payphone one of the locals called the dinosaur, located inside a place called Tommy's Laundromat.

Harry was tipped off to a storied Bayonne pub by his childhood friend, Shea Ryan. Harry went off book and ate and drank himself to an earlier bedtime every night. Nothing genteel, but the food did the trick all right. It was just what the doctor ordered.

Harry and Lolly didn't attract attention nor did they run into any trouble. *How's that for a first?* Harry mused. Harry laid low until Caribbean hurricanes and accumulating political gaffes along the presidential campaign trail pushed his story deep into the background.

There were no signs of his prickly neighbors or the news vans when he returned home. Harry avoided the curbside water basin like a childhood bully. It was late. Harry was looking forward to reintroducing himself to his mattress. He was eager to cook in his kitchen with the sounds of jazz swirling around him.

When Harry poked his head outside the next morning, he noticed his boy genius paperboy, Charlie, had placed the unread newspapers in a neat pile behind a bush. Harry reached for the *Richmond County Register*, which led off with a story about what else? The rotten life and miserable times of Thaddeus Calendar, co-starring Irene Roth and a supporting cast of misfits. Harry threw the newspaper on the pile and called out Lolly's name, politely asking her to join him for a stroll. He heard her tail knocking against the dryer.

"It is time to repudiate my prescription to this newspaper," Harry joked, imitating Slip Mahoney.

Thaddeus Calendar, Robert Devine, and the cop Heastie were remanded into custody. Harry wasn't keeping score. He wasn't following their fate. They crept into his mind, but he didn't want to read anything else about them. His job was over. His Felicity wasn't the angry-go-unlucky drunk they'd made her out to be, tooling recklessly around town until she drowned her car and herself. Her gossipy group had nothing to buzz about. After everything went down, the women began calling him, offering Harry a mixed bag of congratulations, condolences, and crumb cake. He handled them the same way they had previously responded to him. He was curt.

Felicity's legacy was restored. Harry wished he could have restored her life. Four years since she passed, and there were days when Harry struggled to remember the sound of her voice. *Time silences the past*, Harry thought. Not exactly an upbeat bumper sticker.

Lolly limped over to Harry. She yawned sloppily. Harry knelt beside her. She looked old; it happened overnight. Lolly was approaching her next birthday, the beginning of the reverse-mortgage years in the life of a Great Dane. Harry knew the score and wanted to spend all of his time with her, showering her with sappy love and appreciation. He stroked her face.

"Come on, beautiful," he said to her softly. They edged down the path leading away from the house. Ten minutes later, Harry threw up his collar and looked for a place to sit near the ferry terminal.

Harry, who was not confident by nature, *was* confident the evil three would receive substantial jail time. Felony murder, attempted murder, felony burglary, and tampering with evidence. Those were some of the charges Harry recounted; there may have been others.

State Senator Irene Roth was not charged with a crime, but the public response to her behavior came in quickly. She was labeled a hero and a coward. She resigned and put her condo and house up for sale. Then she disappeared.

Harry's ire toward Irene Roth had faded. The dollar-store psychologist that he was, he speculated she'd had a lousy childhood, which kick-started her attraction to a powerful, soulless man like Calendar. Irene Roth was the type of person who would spend her leisure time punishing herself more severely than the public sentiment. Irene Roth didn't kill Felicity – her deranged manfriend did. The same man who was willing to kill his own daughter. Harry wished Roth nothing but a tranquil mind. He wanted the same for himself.

Harry and Lolly continued along on their slow walk. They required easy exercise these days. Harry was banged up, and Lolly continued to stride with a limp. The vet reported she had strained muscles in her hind legs when toppling the former office-holder from Brooklyn. And at Lolly's age, it looked like she had finally earned her very own spoonful of arthritis, the bitter taste of it she would experience for the rest of her years. Easy and quaint walks were manageable, followed by an icepack and/or a heating pad for her, which Harry would sometimes borrow.

Harry was recovering nicely from his concussion; his orbital fracture was a work in progress. His broken pinkie had healed in an unnatural position. It was Harry's own fault, that. He ignored the injury. A recent MRI revealed a torn labrum in Harry's bad hip, which came as no big surprise. Naively resuming an exercise regimen after years of surfing the couch may not have been such a good idea. During the course of his misadventures, Harry became accustomed to living with pain. But the latest discovery, the burning in his hip, the torn labrum, it was a drag. *So much for jogging around the reservoir*, Harry thought.

Harry sat on a public bench and groaned with relief. Lolly managed to jackknife herself into position. No groan from Lolly, but Harry was concerned nonetheless. The old girl couldn't be comfortable on the cement. Harry decided they'd make it a short pit stop and with a little luck, he'd figure a way to get Lolly quickly reacquainted with the heating pad at home.

Harry observed working people rushing toward the ferry terminal. It was another work day for most. Harry took a solemn breath. He had no choice but to look across the street at the remains of Felicity's wine shop. It was boarded up. It would be demolished like Corbin Reece's building.

Harry stared without blinking until it appeared as if he was viewing the shop through an aqueous curtain. He dotted his eyes with his thumbs, took a breath and gave in. He took some seconds before reluctantly asking the great and powerful someone upstairs for the peace and tranquility he was seeking. Harry absently stroked Lolly's head.

"Sorry about the shop, Felicity. I can't rebuild it. The words *customer service* would never be my tattoo of choice. You were so beautifully wonderful at everything. Now that your legacy is straightened out, I don't want to mess anything up. I hope you understand."

Harry was distracted by millennials, a man and a woman who stopped to have themselves an anguished discussion about the election. He remembered it was January 20th, the day of the Presidential Inauguration. There had been a surprise victor, this new president. Not everyone was happy about President Donald J. Trump. The couple, professionally dressed, were shaky on their feet. Harry felt guilty for witnessing their distress. Harry looked over at Lolly for some kind of sign. She ignored Harry and the couple. Harry drummed Lolly's head with his fingers. She uncomfortably unfurled herself. They limped away from the bench.

Harry noticed Emma Kendall's car driving along Bay Street. *What timing*, he thought. It occurred to him that he hadn't seen or heard a peep from Emma in a long time.

"Hey, Emma!" he waved. The car drove past them.

"Oh geez, she didn't see us," Harry lamented to Lolly. "Chrissakes."

Emma Kendall did indeed spot Harry Kavanagh but chose to ignore him. She was in a hurry to pay a visit to her deadbeat ex-husband. There were matters to discuss and a debt to settle.

Chapter Thirty

The flames were burning evenly in the living room fireplace. When Harry entered the kitchen, he noticed the side door was ajar. He danced over and tapped it shut with his toe. Harry was putting the finishing touches on an organic free-range chicken dinner. Chick Corea was playing a dedication to John Coltrane on WBGO, and Lolly was out cold.

It was going to be a good night; Harry was feeling all right with the world. In a few weeks, he would be traveling to Parris Island to see Jake graduate from boot camp. He was quietly bursting inside. The newly minted Marine would have about ten days of liberty to spend in the company of his father and younger brother. Speaking of company. Harry currently had some. Company. There was a woman in his house. She was upstairs using the facilities because Lolly was unconscious on the floor, blocking the entrance to the half-bathroom. On all days, the flush valve made by American Standard decided to become temperamental. The master bathroom was the only way to travel. Rather than wax poetic about a valve, Harry positioned Lolly's blankets in front of the bathroom door in the hopes she would pass out there. Lolly did not disappoint.

In any event, his guest was on the second floor *freshening up*, as they say in the old movies Harry loved so dearly.

"The thing about free-range chickens is they're allowed to go to the gym every day, so they can develop muscles," Harry joked.

"Who goes to the gym every day?"

"Free-range chickens do."

"You're filling this highly educated woman's head with a lot of malarkey," was his guest's response. Harry couldn't stop stealing glances at her. He hoped it didn't show. She tilted her glass slightly before her lips took a satisfying sip.

"You make one hell of a martini, Harry," she said.

Harry, a little nervous and one step behind the conversation, responded, "So, to make sure the chicken is really tender, you have to make a brine and marinate it overnight."

"So, what you're saying is, you've been obsessing about our date for about what, twenty hours or so?"

"Ah, um…" Harry stammered as he slid the beautifully roasted chicken from the oven.

"I'm teasing you. I've been looking forward to this all day."

"Me too," Harry smiled. "I'll take off the oven mitts before we eat. Promise." He held up his hands in mock-surrender.

"You are thoughtful." She made a face at him. "I'm going to take five. I'd like to wash away the hell of day I had today, so I can enjoy this fabulous meal and your company."

"Oh, you can use the powder room upstairs. I don't think you'll be able to get around Lolly there."

"The powder room it is," she said with amusement. And she was off. Harry's plan worked perfectly.

Harry ambled into the living room, sipping a glass of Riesling from Upstate New York, the Finger Lakes area. It was the first glass of wine he'd had in years. A medium-dry Riesling. He thought Felicity would have approved of his choice.

The fire was roaring in the fireplace now. Harry peeked over his shoulder and spied the fire extinguisher propped on the floor beside the built-in bookcase. He breathed easier.

Harry clicked on the TV to check the basketball score. It wasn't like him to flick on a sporting event, but there was a method to his temporary insanity. Harry couldn't care less about the team, but there was money on the line with his buddy Al Manoscalpo. The Cavaliers were in town. Al was bragging the Knicks would defeat LeBron. *Talk about temporary insanity*. Harry had seen enough of the Knicks to bet against them. He had to make the bet interesting for Al to take the bait. He wagered twenty bucks the Knicks would lose by thirty. It was a good-natured wager. If Harry won, he'd take his twenty-bucks worth out on Al's coffee maker. Midway through the fourth quarter, the Knicks were down by thirty-six.

"Ha!" Harry did a little jig. He was feeling loose and silly. His new cellphone rang. It was Will. Harry could barely say hello, because Will was already off to the races.

"Pops, remember the woman who tagged along with Mom?"

"Ay, hello Will, what's up? How's school?"

"Pops, Pops? Listen to me?"

"Wha…what's wrong?"

"Mrs. Kendall, right?"

"Yeah, Emma Kendall. What about her? She was Mom's friend."

"I've been trying to tell you all along, she's a psycho."

"Slow down, what are you talking about?" Harry could hear Will attempting to take some measured breaths.

"I'm going to talk to you slowly, so you can understand," Will said.

"Really?" Harry hemmed and hawed, wanting to object to Will's tone.

"Stop talking! And don't say another word until I say I am finished," Will ordered.

Harry put a finger over his lips, stopping himself from saying something that might escalate the situation.

"One of the really old Hitchcock movies, this long-suffering woman who's in love with this guy says to him, something like, you loved her or something."

"Yeah, maybe it's Joan Fontaine talking to Olivier…" Harry was thinking about the film *Rebecca*.

"Shut up and listen!"

Harry was stung, but not insulted. Something serious was unfolding.

"And he says something like, loved her? I hated her! I'm talking along the same lines here, sort of," he rambled. "The Kendall lady was no friend of Mom's. She was a tagalong freak. Some weird shadow. She wasn't Mom's friend. Mom was afraid of her. She was an adversary. Mom was trying to figure out a way to extract herself…"

"What? Really? I don't…what does this have to do with anything right now?"

Will kept speaking, but Harry didn't hear him because he became hypnotized by the breaking news streaming across the TV screen below the Knicks debacle.

The caption was rolling by, but Harry could only catch some of it…*the forty-nine-year-old man, mutilated, Fort Lee, New Jersey, identified as Michael Little. Police are seeking his ex-wife Emma Kendall in connection to his death. She was last seen leaving his…*

"Pops. It looks like Mrs. Emma Kendall murdered the fucking shit out of her old man." There was a pause. "Pardon my fucking vernacular," Will exhaled. "It just popped up in my news feed."

Harry clicked off the TV. Returning his full attention to his son, he said, "Will, don't worry. I've got Lolly with me. I'm sure she'll be picked up quickly."

"All right, Pops. Jesus. Lock the doors and stay frosty. Call me tomorrow."

Harry shuffled into the kitchen trying to shrug off the shocking news. It wasn't going to be easy. The kitchen door was ajar.

"Jesus."

Harry pushed the door closed with an elbow. He threw the dead bolt for good measure. He was confused. He backed away and saw a key on the countertop. Bloody fingerprints defaced the marble.

Harry turned slowly. Standing a few feet away from him with a leer on her face was the twisted-looking Emma Kendall. Her tangled hair sat high atop her head. She looked like a modern-day Medusa. Her gray roots made it appear as if there were brush fires emanating from her scalp. A jagged mascara path ran from the corner of one eye all the way down to the edge of her lip. Smudged lipstick made it look like she was doing her take on Heath Ledger's Joker. She was wearing the hideous gorilla coat.

"Hello, Harry. I'm returning Felicity's house key."

Harry appeared solemnly disquieted by her appearance.

"I must have forgotten to return it. What's the cute line you always say?"

"Emma, what can I do for you?"

"I blame myself," she said. She removed her right hand from her pocket as she yawned. She coolly displayed a butcher's knife, which was marinated in blood.

"You should never bring a knife to a gun fight, but you don't own a firearm, do you, blossom?" his uninvited guest said.

Harry tilted his head toward his sleeping dog and asked, "Um, Lolly?" The dog didn't budge.

"Despite what the newspapers say, you're not much of a shamus are you Harry?"

"No, I'm no detective. I uh…are people still reading newspapers?"

This was not the time to have a witty conversation. He was experiencing a plummeting chill throughout his body. It should have paralyzed him, but he was obsessed with avoiding Emma Kendall's homerun swing. He was trying to stay frosty. He wriggled the toes inside his shoes. He wanted to be sure his feet would be ready to run.

"I've been spending a little time in your quaint abode while you were out. I've been doping the dog. One sleeping pill in a Manoscalpo's meatball and she's a dope. Haven't you noticed how sluggish she's been?"

"I've been preoccupied."

"Preoccupied, really? But not with me, sadly. This had been a growing issue."

"Preoccupied with trying to stay on my feet." He looked over at Lolly. "I'm very sorry, girl."

"Today you should focus on your breathing."

"Why?" He knelt to check on Lolly, keeping a watchful eye on the intruder.

"Why focus on breathing, or the general question, why? As in, why have I dropped in on you on this fine evening?"

"Let's start with the general question. That response may require a longer explanation. I'm thinking it'll allow me some more time to keep breathing."

Harry carefully got to his feet. The shock of engaging with crazy people was wearing off. He didn't appreciate the intrusion or the threat of violence. And his roasted chicken was languishing. He could taste the disgust in his mouth. He felt the same way in the company of Nicky Sotto.

Emma Kendall unbuttoned her beastly-looking wrap. She let it shimmy to the floor. She stood completely naked before him. Harry remained expressionless. He didn't react to her big reveal, which annoyed her even more.

"I knew my ex-husband was a bastard, a womanizer among many other things. But imagine my dismay when I discovered he gambled all of my money away. All of it! Leaving me nothing but reminders of our shattered life together. You, Harry, became my one last hope." She paused, searching for the right words. "H-o-w-e-v-e-r," she said, elongating the pronunciation of the word. She bit down on her lower lip. She pouted, trying to find her place in the narrative of her oral book report. "Ah," she said, finding her way back. She aimed the tip of the knife in Harry's direction. "In the last four years, the only thing you've given me is a shitty cup of coffee. I'm sick and tired of it."

"My chicken is getting cold. It's time for you to exit the stage."

"You've rejected all my choreography, Harry. Mistaken my kindness and generosity for the coming of a new plague. And now while you're making love with a stranger, I'm left outside in the cold."

"Thanks for dropping by."

Harry was not in a patient frame of mind. He wanted her the hell out. Emma Kendall murdered her ex-husband, and she was about to ruin his evening. His restrained ire was preventing his rising fear from taking off.

She stepped over her coat and said, "You should have drowned in the swill of the storm. I thought I sent you off proper then."

"You were the one who attacked me? That was you?"

"Oh, goodness, yes. That was me. I was having a difficult time of it that day. But I was only thinking of you. Did you hear your wedding song? Bobby Darin? I played the CD in my car. I wanted it to be the last thing you heard."

"Very thoughtful of you," he said.

The muscles in her face tensed. She screwed the tip of the knife into her palm drawing blood. She smeared blood across her breasts and eyed him with a profound look of lovesickness.

"What do you say to me now?" The plea did not move Harry to speak. "I'm asking you out."

"I don't see a future for us," he said.

Her sloppy expression didn't change for several long seconds. The soft lines of her eyebrows lowered and hardened, meeting up like a drawbridge. Her jaw clenched and then she said, "I plan to gut you like the rancid fish you are and then we're going to make love while you bleed out."

"The gutting-of-the-fish comment seems to have had an effect on me," Harry said, seemingly more attentive.

The adrenalin began rushing through his body. Given his prior experiences with crime and punishment, the feeling was not unfamiliar. All of a sudden, something inside was shouting at him to play for time. It wasn't so much an inner conversation as it was an alarm going off inside his head. It was simple. Harry had to keep talking to keep breathing. While he determined sarcasm wouldn't be good for his health, he couldn't help himself. He heard himself say in a dangerously condescending tone: "There are a few things we need to address, Emma."

"Image, you cooking a lovely dinner and it wasn't for me. You need to undress now, or I'll slice your clothing from your skin."

"Number one, why would you gut a rancid fish? And the making love part whilst I'm bleeding will probably not result in a satisfactory outcome for either one of us, now that I'm really thinking about it."

"Did you just *whilst* me, Professor?" Her eyes were on fire. Harry took one anxious step backward.

"Harry, I'd advise against running out the door. In your absence, I might plant my bloody flagpole through the heart of your sleeping dog. I'll chase down your date and stick her face in a food processor."

"I hesitate to ask the question, but what do you suggest I do?"

"I'm no doctor, but I suggest you stand there and take your medicine."

Emma Kendall's blood-soaked body moved in on Harry. He threw up his arms in a defensive position. When he tensed his toes, his left calf began to cramp. He let out a groan as he grabbed his hardening muscle. He was cornered; defenseless. Harry looked on expecting the worst.

That's when he saw a long arm shooting out from the hallway. It began its arc from a low vantage point, heading upward, resembling the path of a beautifully timed uppercut. Harry had seen a lot of punches staged in the movies. This one had the potential of a masterpiece. And talk about choreography? It was expertly articulated, and it swung for the fences. The fist dented Emma Kendall's cheek. Harry heard her teeth shatter. Following the rules of science, Emma Kendall's chassis folded in a dreamlike sequence of stop-motion movements.

When the intruder's head bounced off the kitchen floor, the knife skipped harmlessly into a corner. Harry's night visitor was out cold.

"Jesus Christ, Harry. Some neighbors are content to bring over a cup of sugar," Emily Armstrong said stepping into the room, sizing-up the unconscious body.

"Are you all right?" Harry gushed, rushing over to the physician's side.

"Me? Sure. How about you?" She wrung out the discomfort in her punching hand.

"But she had a knife…and she was naked," Harry blurted, his heart pounding faster than it had moments earlier.

"I see naked bodies and sharp instruments every single day. Blood is part of the deal too. Besides, I owed her one."

"What are you talking about?" Harry hopped on one leg until the muscle in his calf softened. He removed an icepack from the fridge and offered it to her. She pushed it back to him.

"The woman who blindsided me," she said pointing. "That's her. She tapped me on the shoulder and when I turned around she punched me. She warned me to stay away from you. I was too shocked to retaliate."

"Why didn't you tell me? Why the hell would you come here if you thought we were friends?"

"I recognized her. The crazy chick in the depressing gift shop. Everyone knows she's off. I didn't really think you'd have a serious connection with someone like her."

Harry knelt down beside Lolly and began stroking her face. The big girl yawned.

"I planned on kicking her teeth in, because the hell with making a police report. By the time my schedule opened up, her shop was padlocked." She watched Harry wipe tears of laughter from his eyes.

"What's so funny?"

Harry gathered himself and said, "When I saw your face, I thought it was the handiwork of Nicky Sotto."

"Who's that?"

"The owner of the crappy marina restaurant I took you to. Sorry about that," he said shaking his head.

"And I gave you a little bit of an unnecessary run around, I'm sorry. Why would you think that guy hit me?"

"Let's say someone who looked a lot like me went back there and broke his nose."

"You did what? Why?"

"When I saw the bruises on your face, I thought he hit you. I interrupted his breakfast by saying good morning. With a skillet. It was very heavy."

Harry tossed the icepack into the sink. Emily stepped over Emma Kendall's limp body and tugged gently on Harry's hips. She kissed him below his eye. It was a gentle kiss; an inviting kiss, and Harry thoroughly enjoyed it.

"Wow. One heck of an appetizer," he said sounding hypnotized.

"Be quiet." She pretended to inspect his face. "You're healing nicely."

"You think so, Doctor?"

"Harry, chivalry is a touchy subject these days. I can obviously take care of myself."

"Yes, of course," he said, eyeing the unconscious body of Emma Kendall.

"What women want most is kindness and respect. With that said, it was very kind of you to prepare this lovely dinner. And I respect the fact that you know your way around a skillet."

"A very heavy skillet."

"Yes. A very heavy skillet," she repeated.

"Looks like we're having dinner for breakfast," he sighed.

"Yes. I guess we should call the police," she said.

"What do you have in your other hand?"

"Oh, it's your credit card. I found it at the bottom of the steps."

Harry moved in closer. A sudden, purposeful shift of position on her part and he inadvertently brushed the corner of her lips with his. Harry felt a humming sensation in his pocket. He started to reach for his phone before realizing his pocket was empty. His face displayed a sudden blush of red.

"You're a funny man, Harry Kavanagh," she said, nibbling his ear. Harry twitched like a child.

"Be careful there," he said chuckling.

"Oh?"

"Apparently, I bruise easily."

Chapter Thirty-One

"The medicine for my suffering is within me."

— Bruce Lee

The good news of the day: Nando Ricci recovers from his coma. He plans on running for State Senator. The seat vacated by Irene Roth. He was told he would have the support of the small business community, in particular, the majority of the pizza parlors in his district.

Jaycee Singletary strode out of the Manhattan dental office with a flawless smile. No more gap. He paid the dentist in cash.

Sporting a brand-new tooth, he had the bright idea he wanted to take it for a ride and show it off. And oddly, there was a longing building up inside of him. He wanted human contact, some like-mindedness, some comfort; some conversation. Being around Harry Kavanagh and the neighbor's dog he called Swoosie reminded Singletary he may actually be capable of having long-lasting relationships. So, following his desire, he hopped on a Greyhound Bus.

Four hours and change later, Singletary stepped inside the place, leaving the gentle snowstorm behind him. He could admire it through the window over a steaming cup of coffee. As far as he could tell, Mrs. Cronin's Creamery was a neighborhood breakfast haunt. Singletary welcomed the warmth greeting him. He took in the aroma of coffee and saw huge plates of eggs and home fries floating from the kitchen. There was plenty of local banter filling the air. A newspaper was in the skilled hands of a man sitting at the counter. He wielded it like a toreador's cape.

Singletary sat at the only available table. The waitress had her back to his table. She was speaking to a customer. One of her hands reached behind her. Without turning around, she flipped over Singletary's coffee cup and planted it on the saucer. She allowed the chatterer to finish his story. Singletary recognized the woman's hip; it belonged to Irene Roth. Roth wheeled around armed with a coffee pot. She filled his cup.

"Good morning," she said, her eyes finally meeting his. She froze.

He said softly, "How do you like Vermont?" Her lips froze. "After what we've shared, this is no time to be shy."

She responded with a tremor in her voice. "One of the ladies won some Lotto money and we think she's taking the rest of her life off. I ate here so often I got promoted from customer to waitress."

"Congratulations," he said brandishing a complete smile.

"You didn't come here looking for trouble, did you?"

"I came here looking for you." He smiled.

"Why?"

"To say hello. To get reacquainted under better circumstances. If that's okay with you?"

She thought before she spoke. "Where are you staying?"

"I haven't gotten that far yet."

"I'm off in half an hour. Lemme take your order," she said. The flutter in her voice was absent.

"How about some of the apple pie I hear a lot about?"

"How do you take it?" She exhaled. She stood comfortably on her feet. Pleased by the fact she was going to have company. She did a quick inventory: the hard lines on his face were gone. His demeanor, thoughtful and kind.

"You tell me."

"I recommend you have it à la mode with some maple syrup and Vermont cheddar."

"I'm going to take your recommendation."

"By the way, how did you find me?" she asked.

"I'm good at finding people," he replied.

Singletary watched her walk toward the kitchen. He sipped his black coffee and watched the snow fall outside the picture window. He became aware of his entire body: his back fitted nicely into the chair, his feet were poised six inches apart on the wooden floor; he could feel himself smiling. He folded his hands in front of him. The busboy stopped by and topped off his coffee.

"Thank you."

"Everything good today, sir?" The kid smiled at him.

Singletary appreciated good manners. "Just fine. Just fine, thank you," Singletary said in a louder voice than he was used to using. "Everything is in order."

Port Royal, South Carolina was an inhospitable host that January morning. It had been pouring all night and into the morning. When they arrived at Parris Island, they were informed the graduation ceremony would be held indoors if the inclement weather continued. Unfriendly winds and incessant rain whiplashed attendees young and old huddled in the grandstands. So much for the promise of an indoor ceremony. *Well, this is as about inclement as it gets,*

Harry Kavanagh thought. But even the lousy weather couldn't dampen Harry's renewed spirit.

Jake explained the rain-soaked ceremony later on with more than a hint of sarcasm, "It's the Marine way."

The newest Marines were standing statue-still on the parade deck in what was fast becoming an increasingly uncomfortable cloudburst. The Marines were broken up into four companies: Alpha, Bravo, Charlie, and Delta. Each company contained an average of six platoons with approximately 50–70 recruits per platoon. The recruits officially became Marines a week earlier after the successful completion of their 54-hour right-of-passage experience, the Crucible. Jake told his father the guys had a lot of other names for the Crucible. Those epithets wouldn't be repeated around polite company.

"Jake is in Bravo Company," Harry heard Will say. "I can't see him. Can you see him, Pops?"

Puddles of water rose to near ankle-level in the ranks; uniform shoulders were drenched. In the stands, families were clinging closer together, trying to pinpoint their loved ones through water-soaked binoculars.

"They all look the same," Julie marveled.

Harry's mind was at ease. His heart swelled with pride. The sound of the beating rain on his hat made his lips curl into smile. The hat was a gift from his uncle. A reward. Harry, forever self-deprecating, would be more apt to describe it as a bonus for getting up off the couch.

"Wear the goddamn thing, Harry. Every day in all kinds of weather. It don't belong in no movie picture museum. This thing is for what you done. The hat, on one hand, it's a little bit of nothin' and yet giving it to you means everything in the world to me. It's a prize, and you deserve it. What you went through to give our beautiful angel some peace. Wear it until it crumbles between your fingers. Watch the little pieces of fibers float up to heaven to meet me and your beautiful, dear Felicity girl," Uncle Sebe told Harry.

"You have plans? And you think you're going to heaven?" Harry asked his uncle at the time.

"Well, not at the moment, but you never know. The math is not in my favor."

A week prior, Harry had been summoned to Avenue U by his uncle. Harry met Sebastian Brazzano at the familiar spot sitting in his lawn chair positioned between the Korean grocery and the Italian bakery. Sebe was bundled in a winter coat and wrapped in a down comforter for good measure. The tip of his nose was beet red. One of Yoo Jin's nephews was meticulously shoveling snow in front of the storefronts. A younger nephew was following with a broom. Harry and the nephews exchanged several poorly timed nods of hello.

"Uncle Sebe, it's twenty-six degrees. You look like an astronaut."

"Shut up and listen," he barked.

"Take your time, but hurry up," Harry said playfully.

Sebe Brazzano pushed aside Harry's words with an impatient wave of his hand.

"I told you my Bogart story a million times. When I snuck into the old Madison Square Garden for Marciano's last fight? He retired undefeated, remember?"

Harry nodded impatiently. A passing sanitation plow flung snow onto the clean sidewalk. Harry was forced to hop closer to his uncle to avoid the slush. Yoo Jin's nephews had to retrace their steps.

"Apparently, that's what an old bag of doughnuts like me does every day. I tell the same story over and over again. My mouth is like a human re-run."

"Okay, okay. I understand, you're senile."

"Hey, how about some polite talk?"

"Forgive me," Harry said politely.

"And yes, I'm senile, but that's my business."

Harry looked up and saw Mr. Montalbano and Yoo Jin standing side-by-side, arms locked together; beaming at him from inside the warm confines of the bakery. Harry greeted them with a tip of his head and a wan smile. His toes were getting cold and he was befuddled by their demeanor. They looked like old uncles gushing with pride at Harry's graduation ceremony.

"But I never told the whole entire complete honest story."

"Will we be here until April showers?" Harry joked, rubbing his hands together for warmth.

"And look at you, no gloves...tsk...tsk," the old man chided.

Harry made a face at him, pleading with him to please hurry up.

"So, as the one and only Mr. Humphrey Bogart is reminding me that I'm sitting too comfortably in his ringside seat, which he paid for and I did not and that I should get myself lost, he gets this funny look in his eye."

"A funny look in his eye, you say?"

"Yes, a funny look in his eye. He removes his chapeau and hands it to me."

"Humphrey Bogart gave you his hat?"

"He didn't just give me it. He presented it to me in a grand gesture, as a gift. At first, I thought he was taking up a collection for the church. Like I'm supposed to drop some moolah in the hat, but no. He says to me, 'For you, kid. You got moxie.'"

"Moxie, huh?"

"That's right," he said beaming. "And I know you know what moxie is, right kid?"

"Sure. Nerve, grit, chops, balls, if you will. When the boys were younger, they used to say nards."

"That's a good story, Harry," he said dismissing it. "But you get it, right? So, take a look for yourself, smart guy." He stuck a thumb over his shoulder toward the window.

Harry looked over his uncle's shoulder into the storefront window. Mr. Montalbano was displaying Humphrey Bogart's hat in his hand as if it were one of his prized communion cakes. It wasn't a fedora Harry recognized from Bogie's heyday in the 1940s when he played a shamus or a tough guy digging himself out of a scrape. Harry would later learn this hat was called a Railbird. It was made by Stetson, briefly fashionable in the 1950s. It was a gray felt fedora with a thin felt band and feather accent. And it looked brand new; freshly baked, as if it had just come out of the oven.

"Harry, you got moxie. If I ever said you was a lazy husband, I take it back," he said somberly. Then shifting gears completely and with mirth in his voice, he said, "And now I can die. Let's go inside and have some coffee and cake first."

The senior drill instructor dismissed the Marines while Harry was ambling around inside his head. Harry was still in a trance even after the graduates responded with their thunderous response of *oorah*.

Families poured out of the stands and onto the parade deck where hundreds of exuberant exchanges of congratulations were happening simultaneously. The rain continued to lash out, but spirits remained high as the families and their Marines began to evacuate the parade deck in favor of the barracks or the warm confines of a family vehicle crowded into the parking lot.

Harry had his hands in his pockets. An arm hooked itself through his and tugged gently. He smiled at young Julie Lambert. Harry had grown to adore her. Julie took a leave of absence from school to help her mother and younger brother cope in the wake of her father's arrest. Harry hugged Julie's arm back. With a soft smile and a subtle tilt of her head, Julie directed Harry's attention to the parade deck. It had completely emptied save the Kavanagh boys, Will and Jake.

"Oh boy, I must have taken a wrong turn somewhere. How did I miss everything?"

"You didn't miss anything, Mr. Kavanagh," Julie said to him. "This is the most important part."

He looked at her through soft eyes. "Harry, please?"

Will circled Jake, gesturing wildly. Jake was hunched, hands on his knees, listening intently. Jake had been on a news blackout. He had no clue about the dramatic family events that had transpired.

Will's play-acting around his brother was wildly expressive and athletic. It was apparent to Harry that Will was providing Jake with a wild *Reader's Digest* version of how their father caught up with the son-of-a-bitch who murdered their mother.

Jake turned toward the grandstands and looked in Harry's direction. He had heard enough for now.

He was too far away for Harry to read his expression.

"Hold onto your hat," Harry heard Julie say. He looked at her. "No, I mean really. Hold on to your hat."

"I think that's good advice, Julie."

Harry secured his footing as Jake hurdled over a security gate and took the grandstand steps two at a time. Julie stepped away from Harry as Jake leapt into his father's arms.

"Pops, Pops," the young man sobbed.

The last time Harry saw his eldest son, he was 150 pounds soaking wet. The kid who had his father in a bear hug ran about 175. He possessed sturdy shoulders and his hardened arms were forcing the air from Harry's body. Harry could feel Jake's fingers pressing into his spine. Harry was trying to convince himself that this was good pain.

Will caught up and completed the Harry Kavanagh sandwich. Without missing a beat, Harry joked, "I guess this makes me the bologna?"

Will reached out his hand and pulled Julie into their bond.

"That makes you the tomato," Will said to Julie.

"One heck of a tomato," Jake answered.

"Too Bad Lolly's not a part of this jam," Julie said.

"Yeah, I can't wait to see that beautiful girl," Jake replied.

"I miss her too," Harry said. "We'll find her where we left her, asleep on the motel bed." Harry smiled. "She's never too far away."

The four of them hugged there for fifteen minutes, simultaneously laughing and crying; conversing enthusiastically at intervals in nearly undecipherable blabber. After finally freeing themselves, they headed into town. The car windows refused to defog because they roared, giddily speaking over one another. Harry laughed himself into a near convulsion as his sons traded embarrassing stories from their childhood. All the restaurants on Main Street were packed with Marines and their families. They selected the least crowded place and happily settled in for a mediocre lunch. Nothing could dim their spirits. Harry thought about his beloved Felicity and a quick smile washed over him. No tears today. Harry was happy. He hoped it would be the beginning of a trend. There were no more shadows for Harry to follow. Not on this day.

The End